DAVID AND LEIGH EDDINGS

THE TREASURED ONE

Book Two of The Dreamers

HarperCollins*Publishers*

Voyager
An Imprint of HarperCollins*Publishers*
77–85 Fulham Palace Road,
Hammersmith, London W6 8JB

www. voyager-books.com

This paperback edition 2005
4

First published in Great Britain by *Voyager* 2004

Copyright © David and Leigh Eddings 2004

The Author asserts the moral right to
be identified as the author of this work

ISBN 0 00 715763 0

Set in Janson Text

Printed and bound in Great Britain by
Clays Ltd, St Ives plc

PREFACE

PREFACE

It was a time of uncertainty in the nest of the Vlagh, for no word of success had yet reached the nest from the warrior-servants which had followed the burrows below the face of the ground toward the broad water which lies beneath the sunset.

All had gone as it should at first as the warrior-servants had moved down through the burrows toward the land of the sunset, killing the man-things of that land as they went, and the joy of our dear Vlagh had known no bounds, for once the land of the sunset was ours, there would be much to eat, and the Vlagh which had spawned us all could spawn still more, and our numbers would grow to beyond counting, and the overmind of which we are all a part would expand, for it grows larger and more complex with each new hatch.

Impatient was our Vlagh, for none of its servants of whatever form had yet brought word of victory, and without that assurance, our Vlagh could not spawn. Though our Vlagh reached out with its senses toward the land of the sunset to question the overmind about the success of the warriors of strange form, the overmind did not respond, and that was most unusual.

And as the days came and went, our Vlagh grew more and more

irritable as the need to spawn was frustrated by the lack of certainty. 'Go!' our Vlagh commanded the warrior-servants which protect the hidden nest. 'Go and look, and then return and tell me that which I must know.'

Many warrior-servants of venomous fangs hurried away, and those of us which are the *true* servants who care for our Vlagh and the newborns sought to assure our dear Vlagh that all was as it should be.

But it was not so.

The venomous warriors of strange form returned to report that they could not find even one of those of our number which had followed the burrows beneath the face of the ground toward the broad water which lies beneath the sunset, nor had they even been able to find any trace of those burrows. More horrible still, they had felt no sense of the overmind in that region.

And the pain of our dear Vlagh knew no bounds, for the overmind had been greatly diminished, and it would remain so until the burrowers and the warriors with venomous fangs were found and their awareness was rejoined with the overmind.

Then there came to the nest of the Vlagh a burrower with missing limbs and deep burns in its shell, and the burrower spoke of hot light spewing up from the mountains and red liquid hotter than fire running down through the burrows below the face of the ground, consuming all that was in its path. And then the burrower said that which should never be said. 'They are no more. The many which went through our hidden burrows toward the land of the sunset have all been consumed by the red liquid hotter than fire, and we are all made less because they are gone.'

And then the burrower's task was complete, and it died.

And our beloved Vlagh shrieked in agony, for the word of the burrower had torn away the urge to spawn. And *all* of us were made less by those words, for the many were now fewer, and the lands beneath the sunset were now and forever beyond our reach. The grief of our Vlagh was beyond our understanding, and that grief brought us rage.

Now it came to pass that the servants with strange forms and venomous fangs which had gone forth to seek knowledge in the lands of the man-things conferred with one another. The seekers of knowledge are unlike the *true* servants, for their task has altered them. The seekers of knowledge go beyond our Vlagh's immediate commands, and they consider the knowledge which they have found and even sometimes offer alternatives when they carry the knowledge which they have found back to the nest.

And so it was that the seekers of knowledge agreed, each with the others, that the lands of the sunset were now and forever beyond the grasp of the burrowers and the warriors by reason of the liquid fire which was coming forth from the mountains, and they offered the alternative which the knowledge they had found had suggested to them. Might it not be better, they said, to expand toward a different direction than we had before? The mountains above the land of longer summers are quiet, and the need to spew forth liquid fire is not stirring in those mountains, and there are many more things to eat in the land of longer summers than there had been in the land of the sunset. Since the presence of things to eat arouses our Vlagh's urge to spawn, should we not seek out a land where there is much to eat? Should we do so, the urge to spawn will grow much greater, and there will soon be even more of us than there had been when the burrowers had opened the passages below the face of the ground which had led down to the land of the sunset. And thereby the awareness of the overmind which we all share will be increased, lifting it to heights which it has never reached before.

And our beloved Vlagh communed with the overmind concerning the virtue of the alternative offered by the seekers of knowledge, and the overmind found much that was good in that alternative, for it had learned much during our attempt to occupy the land of the sunset. The warriors of strange form had encountered many different creatures as they had moved toward the sunset, and the overmind perceived that those different forms might prove to be most useful in our encounters with the man-things in the land of longer summers, for the man-things are most tenacious and difficult to push aside as we move toward that which is our goal. Then, however, the overmind warned our beloved Vlagh that the greatest danger we would face in the land of longer summers would be – even as it had in the land of the sunset – *not* the man-things who stood in our path, but would rather be sleeping infants and peculiar stones.

And so it was that we turned aside from the lands of the sunset and fixed our attention on the land of longer summers where the two-legged ones produce food from the ground and where there is much room, for food and space will surely once again stir our Vlagh's urge to spawn, and the overmind will grow, even surpassing what it had been before the mountains of the land of the sunset had reduced it, and that will bring joy to all of us, for we all share the benefits of the increase of the overmind.

And surely the time will come when all the lands of the man-things shall be ours, and we shall grow to numbers beyond counting, and our overmind shall expand until all knowledge is ours – and the world as well.

And only then will we be content.

THE DREAM OF ASHAD

During the course of my many cycles I've grown very fond of the mountains of my Domain. There's a beauty in the mountains that no other kind of country can possibly match. My sister Zelana loves the sea in much the same way, I suppose, but I don't think the sea can ever match mountain country. Mountain air is clean and pure, and the eternal snow on the peaks seems to increase that purity.

Over the endless eons I've discovered that a mountain sunrise gives me the most delicious light I've ever tasted, so whenever possible I go up to the shoulder of Mount Shrak at first light to drink in the beauty of the sunrise. No matter what happens later in the day, the taste of a mountain sunrise gives me a serenity that nothing else can provide.

It was on a day in the late spring of the year when the creatures of the Wasteland had made their futile attempt to seize sister Zelana's Domain and had been met by Eleria's flood and Yaltar's twin volcanos that I went out of my cave under Mount Shrak to greet the morning sun.

When I reached my customary feasting place, I saw that there was a cloud bank off to the east, and that always makes the sunrise even more glorious.

I looked around at the nearby mountains, and it seemed that summer was moving up into my Domain a bit more slowly than usual, and last winter's snow was still stubbornly clinging to the lower ridges. It occurred to me that this might be a sign of one of those periodic climate changes which appear much more frequently than the people who serve us seem to realize. The temperatures on the face of Father Earth are never really constant. They're subject almost entirely to the whims of Mother Sea, and if Mother's feeling chilly, Father will get a lot of snow. That can go on for centuries.

After I'd considered the possibility, though, I dismissed the notion. Zelana had tampered with the weather extensively during the past winter to delay the invasion of her Domain by the servants of the Vlagh until her hired army arrived from the land of Maag, and it might take a while for things to go back to normal.

All in all, though, things had gone rather well this past spring. The more I considered the matter, the more certain I became that my decision to rouse the younger gods from their sleep cycle prematurely and to cause them to regress to infancy in the process *had*, in fact, fulfilled that ancient prophecy. Eleria's flood and Yaltar's twin volcanos had forever sealed off Zelana's Domain from any more incursions by the creatures of the Wasteland.

The morning sun rose in all her splendor, painting that eastern cloud-bank a glorious crimson, and I feasted on her light. I've always found early summer light to be more invigorating than the pale light of winter or the dusty light of autumn, and there was a certain spring to my step as I walked on back down the mountain to the mouth of my cave.

My little toy sun was waiting for me at the cave-mouth, and she flickered her customary question at me.

'Just taking a look at the weather, little one,' I lied. She always seems to get all pouty and sullen if she thinks that I prefer the light of the *real* sun to hers. Pets can be very strange sometimes. 'Is Ashad still sleeping?' I asked her.

She bobbed up and down slightly in answer.

'Good,' I said. 'He hasn't been sleeping too well here lately. I think he was badly frightened by what happened down in Zelana's Domain. Maybe you should keep your light a bit subdued so that he can sleep longer. He needs the rest.'

She bobbed her agreement, and her light dimmed. She *had* been just a bit sulky when I'd first brought Ashad into our cave, but that had passed, and she was now very fond of my yellow-haired little boy. She'd never fully understood Ashad's need for solid food rather than light alone, so she habitually hovered near him, spilling light down on him – just in case he happened to need some.

I went on down through the twisting passageway that led to my cave, ducking under the icicle-like stalactites hanging down from the ceiling. They were much thicker and longer than they'd been at the beginning of my current cycle, and they were starting to get in my way. They were the result of the mineral-rich water that came seeping down through Mount Shrak, and they grew perceptibly longer every century. I made a mental note to take a club to them some day, when I had a little more time.

Ashad, covered with his fur robe, was still sleeping when I came out of the passageway into the large open chamber that was our home, so I thought it best not to disturb him.

I was still convinced that my decision to bring our alternates into the tag-end of *our* cycle had been the right one, but it was growing increasingly obvious that they'd brought some of their previous memories with them. I sat down in my chair near the table where

Ashad ate his meals of what he called 'real food' to consider some things I hadn't anticipated. I rather ruefully admitted to myself that I probably should have examined our alternates a bit more closely *before* I'd awakened them, but it was a little late now. I'd *assumed* that the children would respond to any dangers in the Domains of their *own* surrogate parents, so I'd been more than a little startled when Veltan had told me that *Yaltar's* dream had predicted the war in Zelana's Domain. I'd *assumed* that it'd be Eleria who'd warn us. Then when the *real* crisis arose, Yaltar had shoved prediction aside and had gone straight into action with those twin volcanos. That strongly suggested that Yaltar and Eleria had been very close during their previous cycle – a suggestion confirmed by the fact that Yaltar had occasionally referred to Eleria by her true name, 'Balacenia', and Eleria in like manner had spoken of 'Vash' – Yaltar's true name.

'I think there might just be a few holes in this "grand plan" of mine,' I ruefully admitted.

The more I thought about it, the more it seemed that the core of our problem lay in the fact that the Vlagh had been *consciously* modifying its servants over the past hundred or so eons. The modification of various life forms goes on all the time, usually in response to changes in the environment. Sometimes these modifications work, and sometimes they don't. The species that makes the right choice survives, but the wrong choice leads to extinction. In most cases, survival depends on sheer luck.

Before the arrival of the hairy predecessors of the creatures we now call men, vast numbers of creatures had arisen in the Land of Dhrall, but at some point *most* of them had made a wrong turn and had died out.

The Vlagh, unfortunately, had been among the survivors.

Originally, the Vlagh had been little more than a somewhat exotic insect which had nested near the shore of that inland sea which in the far distant past had covered what is now the Wasteland. A gradual climate change had evaporated that sea, and the Vlagh, driven by necessity, had begun to modify its servants. The change of climate had made avoiding the broiling sunlight a matter of absolute necessity, but as closely as I've been able to determine, the Vlagh had *not* simply groped around in search of a solution, but had relied on observation instead. I'm almost positive that it had been at this point that 'the overmind' had appeared. The ability to share information had given the servants of the Vlagh an enormous advantage over their neighbors. What any single one of them had seen, they *all* had seen. The Vlagh's species at that time had lived above the ground – most probably up in the trees. Several other species, however, had lived beneath the surface of the ground, and 'the seekers of knowledge' – spies, if you wish – had observed those neighbors and had provided very accurate descriptions of the appendages the neighbors used to burrow below the surface. Then 'the overmind' had filched the design, the Vlagh had duplicated it, and the next hatch had all been burrowers.

The extensive tunnels had kept the servants of the Vlagh out of the blazing sunlight, but that had only been the first problem they had been forced to solve. As the centuries had passed, the changed climate had gradually killed all the vegetation in that previously lush region, so there was no longer sufficient food to support a growing population.

The Vlagh had continued to lay eggs, of course, but each hatch had produced fewer and fewer offspring, and the Vlagh had come face to face with the distinct possibility of the extinction of its species.

When the burrowing insects had reached the mountains, they'd encountered solid stone, and their progress had stopped at that point. Not long after that, however, they'd discovered the caves lying beneath those mountains, and the species which *should* have gone extinct lived on.

I'm of two minds about caves. I *love* mine, but I *hate* theirs.

Anyway, the servants of the Vlagh had encountered other creatures in the caves and mountains, and evidently the overmind had realized that some of those creatures had characteristics which might prove to be very useful, and it had begun to experiment – or tamper – producing peculiar and highly unnatural variations.

I rather ruefully conceded that the experiment which had produced what Sorgan Hook-Beak of the Land of Maag colorfully called 'the snake-men' had been extremely successful, though I can't for the life of me understand exactly *how* the Vlagh had produced a creature that was part bug, part reptile, and part warm-blooded mammal that closely resembled a human being.

Biological impossibilities irritate me to no end.

I will admit, though, that had it not been for the near genius of the Shaman One-Who-Heals, the creatures of the Wasteland would probably have won the war in my sister's Domain.

Ashad made a peculiar little sound, and I got up from my chair and crossed in the dim light of our cavern to the stone bench that served as his bed to make sure that he was all right. He was nestled down under his fur robe with his eyes closed, though, so I was sure that he wasn't having any problems. Our discovery that our Dreamer-children weren't able to live on light alone had made us all a little jumpy. It wasn't the sort of thing we wanted to gamble with. Then we came face to face with the question of breathing. Veltan's ten eons on the face of the moon had been a clear demonstration of the fact that we didn't really *need* to breathe. Many of our pet people were fishermen, though, and drowning happens quite often. Even though our Dreamer-children were actually gods, their present condition strongly suggested that they needed air to breathe and food to eat, and none of us was in the mood to take any chances.

Ashad was still breathing in and out, though, so I went on back to my chair. I let my mind drift back to Ashad's first few hours here in my cave. If anybody with a cruel mind would like to see a god in a state of pure panic, I think he missed his chance. Panic had run rampant in my family that day. As soon as Ashad started screaming at me, I went all to pieces. Eventually, though, I remembered a peculiarity of the bears which share my Domain with deer, people and wild cows. She-bears give birth to their cubs during their yearly hibernation cycle, and their cubs attend to the business of nursing all on their own. Then I remembered that a she-bear called Broken-Tooth customarily hibernated in a cave that was no more than a mile away.

Still caught up in sheer panic, I grabbed up my howling Dreamer and ran to Mama Broken-Tooth's cave. She'd already given birth to the cub Long-Claw, and he was contentedly nursing when I entered the cave. Fortunately, I didn't have to argue with him. He was nice enough to move aside just a bit, and I introduced Ashad to bear's milk.

His crying stopped immediately.

Peculiarly – or maybe *not* – Ashad and Long-Claw were absolutely positive that they were brothers, and after they'd both nursed their fill of Mama Broken-Tooth's milk, they began to play with each other.

I remained in the cave until Mama Broken-Tooth awakened. She sniffed briefly at her two cubs – totally ignoring the fact that *one* of them didn't look at all like a bear – and then she gently nestled them against her bearish bosom as if there was nothing at all peculiar taking place. Of course, bears don't really see very well, so they rely instead on their sense of smell and after two weeks of rolling around on the dirt floor of the cave, Ashad had most *definitely* had a bearish fragrance about him.

Ashad slept until almost noon, but my flaxen-haired little boy still seemed exhausted when he rose, pulled on his tan leather smock and joined me at our table. 'Good morning, uncle,' he greeted me as he sank wearily into his chair. Almost absently, he pulled the large bowl full of red berries he'd brought home the previous evening in front of him and began to eat them one at a time. His appetite didn't seem quite normal, for some reason.

'Is something bothering you, Ashad?' I asked him.

'I had a nightmare last night, uncle,' the boy replied, absently fondling a shiny black stone that was about twice the size of an eagle's egg. 'It seemed that I was standing on nothing but air, and I was way up in the sky looking down at the Domain of Vash. The country down there in the South doesn't look at all like our country up here, does it?'

There it was again. Ashad obviously knew Yaltar's true name, even as Eleria did. 'The people of the South are farmers, Ashad,' I explained. 'They grow much of their food in the ground instead of concentrating on hunting the way our people do. They had to cut down the trees to give themselves open ground for planting, so the land down there doesn't look at all like the land up here. What else happened in your dream?'

Ashad pushed his yellow hair out of his eyes. 'Well,' he continued, 'it seemed that there were a whole lot of those nasty things coming into the Domain of Vash – sort of like the things that crawled down into Balacenia's Domain a little while ago.' The boy put the shiny black stone down on the table and ate more of the red berries.

There it was again. It was obvious now that the Dreamers were, perhaps unconsciously, stepping over the barrier I'd so carefully set up between them and their past.

'Anyway,' Ashad continued, 'there were outlanders there, and they were fighting the nasty things just like they did in Balacenia's Domain, but then things got very confusing. A whole lot of *other* outlanders came up across Mother Sea from the South, but it didn't seem like they were interested in the war very much, because they spent all their time talking to the farmers about somebody called Amar. The ones who were doing all the talking were wearing black robes, but there were some others who wore red clothes, and they were pushing the farmers around and making them listen while the ones in black talked. That went on for quite a while, and then the outlanders in the South got all excited, and they started to run north toward a great big waterfall, and the other outlanders – the ones who got there first – sort of got out of their way for while, and then when everybody got to that waterfall, it looked to me like everybody was trying to kill everybody else, and no matter how much I tried, I couldn't understand exactly what was going on.'

'I've heard that dreams are like that, Ashad. I don't need to sleep, so I don't really know what dreams are all about.' I hesitated. 'Where did you find that shiny black rock?' I asked, more to change the subject than out of any real curiosity.

'It was in the back of the cave where Mama Broken-Tooth sleeps in the winter,' Ashad replied. 'She had three cubs while she was sleeping this past winter, and while you were busy helping your sister Zelana, I went to her cave to see them. They're sort of the brothers of me and Long-Claw, aren't they? I mean, Mama Broken-Tooth nursed me and Long-Claw when *we* were just cubs, and now she's nursing the three new ones. That sort of makes us relatives of some kind, doesn't it?'

'I suppose so, yes.'

'Anyway, the three new cubs were making those funny little sounds bear-cubs always make when they're nursing, and Mama Broken-Tooth was cuddling them like she used to cuddle Long-Claw and me when we were just cubs.' He picked up the shiny stone. 'This is an agate, isn't it?' he asked, holding it out to me.

I took the stone, but almost dropped it when I sensed the enormous power emanating from it. 'I think you're right, Ashad. Black agates are very rare, though.'

'It's pretty, and I really liked it when I first saw it. I asked Mama Broken-Tooth if I could have it, and she told me to go ahead and take it. I used to carry it with me wherever I went, but then I mislaid it, I guess, but when I woke up this morning, there it was right in my bed with me. Isn't that odd?'

I laughed. 'I think this might just be the year of "odd", Ashad,' I said. 'It seems like every time I turn around there are piles and piles of "odd" staring me in the face. How did the rest of your bears come through this past winter?'

'Just fine, uncle,' Ashad replied. 'There are lots and lots of new cubs.' He suddenly grinned broadly, shaking off his gloomy expression. 'Baby bears are *so* much fun. They do all sorts of funny things that make their mothers terribly grouchy. Just last week Mama Broken-Tooth was scooping fish out of a stream – you know, throwing them up on the riverbank the way bears always do – but her three cubs thought she was playing, so they were swatting the fish back into the stream. When she saw what they were doing, she came running out of the water, gave them a few swats, and then chased them up a tree and made them stay up there for the rest of the day. I laughed, but she growled at me. She didn't seem to think it was funny at all.'

'Will you be all right here by yourself for a few days, Ashad? I need to go talk with my brother and my sisters. There are some things they need to know about.'

'I'll be fine, uncle. I was over in the village of Asmie the other day, and Tlingar promised to teach me how to use a spear-thrower – that long, limber stick the man-things around here use to whip their spears out there a long, long way. Tlingar's just about the best there is with the spear-thrower, isn't he?'

'He keeps the people of Asmie eating regularly, that much is certain,' I agreed. 'I shouldn't be too long, Ashad. If you get tired of throwing spears, you might want to go play with Mama Broken-Tooth's three cubs. If they're as frisky as you suggested, poor Mama Broken-Tooth's probably exhausted by now. Give her a little time to rest up. Like they always say, "Be nice to the neighbors, and they'll be nice to you." I'd better get started. I'd like to talk with Aracia *before* her priests get her involved in all those silly ceremonies.'

'Say hello to Enalla for me, uncle.'

There it was again. Ashad had just used Aracia's Dreamer Lillabeth's real name. Despite all my careful manipulation, the Dreamers kept pulling bits and pieces of reality up through the barriers I'd put between them and the past. I shuddered to think of what might happen if the Dreamers stumbled across some things far more significant than just their names.

I told my tiny, glowing sun to stay behind, and then I went to the long, twisting passageway that led out to the open air.

The morning light of early summer was golden as I came up out of my cave under Mount Shrak. I summoned my thunderbolt and rode on down toward the south-east to the Domain of my elder sister Aracia.

Aracia's Domain is much like the Domain of our baby brother Veltan, with vast wheat fields stretching from horizon to horizon like some enormous green carpet in the early summer sun. I hate to admit it, but the introduction of wheat farming and bread has brought much more stability to the Domains of Aracia and Veltan than the sometimes catch-as-catch-can quality of life in my Domain and Zelana's, where the land is primarily devoted to hunting and fishing. There *has* to be more to life than just munching on a piece of half-moldy bread, though. I'm fairly sure that Aracia and Veltan view me as some sort of primitive antique, but I know better. The people of their Domains are little more than cattle. They move around in herds, and I wouldn't be the least bit surprised to discover that 'moo' crops up in their dialect quite frequently.

The people of my Domain – and of Zelana's – are fiercely independent. *Nobody* – not even me or Zelana – tells them what they *must* do. To my way of looking at things, those farmers more closely resemble the mindless servants of the Vlagh than they do *real* people.

You don't necessarily need to tell Aracia or Veltan that I just said that.

* * *

Where was I? Oh, yes, now I remember. I'm fairly certain that it was farming that ultimately led to religion in Aracia's Domain. Once the spring planting is finished, a farmer really has nothing significant to do until harvesting in the autumn, and that gives him far too much time for speculation. As long as people concentrate on such things as what they are going to eat tomorrow or how they're going to avoid freezing to death when winter rolls around again, there's a certain practicality in their lives. It's when the people have enough free time to begin asking such questions as 'Who am I?' or 'How did I get here?' that things start getting wormy.

I've periodically ranged out beyond the Land of Dhrall to observe the progress of the outlanders, and I've noticed that the more intelligent ones spend a lot of their time brooding about mysterious gods. That isn't necessary here in the Land of Dhrall, of course, since it's very likely that the god of any particular region lives just over the hill or down the street.

Some of the people of Aracia's Domain saw a glorious opportunity there. Aracia could tamper with the weather, if she chose to, and that produced abundant crops, and the displays of gratitude of her subject people were usually grossly overdone. Had one of my people gone to such extremes, I'd have laughed in the fool's face.

Aracia, however really enjoyed all the groveling and excessive displays of gratitude. Deep down, Aracia adores being adored. I'd been the first of our family to awaken during this cycle, so I was nominally in charge of things this time. Aracia had been the second to awaken, but deep in her heart she yearns to be first, so she encourages her people to continue their overdone displays of gratitude, and the more clever among them, sensing that need, exaggerate their thanks to the level of absurdity, erecting temples and altars, and prostrating themselves each time she passes.

Aracia thinks that's *awfully* nice of them.

Aracia's need for adoration has attracted many of the less industrious men of her domain, and over the years this has produced a sizeable town, and that in turn has brought assorted tradesmen to the place. I'm sure that Aracia's temple-town is the closest thing to a city in the entire Land of Dhrall. The large stone buildings are covered with a white plaster and their roofs are made of red tile. The narrow streets have been paved over with large flagstones, and the town is at least a mile wide.

At the very center, of course, is Aracia's enormous temple with gleaming white spires reaching up toward the sky. To be perfectly honest, the whole place seems just a little silly to me.

When my thunderbolt deposited me in Aracia's marble-pillared throne-room, her overfed sycophants either fainted dead away or fled in terror. I smiled faintly. Nothing in the world seems to get everybody's immediate attention more quickly than a thunderbolt.

Aracia's golden throne stood on a marble pedestal, and there were red drapes behind it. 'Have you ever considered letting me know when you're coming, Dahlaine?' my splendidly dressed sister demanded in an icy tone of voice.

'I just did,' I replied bluntly. 'Are your ears starting to fail, Aracia? Any time you hear thunder, it's probably me.' I looked around my sister's throne-room and saw a fair number of wide-eyed clergymen trying to conceal themselves behind the marble pillars at the sides of the vast chamber. 'Let's go find someplace private, dear sister. There are some things you should know about, and I don't have all that much time.'

'You're very rude, Dahlaine. Did you know that?'

'It's a failing of mine. Over the years, I've found that "polite" is a waste of time, and I'm just a bit busy right now. Shall we go?' I've long since discovered that abruptness is the best way to get Aracia's immediate attention. Any time I give her the least bit of slack, she'll lapse into 'ceremonial', and that usually takes at least half a day.

Aracia looked more than a little offended, but she *did* rise up from her golden throne and step down off the pedestal to lead the way out of her ornate throne-room.

'What's got you so stirred up today, big brother?' Aracia asked as we proceeded down a long, deserted hallway.

'Let's hold off until we get to some private place,' I suggested. 'There's trouble in the wind, and I don't think we should alarm the people of your Domain just yet.'

Aracia led the way into a rather plain room and closed the door behind us. We sat down in large wooden chairs on opposite sides of an ornately carved table.

'Are you sure that none of your people can hear us here?'

'Of course they can't, Dahlaine,' she replied. 'This room's one of those "special" places. Nobody'll be able to hear us, because the room isn't really here.'

'How did you manage that?'

She shrugged. 'A slight adjustment of time is all it takes. This room is two days older than the rest of the temple, so we're talking to each other two days ago.'

'Clever,' I said admiringly.

'I'm glad you like it. What's happening that's got you so stirred up, Dahlaine?'

'Ashad had one of *those* dreams last night, dear sister. Evidently the Vlagh didn't learn too much in Zelana's Domain, so it's sending its servants South toward Veltan's Domain – or it will before much longer. Ashad's dream was a bit more complicated than Yaltar's was when he saw the invasion of Zelana's Domain though, and some things were cropping up that I didn't quite understand. He told me about two separate – and evidently unrelated – invasions and a very complex war near the Falls of Vash. That's another thing that kept cropping up as well. Ashad referred to Yaltar by his real name – in much the same way that Yaltar kept referring to Eleria as "Balacenia". I almost choked the first time Ashad said "Vash" when he spoke of Yaltar.'

'I *told* you that bringing in our alternates was a mistake, Dahlaine. If our Dreamers wake up and come to their senses, the whole world might collapse in on itself.'

'They *do* seem to be stepping around some of the barriers I put in place, Aracia,' I admitted, 'but it's too late to do anything about it now. The Vlagh's evidently going to keep trying to overrun us, and we don't have time to raise a new group of Dreamers. Has Lillabeth had any of *those* dreams yet?'

'Not that she's told me about,' Aracia replied. 'I've been a bit busy here lately, though.'

'Does being worshiped and adored really take *that* much time, Aracia?'

'No, but running back and forth to the Isle of Akalla to negotiate with Trenicia does. She's not really interested in gold, so I've had to find something else to get her interest.'

'Who's Trenicia?' I asked curiously.

'She's the queen of the warrior women of Akalla.'

'Do women really make very good warriors?'

'If they're big enough, they do. Trenicia's almost as big as Sorgan Hook-Beak, and she's probably more skilled with a sword than he'll ever be.'

'Impressive,' I conceded, 'but if she doesn't want gold, how are you paying her?'

'With diamonds, rubies, emeralds, and sapphires,' Aracia replied. 'They're warriors, but they're still women, so they love adornment. For a good diamond necklace, a woman from Akalla will kill anybody – or anything – that gets in her way.'

'If the women rule the Isle of Akalla, what are the men doing?'

'They're something on the order of house pets, Dahlaine. If I understood what Trenicia told me correctly, the men of the Isle of Akalla have raised indolence to an art form. On Akalla, *everything* is women's work.'

'Even war?' That startled me.

'Especially war. The men of Akalla are lazy and timid and generally useless – except as breeding stock.'

I chose not to pursue *that* particular comment. 'It just occurs to me that maybe you and I might want to consider taking Queen Trenicia and the horse soldier Ekial with us to the war in Veltan's Domain,' I said. 'They'll probably be fighting the servants of the Vlagh before much longer, it wouldn't hurt for them to see what they'll be coming up against.'

'You might be right, Dahlaine,' Aracia agreed. 'As I recall, the Maags and Trogites weren't *too* happy when Zelana finally got around to telling them about some of the peculiarities of the enemy. Maybe you and I should try honesty rather than deception.'

'What an unnatural thing to suggest, Aracia,' I joked. 'I'm shocked at you. Shocked!'

'Oh, quit!' she said.

And then we both laughed.

My thunderbolt took me across the lower edge of the Wasteland, and I peered down at the sand and rocks rather closely on the off-chance that I might see the servants of the Vlagh moving toward our young brother's Domain, but as far as I could tell, the desert below was void of any kind of life.

The twin volcanos at the head of the ravine above Lattash were still belching fire as I rode my thunderbolt into Zelana's Domain, and I was quite certain the eruption would continue for years. The more I thought about it, the more it seemed that perhaps I should have put some limitations on the capabilities of the Dreamers. They *were* children, after all, and children sometimes get carried away and overly enthusiastic. The only problem I saw with that notion was *how*. Despite their immaturity, the Dreamers had virtually unlimited power over the forces of nature, and I ruefully conceded that they could quite probably step over any barrier I might have tried to put in their way. My original idea had *seemed* to be a perfect solution to a serious problem, but perhaps I should have given it just a bit more thought.

I cast out a searching thought and sensed Zelana's presence about halfway down the north side of the bay, and I directed my thunderbolt to that spot.

Zelana was talking with Red-Beard and Longbow in what appeared to be a village in the final stages of construction some distance down the bay from Lattash. The rounded hills behind that new village had gentler slopes than the steep peaks somewhat to the east of Lattash, there was a patch of woods just to the north of the new village, and a meadow that stretched for miles beyond those woods.

'Do you *have* to do that, Dahlaine?' Zelana demanded peevishly when I suddenly joined them. 'Isn't there some way you can muffle that awful noise?'

'I don't think so, Zelana. Lightning *is* the fastest way to travel, but you have to put up with the noise. Ashad's been dreaming, and it seems that our speculation came pretty close to the mark. Ashad's dream confirmed the fact that the creatures of the Wasteland will attack Veltan's Domain next.'

'Did your boy's dream give you any specifics about just where we'll encounter the servants of the Vlagh?' the archer Longbow asked.

'Somewhere in the vicinity of the Falls of Vash,' I replied. I looked curiously at Zelana. 'I gather that you've changed your mind and decided to help the rest of us defend our Domains,' I suggested.

'The Land of Dhrall is all one piece, brother mine. If the Vlagh wins any part of it, we'll *all* be in danger.'

I hesitated. 'Are you feeling better now, dear sister?' I asked. 'We were all very worried when you suddenly decided to go home to your grotto.'

'No, Dahlaine,' she replied tartly, 'I'm *not* feeling better, but Eleria bullied me into coming back out into the world of chaos.'

'Bullied? She's just a little girl, Zelana. How could she bully *you*?'

'She told me that if *I* didn't want to help Veltan, she'd take over and do it herself. Once she takes off that sweet mask she wears all the time, she can be very cruel. She didn't leave me any choice at all. I think that pearl of hers might have something to do with that.'

'It's possible, I suppose,' I agreed. 'Those jewels seem to be deeply involved in the children's dreams. Ashad has one too, and I think it had something to do with that dream of his.'

'What sort of jewel is it?' Zelana asked curiously.

'A black agate. It's really rather pretty, and Ashad seems quite attached to it.'

'I don't think I've ever seen a black agate. Where did he find it?'

'It was in the back of Mama Broken-Tooth's cave.'

'Who's Mama Broken-Tooth?'

'The she-bear who nursed him when he was a baby.'

'Wasn't it a little dangerous to hand your little boy over to a bear?'

I shook my head. 'Not really,' I replied. 'She-bears give birth to their cubs while they're hibernating, and when they wake up, the cubs are nursing or playing in the cave. They automatically bond with the cubs they nurse, so Ashad wasn't in any danger. Mama Broken-Tooth had already given birth to her cub Long-Claw when I took Ashad to her cave, and Ashad and Long-Claw think of themselves as brothers.' I looked around. 'Where's Eleria right now?' I asked quietly.

'She and Yaltar are out in that meadow just beyond the trees,' Red-Beard told me. 'Planter's looking after them.'

'Who's Planter?'

'She's the one who teaches the women of the tribe how to grow food,' Red-Beard explained, 'and the one the women go to when they have problems. She can be a little blunt sometimes, but she knows what she's doing.'

'You're keeping something from me, aren't you, Dahlaine?' Zelana asked pointedly.

'I was just getting to that, dear sister. Ashad's dream was fairly specific about the invasion of Veltan's Domain by the creatures of the Wasteland, but he mentioned a second invasion that *won't* come from the Wasteland. It's going to come from the sea.'

'That's ridiculous, Dahlaine,' Zelana scoffed. 'Has the Vlagh allied itself with the queen of the fish now?'

'I'm just passing on what Ashad told me, Zelana. Where's Veltan? We'd better go tell him what's afoot.'

'He's out in the bay on the Trogite ship of Commander

Narasan,' Red-Beard replied. 'Longbow can take you out there in his canoe, if you'd like. I'd do it myself, but I'm just a little busy right now.'

'Is there trouble of some kind?'

'Sort of. The fire-mountains destroyed Lattash, so the tribe's busy setting up a new village out here. It might not be as pretty, but it's safer.'

I looked at the partially-completed lodges near the beach. 'Those don't look at all like the ones back in Lattash,' I observed, 'but they seem sort of familiar, for some reason.'

'They should,' Longbow told me. 'They're copies of the lodges up in the north of *your* Domain.'

'It's part of a fairly elaborate deception, big brother,' Zelana said with a faint smile. 'The men of Chief Red-Beard's tribe believe that growing food is "women's work", and that it's beneath them. The women needed help in preparing the ground for planting, and Longbow's chief, Old-Bear, told these two that some tribes in your Domain live in a vast grassland where there aren't any trees, and they build their lodges out of sod instead of tree branches. The men of Red-Beard's tribe built the usual lodges out of tree limbs and then sat around loafing and telling each other war stories. But one windy night these two slipped around pulling down the new lodges. When the sun came up, they walked around with sombre faces telling the men of the tribe that tree limbs weren't sturdy enough for lodges out here, and that they were going to need something more solid. They suggested sod, and the men of the tribe are out in that meadow cutting sod for all they're worth. The women of the tribe are coming along behind them planting seeds. Red-Beard's tribe will have nice sturdy lodges and plenty to eat when winter arrives, and nobody was offended.'

'Clever,' I said admiringly. Then I frowned. 'Has something happened to old Chief White-Braid?' I asked.

'The destruction of Lattash was more than he could bear,' Red-Beard explained sadly. 'He knew that the tribe was going to have to find a new place to live, but he didn't feel up to doing it himself because his sorrow – or maybe even grief – had disabled him to the point that he couldn't make decisions any more. He realized that, so he laid the chore on *my* shoulders. I didn't really want any part of it, but he didn't give me any choice.'

'You'll probably do quite well, Chief Red-Beard,' I told him. 'I've noticed that men who don't really *want* authority and responsibility make better leaders than men who yearn for the position. Let's go talk with our baby brother, Zelana. There are things he needs to know, and I'm not sure how much time he has left.'

Longbow led my sister and me down to the beach where his canoe was resting on the sand. There's a quality about Zelana's archer that I find more than a little awesome. He's a bleak-faced man whose war with the creatures of the Wasteland had begun when he'd been hardly more than a child, and killing the servants of the Vlagh had been his only purpose in life. He was a grim man with very few friends and an almost inhuman level of self-control.

It occurred to me that we might all want to keep this man around. If all went well, we'd turn back the servants of the Vlagh wherever and whenever they attempted to invade our individual Domains, but in all probability, the Vlagh would still be there. Longbow might very well be the answer to that problem. A single venom-tipped arrow would send the creatures of the Wasteland down the road to extinction, and that, of course, was our ultimate goal.

Longbow pulled his canoe down to the water and held it in place while Zelana and I climbed into it, and then he pushed it clear and stepped into the stern all in one motion.

'I think our baby brother's on board Narasan's ship, Longbow,' Zelana suggested.

'Probably so,' Longbow agreed. He paddled us out across the bay to the oversized Trogite ship of Commander Narasan, where the young soldier called Keselo stood waiting for us at the rail. 'Is something wrong?' he asked as Longbow smoothly pulled his canoe in alongside the ship.

'Not really,' Zelana replied. 'We just came by to tell our baby brother that it's time to go to work.'

'Has Eleria been dreaming again?'

'No, young man,' I told him. 'It was *my* little boy, Ashad, this time, and there were some very peculiar things involved. We're hoping that Veltan might be able to explain them for us.' I paused for a moment. 'Now that I think about it, though, *you* can probably explain them even better than Veltan. Why don't you come along?'

'Of course. Your brother's back in Commander Narasan's cabin at the stern.'

'Is Narasan with him?' Zelana asked.

'No, Lady Zelana. The commander's over on the *Seagull* conferring with Captain Sorgan.'

'Good,' I said. 'I'm not sure that Narasan's going to be very happy about some of the peculiarities that showed up in Ashad's dream. Is your commander particularly religious?'

'Not noticeably,' Keselo replied. 'Is that likely to be very significant?'

'We'll get to that in just a few minutes. Let's go talk with Veltan.'

'All right,' the young man replied, turning and leading us back toward the ornate, almost house-like structure at the aft end of the ship. He rapped politely on the door.

'Come in,' Veltan's voice came from inside.

Keselo opened the door and stood aside to let us go on in ahead of him.

The cabin was much more ornate than I'd really expected. In some ways it resembled a room in a house rather than part of a ship. The ceiling wasn't very high, and, since the sailors used the cabin's roof as a deck, there were substantial beams to keep the ceiling from tumbling down on those who slept there. There was also a large window across the back of the cabin to give the people inside the cabin something to look at. All in all, I thought the whole thing was just a bit silly, but I decided not to make an issue of that.

Veltan was seated at a large table examining a map. 'Is something amiss?'

'Not really,' I told him. 'At least not yet. My little boy Ashad had one of *those* dreams last night, and we were right about *one* thing, at least. The servants of the Vlagh *will* be coming your way soon.'

'Did he tell you exactly when?'

'"When" never comes up in these dreams, Veltan,' I told him. 'You should know that by now. Now we come to the complicated part. Ashad told me that there was a *second* invasion in his dream, and *those* particular invaders had absolutely no connection with the servants of the Vlagh.'

'Who were they, then?'

'As closely as I was able to determine, they were Trogites, and they wanted to talk to your people about their gods. How much were you able to discover about somebody called Amar?'

'Not too much, big brother,' Veltan replied. 'Narasan has nothing but contempt for the clergy of the Amarite faith.'

'He's not alone there, Veltan,' Keselo said. 'Anyone in the Trogite Empire with the least bit of decency or intelligence despises the Amarite church. The clergy is corrupt, greedy beyond belief, and totally without honor. It's common knowledge that the "church" is nothing more than an invention of the priesthood designed to swindle the ordinary people of the empire out of just about everything they own.'

'That has a familiar ring, doesn't it?' Zelana observed. 'Our dear sister has a priesthood that behaves in much the same way.'

I shrugged. 'It makes her happy, I suppose.' I looked at Veltan. 'Where's the rest of Narasan's army?' I asked. 'If I understood correctly, the men he brought to Lattash were just an advance force.'

'The bulk of Narasan's army's still in the port of Castano on the north shore of the Empire. Why do you ask, big brother?'

'The second invasion in Ashad's dream almost *had* to involve Trogites, since this "Amar" is a Trogite invention.'

'That's true, I suppose,' Veltan conceded. 'Where are we going with this, Dahlaine?'

I looked inquiringly at Keselo. 'I gather that *most* of the men in Narasan's army share your feelings about this so-called religion,' I suggested. 'Is it at all possible that *some* of them feel differently, but they're keeping it to themselves?'

'Not after what happened in the southern part of the empire last year,' he replied. 'We lost twelve cohorts as a direct result of a deception that we tracked back to a high-ranking clergyman in the Amarite church. That's why Commander Narasan threw his sword away and went into business as a beggar. If any man in the army even suggested that the Amarite church had anything even remotely resembling decency, his comrades would kick the living daylights out of him.'

33

'Let's not dismiss the possibility entirely, Keselo,' Veltan said with a troubled look on his face. 'From what I've heard, the word "gold" sends the Amarite church into a feeding frenzy, and if I remember correctly, there was some extended discussion of gold in the army compound back in Kaldacin. Just for the sake of argument, let's say that some soldier in your army happened to visit a tavern in Castano, and the word "gold" came up during a casual conversation, and somebody affiliated with the Amarite Church happened to overhear the conversation. Wouldn't *that* sort of explain the second invasion in Ashad's dream?'

'It doesn't really fit,' Keselo disagreed. 'The Amarite church might *want* to come here to the Land of Dhrall to harvest gold and slaves, but they'd need to know exactly how to get through all that floating ice, and Gunda and Padan have the only maps.'

'That's true, I suppose,' Veltan conceded, 'but Narasan told me that he could field a hundred thousand soldiers. It'd only take one opportunist to blow away any chance of secrecy. I think *that's* the answer to the origins of that second invasion in your little boy's dream, Dahlaine.'

'It *would* explain it, I guess,' I agreed. Then I looked at Keselo again. 'Just exactly what are "slaves"?' I asked him. 'I don't believe I've ever heard that word before.'

'You've been very lucky, then. It was a fairly standard custom back in the early days of the Empire for the Imperial armies to capture people of more primitive cultures and then sell them to the landowners of the Empire itself, almost as if they were cattle. Then the landowners would hire men with whips to drive the unfortunates to do the actual farming. The practice fell into disuse a hundred or so years ago, but a few decades back the Church realized the she'd been passing up a wonderful opportunity to make money, so the slavers are back in business again, and at least half of them are members of the clergy.'

Veltan's face went dead white. 'If those monsters even come *close* to the shores of my Domain, I'll *destroy* them!'

'No, Veltan,' I told him quite firmly, 'you *won't*. Killing *anything* is absolutely forbidden, and you know it. If you tried something like that, you'd be banished forever, and it wouldn't be to the moon this time. You'd spend the rest of eternity in a place of absolute darkness where the only sounds you'd hear would be your own screams of endless despair. I'm sure we'll be able to find some suitable alternatives, but if you even *try* to kill anything, I'll tie you up in a knot so tight that it'll take you about four cycles just to unlace your fingers from your toes.'

'So *that's* why you people had to rush around hiring armies!' Keselo exclaimed. 'I've never really understood why you didn't just obliterate the enemies with a wave of your hand. It was because you're not permitted to kill *anything*, isn't it?'

'I want you to forget what you just heard, young man,' I told him firmly. 'Do you understand me?'

'Why, yes, I believe I do.'

'Good.' I looked over at my brother, 'You'd better tell Narasan to start moving his fleet, Veltan,' I suggested. 'We've finished everything here in Zelana's Domain, so it's time to move on. Ashad's dream wasn't too specific about time. That seems to be one of the characteristics of these dreams. Our Dreamers can give us all kinds of details about *what's* going to happen, but "when" always seems a little vague.'

'Did Ashad happen to mention *where* the main battle's likely to take place?' Veltan asked.

'He said that it would be in the general vicinity of the Falls of

35

Vash, little brother. He wasn't too specific, and I didn't want to push him.'

Veltan winced. 'That's very rugged country up there, big brother. I don't think the Trogites will like the idea of fighting on ground like that.'

'It can't be much worse than the ravine above Lattash was, can it?' Zelana asked.

'It makes that ravine look like a gentle meadow, sister mine,' Veltan replied glumly. 'It wasn't even *there* at the end of my last cycle. When I woke up, the man-things of my Domain seemed to be very excited about it. I'm not sure exactly why Vash created the falls, but they *are* spectacular to look at. Looking is one thing, but walking around up there's something entirely different. I wouldn't be at all surprised if Yaltar's twin volcanos are an outgrowth of what he'd done when his name was Vash. The river that tumbles over the falls originates in a geyser that spouts up about a hundred feet into the air, and that's got a fairly strong odor of earthquakes and eruptions. There's a fault line just south of that geyser, and it left a sheer face about two hundred feet high a mile or so downstream from the geyser. With all that water tumbling over the edge, it's impossible to climb up that cliff, so anybody who wants to get up there has to take a different route.' Veltan stopped and suddenly snapped his fingers. 'I should have *known* that this was coming!' he exclaimed. 'Last spring Omago told me that some strangers had been asking questions about the Falls of Vash. I had my mind on other things at the time, so I didn't pursue it. Evidently, the Vlagh's been sending scouts out into our Domains for quite a while now.'

'Who's Omago?' Zelana asked.

'He's a very solid, dependable fellow with an extensive orchard near my house. He knows more about farming than anybody else in my Domain does, and he's a very good listener. Other farmers come to him for advice, and they tell him about any unusual things that are happening. Then he passes them onto me.'

'He's the chief, then?' Longbow asked.

'I wouldn't go quite *that* far, Longbow. He gives advice, not orders.'

'It sort of amounts to the same thing, wouldn't you say? A good chief does things that way. Only bad chieftains order their men around. Fortunately, they don't usually last very long.'

'He's got a point there, Veltan,' I agreed. 'You might want to consider getting word to this Omago fellow. Let him know what's in the wind, and have him pass the word along. Your people should know that the creatures of the Wasteland are coming, and they need to start getting ready for war.'

'That's absurd, Dahlaine,' Veltan scoffed. 'My people don't even know what the word "war" means. That's why I had to hire Narasan's army. Omago can probably make certain that the hired soldiers get plenty to eat, but that's likely to be his only contribution during the war.' He smiled faintly. 'Of course, if we can persuade Ara to do the cooking, we might have some trouble persuading the outlanders to go home after the war's over.'

'Who's Ara?' Zelana asked.

'Omago's wife. She's a beautiful lady and quite probably the best cook in the world. The smells that come from her kitchen even tempt me sometimes.'

'Oh, incidentally, Veltan,' I cut in, 'Aracia and I'd like to bring the commanders of the armies we've been hiring down to your Domain to observe. I'm sure they'll be coming up against the servants of the Vlagh sometime soon, and it might not be a bad idea for them to see what they'll encounter.'

'No problem, big brother,' Veltan said with an impudent sort of grin. 'I'll go tell Narasan and Sorgan that it's time to go South, and then I'll have my pet take me home so that I can have a talk with Omago. For right now, that's about as far as we can go. Everything's sort of up in the air at this point, so we might have to make things up as we go along.'

'What else is new and different?' I said sourly. 'Looking back, I'd say that we've been doing that since the very beginning.'

'Of this war, you mean?' Zelana suggested.

'I wouldn't limit it to that, my sister. We've been making things up as we went along since the beginning of time, haven't we?'

'It makes life much more interesting, big brother,' she said with an impish sort of grin. 'Things always seem to get so boring if you know exactly what's going to happen, don't they?'

I chose not to answer that particular question.

THE SOUTHLAND

1

◆━◆━◆

Omago's father owned the fields and orchards lying just to the north of Veltan's huge house, and that proximity had made Omago look upon Veltan more as a neighbor than a ruler – or a god. Veltan didn't make a big issue of his divinity, and so Omago had always felt comfortable in his presence.

As a child, Omago had much preferred working in his father's orchard rather than in the open fields, mostly because it was shady in the orchard, but in the springtime when the fruit trees bloomed, the beauty of the blossoms almost took his breath away.

He soon discovered that he was not alone in that appreciation. When the fruit trees were in bloom Veltan almost lived in the orchard, and as the two of them came to know each other better, they spent many hours talking. Their discussions were wide-ranging, and almost without realizing it, the boy Omago was receiving an education that went far beyond the tedious business of digging, planting, and harvesting.

Veltan's Domain here in the South of the Land of Dhrall, for example, was only a *part* of the entire continent. There were three others that were owned by Veltan's brother and his two sisters. Veltan's descriptions of his kin were so amusing that Omago frequently burst out laughing. He found Veltan's description of the people of the West and North somewhat tantalizing, though. He simply could not imagine a life spent hunting. Some times he'd tried his hand at fishing, but he wasn't really very good at it, and it seemed that hunting and fishing might be a very chancy sort of thing to depend on if somebody wanted to keep eating regularly. Veltan's descriptions of the deep primeval forests, noble deer crowned with antlers, and buckskin-clad hunters stirred some longings in young Omago, though. There wasn't really much in the way of adventure here in the farmland of the South where the primary desire of the inhabitants was stability. Stability was good for farming, but it wasn't really very exciting.

Veltan didn't go into too many details about his *own* peculiarities during those extended springtime conversations, but Omago had already heard about most of them. At first, the stories other farmers passed on had seemed wildly exaggerated to young Omago, but as he came to know Veltan better, he'd been reluctantly forced to accept them. He'd never seen Veltan so much as taste any food, and not once had he even seen him close his eyes.

It was shortly after Omago's ninth birthday when the question of alternate gods came up. The two of them were sitting in the orchard, and a strong breeze was showering them with a near blizzard of apple-blossom petals.

'You don't have to answer this if you'd rather not, Veltan,' Omago said a bit hesitantly, 'but old man Enkar told me that you haven't always been the god of this part of the Land of Dhrall. He said that somebody else used to take care of things around here. Is that really true, or was he just making it up to fool me?'

Veltan shrugged. 'It's fairly close to what really happens, Omago,' he replied. 'It might *seem* that we never sleep, but that's not entirely true. We have cycles of sleep and wakefulness, and after we've been awake for a long time, we start to get a little fuzzy in our minds. We can't remember things, and we start behaving just a bit strange. That's a clear sign that it's time for us to get some sleep – and it's just about at that time that the other branch of the family wakes up. Then they take care of things while we sleep.'

'I guess that makes sense – sort of,' Omago admitted. 'How well do you know these cousins of yours?'

'Cousins?'

'Cousins are the children of your parents' brothers and sisters,' Omago explained. 'Wasn't that what you meant when you said "branch of the family"?'

'It *does* sort of fit, now that you mention it. I'll have to remember that.'

'Do you ever have a chance to talk with them?'

'I don't talk in my sleep, Omago. Actually, about the only thing I know about my cousin is his name – and that's probably only because there's a waterfall up in the mountains that's named after him. You *have* heard of "the Falls of Vash", haven't you?'

'I've heard about them, but I've never seen them. Did your cousin make them, maybe?'

'I couldn't really say, boy. When I woke up this last time, the people around here didn't speak any too well, so about all I could get from them was the name.' Veltan paused and looked speculatively into Omago's young face. 'I think maybe that's about as much as I should tell you for right now. After you've had some time to get used to what I've told you today, you can come by and ask more questions if you really want to.'

'It might take a little while,' Omago admitted. 'Maybe I should be a little more careful with these questions of mine. The answers are kind of scary.'

'You'll get used to them in time, boy. Curiosity's a good thing, really, but you have to be a little careful when you turn it loose.'

'I noticed that,' Omago agreed.

'I thought I noticed you noticing,' Veltan said with no hint of a smile.

As Omago matured, the local farmers became aware of his familiarity with Veltan, and they thought that it might just be sort of convenient. It was much easier for them to look Omago up and tell him about things than it would be to go up to Veltan's house on the hill and tell him in person. Veltan didn't really wave his divinity around, but still—

In time, it became almost like a tradition. During the course of almost every day, two or three local farmers would approach Omago and tell him things they thought Veltan should know about, and as evening approached, Omago would trudge up the hill to Veltan's peculiar house and pass those things on to the local god.

Omago didn't really think of Veltan as a god. It seemed that he was more a friend than some distant divinity. In time, he even came to enjoy those daily conversations. It was a rather nice way to conclude each day, and he'd stop by Veltan's house every evening, even when he had nothing to report.

The seasons turned in their stately march, and it seemed to Omago that the farmland near Veltan's grand house moved in rhythm with those seasons. He'd heard that there were towns and villages farther to the south, but it had always seemed to him that cramming people together all in one place was just a bit ridiculous. His father's farm covered many acres of land spread out over the gently rolling hills, and every crop had its proper place – wheat to the west and south, vegetables to the north, and the orchard close in just to the east of the well-shaded house. Some of the neighboring farmers seemed to think that shade-trees were just a waste of time and space – up until about midsummer, when it turned hot and the sun beat down on them.

The houses stood far apart in this region, each of the thatch-roofed homes standing in the approximate center of each farmer's land. That seemed most practical to Omago. Daylight was a time for work, not for walking.

By the time he'd reached his twenty-first birthday, Omago had come to know all the local farmers very well, and he passed his assessments on to Veltan along with whatever those farmers had told him.

'I wouldn't really take anything Selga comes up with too seriously, Veltan,' he said one evening.

'Oh?'

'Selga's got a sort of a problem. He isn't very tall, and people tend to overlook him. He *really* wants to be noticed, so he comes by almost every day to tell me about something – anything – that he wants me to pass on to you. All I have to do to make him feel good is to pretend that I think what he just said was terribly important and that I'll pass it on to you the first chance I get, *and* assure him that I'll tell you that *he* was the one who brought it to my attention.'

'That's sad,' Veltan sighed.

Omago shrugged. 'Everybody's got problems of some kind, Veltan. It's nothing to get all weepy about. People come, and then they go. You know that, don't you?'

'You can be a very cruel person sometimes, Omago.'

'I don't make the rules, Veltan. All I do is follow them.'

'How's your father been lately?'

That startled Omago. No matter how hard he tried to conceal things from Veltan, his friend always saw right through him. 'He's not getting any better, I'm afraid,' he replied sadly. 'Sometimes he can't even remember his own name. He keeps asking for mother, though. I don't think he remembers that she died last year.'

'I'm sorry, Omago,' Veltan said with great sincerity. 'I wish there was something I could do to help him.'

'I don't really think you should, Veltan. I think father's getting very tired, and if we keep him here, it'll just make him more sad. Why don't we just let him go? I think that might be the kindest thing we can do for him.'

The following spring Omago was in his orchard when a vibrant woman's voice came from just behind him. 'Why are you doing that?'

Omago, startled, spun around quickly.

'I'm sorry,' the woman apologized. 'I didn't mean to frighten you. Why are you picking all those little green apples?' She was quite tall, she had long, dark auburn hair, soft green eyes, and she wore a blue linen dress.

Omago smiled. 'Apple trees always seem to get carried away in the spring,' he explained. 'They want to have lots and lots of puppies. If I don't thin out the baby apples in the spring, there won't be any of them much bigger than acorns when they ripen. I've tried to explain that to my trees, but they just won't listen. It's awfully hard to get a tree's attention, particularly in the spring-time.'

'You're Omago, aren't you?'

'That's what they call me.'

'You're quite a bit younger than I thought you'd be. You *are* the same Omago people come to when they want to let Veltan know what's happening, aren't you?'

Omago nodded. 'Was there something you wanted me to tell him?'

'Not right now, no. I just wanted to be sure that I'd recognize you in case something came up that I needed to let him know about.'

'You could always go on up to his house and tell him yourself, you know.'

'Maybe, but people tell me that he'd rather hear you tell him these things. How did you get to know him so well?'

'He used to come here to this orchard when the trees were blooming. An orchard in bloom is prettier than any flower-garden. This was my father's orchard back then, and I was only a little boy. Veltan and I used to talk for hours and hours, so I probably know him better than anybody else around here. That's most likely why the local farmers decided to use me as their messenger boy. You don't live around here, do you?'

She shook her head. 'No. I live quite a ways away. I was very sorry to hear that your father died recently.'

Omago shrugged. 'It didn't really come as a surprise. His health hadn't been too good for the past several years.'

'You're busy,' she said, 'and I'm just underfoot. It was nice meeting you.' She turned to walk away.

'What's your name?' he called after her.

'Ara,' she replied back over her shoulder.

For some reason, Omago couldn't get the strange girl out of his mind. He realized that he didn't know very much about her. She hadn't even volunteered to tell him her name until he'd come right out and asked her.

She was obviously several years younger than he was, but her manner of speaking was hardly adolescent. She'd managed to get a great deal of information from him, but she hadn't given him very much in return.

He tried to just shrug her off, but the memory of their brief conversation kept coming back, and it wasn't only the conversation. She was far and away the prettiest girl he'd ever met. Her lush auburn hair reminded him of autumn, and the memory of her vibrant voice sang in his ears. He felt an almost desperate need to find out more about her.

It was spring, and there were all kinds of things he should be doing right now, but he just couldn't keep his mind on his work.

'I can't seem to think about anything else, Veltan,' he confessed a few days later.

Veltan smiled. 'Is she still in the general vicinity?' he asked.

'That's what people tell me,' Omago replied. 'I haven't seen her myself, but several other farmers have. They all tell me that she's been asking a lot of questions – most of them about me. You don't suppose she'll just turn around and go on back home again, do you? She didn't even tell me the name of the village where she lives. How in the world am I ever going to find her again?'

'I wouldn't really worry too much about that, Omago. She isn't going anywhere.'

'How do you know that for sure?'

Veltan grinned broadly, but he didn't answer.

'I think its time for us to do something about this, Omago,' that vibrant voice said quite firmly.

Omago dropped his hoe and spun around. 'Where have you *been*, Ara?' he demanded. 'I've been looking all over for you.'

'Yes, I know. Neither one of us is going to get anything done until we settle this. My name is Ara, I'm sixteen years old, and I *want* you.'

Omago almost choked. 'Is everybody in your village *this* blunt, Ara?' he asked her.

'Probably not,' she replied, 'but I hate to waste time. Are you interested?'

'I can't really think about anything else,' he confessed.

'Good. Is there anything we have to go through before I come to live with you?'

'I'm not really sure. I've never been very curious about this sort of thing before.'

'That's nice,' she said with a sly little smile. 'Let's go talk with Veltan. If there's supposed to be a ceremony of some kind, let's get it out of the way. I'll need some time to prepare supper for you.'

And so it was that Omago and Ara were wed that spring, and Omago's life wasn't ever the same after that. He never actually found out very much about her, but as the seasons passed that became less and less relevant. The wonderful smells coming from her kitchen seemed to put his curiosity to sleep, but they definitely woke up his appetite.

2

❖━━❖

It was on a blustery spring night about ten years after the joining of Omago and Ara when Veltan came to the door. It seemed to Omago that his friend was almost in a state of panic. 'I need help,' he said desperately.

'What's the problem?' Omago asked.

'This is,' Veltan replied, holding out a fur-wrapped bundle. 'My big brother came by and foisted this off on me, and I haven't the faintest idea of what I'm supposed to do about it.' He turned back a corner of the robe to reveal a very small infant. 'I think he's going to need food, and I don't know the first thing about that.'

Ara firmly took the baby away from the distraught god and cuddled it to her. 'I'll take care of him, Veltan,' she told him.

'He doesn't seem to have any teeth, Ara,' Veltan said. 'How can he eat without teeth?'

'I'll take care of him,' she said again. 'There are several women nearby who are nursing. I'm sure I can persuade them to feed your little boy.'

'Nursing?' Veltan asked curiously. 'What's nursing?'

'Oh, dear,' Ara said, rolling her eyes upward. 'Just go back home, Veltan. I'll see to everything.'

'Are they always this small?' Veltan asked. 'I don't think I've ever seen one at this stage before.'

'Just go home, dear Veltan. Everything will be just fine.'

'I feel like such an idiot,' Veltan confessed. 'My brother knocked on my door, told me that this little boy would be one of the Dreamers, and then he left without saying very much more. I've never really paid much attention to infants, so I don't know the first thing about them. He *will* grow some teeth before very much longer, won't he?'

'He'll be just fine, Veltan. Go home – *now*.' Ara imperiously pointed at the door.

Omago didn't get too much sleep for the next month or so. Babies tend to be very noisy, he discovered, and Veltan seemed to be underfoot every time Omago turned around. It occurred to him that it was probably time to add a room to his cottage – or maybe two or three. He began mixing clay and straw to make the sun-dried bricks that were customary here in Veltan's Domain. He realized that he was going to have to extend the roof, but that wouldn't be too much of a problem. He had fairly extensive wheat fields to the west and south of his orchard, so he'd have plenty of straw for thatching after harvest-time.

Veltan conferred with Ara, and between them they decided that Yaltar might be an appropriate name for the young Dreamer. Omago wasn't really sure just exactly where the term 'Dreamer' had originated, but he had too many other things on his mind just then to sit around brooding about it.

Yaltar began toddling about Omago's cottage when he was not even a year old, but he didn't talk yet. It took Ara quite some time to explain this to Veltan. 'Learning how to speak is probably the most important thing a baby does during his first few years,' she told him.

'I thought it was just there,' Veltan protested. 'Are you saying that every baby in the world has to learn how to talk?'

'I've never heard of one who was born talking,' Ara replied.

'Birds seem to know how to peep and chirp without much help.'

'The language of people is a little more complicated, dear Veltan,' Ara reminded him. 'I don't think people could explain very much with peeps and chirps, do you?'

'Well—' Veltan seemed to be having a lot of problems with his little boy. 'I don't know why Dahlaine had to hand Yaltar to me before the boy could even function.'

'Look upon it as a learning experience, Veltan. You'll understand people much better after you've raised Yaltar from early childhood.' Ara smiled slyly. 'Won't that be fun?' she asked him.

'I'm not having all that much fun right now.'

'That'll probably come later, dear Veltan. I wouldn't hold my breath, though.'

When Yaltar was about three years old, Veltan began to take him up the hill to his stone house for several hours each day, but he still depended upon Ara to keep him clean and prepare the little boy's meals.

'Is it *really* necessary for him to eat so often?' Veltan asked Omago's wife one evening.

'You eat light, don't you?' Ara asked him.

'Well, I wouldn't exactly say "eat", Ara,' Veltan replied.

'All right, let's say "absorb", then. The sun's up there in the sky for a good part of every day, so you're soaking up light for much, much longer than Yaltar spends eating, aren't you?'

'I guess I hadn't really thought of it that way,' Veltan admitted.

'You might want to consider cutting down on that, dear Veltan. If you keep absorbing light for so much of every day, you'll start to get fat, and I don't think the people of your Domain would like that very much. Nobody would take a fat god very seriously, you know.'

Veltan frowned slightly, and he absently ran his hand across his abdomen.

'I'm just teasing, dear Veltan,' Ara told him with a fond sort of smile. 'If you start getting a bit portly, just stay out of direct sunlight for a little while.' She glanced at Yaltar, who was vigorously concentrating on his supper. 'Has he had any dreams yet?' she asked very quietly.

'Not that he's mentioned,' Veltan said. Then he gave Ara a startled look. 'How did you know about that?'

'The old stories are still out there, dear Veltan, and old men are very fond of telling old stories. The old men of my village could go on and on about the Dreamers for hours on end. If their stories came anywhere close to what's *really* happening, Yaltar should start dreaming before much longer, and that'll be a sure sign that there's trouble in the wind. You might want to have a talk with your big brother about that. When Yaltar *does* start having those significant dreams, I don't think you should make a big fuss about it. Don't alarm the boy. If you frighten him, he might have trouble sleeping, and if he doesn't sleep, he won't dream. You don't want that to happen, do you?'

'Not even a little bit,' Veltan agreed. 'You're very, very good at this sort of thing, aren't you?'

'It's a gift,' she replied. And then she laughed for no reason that Omago could see.

* * *

As the seasons progressed, Yaltar spent more and more of his time with Veltan in the house on the hill, and Ara took to carrying the little boy's meals up the hill to Veltan's house.

'You miss him, don't you, Ara?' Omago asked her.

'Sort of. He's doing what he's supposed to be doing, though, so I won't interfere. What would you like for supper this evening, Omago?'

'Anything you want to cook, dear,' Omago replied. 'Surprise me.' He grinned at her.

'Very funny, Omago,' she said tartly.

It was not long after Yaltar's sixth birthday when Veltan stopped by one morning to tell Omago and Ara that he'd be gone for several weeks on a matter of some importance.

'Go ahead, Veltan,' Omago said. 'We'll take care of Yaltar while you're gone.'

'I knew that I could depend on you two,' Veltan said. And then he left rather hurriedly.

Ara frowned, but she didn't say anything.

Nanton was a tall, bearded shepherd who had a large flock that grazed in the meadow above the Falls of Vash. Nanton seldom came down to the farmlands, since the voracious appetite of his sheep made the local farmers very nervous.

'They're asking a lot of questions that don't seem to have anything to do with what they're *supposed* to be interested in, Omago,' Nanton reported in his quiet voice. 'They claim to be traders from Aracia's Domain, but as far as I could see, they didn't have anything with them for trades.'

'Why would traders be wandering around up in the hills?' Omago asked with a puzzled frown.

'Exactly. The only people up there are shepherds like me, and we certainly don't need any of those trinkets the traders from the East keep trying to foist off on silly farmers and their wives. There's something else, too.'

'Oh?'

'They don't really *look* like real people. They're very short, and they all wear grey clothes – with hoods that cover most of their faces – and they mumble.'

'Mumble?'

'They don't speak clearly, and they all seem to have some kind of lisp.'

'Peculiar. You said that they were asking questions. What sort of questions?'

'They wanted to know how many people live in the vicinity of the Falls of Vash. I didn't really think that was any of their business, so I lied to them.'

'Nanton!' Omago exclaimed.

'Grow up, Omago,' Nanton said. 'I was catching a strong smell of "unfriendly", so I gave them something to worry about. I told them that there were thousands of us wandering around in those hills, and that we are all armed. I was going to give them a quick demonstration with my sling, but I decided to keep it out of sight. If my nose was right about "unfriendly", the less they know about us, the better.'

'You could be right, I suppose. Did they ask you any other questions?'

'None that made very much sense. For some reason, they seemed to think that our Veltan and his sister Zelana hated each other, and that there was a perpetual war going on between her people and us. The answer I gave them was just about as vague as

55

I could make it. I told them that over the years I've killed dozens of enemies. Of course, I sort of glossed over the fact that the enemies I've killed were wolves, not people, so I think they swallowed it whole. Is Veltan going to be gone for much longer?'

'I don't know for certain, Nanton. He wasn't too specific when he left.' Omago frowned. 'Where's your flock right now?'

'Up in the hill-country. My nephew's watching over them while I'm gone.'

'You won't be going back up into the mountains with your sheep very soon, will you?'

'Not until the snow melts off and I've got them sheared. My flock produced a *lot* of wool this past winter.'

'Good. You usually graze your flock up near the Falls of Vash, don't you?'

'Almost always. There's good grass up there and plenty of water.'

'Keep an eye out for these strangers, will you? And if they come back again, I'd really appreciate it if you'd send your nephew down here to tell me about it. This is something that Veltan should really know about.'

'I'll take care of it, Omago.' Nanton hitched up his belt. 'I'd better get on back to my flock,' he said. 'There's a young shepherdess near where my flock's grazing, and my nephew's breaking out in *that* sort of rash, so he's not paying much attention to the flock.'

'That's been going around quite a bit here lately,' Omago said with no hint of a smile.

'I think spring has a lot to do with it, and spring isn't really all that far away.' Nanton shrugged. 'It helps to increase the flock, I guess.'

'Are we talking about people or sheep?'

'Both flocks, probably. As long as there's good grazing, it doesn't really hurt anything, I guess. Babies are *almost* as pretty as lambs, and once they grow up, we can put them to work. Have a nice day, Omago.' And then he turned and walked away.

'I think you'd better tell Veltan about them, Omago,' the little flax-farmer Selga suggested a week or so later. 'They don't really belong around here, and they talk sort of strange.'

'Oh?' Omago said. 'Just exactly what do you mean by "strange", Selga?'

'It sort of sounded to me like their teeth were getting in the way of their tongues. I think people call it lisping. Anyway, they're awfully short. I'm not very tall myself, but their heads didn't even come up as high as my shoulder, and those grey, hooded smocks they wore weren't made of linen or wool. It was something else entirely. They were asking all kinds of odd questions, but I saw right off that it wasn't any of their business, so I didn't give them any straight answers. You might want to tell Veltan about that. If these dinky little strangers are planning to give us trouble, they didn't get much help from me.'

'I'm sure he'll appreciate that, Selga. Were you able to find out which direction they came from?'

'As close as I could tell, they came down from out of the mountains near the Falls of Vash. If I happen to come across any more of them, I'll ask them about that. Tell Veltan that I'm keeping my eyes open, and I'll find out as much as I can about them.'

'I'm sure he'll appreciate that, Selga.'

Omago was certain that Veltan should be aware of these strangers, so before supper that evening he went up through the twilight to Veltan's house to have a word with Yaltar. He went on in, climbed the stone stairway, and rapped on the little boy's door. 'It's only me, Yaltar,' he called.

Yaltar opened the door. 'Come inside, Omago,' he said.

'Do you have any idea of when he's coming home?' Omago asked, looking with a certain disapproval at the boy's cluttered room and unmade bed.

'He didn't say for sure, Omago,' the boy replied. 'I guess there are some things going on that need his attention.'

'As soon as he comes home, tell him that I need to talk with him, Yaltar,' Omago told the little boy. 'Some peculiar things have been happening here lately, and I think he should know about them.'

'I'll be sure to tell him, Omago,' the boy replied, fingering the peculiar-looking stone he had hanging on a leather thong around his neck like a pendant.

'How did you manage to come by that opal, Yaltar?' Omago asked.

'I found it just outside the front door,' Yaltar replied. 'Isn't it pretty?'

'Beautiful,' Omago agreed. 'It's a bit peculiar that you found it, though. As far as I know, there aren't any opals around here.'

'Maybe it was wandering around and got lost – or maybe it started feeling lonesome.'

'Rocks almost never get lonesome, Yaltar. Ara's cooking supper right now. Come along, and we'll go eat.'

'That sounds like a great idea, Omago.'

Veltan came home a week or so later, and he stopped by Omago's house quite early one morning. 'Yaltar said that you wanted to tell me something,' he said. 'He seemed to think it might be important.'

'It could be,' Omago replied and he repeated what Nanton and Selga had told him about the strangers and their questions.

'I have to go talk with my brother,' Veltan said. 'Keep your ears open, and let me know about any more visits when I come back.'

'I'll do that,' Omago promised.

The spring thaw that year produced a near disaster. The snow pack in the mountains had been much deeper than was usual, and the spring wind that melted off the snow each year wasn't just warm; it seemed even hot. All the streams coming down out of the mountains overran their banks overnight, and then the floods began. To make things even worse, Veltan and Yaltar were away, so Veltan wasn't there to control the floods, and the farmers couldn't do anything except wring their hands as they watched the flood engulf their fields.

The shepherds who customarily grazed their flocks in the region to the west of the Falls of Vash began to bring word of some serious trouble in the Domain of Veltan's sister Zelana, but the messages were sorely lacking in details.

As the flood began to subside, a few more shepherds stopped by, but their stories about events in Zelana's Domain were so lurid that Omago viewed them with profound skepticism.

And then one night after the apple trees had begun to bloom, a clap of thunder woke Omago out of a sound sleep.

'Veltan's back, love,' Ara told him. 'I think we'd better go on up to his house. He'll be able to tell us what's *really* going on in his sister's Domain.'

'You're probably right, Ara,' Omago agreed. 'The wild stories we've been hearing are starting to make me a little cross.'

'I'll go with you, dear heart,' Ara said briskly. 'I'm just as curious as you are.' That struck Omago as a bit strange, but he let it pass.

They rose from their bed, dressed themselves and went on up the hill in the warm spring darkness. When they reached the house, Veltan was standing in the doorway. 'I was hoping that you'd stop by,' he said. 'Please come in. I have a great deal to tell you, and I don't have much time.'

'I'm glad you came home, Veltan,' Omago said as he and Ara followed Veltan up the stairs to the room where Yaltar spent most of his time. 'The shepherds up near the border of your sister's Domain have been telling me all sorts of wild stories, and I'd like to know what's *really* going on up there.'

'You might want to know, Omago,' Veltan said bleakly, 'but I don't think you're going to like it very much.'

They went into the cluttered room, and Ara looked around. 'Where's Yaltar?' she asked.

'He's presently in the care of my sister,' Veltan replied. 'I don't think he's quite ready to ride my pet just yet.'

'Good thinking,' Ara replied.

'All right, then,' Veltan said, 'as it turns out, Yaltar *is* indeed one of the Dreamers, and his dream gave us a glimpse of the future. The creatures of the Wasteland have invaded Zelana's Domain, but Yaltar's dream gave us time to make some preparations. Zelana went off to the west and hired an army of Maag pirates to fight the war in her Domain, and I went south and hired some professional soldiers to help us defend *this* part of the Land of Dhrall. I took an advance party of Trogite soldiers up to Zelana's Domain to lend her a hand.'

'Some of the shepherds told me about that,' Omago said. 'I thought they were just making it up.'

'No, Omago, it's really true. The outlanders are more advanced than we are, and their weapons are made of iron – or bronze in some cases. All of the tools and weapons here in the Land of Dhrall are made of stone or animal bones, but metal weapons are much better.' Veltan took a knife out from under his belt and handed it to Omago. 'That's an iron knife, and I'm sure you can see how much stronger it is than flint or bone could ever be.'

Omago took the peculiar-looking knife and carefully rubbed his thumb across the edge. 'Extremely sharp, isn't it?' he observed.

'Indeed it is,' Veltan agreed. 'Did the flood do much damage down here?'

'It could have been worse, I suppose,' Omago reported. 'A fair number of people lost their houses, and I've heard that quite a few on to the south of here were drowned. It's subsiding now, so I should be able to get some more accurate numbers before too much longer.'

'The flood was a bit extreme, perhaps, but it *was* necessary. The bug-like creatures that serve the Vlagh were invading my sister's Domain, and Zelana's Dreamer conjured up that flood to stop them until our hired armies were ready to meet them. The flood drowned thousands of them, and the Vlagh had to send new forces out of the Wasteland. The enemy force was using a ravine as their invasion route, and our forces have managed to block it off. We can't really be sure how long the enemy forces will keep trying to break through. They aren't really very bright, but sooner or later, I think they'll give up and change direction. If they come South, we'll have to be ready to meet them – probably up near the Falls of Vash.'

'Do you think your hired army will have enough time to get here before we're overrun?' Omago asked.

'I'm sure they will. They have large ships, so they'll come by sea rather than marching overland. I'm going to try to persuade my sister to send some help as well. Her people are hunters, and they're excellent archers. The commander of the army I hired is a brilliant strategist, and once he gets his people in place, it's not very likely that our enemy's going to be able to get past him.'

'I don't think we'll be of much help, Veltan,' Omago said dubiously. 'We should be able to provide food for your outlanders, but we don't even have anything resembling weapons. The shepherds use slings to protect their flocks from wolves, but other than that—' Omago left it up in the air.

'We'll see, Omago. Talk with the other farmers and see how they feel about this. I think the most important thing right now is to start gathering up supplies. The Trogite army I hired has about a hundred thousand men, so we'll need a *lot* of food.'

'I'll pass the word along, Veltan, and we'll get started.'

'I knew I could count on you,' Veltan replied. 'I think I'd better get on back. I wanted to warn you about what's probably coming, but for right now, the war's going on in Zelana's Domain, so I want to be there in case she needs me.'

Omago had a growing sense of apprehension. Nothing in his background had anything to do with war, so he didn't have the faintest idea of what to expect.

'Don't worry so much, dear heart,' Ara told him as they went on back down the hill. 'Just do the best you can and let Veltan do the worrying.'

'For the moment, helping him worry is about the only thing I can manage, Ara,' Omago replied glumly.

3

The metal knife Veltan had given Omago opened some enormous possibilities for him. He immediately saw dozens of ways to improve common tools, but that would probably come later. For the moment he felt obliged to concentrate on weapons. As nearly as he was able to determine, a weapon should serve two functions – hurt your enemy, and prevent your enemy from hurting you.

The metal knife could probably damage any enemy who came too close, but if the enemy had weapons of his own, things might start to get a little sticky.

'I wish this thing had a longer handle,' he muttered. Then he suddenly felt just a little foolish. Many of his own tools – particularly in his orchard – consisted of long poles with a cross-piece firmly attached so that he could pull the branches of his fruit trees down and pick the fruit without climbing up the tree. The longer handle he needed was right there in his tool shed.

As a sort of experiment, Omago removed the crosspiece from one of his harvest poles and firmly lashed the knife to the tip. The pole stopped being a tool at that point and became what might be called a weapon. Omago tried a few practice jabs with his modified pole, and it seemed that it definitely had some potential. If his enemy came running at him, a jab in the belly or the face with that sharp knife would most likely hurt the enemy, and it might even kill him. Not only that, the length of the pole would keep his enemy from getting anywhere at all close to him.

'Well, now,' he murmured. 'Isn't *that* interesting?'

The notion of deliberately hurting people was completely alien to the farmers of Veltan's Domain, but if the stories Omago had been hearing lately came anywhere near to the truth, the approaching enemies were *not* people. A few of them might *look* like people, but that was probably just a hoax. The term that had sort of drifted down from Zelana's Domain had been 'bug-men', and that might be very useful. If Omago stressed the word 'bug' when describing their enemies, the local farmers wouldn't feel at all guilty about exterminating them. On occasion, swarms of locusts had attacked the fields, and the local farmers had found that grass fires were a fairly effective way to deal with them. It occurred to Omago that the word 'bug' might be even more useful than metal weapons. Farmers start feeling belligerent every time they hear that word.

All sorts of possibilities were coming to the surface and Omago went home to supper filled with enthusiasm.

'What are you grinning about, Omago?' Ara asked as he sat down at the table.

'I don't think we farmers are going to be *quite* as helpless as Veltan seems to believe. Turning tools into weapons isn't nearly as difficult as I thought it might be, and I think I've stumbled across the solution to a much bigger problem.'

'Oh?'

'Farmers will go to any lengths to protect their fields from bugs, and if I understood what Veltan was telling us about these invaders correctly, they're at least part bug. All I'll have to do is stand on a hill and shout "Bug!" As soon as they hear that word, every farmer in Veltan's Domain will come running to help me stamp them out.'

'That's very interesting, dear heart,' she said. 'Now eat your supper before it gets cold.'

Omago sent word to several of his friends, and that evening they came across the fields to his house. He took them out to his tool shed and showed them his improvised weapon. They all seemed quite interested.

'Do you think Veltan could get any more of these knives for us, Veltan?' the bulky wheat-farmer Benkar asked. 'If we all had metal knives like that one of yours, we could tie them to poles like you did, and then we could lend the outlanders a hand when those bug-men come down out of the mountains.'

'I'm not all that sure, Benkar,' Omago said a bit dubiously. 'The outlanders might not want us getting in their way when the fights start, and I don't really have any idea of just how valuable this knife really is.'

'It's something to think about, Omago,' the bearded shepherd Nanton said. 'If all of you farmers had sharp poles like that one you've got, you could slow the bug-men down, and then me and my shepherds could rain rocks on them with our slings. Not very many of them would come out of a meeting like that alive. Some of the stories that came down from Zelana's Domain suggested that the outlanders sort of looked down their noses at her people – right up until her bow-and-arrow men started killing bug-people by the hundreds.'

'If somebody tries to look down his nose at me, I'll knock his teeth out!' the small farmer Selga flared.

'We'd have to practice for a while,' the farmer Eknor said.

'How can we practice if Omago's got the only iron knife in the whole of Veltan's Domain?' Benkar demanded.

'It's the *pole* that does most of the work, Benkar,' Eknor said. 'We can practice jabbing with just the poles. Then when the outlanders get here, they can give us knives to tie to the end of the poles and we'll be ready to go to work. It won't really be too much different from what we do when we harvest wheat. All we have to do is walk side by side in a straight line – harvesting bug-men instead of wheat.'

Omago managed to conceal his grin. This was turning out even better than he'd hoped it would. The word 'bug' had brought all the local farmers to his side almost immediately, and they were obviously feeling very belligerent. It was entirely possible that they weren't nearly as helpless as Veltan seemed to believe they were. Nanton and Eknor had responded to the threat exactly as Omago had hoped they would. Things were *definitely* looking up.

As the days passed, Omago's 'bug-men' warning brought more and more farmers and shepherds in from the surrounding territory to join the impromptu army. Eknor instructed the farmers in the business of holding their still-harmless poles steadily out to the front and keeping their lines straight while Nanton gave the shepherds extensive training in the art of hitting targets with their sling-thrown rocks at increasingly longer distances.

They'd been at it for more than two weeks when on a sunny afternoon a crash of thunder shook the ground and Veltan was there. 'What are we doing here, Omago?' he asked.

'It sort of came to me that my knife needed a longer handle,' Omago explained, 'so I tied it to a long pole, and it started to look more like a weapon than just a tool. The other farmers thought that was very interesting, and we're hoping that the outlanders might give us more of these knives.' He looked around to make sure that none of the other farmers were close enough to hear him. 'I cheated just a little,' he said quietly. 'After you told me that our enemies were part bug, I started calling them "bug-men". Farmers get very belligerent when somebody says "bug", and when word got out, they all came running to join the fight. Then Nanton and the shepherds joined us with their slings. I think the outlanders might be a little surprised when they find out that we're not *quite* as helpless as they might have thought we were.'

'Very good, Omago,' Veltan said. 'As soon as Rabbit gets here, I think I'll be able to persuade him to make regular spear-points for our farmers. They work better than just tying a knife to the end of a pole.'

'Who's Rabbit?'

'He's a little Maag who works with metal. Once your men have metal spear-points – and venom – I don't think any of the enemies will be able to get past you.'

'What's venom?'

'Poison. The creatures of the Wasteland are part snake, and their fangs are venomous. Up in my sister Zelana's Domain, all her hired soldiers dipped the points of their weapons in that venom. It killed hundreds of the servants of the Vlagh. Anyway, Dahlaine's Dreamer, Ashad, had one of "those" dreams, and the enemies are *definitely* coming this way. I don't think we need to worry much, though. The outlanders will almost certainly be here in time to help us hold off our enemies.'

'I hope so,' Omago said. 'The farmers and shepherds here are getting better, but I don't think we're quite ready to fight this war all by ourselves.'

'We'll see, Omago,' Veltan said. 'I'll go see if I can hurry the Maags along.'

Now that the planting was done, more and more farmers were drifting in, drawn by the stories that had been going around. As Omago was fairly certain would be the case, the visiting farmers were all extremely curious about the iron knife Veltan had given him, and terribly disappointed when he couldn't tell them where they could find what Veltan had called 'metal'. Quite a few of them just turned around and went home at that point, but enough of them remained to expand Omago's growing army. Training the newcomers was very tedious, but Omago was fairly sure that it'd be worth the trouble, so he stuck with it for the next several weeks.

Then, early one morning, the familiar crash of thunder announced that Veltan had come home again.

Omago dressed himself, and then he and Ara went up the hill to Veltan's oversized house to ask him how the war in the West had turned out.

'Everything turned out even better than we'd expected,' Veltan told them. 'We lost the village of Lattash, unfortunately, but I guess that was a small price to pay for our victory. The Maags and Trogites are coming here to help *us* now. If things turn out as well here in the South as they did in the West, we'll win this war too, and that might persuade the creatures of the Wasteland to go back where they came from.'

'Wishful thinking, dear Veltan,' Ara said. 'Bugs aren't really that clever.'

'When do you think the outlanders will get here?' Omago asked. He wasn't very comfortable with the notion of having alien helpers in the upcoming war.

'Probably within the next day or so,' Veltan replied. 'Zelana's been tampering a bit, so the winds are being very cooperative.' He frowned slightly. 'You might want to warn the womenfolk, Ara. Narasan has his soldiers pretty well under control, but Sorgan's Maags are sort of rowdy, and they get ideas when they see young women.'

'I'll pass that along,' Ara promised.

'How long do you think it's going to take for us to get our hands on more of these metal knives?' Omago asked.

'We'll talk with Rabbit as soon as he arrives,' Veltan replied. 'Don't lock the notion of "knife" in stone, though. I've noticed that Rabbit can be very creative. If you tell him what you want the weapon to do, he'll come up with the best form to get the job done. The metal arrowheads he made for Longbow and the other archers were much more advanced than the flint ones they'd used in the past.'

'I'll keep that in mind,' Omago said.

4

'Did you want me to take my men on down to the beach before the outlanders arrive tomorrow, Veltan?' Omago asked just a bit dubiously.

'I gather that you're not very enthusiastic about it,' Veltan observed.

'Well, not really,' Omago conceded. 'These strangers are professionals, and when you get right down to it, my men are still stumbling quite a bit. The outlanders might laugh when they see us pretending to be soldiers, and I'd probably lose half of my men right then and there. Wouldn't it be better if you had a chance to talk this over with the strangers first?'

'I see your point, Omago. All right, then. You and I'll go down to the beach by ourselves.'

'Ara wants to go, too. She hasn't seen Yaltar for quite some time, and she misses him.'

'Good idea. I want her to meet my sister anyway.'

'When do you think we should leave?'

'After you've had breakfast should be soon enough. Zelana advised me that the fleet won't arrive until about mid-morning, and it's only about two miles to the beach.' Veltan squinted for a moment. 'Now that I've had some time to think my way through this, I'm having some second thoughts about bringing those entire armies here. I'll need to bring a few of the officers, but I think maybe we should leave the rest of the outlanders on board their ships until we decide to march them on up to the Falls of Vash. Let's keep the possibility of unpleasant confrontation to a minimum if we can.'

'Whatever you think best, Veltan,' Omago agreed.

The first hint of the approaching fleet was the mass of sails along the horizon, and the sheer numbers indicated by those billowing sails stunned Omago. Ara, who stood at his side, however, didn't appear to be overly impressed. Ara's reactions to things were sometimes very peculiar.

As the fleet drew closer in the golden summer sunlight, Omago noticed certain differences. Some of the ships appeared to be very fat, while others were as skinny as saplings. 'They don't seem very much alike, do they?' he said to Veltan.

'They were built with different purposes in mind,' Veltan explained. 'The wide, slow ones were built to carry large numbers of people or cargo. The slender ones were built to go fast so that they can catch the slow ones and rob them.'

'Wouldn't that make them enemies, dear Veltan?' Ara asked.

'They didn't get along too well right at first,' Veltan conceded, 'but the threat of the creatures of the Wasteland sort of united them.'

There was a much smaller boat that was moving rapidly toward the beach, and Veltan looked at it with a certain affection. 'That's my sloop,' he told Omago and Ara. 'She moves right along, doesn't she?'

'What was that one built for, dear Veltan?' Ara asked. 'It doesn't seem to fit in with the others.'

'She moves very fast,' Veltan said proudly. 'I use her when I want to go someplace in a hurry.'

'Isn't that what your lightning bolt's supposed to do?'

'My pet's fast, but she's very noisy. Sometimes quiet is more important than fast.'

There were four men on the sloop. One of them seemed quite small, another was medium-sized, and the last two were fairly tall and were dressed in leather clothes.

'The little one's that Maag named Rabbit that I've told you about, Omago,' Veltan said. 'The young fellow's a Trogite soldier named Keselo, and the two others are Longbow and Red-Beard, archers from Zelana's domain.'

'They're hunters, aren't they?' Omago asked.

Veltan nodded. 'Very *good* hunters,' he said. 'Red-Beard's not *quite* as good as Longbow, but then, nobody's as good as Longbow is. As far as I know, he's never missed. His arrow *always* goes where he wants it to go.'

Omago smiled faintly. 'When I was a boy, I used to dream about being a hunter. It must be a very exciting life.'

'I suppose it is, Omago, but Longbow isn't just an ordinary hunter. *His* war with the creatures of the Wasteland started a long time ago. He hates them, and he kills every one he sees. Technically, I suppose he's working for my sister Zelana, but he doesn't take orders very well. Eleria's about the only one he really listens to, and he'll even jerk her up short every now and then.'

'Doesn't that make your sister angry?' Ara asked.

'Not really. Zelana knows that he's loyal and that he's doing his best to help her, but he does things his own way.' Veltan shrugged.

'It's the results that really matter. The method isn't all that important.'

'Where's Yaltar?' Omago asked.

'He's traveling with Zelana and Eleria on the *Seagull* – that's the ship of Sorgan Hook-Beak, the commander of the Maags,' Veltan replied. 'Someday I suppose I'll take him for a ride on my pet thunderbolt, but he might be a little young for that right now.'

'*Much* too young,' Ara said firmly.

The small ship Veltan had called a 'sloop' came ashore somewhat in advance of the rest of the fleet, and Veltan introduced Omago and Ara to the men who'd been on board. 'This is the one I've been telling you about, Omago,' Veltan said, putting his hand on Rabbit's shoulder. 'If you tell him what you need, I'm sure he'll be able to hammer whatever it is out of metal.'

'I hope so,' Omago replied, looking at the little man Veltan called Rabbit. 'Veltan came by a while back,' he told the Maag, 'and he told me what was happening in his sister's Domain. Then he gave me a knife to show me what he was talking about when he used the word "metal". I got to thinking about it, and it seemed to me that if I lashed the knife to the front end of a long pole, it might make a fairly useful tool when we come up against the creatures of the Wasteland.'

'We call those tools "spears", Omago,' Rabbit said, 'and they've been around for a long, long time.'

'Really? I sort of thought that I'd come up with the idea all by myself. We don't know all that much about wars, though.'

'This one's very quick, Rabbit,' the young Trogite Keselo said. 'If he's never seen a spear or even heard about one, it seems that he invented it right on the spot.'

'It does sort of look that way, doesn't it?' Rabbit agreed with a

73

slight frown. 'If you come up with any more of these ideas, Omago, describe them to me. Then I'll hammer one out and we'll see how it works. How did the idea of the spear come to you?'

Omago shrugged. 'I've got an extensive orchard, and I use a long pole with a crosspiece tied to the tip to pull down the higher limbs so that I can pick the fruit without climbing up the tree. I was standing there with the knife in one hand and the pole in the other, and the notion of putting them together sort of popped into my head.'

'Any time you hear one of those "pops", let me know about it,' Rabbit said.

'Some skiffs are coming in,' the tall archer Longbow said. 'Sorgan, Narasan, and a few of the others will be here soon.'

'Good,' Veltan said. 'We've got work to do, and we haven't got much time.'

Omago was more than a little surprised by the hulking Maags. He'd never seen people so tall before, and the assorted metal weapons they had hanging from their belts were quite intimidating. The Trogites were shorter and somewhat darker, but they were also well-armed.

Then Omago saw Yaltar trailing somewhat to the rear with a beautiful lady who was almost certainly Veltan's sister Zelana, and perhaps an even more beautiful little girl, who was obviously Zelana's Dreamer, Eleria.

Ara rushed down toward the water and embraced the boy, and Yaltar clung to her as if something terrible had recently happened.

'Nice country, Veltan,' a Trogite with silver-touched hair at his temples observed.

'Thank you, Narasan,' Veltan replied. 'Where's Gunda?'

'I sent him on back to Castano to bring the rest of the army here,' the Trogite replied. 'I'm hoping that the open channel through the ice is still there.'

'It is,' Veltan assured him. 'Did you run into any problems on the way here?'

'No, the only problems we encountered cropped up *before* we set sail. Red-Beard's tribe wasn't very happy when he told them that he'd be gone for a while. His elevation to the rank of chief was fairly recent, and he's been quite open about his dislike for the whole idea. They're convinced that he seized on the idea of sailing south as a means of escape. There's a lady in his tribe named Planter, and she said some *very* uncomplimentary things to him before we left.'

'Just let it lie, Narasan,' the red-bearded fellow who'd come ashore from the sloop growled.

'Just trying to explain a few things, Red-Beard,' Narasan replied. 'My employer has a right to know about these little squabbles, wouldn't you say?'

Red-Beard turned and stalked away, muttering to himself.

'This is Omago, Commander,' Veltan said. 'I've known him since he was a little boy, and the other farmers and the shepherds all seem to bring their problems to him.'

'He's quite gifted, Commander,' Keselo reported. 'Veltan brought him an iron knife to show him what the word "metal" really means, and he turned right around and invented the spear.'

'The spear's been around for centuries, Keselo,' a very thin Trogite scoffed.

'Not around here, it hasn't, Jalkan. The farmers around here don't even know what the word "war" means, so they've never needed weapons of any kind. Omago refers to his spear as a "tool".

That suggests an entirely different sort of mind, wouldn't you say?'

'The other farmers were quite impressed when Omago showed them his spear, Commander Narasan,' Veltan said, 'and they'd really like to have spears of their own.'

'What does a farmer need a spear for?' the thin Trogite Jalkan demanded with a faint sneer.

'That's about enough of that, Jalkan,' Commander Narasan said very firmly.

'It's a legitimate question, Commander,' Veltan said. 'I'd mentioned that our enemies are part bug, and some accounts of the war in Zelana's Domain drifted across the border between our two Domains, and Omago heard a few references to "bug-men". Any time a farmer hears the word "bug", he starts to feel very belligerent. A swarm of locusts can devour a whole year's crop in less than a day. After Omago had shown the other farmers his spear, they sort of volunteered to join us in the upcoming war.'

'If we showed them how to form a phalanx, they could be very useful, couldn't they, Commander?' the young soldier Keselo suggested.

'They might at that,' Narasan agreed. 'They'd need shields, though.'

'What's a shield?' Omago asked the commander.

'It's a metal plate we strap to our left arms. We use it to protect our bodies from enemy weapons.'

'Sorgan's coming, sir,' Keselo advised.

'Good.' Narasan looked at Veltan. 'Where do you think we should set up our camp?' he asked.

'That's something I wanted to talk over with you, Commander,' Veltan replied. 'I don't want to offend you, but it seems to me that we might want to keep your army – and Sorgan's as well – on board your ships. *Your* men are well-disciplined, but Sorgan's Maags—? Well, I'm sure you get my point.'

'It's crystal clear, Veltan. Peacetime brings out the worst in the Maags.'

'We'll be moving up to the Falls of Vash before long anyway,' Veltan continued, 'so setting up a temporary camp would just be a waste of time and labor. My people have been gathering food for your armies, and I'll have them bring it here to the beach. In the meantime, I'll take you and Sorgan and some of the others to my house to have a look at my map. I filched Rabbit's idea of a lumpy picture, so you'll be able to get some idea of the terrain near the falls. My big brother's Dreamer said that we'll be fighting this war up there, so you'll need to be familiar with the territory.'

A towering Maag came up from the water's edge to join them. 'The country around here looks a lot flatter than it was off to the West, Narasan,' he said, 'and there aren't so many trees.'

'That doesn't hurt my feelings too much, Sorgan,' Narasan replied. 'Fighting a war in the bushes irritates me. This is Omago. He's sort of in charge here.'

'The chief, you mean?'

'We're a little less formal here, Sorgan,' Veltan said. 'Omago doesn't give orders to the other farmers. He makes suggestions sometimes, but that's about as far as it goes.'

'Veltan thinks that we might want to leave our men on board the ships for now,' Narasan said. 'We'll be marching on up into the mountains in just a few days anyway, so there wouldn't be much point in having them come ashore and set up a camp.'

'I'll go along with you there, Veltan,' Sorgan agreed.

'I *will* want to take you and Narasan – and any others you might want to bring along – up to my house,' Veltan added. 'I've put

77

together a map that you'd better have a look at. The terrain where we'll be fighting this time's much steeper than the ravine above Lattash was.'

Sorgan shrugged. 'I'll bring Ox and Ham-Hand,' he said. 'When you get right down to it, though, this is Narasan's war. I just came along for the ride.'

'That's not true, and you know it, Sorgan,' Narasan flared.

'Maybe not,' Sorgan replied with a wicked grin, 'but this time we're going to do things *your* way. That means that I get to blame you when things go wrong.'

'You're all heart, Sorgan,' Narasan said sourly.

'I thought you might have noticed that,' Sorgan replied, grinning even more broadly.

Omago saw that the two widely different men had apparently developed a strong friendship during the course of the war in the West, and he believed that would probably be very useful when trouble arrived.

'Just exactly how's the church organized here in the Land of Dhrall?' the thin, leather-clad Trogite called Jalkan asked Omago curiously as they were all following the path from the beach through the wheat fields to Veltan's house.

'I'm not sure I follow you,' Omago replied. 'What exactly do you mean by "church"?'

'Priests. The ones who lead the people in their prayers and make sure that they aren't violating the articles of the faith.' Jalkan seemed very curious about this.

'We don't have anything like that here in Veltan's Domain,' Omago replied. 'I've heard that there's something along those lines over in the Domain of his sister Aracia, but Veltan doesn't seem to think we need anything like that here in the southland. If someone wants to ask Veltan a question, they can just go up to his house and talk with him about it, but they usually go through me for some reason.'

'Are you saying that you talk directly with your god?' Jalkan demanded in a shocked voice.

'That's why he's there, isn't it?'

'But—' Jalkan floundered.

'Different places have different customs, I guess,' Omago said. 'We're fairly relaxed here in the South.'

'Where are all the gold mines located?' Jalkan quickly changed the subject. 'That's what this war's all about, isn't it? I mean, these invaders we'll be fighting are coming here because they want your gold, don't they?'

'I doubt it. I don't think the servants of the Vlagh are very interested in the yellow metal some people use for trinkets. The Vlagh wants our land and the food we grow.'

Jalkan's expression turned suspicious, and he abruptly stalked away.

'I wouldn't answer too many of that one's questions, Omago,' the tall archer Longbow suggested quietly. 'The other Trogites don't like him very much. He's very greedy, and he doesn't treat his men too well.'

'These outlanders are peculiar, aren't they?'

Longbow smiled faintly. 'They seem to think that *we're* the peculiar ones. Their lives are very complicated, but we try our best to keep everything simple. I'm not sure exactly why, but that seems to offend them for some reason.'

'I'll be glad when this is all over and they pack up and go home.'

'You're not alone there, friend Omago.'

* * *

'That's impossible!' the Trogite called Padan exclaimed, staring in awe at Veltan's house. 'It's all one solid rock!'

Veltan shrugged. 'It keeps the bad weather out,' he said. 'I noticed back in Kaldacin that most of the fancy buildings down there let in a lot of cold air.'

'How did you *do* that?'

'Are you sure that you really want to know, Padan?' Veltan asked with a sly little grin.

Padan gave him a quick, slightly startled look. 'I don't think so,' he said after a moment. 'I'm getting a strong notion that I won't sleep too well if you tell me exactly *how* you made it.'

'Let's all go on inside, friends,' Veltan said to the outlanders. 'I stole an idea from Rabbit and made a detailed map of the region where we'll probably meet the enemy. I think you should all have a look at it so you'll know what we'll be coming up against.'

Omago waited near the door until Ara joined him. 'How's Yaltar?' he asked his wife quietly.

'Not all that well, dear,' Ara replied. 'As I understand it, he had to do something fairly awful up there in Zelana's Domain, and it's really bothering him. Zelana's doing what she can to calm him, but about the only thing that helps him is holding Eleria's hand.'

'Are you going to stay with them?' Omago asked her.

'I think I'd better, dear. We'll be in the kitchen. I'll need to fix supper for these outlanders anyway, and the smell of cooking food usually makes Yaltar feel better.'

Omago smiled. 'The smell of *your* cooking makes *everybody* feel better, dear heart,' he said fondly.

'It seems that way, doesn't it? Run along, dear. Veltan might need some help explaining things to the strangers.'

Omago rejoined the others, and they trailed along behind Veltan and entered a large room that so far as Omago could recall he'd never seen before. That wasn't really unusual, though. Every now and then Veltan rearranged his house, switching the locations of various rooms for no particular reason.

'This is my map-room,' Veltan announced with a certain pride. 'It's sort of based on your war-room back in Kaldacin, Commander Narasan, but there are a few variations.'

'I noticed that,' the Trogite commander said with a kind of awe in his voice. The room was circular, and the doorway opened onto a sort of balcony that was perhaps ten feet above the floor. The map Veltan had constructed lay down below, and so far as Omago could determine, it was a perfect duplicate of the mountainous country around the Falls of Vash. Omago knew that Veltan was gifted, but the map was astonishingly accurate.

'Where's all that water coming from?' Sorgan Hook-Beak asked. 'I don't see any little streams leading into that river that's tumbling over the edge of the cliff.'

'It comes up from beneath the ground,' Veltan explained. 'It's a bit quiet right now. Every now and then it gets sort of excited, and the water spurts about a hundred feet up into the air.'

'Did you put that there, Veltan?' the young Trogite Keselo asked.

Veltan shook his head. 'I think an earthquake might have caused it. The ground's a bit unstable under those mountains.'

'The ground up there by that waterfall's a whole lot steeper than what we encountered in the ravine above Lattash,' Sorgan observed. 'That might give us a bit of trouble on down the line.'

'Could you come up with a notion of just when we can expect the enemy to reach that area, Veltan?' Commander Narasan asked.

'We're encountering the same problem we came up against in

the ravine above Lattash,' Veltan replied. 'My brother's Dreamer told him *where*, but he couldn't be very specific about *when*.'

'If they've been boring tunnels under the ground, they might be up there waiting for us already,' Padan suggested.

'No,' the young Trogite Keselo disagreed. 'It took them centuries to bore their way through the rock from the stairway to the caves leading to those ancient villages in the ravine. They haven't had enough time to get to that waterfall yet.'

'I think Keselo might be right, Padan,' Narasan said. 'If the tunnels were already there, the enemies would probably have invaded both regions at the same time. I don't think we're going to encounter tunnels this time. It seems to me that *this* invasion is an act of desperation. The volcanos closed off that ravine permanently, and *something's* driving the enemy to seize new land, and it doesn't seem to matter which region the new land lies in. Does that sound about right to you, Sorgan?'

'I hadn't really thought about it that much, but it *does* sort of make sense,' Hook-Beak conceded. 'If that's the way it *really* stands, we'd better hustle right along. As soon as we get up there, we'll probably have to start building forts and such. We don't want to come up against those snake-men on open ground if we can avoid it.'

'I think you're right, Sorgan,' Narasan said. 'The rest of my army should be arriving fairly soon, but let's get some advance forces up to the top of the falls as quickly as we can. I *definitely* don't want those snake-men creeping up behind me like they did last time. I'm getting just a little too old for surprises.'

5

A ra came through the door of the round room about an hour later. 'Supper's ready,' she announced. 'Come along and eat it before it gets cold.'

'I think you're in for a treat, gentlemen,' Veltan said with a note of pride. 'Ara's probably the best cook in the whole wide world.'

'I'd say that she's wasting her *real* talent, then,' Jalkan declared with an obscene leer. 'A woman with a body like hers could make a fortune in Kaldacin.'

A chill came over Omago. 'I'm not quite sure what you're getting at, Jalkan,' he said in a flat, unemotional tone.

'Are you blind, man? This servant sets my blood to boiling. I'd pay good gold for the chance to get her in bed.'

Without even thinking, Omago drove his fist into the scrawny Trogite's mouth, knocking him flat on his back.

Jalkan stumbled back up, spitting blood, teeth and curses as he clawed at his knife-hilt.

Keselo's sword, however, came out of its sheath more smoothly and rapidly. The young man put the point of his sword against the bone-thin Trogite's throat. 'Drop it Jalkan,' he said quite firmly. 'Drop the knife, or I'll kill you right here on the spot.'

'But this peasant just hit me!' Jalkan screamed. 'That's a hanging offence! I'm an *officer*!'

'Not any more, you aren't,' Narasan declared in a flat tone of voice. 'I've put up with you for much too long already, and you've just given me something that I've been waiting for. Your army career is finished, Jalkan, and good riddance.'

'You can't do that!' Jalkan screamed at Narasan. 'I paid gold for my commission! *Gold*!'

'You just forfeited the gold, Jalkan. You're done.' Narasan turned. 'Padan, chain this scoundrel and take him back to the beach. I'll decide what to do with him later – *after* I get my temper under control.' He turned to Omago. 'Did you want to deal with this yourself, or would you rather that I did it? I'm not too clear about the customs here in the Land of Dhrall. It was *your* wife he insulted, though, so I think it's only proper that you should decide his fate.'

'Just get him out of my sight, Commander,' Omago said, clenching and unclenching his fists.

'I'll take care of it, then.' Narasan looked at Padan. 'Get this scummy lecher out of here,' he ordered.

'My pleasure, Commander,' Padan said with a broad grin. 'Did you want to go peacefully, scummy lecher? Or would you rather have me kick your behind every step of the way back to the beach?'

'Nicely put, Padan,' Red-Beard said admiringly.

'I've always had this way with words,' Padan replied modestly.

There were several strangers in the round map-room with Veltan the next morning when Omago arrived.

'Ah, there you are, Omago,' Veltan greeted him. 'There are some people here I'd like you to meet.' He gestured at an imposing, grey-bearded man wearing clothes made of furry animal skins. 'This is my older brother, Dahlaine of the North.'

'Omago,' the bearded one said, briefly nodding.

'I'm pleased to meet you,' Omago replied a bit uncertainly. There was something about Veltan's brother that made Omago just a bit nervous.

'You've already met my sister Zelana,' Veltan continued, 'but this is my other sister Aracia.'

Aracia wore splendid clothes and a superior expression.

'Ma'am,' Omago said politely.

'Dahlaine and Aracia thought it might be wise to bring the leaders of the armies they've hired here so that they can observe,' Veltan said. 'They'll almost certainly be coming up against the creatures of the Wasteland before much longer, and it won't hurt if they know what they'll be facing.'

'Let me take care of this, Veltan,' the bearded Dahlaine said. He turned back to Omago. 'Veltan tells us that you're the leader of his army,' he said.

'I don't know if I'd go *quite* so far as to call my people an army,' Omago said. 'We aren't really all that familiar with weapons, but Commander Narasan's promised to see to it that we'll get the training we're going to need.'

'Have you ever heard of horses?' Dahlaine asked.

Omago frowned. 'I don't believe I have,' he admitted.

'A horse is something like a cow – except that it doesn't have horns, and it can run much faster than a cow,' Dahlaine explained. He reached out and put his hand on the shoulder of a lean man with a scarred face. 'This is Prince Ekial, the leader of the horse-people. Quite some time ago, Ekial's people tamed the horses and taught them how to carry things. After a while, it occurred to some clever fellow that if a horse could carry heavy bags of grain or loads of firewood from one place to another, it could probably carry people just as well – and a horse can run much faster than a man can. The horse people did that for quite some time, and then a war came along. The horse people found that fighting from the back of a horse could be very effective. Since there aren't any horses here in the Land of Dhrall, the servants of the Vlagh won't have any idea of what they're encountering. I'm fairly sure that they aren't going to like horses and the men who'll be riding them very much at all – that's the ones who'll survive, and I don't think there'll *be* very many survivors.'

'Do you actually sit on an animal's back when you want to go somewhere?' Omago asked the scar-faced Prince Ekial.

Ekial shrugged. 'It's easier than doing the walking ourselves,' he replied, 'and horses love to run. If you've got a good horse, you can go from here to there about five times faster than you could if you did the walking yourself.'

'Can we get on with this?' Aracia said abruptly. 'I have other things I need to attend to.' She turned to look at Omago. 'Please don't get all excited, Omago,' she said. She pointed at a tall woman who had a very long knife hanging from the leather belt encircling her waist. 'This is Trenicia, the queen of the warrior women of the Isle of Akalla. Different places have different traditions and different customs. On the Isle of Akalla, the women rule, and the women do the fighting.'

'What do the men do?' the horseman Ekial asked curiously.

'As little as they possibly can,' the warrior woman said in a sardonic tone. 'Over the years, they've foisted just about everything off on us. We have to grow the food, hunt the meat, and fight the wars. The men sit around getting fat and arguing with each other about something they call "philosophy" – most of which is pure nonsense.'

'Isn't your sword just a little slender?' the horseman asked curiously. 'I wouldn't think it's quite strong enough to cut through any kind of armor.'

'Why would I want to waste my time banging on somebody's armor?' Trenicia asked scornfully. 'The important part of my sword is the point. It's very sharp, and it slides through an enemy quite smoothly. There are all sorts of important things in an enemy's belly or head. My enemy always seems to lose interest in a war after I've slid my sword through her a few times.'

'Are you saying that you fight wars with other women?' Zelana asked with a certain surprise.

'We almost have to,' Trenicia replied. 'The men of Akalla don't really know which end of a sword is which. There was an argument on the Isle a few years back about who was *really* the queen. We don't have to argue any more, though. Everybody who's still alive wholeheartedly agrees that *I* am queen, and *I* give the orders.' She smiled a sunny sort of smile. 'Isn't that just lovely?' she asked them.

For some reason the warrior queen made Omago turn cold all over. There was a savagery just below her surface that was very frightening.

Dahlaine motioned Veltan off to one side, but Omago was close enough to hear their quiet talk.

'Have you told any of these mercenaries about that second invasion that turned up in Ashad's dream?' Dahlaine asked quietly.

'Not as yet,' Veltan replied. 'I can't for the life of me think of a way to mention it to Narasan without offending him. I'm hoping that I'll be able to deal with it on my own – or possibly get some help from Zelana. She's very good at dealing with winds and tides, and she could probably freeze any approaching fleet in place for the next few centuries.'

'I wouldn't set that in stone, Veltan,' Dahlaine cautioned. 'Ashad's dream *definitely* put that second invasion ashore in the southern part of your Domain.'

'That doesn't necessarily lock it in place, Dahlaine,' Veltan disagreed. 'Eleria's dream over in the Land of the Maags supposedly killed Sorgan and all his men, but Longbow stepped in and prevented that dream from taking place right there on the spot. As I understand it, these dreams are sometimes warnings rather than absolute certainties.'

'Well, maybe,' Dahlaine conceded, 'but keep your eyes and ears open.'

'This rounded shank fits right over the tip of the spear-shaft, Omago,' the small Maag called Rabbit explained the following day when the two of them were working in Omago's door-yard. 'Then I whack it a few times with my hammer to sort of lock the spear-point in place.'

'That probably would work better than just lashing a knife to the tip of the pole,' Omago conceded. 'I was mulling things over last night,' he said, 'and something sort of came to me.'

'Another one of those pops of yours?' Rabbit asked with a sly grin.

'Well, sort of. It seemed to me that if a spear had more than one point it might be more effective.'

'I don't think I've ever seen a spear with more than one point.'

Omago went into his tool shed and picked up his wooden hay-rake. 'We use this tool to clear away the straw after we've harvested our wheat,' he said, holding the rake out to Rabbit. 'If the points were sticking straight out instead of angling down, wouldn't that be more effective than just a single point?'

Rabbit squinted, absently tapping his hammer on his anvil. 'You might have just come up with something, Omago,' he agreed. 'An ordinary spear only has one point, because you're only trying to kill one enemy at a time, but if you've got that venom we used back in the ravine, you could kill three or four snake-men with one poke. Let's try it and see what the Cap'n and Commander Narasan think about it. If your people are all lined up the way you told us they'd be, that'd put a *whole lot* of poisoned points out to the front.'

'Who came up with the idea of dipping the points of your war-tools in venom?'

'Longbow – or maybe it was One-Who-Heals – I'm not really sure which one. Longbow's been killing snake-men since he was just a boy. You wouldn't *believe* how good he is with that bow of his.'

'Did he ever tell you just why he hated the snake-men so much?' Omago asked.

'*He* didn't, but I was talking with one of the men from his tribe back in Lattash, and he told me that a snake-man killed the girl Longbow was going to marry, and after that, killing snake-men was about the only thing Longbow thought about. Let's hammer out one of those rake-point spears and see what the Cap'n and Narasan think about it. If it works even half as good as it seems to me that it will, I think they'll really like the idea. Every time you turn around, you seem to come up with a new idea.'

Omago smiled faintly. 'It's probably because I'm just a bit lazy, Rabbit. Maybe someday I'll come up with a tool that'll do all my work for me. Then I'll be able to stay in bed until noon.'

'Now *that's* the tool I've been looking for since the first day when I had to go to work,' Rabbit said with a broad grin.

* * *

Keselo turned the large metal shield over and showed Omago the back of it. 'You have to slide your left arm under this leather strap and take a firm grip on the bar. That makes the shield a sort of extension of your arm, and you can block the strokes of your enemy's sword or the jabs he makes at you if he's using a spear. The creatures we came up against in the ravine didn't have any weapons except their fangs and stingers, but the shields held them back far enough so that they couldn't reach us. I talked this over with Rabbit earlier this morning, and he agreed with me that wooden shields would work as well as metal ones, since the snake-men don't have swords or axes. We wouldn't be able to gather up enough metal to make shields for all of your men anyway, and wood's lighter and easier to carry than iron or bronze.'

'And if the shield was made of wood, Rabbit could probably attach a spear-point to the middle of it, couldn't he?' Omago suggested.

Keselo blinked. 'I never thought of that!' he exclaimed. 'How in the world did you come up with *that* notion, Omago?'

'The two things just sort of connected,' Omago replied. 'I wasn't trying to make a joke of it or anything like that, but if there's a spear-point that's been dipped in that venom, you'd have something to protect yourself with if one of the snake-men happens to duck under the spear-points lined up out in front.'

'You're an absolute genius, Omago!'

'I wouldn't go *that* far, Keselo,' Omago replied, feeling slightly embarrassed by the young Trogite's enthusiasm. 'As I see it, this phalanx thing your commander mentioned is going to take quite a bit of practice to get used to.'

Keselo nodded. 'Several weeks at least,' he agreed. 'Now, when we take up the phalanx formation we overlap our shields to put a solid wall to the front. Then we tuck the butt of the spear under our right armpit and take hold of the shaft with our right hand. You have to hold the shield bar tightly with your left hand and the shaft of your spear just as tight with your right. The muscles in both your arms will be a little sore by the end of the day at first, but that'll go away after a while. The secret of the whole thing is that your soldiers aren't working as individuals. They're a unit, and they're very closely coordinated. When you use the phalanx formation, your men have to lock their spears in place and then walk forward in unison. They *walk* the spear-point into the enemy instead of jabbing or poking.'

'That might take a bit of getting used to,' Omago said a bit dubiously.

'Yes, it does. We'll start by teaching your men to march. That involves walking in unison. We want everybody's left foot to come down on the ground at the same time. After a while, it gets to be second nature, and they'll be able to do it in their sleep – well, almost.'

'Being a soldier's a little more complicated than I thought it might be,' Omago observed.

'It beats doing honest work,' Keselo replied with a slight grin.

'My ships are a lot faster than yours, Narasan,' Sorgan Hook-Beak said that evening at the supper table. 'I'll be able to bring Lady Zelana's archers here in about half the time it'd take those scows of yours.'

'And only bring back half as many,' Narasan added dryly. 'We could probably argue all night about which would be better – fast or many.'

'You've got a very warped sense of humor, Narasan.'

'Nobody's perfect,' Narasan replied blandly.

'Just exactly where's the border-line between your Domain and Zelana's, Veltan?' Longbow asked.

'I don't know if I'd call it a line, exactly,' Veltan replied. 'Why do you ask?'

'Most archers are hunters, and hunters can run quite a bit faster than people who spend their time sitting in one place. Any ship – either Sorgan's or Narasan's – will have to take the long way around to get back to Lattash. The archers could come across country, though, and if I remember your lumpy picture correctly, a straight line from Lattash to your house here would be less than half as far as a ship would have to travel.' He looked at Sorgan with a faint smile. 'We could race, if you'd like, and maybe even make some kind of wager on it.'

'I think I'll put my money on Longbow, Sorgan,' Narasan declared.

'Not against *me*, you won't,' Sorgan said sourly. 'The main thing I've learned about Longbow is never to try to beat him – at anything.'

The following morning a balding Trogite named Gunda came up from the beach to confer with Commander Narasan. 'I had a clerk draw a copy of my map for Andar,' he reported, 'and he'll bring the rest of the army on up through that channel through the ice. Then I bought a sloop so that I could come up here and find out exactly where we want the army to come ashore. Then I'll go on back down to the upper end of the channel and lead Andar on up here.'

'How long is it likely to take, Gunda?' Narasan asked.

'Probably about another two weeks. Have things started to heat up here yet?'

'Not as far as we know,' Narasan replied. 'Of course, when you're dealing with those snake-men, you can never be sure. Why didn't you bring Padan up here with you?'

'Well, he's just a little bit nervous, Commander,' Gunda replied. 'When he gets here, he's going to have to report a couple of things that aren't going to make you any too happy.'

'Such as?'

'Could I take that as an order, sir?' Gunda asked. 'I wouldn't want Padan to start calling me a snitch.'

'Consider it to be an order then, Gunda. What's been going on down there at the beach?'

'Well, sir, when Padan woke up yesterday morning, he noticed right off that Veltan's sloop wasn't there any more.'

'You said *what*?' Veltan demanded.

'It's gone,' Gunda replied, 'but this gets even better. Padan told me that Commander Narasan had stripped Jalkan of his commission and had him put in chains. After a while, Padan put a couple of things together and he ran down to the little room in the hold of the ship where Jalkan had been chained to the wall – and guess what? Jalkan wasn't there any more either. I suppose it *might* just be a coincidence that the sloop and Jalkan both vanished on the same night, but I don't think I'd want to wager a month's pay on it.'

'Are you just about through joking around, Gunda?' Narasan demanded.

'I was just reporting what had happened, sir. If I remember correctly, you *did* order me to tell you about this, and a good soldier always obeys orders.' He feigned a look of wide-eyed innocence.

And then he burst out laughing.

* * *

Upon reflection, Omago realized that the outlanders were quite a bit more advanced than the people of the Land of Dhrall, but their social structure left much to be desired. They were very much like children – except that they all carried deadly weapons, and they'd go to war on almost any pretext.

That childish aggressiveness *did* work to the advantage of the people of the Land of Dhrall, though. The current situation required many hired killers, and it appeared that Veltan and his sister had found exactly the ones best qualified to meet the servants of the Vlagh.

Omago smiled faintly. The outlanders had all appeared to be astonished by several of the innovations he'd suggested. Evidently they all had the notion of 'primitive savages' locked in stone in their minds. The possibility that anybody in the Land of Dhrall could come up with improvements in weaponry was beyond their comprehension.

To some degree, perhaps, that blank spot in the minds of the outlanders *could* have grown out of their lack of awareness – or interest – in the extensive education Omago had received from Veltan since his early childhood. He was fairly sure that no outlander from the Trogite Empire or the Land of Maag had ever had a god for his teacher. The 'connections' which had come to Omago had been second nature, actually. Omago habitually moved from 'effect' to 'cause', and that seemed to be unnatural for the outlanders. They always seemed to think in the opposite direction. Evidently it had never occurred to them that the source of most inventions was 'I need something that will do *that*,' not 'I wonder what I'll be able to do with this thing if I make it.'

Omago was forced to concede that he *had* made a serious blunder, however. Jalkan's insult had been a perfect opportunity to eliminate what might well turn out to be a serious danger down the line. 'I should have killed him right there on the spot,' Omago muttered regretfully. 'Narasan even went so far as to offer me the opportunity, and I passed it up – probably because I didn't want to offend the Trogites. I'm almost certain that we haven't seen the last of that foul-mouthed lecher.'

Then a peculiar notion came to him. Could it be that Ara had deliberately instilled that lust in Jalkan? Omago was almost positive that she could have done that. She'd certainly done it to *him* when they'd first met in his orchard. Just the sight of her had made him her captive. If she *had*, in fact, set Jalkan's mind to moving in *that* direction, it was quite obvious what she'd been after. Omago cursed himself. He'd failed her. She'd almost certainly have wanted him to respond in the most primitive way – bashing Jalkan's brains out or ripping him up the middle with that iron knife.

'If that's what she really wanted, I wish she'd told me what she had in mind.' He shrugged. 'Ah, well,' he sighed. 'Maybe next time.'

THE BETRAYAL

1

—◦—

Jalkan of Kaldacin was the sole remaining member of a once-prominent family of the Trogite Empire. Many of his ancestors had served with honor and distinction in the Palvanum, and others had been advisors to historically significant emperors. The family had accumulated wealth, prestige and power over the years, and the names of several members were prominently displayed on various public monuments.

In the past century, however, Jalkan's family had gone into a steep decline. Various ne'er-do-wells had squandered away the family's wealth in wanton debauchery, gambling and drinking to excess. Moneylenders pursued them, and a fair number of Jalkan's recent ancestors had spent their final years in assorted debtors' prisons.

By the time Jalkan himself reached maturity, the family's reputation had been irrevocably tarnished, and there were very few career opportunities available to him.

He considered the possibility of joining the ranks of the assorted Trogite syndicates that were currently amassing vast fortunes in the Land of Shaan. The notion of swindling ignorant savages out of their gold had a certain appeal, but he quickly discarded that idea when word of a colossal disaster reached Kaldacin. Evidently some idiot, far gone in drink, had boasted about his success in the wrong place and in front of the wrong people, and the natives of the Land of Shaan had gone on a rampage, slaughtering (and feasting on) every Trogite they could lay their hands on.

Jalkan, now facing the prospect of hard, honest work for scant pay, turned instead to the last refuge of the scoundrel. Dressed in his most sober clothing and wearing a somberly pious expression, he began to attend holy services in the local Amarite convenium three or four times a day.

In due time, one of the minor Hieras in the hallowed convenium noticed Jalkan and brought him to the attention of the Oran as a potential member of the clergy. The Oran interviewed Jalkan and enrolled him as a novice, demanding scarcely more than a third of Jalkan's very limited remaining assets as a sign of good faith.

Jalkan winced, but finally agreed.

His first few months as a very junior member of the clergy were moderately unpleasant, since the Amarite hierarchy devoted much effort to weeding out apprentices who were excessively unworthy. Jalkan was clever enough not to steal *too* much *and* to discredit those of his fellow novices who were overly honest or obviously more clever than he was.

His cunning was noted by his superiors, and it generally met with their approval.

Jalkan's most immediate goal as a novice had been to take the next step up to the rank of Hiera. A Hiera in the Amarite faith was not required to do much hard labor, and he was even assigned his own room. The rooms of the Hieras were called 'cells', and they were very tiny, but they were far better than the rank-smelling first-floor dormitories where the novices were crammed together like cattle.

Because he was marginally literate, Jalkan's duties as a Hiera were largely limited to administration, and he was somewhat startled to discover that nearly half of the Empire belonged to the Amarite church. The vast church estates produced much of the Empire's food – for a handsome price – and the annual rent on various buildings in the capital city of Kaldacin brought in staggering amounts of money.

It was on a gloomy afternoon in late winter that Jalkan came across an ancient document that gave an account of the closing of a rundown convenium in one of the poorer districts of the imperial city of Kaldacin. If the time-faded document was correct, the structure had been closed for nearly a century, and the financial records of the church showed that it had not brought in so much as a single copper penny in all those years. If that were indeed the case, Jalkan realized that he could very well be the only man in the world who even knew of the existence of the building.

Overcome with curiosity, Jalkan bundled himself up in his heavy cloak and walked across town to the district where the convenium was supposedly located.

There was a crumbling old stone wall surrounding the tired-looking structure, and the building itself was quite nearly hidden by trees and bushes.

Jalkan was very disappointed. He'd hoped that the abandoned convenium might prove to be of some value, but it was quite obvious why the place wasn't bringing in any money. A good sneeze would probably bring it tumbling down.

Then, even as he was turning away in disgust, his eye caught a faint glimmer of light coming through a crumbling board that partially covered one of the windows. Unless it happened to be on fire, the ancient building was obviously not as deserted as it had seemed at first glance.

That might turn out to be useful, so Jalkan clambered over a low place in the crumbling wall and approached the disreputable structure. As he drew closer, he began to hear some people talking inside. He raised up on his tiptoes to peer through the cracked board that covered the window.

Inside the supposedly empty convenium there was an extremely fat man seated at a rough table with a smoking lamp at one end, and the fat man was holding up a rather splendid metal tray. 'This is solid silver, Esag. It's worth a lot more than just one gold crown.'

'I could maybe go as high as one and a half, Rabell, but it's got that coat of arms engraved on it, so I can't just put it in the window of my shop. If that silly aristocrat your people stole it from happens to walk by and sees it there, he'll have the law on me before the sun goes down.'

Jalkan nearly choked. 'It's a den of thieves!' he gasped, 'and they're not paying us so much as a penny for its use!'

'I can let you have the tray for two crowns, Esag,' the fat man conceded, 'but that's as low as I'll go.'

'You're an out and out swindler, Rabell,' Esag grumbled.

'You don't have to buy it if you don't want to, Esag,' the fat man said. 'I've got a lot of other customers.'

Esag took two gold coins from his purse, slapped them down on the table, and left with the silver tray.

Then a burly-looking ruffian with a little girl at his side came out of the shadows. 'You bargain real good, Rabell,' he said in a raspy voice.

'I could have that idiot for lunch any day of the week, Grol,' Rabell sneered. He held out one of the gold crowns. 'Here's your half, good friend.'

'I've been meaning to talk with you about that, Rabell,' the ruffian said. 'It seems to me that your arrangement just ain't none too fair. I mean, Baby-Girl and me are sort of partners, and she ain't getting her fair share.'

'That's between you and her, Grol. Half and half is our standard arrangement. You and Baby-Girl steal it, and I sell it.'

Grol grumbled a bit, but he *did* take the gold coin. 'I don't know how much longer Baby-Girl's going to be able to do our stealing for us, Rabell,' he said. 'She's growing awful fat for some reason, and it's getting harder and harder for her to wiggle through them little windows to get inside them houses to steal stuff. It ain't going to be too much longer afore I'll have to find some new little child to do the stealing.'

'That's *your* problem, Grol,' Rabell replied. 'Now move along. There are quite a few other people waiting to show me what *they've* stolen.'

Jalkan did not sleep well that night. As a member of the clergy, it was his duty to bring the matter to the attention of his Oran, but he knew his superior well enough to be fairly sure that Oran Paldor would most probably approach the fat thief Rabell who was operating the business in the abandoned convenium and demand a sizeable share of the profits. He was almost positive *also* that Paldor would neglect to tell his superiors about the arrangement. Paldor would be most grateful to Jalkan, of course, but not *quite* grateful enough to share the profits.

There was an alternative, of course, and the alternative was much, much more attractive than doing his duty.

'This is church property, Rabell,' Jalkan told the fat man the next afternoon in the crumbling old convenium. 'You can't just walk in off the street and take it over without church permission. I think you might just be in a lot of trouble.'

'Don't get excited,' Rabell told him with a note of resignation. 'I'll be out of here before the sun goes down.'

'I didn't say that you have to leave, Rabell. All I meant was that you should pay the church for the use of this splendid convenium. I think the term is "rent". You can stay if you pay.'

'Get to the point, Jalkan. How much do you want?'

'Oh, I don't know. Half sounds about right to me.'

'Forget it. I can set up shop in some other place.'

'Don't get excited, Rabell. That was only a suggestion. It's open to negotiation.'

'Not until you stop lying to me, it isn't. The church has no part in this, and all the money I give you will go into your own purse. Isn't that what you've got in your greedy little mind?'

'Well—'

'I thought so. Don't blink, Jalkan, because if you do, I won't be here when you open your eyes again.'

'I can really make it worth your while, Rabell,' Jalkan said a little desperately.

'You'd better make it good,' Rabell growled.

'I'm a Hiera in the Amarite church, and I've frequently been inside the palaces of the higher-ranking clergymen. I can tell you exactly where in those palaces the valuables are kept. That should be worth *something*, wouldn't you say?'

'Well, maybe. I'd also need to know how well those palaces are guarded. The little children we use to do the stealing for us are extremely valuable, so I won't take any chances with them.'

'How in the world did you ever come up with this idea?' Jalkan asked curiously.

'Where have you been, Jalkan?' Rabell demanded. 'This has been going on for generations. When I was just a little boy, I was the best thief in the whole city of Kaldacin. I could wriggle through the bars on any window in town, and if there weren't any windows, I could crawl in through rat holes.' He reached down and put his hands on his paunch. 'I've gained quite a bit of weight since then, though.'

'I noticed that, yes. What do you think, Rabell? Would the information I give you about the location of valuables be worth a fair share of the loot?'

'We can give it a try, I suppose – but *only* what we get from those places *you* tell me about. I've got quite a few teams out there, and they're robbing fancy houses all over town.'

'There's something I don't quite understand there, Rabell,' Jalkan admitted. 'Couldn't you make more money if you eliminated the ruffians who tell the children which houses to rob?'

'You want *me* to stand guard out in the street while the children are inside the house stealing anything they can lay their hands on? Are you out of your *mind*?'

'Ah,' Jalkan said. 'I guess that *does* make good sense.'

'Let's get down to business here, Jalkan,' the fat man suggested. 'I'll need to know quite a bit about one of these church palaces *before* I risk one of the children.'

'I know just the place, Rabell,' Jalkan said, rubbing his hands together.

'How are things going, Rabell?' Jalkan asked the fat man a few days later.

'Better than I'd expected,' Rabell replied. 'That house you pointed out to me was almost a gold mine. I turned that one over to Grol and Baby-Girl. She had to make eight trips from the kitchen to the window to haul out all the loot. That set of dishes and the silverware brought in a lot of money.'

'I've been looking into a few other houses,' Jalkan said. 'There are a couple of them that we might want to consider. Let's settle accounts, and then we can talk about them.'

2

◄—►◄—►

'I think I must have offended my Oran,' Jalkan complained to the elderly servant in Adnari Radan's palace. 'He *claims* that we need exact measurements of every church building in all of Kaldacin for church records, but I think he's lying through his teeth. This is the most tedious chore I've ever had laid on me since I first entered the church, and I'll be old and grey before I get even halfway through it.'

'We live but to serve,' the servant said piously.

'Of *course* we do,' Jalkan agreed sardonically. 'Is this the Adnari's study?' he asked, pointing at an ornate door. 'I wouldn't want to disturb him.'

'He's over in the convenium right now.'

'This won't take more than a few minutes,' Jalkan said. 'I'm sure you have other matters to attend to. I won't disturb anything, and I'll close the door when I leave.'

'I *do* have some chores to take care of, Hiera Jalkan,' the old man said. 'Are you sure you won't need me?'

'I've been doing this for weeks now, my friend,' Jalkan replied. 'A few more times and I should be able to do it in my sleep.'

The old man smiled and went off down the hall. Jalkan went

into Adnari Radan's study and looked around. *This* one seemed to be filled with all sorts of valuable items. Jalkan quickly began to scribble notes describing some of the more valuable objects. It appeared that Adnari Radan had some very expensive tastes. He *had* to get this place on Rabell's list.

He was whistling as he returned home and bounded up the stairs to his second-floor cell.

Then he stopped suddenly. There were three iron-faced men in the distinctive uniforms of the church Regulators, the internal police of the Amarite church, waiting.

He turned to run back down the stairs, but the Regulators were too quick for him. They seized him and slammed him up against the wall. 'You're under arrest, Hiera Jalkan,' one of them announced in an almost bored tone of voice.

'But I haven't done anything!' Jalkan protested.

Almost casually, one of the Regulators drove his fist into Jalkan's belly, knocking the wind out of him. Then, while he was gasping for breath, the Regulators slapped him into chains.

'You're in custody now, Hiera Jalkan,' another Regulator declared. 'You *will* come with us, and if you give us any trouble, the three of us will beat you to within an inch of your life.'

'What are the charges?' Jalkan demanded.

'That's none of our concern,' the Regulator replied. 'We were told by Adnari Estarg to bring you in, and that's exactly what we're doing.'

Jalkan began to tremble violently. Adnari Estarg was the most powerful man in the Amarite church, and he had a fearsome reputation. Church law forbade the death penalty for priests and even for novices, but it was widely known in Kaldacin that Adnari Estarg could come up with forms of punishment that made the death penalty seem almost preferable.

The Regulators dragged their violently trembling prisoner through the streets of Kaldacin to the splendid palace adjoining the huge, ornate convenium that marked the center of the Amarite faith. Then they took him up an ornate marble staircase to a splendidly furnished study on the second floor of the palace. They pushed him down onto his knees before the throne of a portly man garbed in the crimson robe of an Adnari of the church.

'The prisoner Jalkan, your Grace,' the Regulator who'd done most of the talking announced.

'Excellent,' the chubby churchman said, rubbing his hands together. 'That'll be all gentlemen. I'll deal with this miscreant myself.'

'As you wish, your Grace,' the Regulator said with a slight bow, and then the three of them left the study, closing the door behind them.

'Shameful, Hiera Jalkan,' Adnari Estarg said. 'Shameful, shameful, shameful. What *am* I going to do with you, you naughty boy?'

The Adnari's tone actually sounded almost amused. 'You *do* realize that you've profaned a sacred convenium by turning it into a den of thieves, don't you?'

'It's been long abandoned, your Grace,' Jalkan protested.

'That doesn't mean that the sanctification's been revoked, Jalkan,' the Adnari insisted.

'It wasn't originally my idea, your Grace. The old convenium had been long deserted, and the leader of a group of thieves just moved in and set up shop without anybody's permission.'

'Why didn't you report that to your Oran?'

'Well—' Jalkan desperately groped for some sort of explanation that wouldn't get him deeper in trouble.

'I'm waiting, Jalkan.'

'I lost my head, your Grace,' Jalkan confessed. 'The thieves are making *heaps* of money, and—' Jalkan faltered.

'And you seized the chance to take most of it away from them, didn't you?'

'Only a quarter, your Grace,' Jalkan protested. 'I thought at first that I could get more, but Rabell wouldn't stand for it.'

'Rabell?'

'The fat man who hires the thieves. They steal and he sells what they've stolen. The really clever part of the business is the use of children.'

Adnari Estarg's head came up sharply. 'Children?' he exclaimed. 'What part could children play in this?'

'They're the ones who do the actual stealing, your Grace. As I understand it, the thieves have been using children for years and years. People with valuables in their houses usually have barred windows, but the children Rabell hires are so small that they can slip right between the bars and get inside with almost no trouble at all. Rabell tells me that when *he* was a child, he was the best thief in all of Kaldacin.'

'And just exactly what part do *you* play in this grand scheme, Hiera Jalkan?'

'Ah – I'd really rather not say, your Grace,' Jalkan replied nervously.

'I'm sure that the Regulators can come up with a way to make you change your mind, Hiera Jalkan,' the Adnari said ominously.

'Well—' Jalkan said nervously, 'I sort of find houses and such with lots of valuable things inside.'

'And just exactly how do you gain entrance into these various houses?' the Adnari pressed.

'Well, they're mostly the houses – and palaces – of the wealthier members of the clergy, your Grace. I told them that the church scholars had issued a rule that the exact dimensions of every piece of church property and all church buildings must be recorded in the church register. That opens a lot of doors for me, and I'm able to have a look around inside every building owned by any member of the clergy. When I come across a place with a lot of valuables inside, I go tell Rabell about it, and he arranges the robbery. I get a quarter of all the money the robbery brings in. He has thieves robbing other places as well, he tells me, but I only get paid for the ones I tell him about.'

'Ah, now it's starting to make some sense,' Adnari Estarg said. 'You're very clever, Hiera Jalkan, but you *do* know that you've committed a serious offense, don't you?'

Jalkan began to tremble violently again.

'Don't shake so much, dear boy,' Adnari Estarg told him. 'I think I've come up with a way for you to expiate this naughty sin you've committed – for a price. Everything has a price – or had you already noticed that?'

'I'll pay *anything*, your Grace,' Jalkan vowed in a trembling voice.

'You will indeed, Jalkan. Now, then, let's get down to business here. How many of these tiny children can this scoundrel Rabell put his hands on?'

'I'm not really sure, your Grace. I haven't had much contact with their handlers.'

'Handlers?'

'They're the men who more or less own the children. They decide which house they want to rob and stand guard outside while the child is inside stealing.'

'Our business seems to be very well-organized.'

'*Our* business?'

'You might want to advise Rabell that I'm the senior partner now. I'll put together an order about recording dimensions of church buildings and put my seal on it. That'll get you into some houses and palaces you probably don't even know about. Our glorious Naos, Parok VII, is so senile now that he doesn't know night from day. That means that I, as the senior Adnari, am running the church, so what *I* say is the law. I think our first step should be to put these "handlers" you mentioned into the uniforms of church Regulators. That should be very useful. *Nobody* argues with the Regulators. You'd better go advise your fat friend that the situation's changed just a bit.'

'Ah, your Grace,' Jalkan said. 'I can't really go anyplace just now. I'm all chained up, remember?'

'Why, so you are, Jalkan,' Adnari Estarg replied with feigned astonishment. 'Isn't it peculiar that I didn't notice that myself?'

'Things have changed just a bit, Rabell,' Jalkan announced when he returned to the ancient convenium.

'Changed? How?' the fat man demanded suspiciously.

'Right after I checked out Adnari Radan's palace, I went back to my cell to put the notes I'd taken into some kind of order, but there were three Regulators waiting for me.'

'*Regulators*?' Rabell exclaimed. 'How is it that you're still alive?'

'The Regulators aren't quite *that* savage, Rabell. They chained me up, of course, and then they dragged me across town to the palace of Adnari Estarg.'

Rabell's face went suddenly pale, and he started to tremble.

'The Adnari had evidently heard some rumors about what we're doing, so he wrung the truth out of me.'

'If we hurry, we can be out of Kaldacin by sunset,' Rabell said in a squeaky kind of voice.

'Don't get excited, Rabell. After the Adnari had heard the details of what we've been up to, he declared that from now on, we'll be taking orders from him.'

'Is this all some kind of elaborate joke, Jalkan? If it is, you'll notice that I'm not laughing very much.'

'Stay with me, Rabell. He told me that he was going to issue a proclamation to the effect that all church property and buildings are required to be listed in official church documents, *and* that the exact dimensions of every single room in all those buildings must be included. That proclamation will have *his* seal on it, and I'll have it in my pocket. Whoever happens to be living there right now will be *required* to open the door and let me in. A week or so from now our people will be robbing houses we didn't even know existed – *and* the handlers who take care of the children will be wearing the uniforms of church Regulators, so nobody in his right mind will interfere in any way at all.'

A look of astonished wonder came over Rabell's face. 'We're going to get rich, Jalkan!' he chortled. 'We're going to go way, way *past* rich! If I happen to be just dreaming, please don't wake me up!'

'I wouldn't dream of it, my dear friend,' Jalkan promised.

And then they both howled with laughter.

The Regulator who'd arrested Jalkan a few months earlier tapped politely on Jalkan's cell door, and he was much more civil this time. 'Adnari Estarg would have a word with you, Hiera Jalkan,' he said mildly.

'I'll come at once,' Jalkan said, rising quickly to his feet.

They moved through the streets of Imperial Kaldacin to the

palace of the Adnari, and Jalkan was immediately admitted to Estarg's study.

'Ah, there you are, Jalkan,' the fat churchman said. 'Things might be looking up for us.'

'Oh?'

'Holy Naos Parok VII seems to be having some serious health problems. His assorted physicians have advised me that he won't be around too much longer.'

'I'll pray that he recovers, your Grace,' Jalkan declared piously.

'We all will, of course,' Estarg agreed, 'but let's not overdo it. Divine Amar's very busy right now – changing the seasons, making sure that the sun rises and sets when she's supposed to – all those tedious little details that take up so very much of a god's time. Parok VII has had a full life, and he's done very well. The church will miss him terribly, of course, but time moves on, and as soon as the holy old fool dies, he'll have to be replaced.'

'I've got a fair idea of who's going to ascend the holy throne when dear Parok leaves us,' Jalkan declared.

3

As it turned out, however, things didn't go exactly as Hiera Jalkan and Adnari Estarg had been most certain that they would. All right-thinking men know that mighty Kaldacin is the very center of the universe, and that Divine Amar had intended it to be so since the beginning of time.

There *were* heretics, however – mostly in the southern reaches of the Empire – who steadfastly refused to accept the desires of Divine Amar. Rational men knew that Divine Amar had, in his infinite wisdom, chosen Adnari Estarg to succeed Holy Parok VII as Naos of all the world, but the heretics of the south turned away and, without consultation of any kind, they elevated a little-known Oran named Udar to the holy throne of the Naos.

The churchmen of mighty Kaldacin thought that was terribly funny, and they laughed long and hard at this colossal absurdity.

The laughter faded, however, when twelve armies marched up from the south and surrounded mighty Kaldacin.

The citizens of Kaldacin didn't think that was very appropriate, so they turned to the various armies whose compounds lay within the city walls.

The armies, however, followed the advice of the well-known

Commander Narasan when he declared, 'We don't get involved in religious squabbles.'

'But what are we going to do?' the civil and religious authorities wailed.

'I'd strongly advise capitulation,' Narasan replied. 'That's entirely up to you, though.' And he turned around and walked away.

The imperial government collapsed about then, and the armies of the south met little resistance as they marched through the gates. They occupied the imperial palace and the holy convenium of the Amarite church. The heretics of the south delivered several ultimatums to the *true* church hierarchy. The ultimatums were couched in formal terms, of course, but the meaning was fairly clear. 'If you don't do exactly as we tell you, we'll kill you,' gets right to the point.

The ceremony that elevated the little-known Udar to the position of Naos took less than half an hour, and the acceptance speech of Naos Udar IV took even less time. He said, 'Divine Amar has sent me here to cleanse the church, and I will obey him. If anybody here gets in my way, I'll trample him into the dust.'

A sudden chill came over Jalkan at that point.

'Will anyone here speak in the defense of this foul miscreant?' the ornately robed Amarite judge demanded, giving the chained prisoner Jalkan a look of profoundest contempt.

Jalkan cringed, looking hopefully at his friend, Adnari Estarg.

Estarg however, turned his eyes away, and Jalkan's last hope faded.

'I didn't really think so,' the judge declared. 'Unfortunately, church law forbids a sentence of death for *any* member of the clergy

– even one of such low rank as the accused. It is therefore the decision of this court that the accused shall be taken hence to a public square and there he shall receive fifty lashes and then be stripped of his membership in the clergy. Let it be known further that no adherent of the Amarite faith shall have any contact with this vile beast, nor will shelter or food be made available to him for so long as he lives. Now get this trash out of my sight.'

The Regulators stripped Jalkan down to his loincloth, chained him to the post in the middle of the square, and then flogged him to within an inch of his life with long whips, ignoring his screams and shrill cries for mercy.

He was blubbering and bleeding profusely when they unchained him. He snatched up his clothes and fled with the mocking laughter of the crowd of commoners who had gathered to watch his punishment following him.

He went into a secluded alley and pulled on his clothes, muttering curses all the while. Everything had been going so well, and then that cursed Udar had usurped the divine throne of the Naos, and Jalkan's world had all gone to pieces.

Adnari Estarg had betrayed him to protect himself, but the high churchman probably hadn't had much choice in the matter.

Right now, Jalkan had something much more important to attend to. It was absolutely essential for him to return to his cell in the church dormitory to gather up his clothes and other belongings before word of his ejection from the church became general knowledge. Far more important than clothes, however, was the carefully concealed purse under his cot. In his present circumstances, that money was an absolute necessity. Without the purse, he'd be a pauper with no prospects whatsoever.

As luck had it, the novice who was guarding the door of the church dormitory was half-drunk, and he waved Jalkan through without any questions. Jalkan nodded briefly and went directly to his cell.

He heaved an enormous sigh of relief when he entered. Nothing had been disturbed – yet. He was certain that when word of his recent dismissal got out, people would be standing in line waiting for the opportunity to rummage through his cell. Wincing in pain, he crawled under his cot and retrieved the worn-out old shoe lying against the back wall. The weight of that discarded shoe brightened an otherwise gloomy day.

Jalkan discarded his clergyman's robe and garbed himself in his best clothing. Then he took the heavy purse out of the tired old shoe and tucked it down into the top of his boot. He gave his cell a final look. All in all, his career in the church had been quite profitable, but it was obviously time to move on.

The recent refusal of Commander Narasan to become involved in church squabbles raised an interesting possibility. Jalkan was fairly sure that his purse filled with gold crowns would get Commander Narasan's immediate attention, and a career as an army officer might be even more exciting than a career in the church. 'I guess it's worth a try,' he muttered to himself as he left the dormitory. 'I think I've just about exhausted the possibilities the church has to offer, and I was getting more than a little tired of all the praying and groveling anyway.'

4

<hr/>

Jalkan had a bit of trouble adjusting to military life. There hadn't been much physical activity involved in being a member of the clergy, so he wasn't really in very good shape. Running five miles before breakfast every morning corrected that after a few weeks, but he still didn't like it very much.

Then there'd been his training in swordsmanship, and after a very short time he'd come to hate the balding officer named Gunda, who was his instructor. Jalkan had assumed that his very expensive commission as an officer in Commander Narasan's army had bought him a certain amount of respect, but Gunda didn't seem to understand the meaning of the word 'respect', and his vocabulary was quite colorful. Every time Jalkan made the slightest mistake, Gunda showered him with curses and ridicule.

In time, however, Jalkan became more proficient, but he still couldn't see why it was necessary. He *was* an officer, after all. He was supposed to give orders, not become involved in the actual business of killing people. That was the job of the ordinary soldiers, not the officers.

It was about a month after Jalkan had bought his commission that Commander Narasan's army had been hired to take part in a small war off to the East of the empire. The officer named Padan referred to the war as 'a slight unpleasantness'. Padan, Jalkan felt, had a very warped sense of humor. To Jalkan's way of looking at things, 'unpleasantness' was a gross understatement.

After a year or so, Jalkan became better adjusted to the life of a soldier, and he even began to enjoy it. Because Commander Narasan was perhaps the finest and most skilled strategist in all the Empire, the various wars his army was hired to undertake were usually quite short, and the eventual outcome was quite predictable – so predictable, in fact, that it was not unusual for the opposing army to capitulate as soon as they realized that they'd be fighting against Narasan's army.

Jalkan definitely approved of that. The pay was good, and there wasn't much danger involved. It occurred to him that the time he'd spent as a clergyman had actually been wasted. He was born to be a soldier.

It was during Jalkan's third year in Narasan's army that the father of young Keselo purchased a commission for his son. At first, Jalkan was quite sure that he and the rather stuffy young aristocrat would become close friends, but Keselo remained aloof. Evidently, Keselo's years as a student at the University of Kaldacin had given him an exaggerated opinion of himself. Jalkan had encountered that often during his years in the Amarite church. Some men simply could not accept the fact that their education had not really ennobled them. Jalkan turned his back on Keselo at that point. He didn't really *need* friends anyway.

Then in the spring of Jalkan's fifth year as an officer in Narasan's army, a duke from the southern part of the Empire approached

Commander Narasan with a very generous offer. As nearly as Jalkan was able to determine, an old baron had recently died without an heir, and the rulers of two nearby duchies had been squabbling for almost a year about which one of them should annex the barony as 'a protectorate'.

The duke who'd approached Commander Narasan had evidently grown tired of the endless argument, and he'd decided to take a more direct approach.

The money was good, and Commander Narasan had quickly agreed.

Jalkan, however, had a few doubts. The southern reaches of the Empire had given rise to the heresy that had placed the usurper Udar IV on the holy throne of the Naos of the Amarite faith, so Jalkan had good reason not to trust *anybody* who came from that region.

As it had turned out, Jalkan's doubts had been even more valid than he'd thought. The opposing duke had secretly hired *three* armies to oppose Commander Narasan's force, and the results had been disastrous.

Jalkan never fully understood Narasan's reaction to the unfortunate events in the south of the Empire. Twelve cohorts had been slaughtered during the battle, but very few *officers* had fallen. The vast majority of the casualties had been common soldiers, so they weren't really all that significant. Narasan, however, had gone into deep mourning. Then he'd broken his sword and left the army compound to take up begging in a scruffy part of the city of Kaldacin.

That raised a number of very interesting possibilities. There were several officers who outranked Jalkan, of course, but that wasn't really a major obstacle. Jalkan knew quite a few professional assassins who normally worked for the higher-ranking churchmen. Once Gunda, Padan – and most certainly Keselo – were out of the way, Jalkan would be the logical successor to Narasan.

That lit a warm little fire in his heart, and he began to work on his agenda. Quite obviously, the common soldiers in the army were being grossly overpaid. Once Jalkan assumed command, his first order of business would be to reduce those wages by half at the very least, and after he'd made examples of the more vociferous objectors, the rest of the army would accept the decrees of their new commander. If everything went according to his plans, Commander Jalkan would soon be collecting as much or more money than even Adnari Estarg had been raking in.

Jalkan felt that was only right and proper. His future was beginning to look brighter and brighter.

Some months later, the cursed foreigner Veltan arrived in Kaldacin, and in less than a week Jalkan's grand plan tumbled down around his ears. Commander Narasan returned to the army compound and snatched Jalkan's glorious future right out from under him.

Jalkan tried his best to conceal his disappointment, but when he was alone, he spent much of his time inventing new curse-words.

5

———✦———

Jalkan had been quite certain that the foreigner Veltan had deceived Commander Narasan during their negotiations, but when the advance force reached Castano after the long march from Kaldacin, Veltan sailed into the harbor in a rickety fishing sloop and delivered ten blocks of what appeared to be pure gold.

That definitely got Jalkan's attention, and he made a point of being in Narasan's cabin on board the large Trogite vessel Narasan had hired to carry most of the officers off to the north when the commander carried the blocks on board. Jalkan *definitely* wanted to know just exactly where that gold was located.

Commander Narasan put the blocks inside the large trunk at the bottom of his bed almost indifferently, and then handed a large map to Jalkan. 'Give this to Gunda,' he said. 'It'll show him the path to follow that'll get the fleet through that belt of ice-floes lying between here and the Land of Dhrall.'

'Yes, sir!' Jalkan replied crisply, coming to attention and saluting smartly. He was fairly certain that a pose of strict military behavior was appropriate just now. A number of very interesting possibilities had turned up, and Jalkan thought it might be best to keep his interest in that gold strictly to himself.

After Commander Narasan and Veltan had sailed north in the fishing sloop, Gunda took charge of the advance force and they made preparations to sail from Castano.

Jalkan agonized over the monumental choice that was facing him at that point. He knew exactly where those ten blocks of gold were stored, and Commander Narasan hadn't even bothered to lock that trunk. On the other hand, Veltan had told them that the Land of Dhrall had whole mountains of gold just sitting there waiting for somebody to gather it up. To be sure, Jalkan could quite easily appropriate those ten blocks and be gone before anyone noticed, but that would forever put the mountains of gold in the Land of Dhrall beyond his reach. A kind of paralysis came over him, and he was unable to make the choice.

And then the fleet sailed, and the choice went out the window.

He began to seriously regret that when the fleet of ships reached the band of ice floes that lay between the Empire and the Land of Dhrall. The term 'ice floe' was a gross understatement to Jalkan's way of thinking. 'A mountain range of floating ice' would come much closer. The channels the fleet followed were disturbingly narrow, and the towering cliffs of blue-white ice rose up and up and up until they seemed to blot out the very sky. A lot of 'ifs' came unbidden into Jalkan's mind as the fleet carefully made its way north. 'If the current changes' seemed to argue with 'if the wind comes from a different direction' in Jalkan's imagination. He realized that the cause wouldn't really matter, since the effect would be the same. The ice-mountains would slowly, but inexorably, come together, crushing the ships

– and everybody on board the ships – slowly into splinters and bloody pulp.

Jalkan went below decks at that point and refused to even look at the mountains of ice on all sides of the fleet.

The weather had cleared off somewhat when the advance fleet sailed into the harbor of a native village called Lattash, but there appeared to be a great deal of snow in the mountains that reared up behind the village.

Commander Narasan was standing on the beach when the ships dropped anchor, and he greeted his officers as they came ashore.

To Jalkan's eyes the village of Lattash was so primitive that he half expected to see the natives walking on all fours like dogs, and the scruffy-looking Maag pirates weren't much better. It *did* raise some interesting possibilities, though. A well-trained army could take just about anything of value from these primitives without so much as working up a sweat. Jalkan was very happy that he hadn't just stolen those few blocks of gold and run off while the fleet had still been in the harbor at Castano. It appeared that there were all sorts of opportunities here.

He almost burst out laughing when Commander Narasan led them into a cave to meet Veltan's sister. A cave took 'primitive' all the way down to the bottom rung of the ladder.

Then he saw Zelana for the first time, and just the sight of her almost stopped his heart. She was by far the most beautiful woman he'd ever seen.

The pirate leader Sorgan was quite another matter. Jalkan had never seen a man so large, and the ones called 'Ox' and 'Ham-Hand' were even bigger. For some unknown reason, Commander

Narasan seemed to think the small, wiry Maag known as 'Rabbit' was somebody special.

After a bit of discussion, Commander Narasan and the pirate decided to leave their men on board the ships in the harbor, and that didn't particularly bother Jalkan. The less he had to do with pirates and savages, the better.

Time seemed to pass very slowly as they all waited for the snow in the mountains to melt off, but Jalkan wasn't in any particular hurry.

And then the day came when an old man from one of the native tribes told them all a wild story about people who were part snake and very dangerous. Jalkan dismissed all of that as pure nonsense. The less he had to do with these superstitious savages the better.

Jalkan's hideous discovery of the *true* reality that lay behind this dreadful war quite nearly dislocated his mind. He spent most of his time devoutly praying to Amar to protect him – not only from the evil snake-men, but more importantly from the witch Zelana. There were several gestures he knew of that would hold evil at bay, and his fingers were moving almost constantly as the army marched on back to the village by the bay.

After what seemed to Jalkan almost an eternity, the army of Commander Narasan boarded the ships in the harbor and set sail for the southern reaches of the Land of Dhrall to fight the war they were being paid for. Jalkan privately wished that they'd just keep on going south. Everything here in the Land of Dhrall seemed so hideously unnatural.

Jalkan found the Domain of Veltan much more attractive than the region controlled by Veltan's sister. The forests of Zelana's Domain had frightened Jalkan, and the savage hunters who lived there appeared to have little respect for those of superior rank. The fact that Jalkan *was* an officer and a gentleman seemed to have escaped them. At least the peasants of Veltan's Domain seemed to know their place.

Jalkan carefully questioned a peasant named Omago about the religious beliefs of the natives, and he was more than a little shocked to discover that the ignorant savages had nothing even resembling a church, and they were permitted to speak directly with their god without benefit of the clergy.

Jalkan concealed his outrage and rather slyly asked the crude bumpkin where the gold mines were located, but the fellow feigned ignorance. Jalkan swore under his breath and stalked away. He was fairly certain that in time he'd be able to find *some* peasant who'd be more forthcoming. There were unbelievable opportunities here in the Land of Dhrall, but Jalkan needed more information before he'd be able to exploit them.

After they'd walked a goodly distance up from the beach, they reached the castle of Veltan, and their host led them to what he called his 'map-room'.

Then Commander Narasan and the pirate Sorgan became involved in a lengthy discussion of the terrain and probable tactics which might – or might not – be involved in their campaign, but Jalkan paid very little attention. It was fairly clear by now that the region around the Falls of Vash was most probably rich in gold. There was no other reason to defend the area, and it was equally obvious that it was *also* the reason for the enemy invasion. That made everything crystal clear. The volcanic eruption in the Domain of Veltan's sister Zelana had buried any gold deposits at the head of the ravine, so now the people of the Land of Dhrall were desperate to protect the deposits here in Veltan's Domain.

Now that Jalkan knew what was *really* happening here, his next logical step was to find some way to profit from that knowledge.

After a while, a peasant woman who was remarkably attractive came through the door to announce that the evening meal was ready, and Jalkan made a few complimentary remarks. Any peasant woman in the Empire would have felt quite flattered by his observations, and no peasant man would have found them the least bit objectionable, but the peasant Omago had the gall to respond with violence. Without so much as any kind of warning, Omago drove his fist into Jalkan's mouth, knocking him flat on his back with a single blow.

Jalkan came to his feet, grabbing at his knife-hilt, but the insolent young Keselo drew his sword and began making threats.

Jalkan appealed to Commander Narasan for justice. The law was very clear in these circumstances. Any peasant who struck one of his superiors was supposed to be executed on the spot.

Commander Narasan, however, refused to uphold the law, and he even went so far as to revoke the commission Jalkan had bought and paid for.

Jalkan protested vigorously, but Commander Narasan ignored his fully justified protests, and then, to Jalkan's utter disbelief, Narasan ordered Padan to chain him and take him back to the harbor where the fleet was anchored to await a final decision.

The thing that none of them seemed to realize was that Jalkan's comments had been intended as compliments.

6

❧

The rank injustice of the entire affair filled Jalkan with a sense of outrage. His rights and privileges as an officer had been violated again and again, but not one fellow officer had come forward to lodge a protest.

It was quite obvious by now that Narasan had agreed to sell Jalkan his commission only to get his hands on all that gold, and he'd seized on the opportunity in Veltan's palace to revoke the commission and keep the gold for himself. Now Jalkan was filled with a towering resentment and a hunger for revenge.

He considered the matter, and he soon realized that there was an extremely simple solution. He was very familiar with certain high-ranking members of the Amarite clergy, and he was certain that the word 'gold' would get their immediate attention. The only problem there lay in the fact that sooner or later he'd have to *show* them gold to gain their support. That wouldn't be much of a problem, though. He knew exactly where he could get his hands on more gold than any churchman had ever seen all at one time.

He was still chained up in the hold of the ship that served as Commander Narasan's floating headquarters, but that wouldn't really be much of a problem. During his novitiate in the Amarite faith he'd frequently dealt with locked doors, and the lock on the chain that held him wasn't all that complex. Despite Padan's thorough search of him when he'd been confined here in the hold of this Trogite ship, Jalkan still had several small weapons concealed about his person, and the little stiletto tucked away in his boot had unlocked any number of doors during his early years in the church. Freedom was within his grasp.

Freedom here in the Land of Dhrall wouldn't mean very much, though, but the solution to *that* problem was anchored not far from his prison. Jalkan smiled. There was a certain kind of justice involved. Veltan hadn't stepped in or objected when Narasan had violated Jalkan's rights, and Veltan was very proud of that little sloop of his.

Jalkan waited for a few days, and then he pulled off his boot, took out his hidden stiletto, and unlocked the chain that held him. He put his ear to the wall of his temporary prison and listened to the gradually diminishing sounds of activity. When all seemed quiet, he opened the door and climbed the ladder to the upper deck. He crouched in the shadows for a while longer, and then he moved on silent feet toward the stern and Commander Narasan's locked cabin. He probed at the lock with his little stiletto and he was soon rewarded with a loud click.

The trunk at the foot of the bed was still unlocked, and Jalkan felt around in the trunk until he found one of the blocks Narasan had casually stored there.

Then Jalkan agonized over a cruel decision. He knew that he was going to have to swim to reach Veltan's sloop, and gold was very heavy. There was just no getting around the fact that he couldn't possibly take *all* the gold, since that much weight would pull him under. The decision to take only two of the blocks made him almost break down and cry.

Cursing under his breath, he left the cabin, unrolled one of the rope ladders, and silently climbed down.

The water was very cold, and the weight of the two gold blocks made it extremely difficult to keep his head above water. He was shivering violently with cold and exhaustion when he reached the sloop. He climbed on board and lay panting on the deck until he got his breath back. Then he sawed at the thick anchor-rope with one of his small, concealed knives for almost a quarter of an hour. When the rope finally gave way, Jalkan felt a surge of elation. He was finally free.

He sat on the bench in the center of the sloop, put the oars in place and rowed in the general direction of the open sea.

It was almost dawn before he was far enough away from the anchored fleet to feel at least partially safe, and the light breeze coming down from the north allowed him to set aside the oars and raise the single sail.

The Empire lay to the south, and Jalkan settled himself at the tiller, steering in the direction of incalculable wealth.

Adnari Estarg sat in stunned disbelief as he hefted the gold block Jalkan had just given him. 'Why do they cast their gold in blocks like this, Jalkan?' he asked. 'Wouldn't coins be more useful?'

'They don't use it as money, Your Grace,' Jalkan explained. 'They're primitives, and as far as I was able to determine, they don't really understand what gold is worth. They'd make fairly good slaves, though.'

'Converts, Jalkan, converts,' the Adnari corrected.

'Doesn't that mean the same thing?'

'It *sounds* nicer, and if we keep waving the word "convert" around, it'll justify what we're doing in the eyes of Holy Udar IV.'

'Is he still alive?' Jalkan asked with a certain surprise. 'I heard some rumors before Narasan's army sailed off to the Land of Dhrall – something to the effect that the higher clergy had decided to eliminate him.'

'He's surrounded by fanatics, Jalkan. Our assassins can't get anywhere near him.' The Adnari squinted thoughtfully. 'I think this Land of Dhrall you've described might just be too good an opportunity to pass up. There's gold there – and thousands of potential slaves. That's all very nice, but I think "distance" might be even more important.'

'I don't quite follow that, Your Grace.'

'The Naos has his hands in every churchman's purse, and he's robbing us all blind. I suppose he's entitled to a fair share, but his definition of "fair" goes *way* beyond what's always been customary. Worse yet, he's got spies everywhere, so it's almost impossible to hide our profits from him. From your description, this Land of Dhrall is far enough away to keep his snoops out of our hair. We'll see how it works out, but I'm beginning to catch a strong odor of "separation" here. We'll still worship Amar in our new church, but we won't be sending any of our money back here to Kaldacin. The merchants and traders will be very welcome, but the agents of Holy Udar will start having unfortunate accidents when they come to visit. After a decade or so, we'll cut all ties with the church here in the Empire and strike out on our own.'

'He'll expel you and your friends from the church, won't he?' Jalkan suggested.

'He can *try*,' Adnari Estarg replied slyly, 'but we'll ignore his proclamations and kill every Regulator he sends to *our* part of the world to enforce those commands. He'll get the point – eventually. How many armies do you think we'll need, Jalkan?'

'I gave it quite a bit of thought on my way home, Your Grace,' Jalkan said. 'I think we should start out with five, at least. A half-million men should be able to occupy the southern portion of Veltan's Domain. That'll give us a good foothold. Veltan's concentrating on an invasion from the north, so it's highly unlikely that he'll divert many troops to meet *us*.'

'We'll start out with five, then,' the Adnari agreed. 'If it happens to turn out that we need more, we'll hire more.'

'I thought that Naos Udar has the church treasury heavily guarded.'

'Indeed he does, Jalkan,' Adnari Estarg said with a faint smile, 'but there wasn't really very much money in that treasury when Udar usurped the holy throne. I'd pretty well cleaned it out when I first saw those twelve armies of his marching up from the south. I've got it stored in a well-concealed place, and *I'm* the only one who knows the location.' He paused for a moment. 'We didn't really treat you very well during your trial, did we, Jalkan?' he asked rather apologetically.

'I don't see that you really had much choice, your Grace. The new Naos was trying his best to purge the church of *all* clergymen who didn't come from *his* part of the Empire. If any of you had tried to come to my defense, you'd have ended up chained to the whipping post right beside me.'

'We *will* reward you for your discovery, Jalkan.'

'Yes, your Grace, you *definitely* will,' Jalkan replied very firmly. 'Since I'm the only one who knows how to reach the Land of Dhrall, I'm very valuable, wouldn't you say?'

The chubby Adnari looked at Jalkan sharply.

'Did you actually think I was just going to roll over and play dead, Your Grace?' Jalkan asked. 'How does twenty percent sound to you?'

'Twenty percent of what?'

'Of everything, your Grace – the gold, the slaves, the land, everything.'

'That's outrageous!' Estarg exploded.

'That's my price, your Grace,' Jalkan said bluntly. 'Take it or leave it. If you don't want to play the game my way, my memory of the route back to the Land of Dhrall might start to fade. I'm not a churchman any more, your Grace, so I don't automatically obey those who outrank me now. That means that *I'll* be the one who makes up the rules this time around.' Jalkan felt a warm sort of glow when a look of consternation came over Estarg's face.

Jalkan was riding north to the port of Castano seated in an ornate sedan chair carried by eight slaves, and he was considering matters of personal safety along the way. He was fairly sure that the high-ranking churchmen Adnari Estarg had recruited would look upon him as redundant once their forces reached southern Dhrall, so it was an absolute necessity for him to remain a vital part of the operation.

The answer was really quite simple. He was the only one in this expedition who'd seen Veltan's map of the region around the Falls of Vash, and since it was obvious that the gold-mines of southern Dhrall were located there, his familiarity with that map virtually guaranteed his safety. He was going to have to make an issue of that once they reached the coast of Dhrall.

The guarantees would probably start to slip once their forces located the mines, though. Jalkan cudgeled his brain trying to come up with a solution. The answer was quite obvious, but it didn't sit too well with him. He'd have to hire – and pay – a large number of professional soldiers to serve as bodyguards, and the wages of those bodyguards would be exorbitant. Worse yet, if he tried to swindle them, they'd almost certainly either walk away and leave him unprotected – or even turn on him and kill him themselves. Protecting himself – and his money – was likely to be *very* expensive.

Jalkan sighed mournfully. Wealth appeared to be terribly inconvenient.

'Ah, well,' he murmured with a note of resignation. 'The price of fame and fortune is evidently very high.' He shrugged. 'It's a lot better than being poor and despised, I guess.'

INTERLUDE IN THE LAND OF DREAMS

Eleria's sleep was troubled that night. The Beloved seemed almost to be her old self, but there were a few hints that the disorder which had driven her to flight after Yaltar's twin volcanos had erupted at the head of the ravine was still there. The Beloved's cycle was nearing its conclusion anyway, and her need for sleep was obviously clouding her mind.

Under normal circumstances, this would not be a problem of any significance, but things in the Land of Dhrall were anything *but* normal right now, so it was time to take certain steps. Eleria regretfully decided that playtime was over, and the time for 'serious' had arrived.

The barriers Dahlaine had set in place when he'd roused the younger gods from their sleep and pushed them back to infancy were not really very substantial, so Balacenia pushed them aside quite easily, and reality came flooding in. The sense of duality – of being two separate and distinct individuals – was a bit disturbing at first, but Balacenia, who had never *had* a childhood, found joy and delight in Eleria's memories, and Eleria's love and adoration for Zelana brought tears to Balacenia's eyes. For a time she lingered there, but she finally set her reverie aside and reached out to her siblings.

Vash, of course, was the first to answer, since he and Balacenia had been very close since the world had been born. 'Were you calling me, Eleria?' he responded in a sleep-dulled voice.

'Don't play Dahlaine's silly game, Vash,' Balacenia told him. 'If you step around his makeshift barriers, your own memories will return, and you'll know your true identity. We need to talk about something that's very important, but we can only do that while we're dreaming. I don't think we want our elders listening in.'

She heard Vash gasp as reality crashed in on him.

'That was quick,' she observed.

'This is *unreal*!' he exclaimed.

'Don't let go of Yaltar, dear Vash,' Balacenia suggested. 'His memories are yours now, and they're all you have in the way of a childhood. Go to that imaginary place where we used to meet and wait there. I'll bring Dakas and Enalla as soon as I've opened their eyes.'

'I'll be there, dear sister,' he promised.

Balacenia reached out to Dakas, and she was a bit surprised to discover that he'd already summoned reality on his own. Of course, Dakas was closer to Dahlaine than any of the rest of them were, so he'd already realized how deceptive the eldest of their alternates could be. 'Just exactly where's this place where we'll meet?' he asked.

'It isn't a real place, Dakas. It's a product of the imagination. Vash and I built it so that we could visit each other. It's quite a bit prettier than the real world. Reach out to Vash, and he'll guide you there.'

'I'll be there, big sister.'

Enalla was a bit more difficult. She clung to the childhood memories of Lillabeth with a kind of desperation. Of course, Aracia had spoiled Lillabeth outrageously, and Enalla obviously hated the idea of growing up and accepting her *real* identity. It took a little while, but Balacenia's upcoming status as the eldest of the gods gave her all the leverage she needed. Enalla *was* a bit sulky when they joined their brothers, however.

The place where Balacenia and Vash had frequently met during their previous cycle existed only in their joined imaginations, and it was far more beautiful than any place in mundane reality. The aurora seethed through the starry sky above a dark forest and the Dreamers floated there absorbing that beauty in sheer delight.

'How did you two *do* this?' Dakas asked in a voice filled with wonder.

'Combined imagination, dear brother,' Balacenia explained. 'It took us quite a while to get it right, but I guess it turned out to be worth the trouble.' She looked around and then sighed. 'I think we'd better get on with this,' she said with regret. 'I'm sure that we all agree that Dahlaine's clever scheme was extremely dangerous, but there's not much we can do about it now.'

'You're probably right, dear sister,' Vash agreed, his face illuminated by the flickering aurora. 'Since you'll be the eldest during our next cycle, I think we'd be wiser to let *you* decide how we should deal with this.' He looked at Dakas and Enalla. 'Would either of you object?' he asked.

'I'll be more than happy to lay *that* burden on our divine sister's shoulders,' Dakas replied. 'It almost broke my back during our last cycle.'

'I won't argue either,' Enalla agreed almost absently as she gazed up at the swirling light in the night sky. 'That's the loveliest thing I've ever seen,' she declared.

'Wait till you see it at sunrise, Enalla,' Vash said proudly.

'All right, then,' Balacenia said. 'We'll have to be very careful not to upset the balance of the world while both we and our elders are awake at the same time. Evidently, we *can* tamper with natural forces while we're dreaming without splitting the world right down the middle, but I don't think we'll dare try anything like that while we're awake.'

'I *still* think Dahlaine was taking an awful chance,' Enalla said. 'The extra weight *could* have made the world fall into the sun, you know.'

'The alternative wasn't very attractive, sister mine,' Dakas reminded her. 'The Vlagh – or whatever it is that's guiding the creatures of the Wasteland – has been violating the natural order of things for a long, long time, so we might have to take a few chances.'

'We're wandering here,' Balacenia noted, 'and we probably don't have too much time left before one of us wakes up. I'm getting a strong suspicion that if we start to overtly tamper with the natural order of things, the results might be disastrous. We can do almost *anything* while we're asleep and dreaming, but once we wake up, that stops. No matter what happens while we're awake, we'll have to endure it until one of us goes back to sleep.'

'That's easy, big sister,' Vash said with a broad grin. 'One of us has to be asleep during every hour of the day. The outlanders call that "sleeping while you're on guard duty", and they seem to think it's a mortal sin. We'll just do it in reverse, that's all. If each one of us sleeps for six hours, we'll have somebody guarding the rest of us all the time.'

'It makes sense, Balacenia,' Enalla said. 'Dear Vash can be terribly clever – once in a great while.' She gave Vash a sly, sidelong smirk.

'Be nice, Enalla,' Balacenia chided.

'I'm *always* nice, dear sister – even though it's terribly boring. "Nice" isn't really very much fun.'

'I wouldn't wave that in Aracia's face, Enalla,' Dakas warned. 'She's got all those fat, tedious churchmen around watching her every move. If you get her interested in "not nice", the church of Aracia could start to crumble.'

'It's going to do more than crumble as soon as Aracia goes to sleep, Dakas,' Enalla replied. 'Those fat, lazy priests make me sick, so the very first thing I'll do when I wake up will be to smash those stupid temples. Then I'll tell them that I don't ever want to see them again. I'm sure they'll have to go out and find honest work at that point.'

'I think Vash found the answer to most of our problems,' Balacenia told them. 'If one of us is asleep, *that* one can be ready to respond to the moves of the Vlagh almost instantly. It's quite obvious that the Vlagh deliberately waited to make its move until our elders had lapsed into their dotage. I occasionally had to push Zelana very hard to get her to respond, and I didn't like that one little bit. Have any of you noticed any signs of similar behavior in *your* elders?'

'Dahlaine *has* been sort of vague lately,' Dakas replied. 'Sometimes he forgets that Long-Claw and I are sort of like brothers, and he has trouble keeping track of the chiefs in some of the villages.'

'Veltan *seems* to be all right,' Vash said a bit dubiously. 'He's always been just a little silly, though. I get *so* tired of listening when he goes on and on about the time he spent on the moon, but Ara always tells me to mind my manners when he does that.'

'You're very fond of Ara, aren't you, Vash?' Enalla asked him.

'*Everybody* loves Ara. Omago's probably the luckiest man in the world, since she's his wife.'

'She's a wonderful cook, that much is certain,' Dakas agreed. 'Our elders don't know a thing about food.'

'Neither did we until recently,' Enalla reminded him. 'I think we've been missing one of the better parts of life.'

'Has Aracia been herself lately?' Balacenia asked her sister.

Enalla shrugged. 'She's been irritable, and her priests have been exaggerating those tiresome ceremonies to stay on the good side of her.'

'It seems that they're all beginning to slip just a bit,' Balacenia said. 'Ordinarily, that wouldn't be much of a problem, but we're in the middle of a war right now, so we might have to step in – subtly, of course – and cover for them. There *have* been a few occasions when I've had to go directly to Longbow to get things done.'

'Persuading Longbow to do something might be even more difficult than bringing Zelana around,' Vash said.

'He *did* take a bit of getting used to,' Balacenia agreed. She frowned slightly. 'I think we're going to have to stay in much closer contact with each other than we usually do,' she told them. 'The Vlagh seems to specialize in surprises, and we'll have to be ready to respond immediately.'

'Did Dahlaine get everything right when he told all of us about *your* dream, Dakas?' Balacenia asked.

'Pretty close,' Dakas replied. 'Of course, it didn't make too much sense to *me* when I woke up. I can't for the life of me make any sense out of that second invasion.' He looked at Vash. 'I thought that the Trogites were working for Veltan.'

'They are – at least *Narasan's* army is,' Vash replied. 'Veltan didn't get into too many details when he told me about how he'd managed to hire an army in the land of the Trogs, so I don't really understand how things work down there.'

Balacenia glanced off to the east and saw a faint light along the horizon. 'It's almost morning,' she told the others, 'so most of us will be waking up soon. I'll stay here until noon at the earliest. I need to think my way through this. I don't *think* we'll encounter any emergencies this early, but I'll be here if any of you happen to need me.'

'And when you get sleepy, call *me*,' Dakas suggested. 'I can go to sleep almost any time of day. I think that might be the result of growing up with bears.'

'And when you wake up, you can call *me*,' Enalla said. 'I'll sleep a while, and then call in Vash. Then it'll be Balacenia's turn again.'

'One more thing before you leave,' Balacenia said. 'Be very careful when you're speaking with the elders. Both Vash and I blundered and referred to each other by our *real* names. If that happens too often, the elders will start getting very suspicious. Let's keep them happy – and drowsy. We *don't* want them to know that we're awake, do we?'

The others all agreed, and then they faded from the imaginary world.

Balacenia wandered alone through the glowing aurora as the eastern horizon grew lighter and lighter. Then the sun rose in stately magnificence, touching the sky with rose-tinted crimson. Balacenia's heart was filled with sadness. The Beloved was deeply troubled, and her pain weighed heavily on Eleria's side of Balacenia's awareness.

And then something quite impossible occurred. The figure of a woman came walking out of the sunrise into the place that existed only in the combined imaginations of Balacenia and Vash.

'That was very nicely done, dear one,' the woman said to Balacenia in a rich, vibrant voice.

Balacenia immediately recognized the voice and for some reason she was not the least bit surprised that Ara had appeared here out of nowhere. It seemed very right somehow. She nodded politely to Omago's beautiful wife. 'There's something I've been meaning to ask you, Ara,' she said, 'and maybe this is the proper time and place. I've had this nagging feeling that I've met you before. That actually *did* happen, didn't it?'

'Oh, yes,' Ara replied with a fond smile, 'but it was a very, very long time ago – even for you.' She held out her arms, and Balacenia automatically went to her.

'You're doing just fine, Balacenia,' Ara said, warmly embracing her. 'I wasn't at all sure that Dahlaine's scheme would actually work, but you just managed the transition so smoothly that there wasn't even a hint of what was actually happening when you realized who you *really* are.'

'It just seemed to me that Dahlaine's little scheme didn't go quite far enough, Ara. That was sort of nagging at Eleria. When you get right down to it, this was all the idea of the Eleria part of me. She knew that she and the other Dreamers were going to need help, so she called me.' Balacenia smiled. 'I've never had anybody wake me before, and her childhood memories brought tears to my eyes.'

'You have to be a little careful when Eleria unleashes her charm on you. In many ways, she's you, but she has her own little idiosyncracies. Playing with the dolphins might have had something to do with that. You'll get used to her, but it's going to take a while. In the meantime, look after Zelana. She's not herself right now.'

'She *will* get better, won't she?' Balacenia asked, greatly concerned.

'Probably not this time, dear Balacenia. She's moving toward her sleep cycle right now, and she's going quite a bit faster than Dahlaine had anticipated, but I can deal with that. For now, comfort your Beloved and keep her safe, and leave the rest to me. Now go back to sleep, dear child. Tomorrow's another day.'

And then Balacenia awoke and found herself in Eleria's bed.

THE MAN OF HONOR

1

❖——❖——❖

Narasan was born in the compound of his father's army, and so in a certain sense he'd been in that army for his entire life, and the notion of becoming a merchant or a member of the government had never even occurred to him.

The army compound had originally been established on the outskirts of the city of Kaldacin, the imperial capital of the Trogite Empire, and it covered several hundred acres. As the imperial city had expanded, it had gradually come to surround the compound, and various high-ranking members of the government had hungrily eyed those prime acres as a possible source of vast amounts of wealth. There had been frequent offers over the past several decades, but a long line of Narasan's ancestors had steadfastly refused to even discuss the matter.

The compound of his father's army was in many ways a fair-sized city, with administrative buildings, officers' quarters, soldiers' barracks, armories, and storehouses conveniently situated among drill fields, parade grounds, and training areas that duplicated virtually every type of terrain the army might encounter in any war anywhere in the Empire. It was separated from the surrounding city by high, sturdy walls and well-guarded gates. The stone structures within the compound were all of a uniform size with stucco-covered white walls and red-tile roofs, and everything was plumb and square with a sense of permanence that the constantly changing city beyond the walls could never match. Narasan had occasionally looked out at the surrounding city as a child, but he saw no real need to go there. Everything he wanted or needed was here in the compound, so why should he bother going out into the city?

There were well-supervised children's playrooms inside the buildings that housed the officers' families, but after the children reached a certain age, the boys no longer played in the same rooms with the girls. Officers' wives had opinions about that, for some reason.

It was perhaps for the same reason that the outside playgrounds for the children had always been somewhat separated from the drill fields and practice grounds of the soldiers. Mothers found some of the language used by soldiers very offensive, so they went to great lengths to protect their young.

Narasan and his friends spent most of their time playing soldier during their early years, armed with wooden swords and shields and under the watchful eyes of old disabled veterans who gave them instructions in marching and swordsmanship and kept them from hurting each other with their toy weapons.

Narasan's closest friends during his boyhood had been Gunda and Padan, the sons of a couple of sub-commanders in his father's army. Gunda was somewhat stout, and even as a child he'd demonstrated a fair degree of skill with his toy sword. Padan was more lean than Gunda, and he seemed to find amusement in things that Narasan didn't think were very funny at all. Narasan decided quite early that he shouldn't make an issue of his father's rank as the three of them played soldier. It seemed to him that waving his father's status in the faces of his friends would be highly inappropriate – and maybe even just a bit dishonorable.

In time, Narasan began to realize that their playground in the shadow of the large, white-walled officers' quarters was not all that much different from the drill-fields of the regular soldiers. In a very real sense, army children *played* at being soldiers until they were old enough to become *real* soldiers.

That seemed very appropriate to young Narasan.

'My papa didn't tell me how it happened, Narasan,' Gunda said one frosty morning when they were out on the playground. 'All he said was that Padan's papa got killed during this last war down south. That's probably why Padan hasn't been around for the past few days.'

Narasan was stunned. He'd known that soldiers sometimes were killed in wars, but this was the first time anything like that had ever happened to the father of one of his close friends. 'What do you think we should say when Padan comes back, Gunda?' he asked.

'How should I know?' Gunda replied.

'Maybe we shouldn't say anything about it at all,' Narasan said a bit tentatively.

'Talk about the weather, or something?'

'I don't know. Maybe we should talk to one of the sergeants about it. People *do* get killed during wars, I guess. That's what wars are all about, aren't they? I'm sure it's happened before, so some old-time sergeant could tell us the best way to handle it.'

'You're probably right. Those old sergeants know just about everything that has to do with wars. After we grow up, though, maybe we'll be able to come up with some way to pick a fight with the army that just killed Padan's papa. If we stomp all over them, that might make Padan feel better, don't you think?'

'You might be right, Gunda,' Narasan agreed. 'I'll find out which army did it, and we'll get back at them when *we're* the ones in command.' He squinted across the playground. 'I don't know that we need to tell anybody about it, though. They might not think it's very honorable to hold grudges like that.'

'That's all you ever think about, isn't it, Narasan?' Gunda said. 'I suppose we should be *sort* of honorable, but when somebody hurts one of our friends, honor goes out the window, and getting even takes over.'

'You're probably right,' Narasan agreed, 'but I don't think we should come right out and *say* that's what we're doing.'

'You're going to be the commander, Narasan, so we'll do it any way you want us to.'

'It was – oh, maybe fifty or sixty years ago – when the armies decided that they didn't want no more part of workin' for the Emperor or the silly Palvanum – all them Earls and Barons that spend all their time makin' speeches,' the wrinkled old Sergeant Wilmer told the boys one rainy afternoon when it was too wet to go outside and play. 'It all started, I bin told, when them thick-headed Palvani all put their heads together and decided that us soljers was gettin' paid *way* too much. Of course, it was peacetime back then, so the soljers didn't have nothin' to do except polish their swords and play dice. The Palvani didn't like that one little bit, so they ups an' cut the soljers' pay in half – and then, as the soljers found out later, the Palvani decided that *they* warn't gettin' *near* enough pay fer all that speech-makin', so they got together one night an' gave theirselves a whoppin' big pay-raise – which it was as they kept purty much a secret.'

'Can they *do* that?' young Padan exclaimed. 'Can they just reach in and take as much money as they want out of the treasury?'

'Well, it seems as how they *thought* they could. When the army commanders got wind of it, though, they all got together and decided that workin' fer the gummint warn't no fun no more, so they all just upped and quit. They *did* hang onto the army compounds, though. Well sir, things was a little tight fer a while, but then some dukes an' barons in the eastern provinces decided that they didn't want no more part of the Empire, so they quit payin' taxes, slammed their borders shut, and hung every tax-collector they could lay their hands on.'

'Isn't that sort of against the law?' Gunda asked.

Sergeant Wilmer laughed. 'The gummint didn't have no armies no more, boy,' he said. 'There warn't nobody around to go to them eastern provinces an' tell them dukes an' barons an' such that they was a-breakin' the law. Well, now, the Palvani all started a-makin' speeches an' scribblin' out orders tellin' the armies t' run over to them eastern provinces an' whomp on them dukes an' barons until they started payin' their taxes again, but the army commanders told them gabby Palvani what they could do with them orders, an' the armies just sat tight an' waited.'

Narasan and the other boys all laughed.

'Well,' the sergeant continued, 'it didn't hardly take no time at all fer them dummies in the Palvanum t' figger out which way the wind was blowin', so they come here to the army compounds an' tole the soljers that they'd be more'n happy t' go back t' payin' 'em what they'd been a-payin' 'em back afore the pay-cut, but the soljers said no. Then they said that it'd take about twice as much t' make 'em even a little bit interested. Let me tell *you*, you ain't never *heard* so much screamin' an' yellin'! Them half-wit Palvani jumped up an' down makin' threats an' tryin' t' order the armies t' obey them there wrote-down commands an' all sorts of other foolish stuff, but the soljers just slammed the gates shut an' wouldn't even answer when the Palvani started a-poundin' on them.'

'That sounds like clear win for our side, Sergeant,' Gunda declared.

'It gets better, boy,' the sergeant said, leaning back in his chair and taking a long drink from his beer tankard. 'Them high-toned Palvani all went back t' their fancy meetin' place an' made speeches t' each other for a week or so, an' then two more of them eastern provinces joined up with the others, an' the limp-brains in the gummint suddenly woke up. The way things was a-goin', in about another month or so there wouldn't *be* no Empire no more. They all come a-runnin' back t' the army compounds an' tole our commanders that they'd pay as much as the soljers wanted, but the commanders come right back an' tole 'em, "We don't march until we see the money". That started a bunch of new screamin', but the Palvani knowed by then that our commanders meant exactly what they'd said, so the gummint finally gave in an' paid the soljers what they had a-comin' to 'em, an' that ended that.'

'How did the war turn out, Sergeant?' Narasan asked curiously.

Sergeant Wilmer snorted. 'It warn't no *real* war, boy,' he replied. 'When them dukes an' barons an' such off t' the east saw ten armies a-marchin' in their direction, they went belly-up right then and there.' The old sergeant took another drink from his beer tankard and looked around at the young boys gathered in front of him in the day-lounge as the gusty wind outside spattered the windows with hard-driven rain. 'When you young gentlemen start receiving your formal education, your teachers are likely to tell you an entirely different story,' he told them quite seriously, dropping his colorful dialect, 'but what I just told you was what *really* happened. My sergeant told me the story when I wasn't much older than you boys are now, and he was here when it actually happened. Every now and then, teachers try to clean up the past, but usually the *real* events are pretty much down and dirty. The real world out there isn't nearly as nice as some people would prefer it to be, so don't swallow everything your high-born teachers tell you without taking a long hard look at it yourselves.'

Narasan stored that notion away for future reference as he pulled on his cape and left the day-lounge to go on home to his family's quarters.

Narasan had heard that *some* army commanders lived in palaces and pretended to be members of the nobility, but Narasan's father disapproved of that, since it wasn't very honorable.

Narasan's father was a lean, but well-muscled man in his early forties. The burden of command weighed heavily upon him, and his glossy black hair was touched with silver at the temples. There was much work involved in the command of an army, but Narasan's father always listened when his son came to him with questions.

When Narasan reached home, he went to his father's book-lined study. Sergeant Wilmer's story had disturbed him just a bit, since it put a whole new light on his intended career. 'Have you got a moment, father?' he asked.

'You seem troubled, son,' his father replied, setting aside the document he'd been reading. 'What's bothering you?'

'Well, when it started raining hard this afternoon, our instructor sent us to the day-lounge to get us in out of the weather, and old Sergeant Wilmer was there. Sometimes he talks real funny, doesn't he?'

Narasan's father smiled slightly. 'It's a pose, my boy. He talks that way right at first to get your attention. I take it that he told you the story about the origins of our army.'

'How did you know that, father?'

'He's been telling that story to army children for a long time now. Sooner or later, every army boy hears Wilmer's account of where we came from quite a long time ago.'

'I thought he was just making it up.'

'It wasn't fiction, Narasan. Wilmer's account comes very close to what really happened back then. The armies of that era *were* attached to the imperial government, and they *did* detach themselves during a dispute with the Palvanum about the pay-scale of the non-commissioned soldiers. We want our sons to know exactly how it came about, so we turn Wilmer loose on every class of our children.' He leaned back in his chair, and the light from the candle on his desk touched his silvery hair. 'Every member of our supposedly noble Palvanum has his own agenda for how the government should spend the money in the treasury, and paying the armies is usually way down at the bottom of the list.'

'That isn't fair at all, is it?'

'Fairness has always been an alien concept for the Palvanum, Narasan. When there's a war in the works, the Palvani all make glowing speeches about the bravery of Trogite soldiers, but when peace rolls around again, they'd rather not think about us. Basically, that's why we went into business for ourselves. That's the whole point of Sergeant Wilmer's story.'

On a sudden impulse, Narasan broached a subject that had been bothering him for several months. 'I wasn't going to say anything about this, father, but Gunda and I were talking after Padan's father was killed in that war last winter, and we sort of thought that maybe some day we might want to pick a fight with the army that killed him to get even with them for what they'd done. It's been worrying at me ever since we talked about it. Would something like that be honorable? I mean, soldiers *do* get killed when there's a war, and it sort of seemed to me at first that holding grudges like that might be kind of improper.'

Narasan's father shook his head. 'A soldier's first loyalty should always be to his comrades. That's where honor begins, my boy. Right, now, *I'm* waiting for the opportunity to kick the daylights out of the army that killed your friend's father myself.'

'You're going to whomp them?' Narasan asked eagerly.

'I see that you paid close attention to Sergeant Wilmer, Narasan,' his father said with a broad grin. 'Yes, as a matter of fact. I *am* going to whomp them. I'll whomp them so hard that their grandchildren will run and hide every time somebody mentions my name. It won't make me very popular with certain members of the Palvanum, since that particular army's one of their favorites, but that's just too bad.'

'Aren't there *any* honest men in the government, father?'

'"Honest" and "government" probably shouldn't show up in the same sentence, Narasan. They're contradictory terms.'

'I'm glad that I'll be in the army when I grow up, then,' Narasan declared. 'From what I've been hearing here lately, we're the only honest people in the whole Empire.'

'That pretty much sums it up, yes,' his father agreed with a wry smile.

It was perhaps a year or so later when Narasan, Gunda, and Padan began their more formalized education, and of course, their teachers were all professional soldiers, and 'We don't march until we see the money,' seemed to turn up in every class they attended.

Padan, whose sense of humor was perhaps a bit warped, frequently suggested that it might very well be an excellent motto to be added to the army banner. Narasan was a little startled when their instructors appeared to give Padan's silly proposal some very serious thought.

The studies associated with their classroom education were extremely tedious, and the boys in Narasan's class much preferred their training on the drill-field. Steel swords were heavier than the wooden toy swords of their childhood had been, and it took the boys a while to toughen up their muscles. The phalanx was the central part of Trogite tactics at that particular time, and the boys spent endless hours growing accustomed to marching in unison with their shields overlapping and their long spears locked in place. Unification lies at the core of the phalanx formation, and the drill sergeants kept shouting. 'Unification! Unification!' at the boys until Narasan got tired of hearing it. He soon came to realize that if he held his shield no more than an inch out of line, the drill sergeant would start screaming at the top of his lungs.

It was shortly after Narasan's eighth birthday when his father's army was hired to put down a slave rebellion off in one of the provinces in the western part of the empire. Narasan's father had never actually said as much, but Narasan rather suspected that his father disapproved of slavery. Narasan himself had never even *seen* a slave, but rumor had it that a fair number of the soldiers in his father's army were former slaves. When a young man appeared at the gate of the army compound and announced that he was interested in a military career, nobody asked him too many questions. There were also rumors that a goodly number of the soldiers in the compound had spent their early years involved in various criminal activities, but nobody asked *those* men any embarrassing questions either.

When the army returned from the campaign in the west, Narasan's uncle Kalan was marching at the head of the column, and that sent a sudden chill through Narasan.

'It was one of those ridiculous things that should never happen,' Kalan sorrowfully told Narasan and his mother later that day. 'A runaway slave had somehow found a broken spear that only had about half of its shaft. We didn't even know that he was hiding in the bushes when we marched up that hill. When he saw us coming, he jumped up, threw the spear in our general direction, and then ran off like a scared rabbit. I don't think he'd ever so much as had his hands on a spear before, but the cursed thing took my brother right in the throat, and he died almost immediately. I'd venture to say that rascal could have thrown that broken spear a thousand times and never duplicated that first cast.'

'Did you chase the slave down?' Narasan's mother demanded in a bleak-sounding voice.

'Oh, yes,' Kalan replied grimly, 'and it took him a long, long time to die.'

'That's something, I guess,' Narasan's mother said.

'It's not much, dear,' Kalan apologized, 'but it's about all I can give you. We put down that stupid rebellion in short order after that. The men were *very* unhappy about what'd happened to your husband, so they made examples of every runaway slave they got their hands on. I'm fairly sure that the slave-owners will have to do their own farming for the next few years, because we didn't return very many live slaves to them when it was all over.'

'That's just too bad,' Narasan's mother replied. Then she rushed from the room, and Narasan could hear her wails of grief coming from the adjoining chamber.

* * *

During the next days and weeks, Narasan's mother grew increasingly distraught. Narasan was trying, without much success, to deal with his own grief, but in time his uncle Kalan helped him through the worst of it. As his mind returned to some degree of normalcy, he came to realize that his mother was no longer rational. It was quite obvious that her grief had unhinged her mind. Narasan decided at that point that he should never marry. A soldier's life could end quite abruptly, but the grief of a soldier's wife could obviously go on forever. Narasan saw quite clearly that a real soldier was married to the army anyway.

Narasan's uncle Kalan had filled his brother's shoes as the commander of the army, and he kept a close eye on his nephew.

When Narasan reached his twelfth birthday, army custom placed him in the ranks of the cadets – he boys with army backgrounds who were extensively trained so that they'd be ready to receive commissions when they reached a certain age. Narasan excelled as a cadet, and when he turned fifteen, he was offered a commission as a very junior officer in his uncle's army.

He went through several wars before he turned twenty, and it was quite obvious that he was going to go far and fast – assuming, of course, that he'd live long enough to move up through the ranks.

He'd reached the rank of sub-commander by the time he turned thirty-five, and his boyhood friends, Gunda and Padan were not far behind him. The three of them served very well, much to the satisfaction of Commander Kalan. Narasan was fully aware of the fact that his uncle was keeping a close eye on his progress, so it came as no great surprise when, as the climax to the celebration of Narasan's fortieth birthday in the officers' lounge, his uncle rose to announce that he was retiring, and that Narasan would replace him as army commander.

'I'm not really ready for command yet, Uncle Kalan,' Narasan protested.

'You'd better *get* ready then,' his uncle declared, 'because like it or not, you *will* be the commander when the sun comes up tomorrow.'

'How do you plan to spend your retirement, Commander Kalan?' Narasan's friend Gunda asked.

'I thought I might catch up on my sleep,' Kalan replied. 'Since I won't be a soldier any more, I won't have to roll out of bed at first light the way I've been doing for the last forty years. Noon sounds about right to me. Then I'll grab a quick bite to eat and go back to bed until supper-time.'

'You're a cruel man, Commander,' Narasan's friend Padan protested. '*We'll* still have to get up at daybreak but you'll spend the whole morning rattling the walls with your snoring.'

Commander Kalan grinned at him. 'Just knowing that *you'll* have to be up and moving when the sun rises will make my sleep all the more pleasant, Padan,' he replied.

Narasan had been groomed for leadership since his early childhood, and despite feeling that his recent promotion was premature, he found his new status as comfortable as an old boot.

After a few minor wars, Narasan's reputation began to grow, and other army commanders let it be generally known that their price would double if the opposing army happened to be commanded by 'that Narasan fellow'.

To make matters better, even when the renters of opposing armies tried to conceal Narasan's likely appearance on the battlefield, his opponents always sent scouts out to make sure that Narasan was nowhere in the vicinity. If it turned out that he *was* there, the opposing army would immediately surrender.

That made for a lot of easy wars.

One of an army commander's more important duties involves the selection of the man who should replace him in the event that he happened to be killed in action. Narasan already had a candidate in mind – even though his youthful nephew had not even been commissioned as yet. Though it pained Narasan to admit it, his nephew Astal was at least twice as gifted as *he* was. Should the young fellow survive his early campaigns, there was the distinct possibility that he *might* be able to reunite the scattered armies of the Empire and change the course of history. The current government of the Empire was so corrupt that it very nearly made Narasan ashamed to even *be* a Trogite. A strong military could ram ethics down the collective throats of the Palvanum and place certain insurmountable barriers between the greedy church and the government. A supreme army commander could slap things into shape in almost no time at all. 'I might even show up in a few history books as the man who engineered the saving of the Empire,' he mused. 'God knows that sooner or later *somebody's* going to have to do that.'

2

❧

'I'd be willing to pay you ten thousand gold crowns, Commander Narasan,' the Duke of Bergalta declared. 'Your reputation alone should settle the matter once and for all.'

'That's a very generous offer, Your Grace,' Narasan replied, looking out across the drill-field at the center of the army compound. 'Is that barony really worth all this trouble?'

'Well, not really, I suppose. What it all boils down to, I guess, is that it's high time to jerk the Duke of Tashan up short. That halfwit seems to believe that he can get away with just about anything. When old Baron Forlen died without an heir, Tashan brazenly announced that he was annexing that barony as "a protectorate", and that rubbed me the wrong way. Then too, the barony has always been a sort of buffer state between my duchy and Tashan's. If I let him get away with this, he'll be camped right on my eastern border.'

Narasan rather ruefully conceded to himself that the growing reputation of his army was attracting more and more of these petty little squabbles. He shrugged. Probably all that was going to be involved in this one would be a leisurely march to the region in question and a bit of muscle flexing to persuade Duke Tashan to come to the bargaining table. The pay was good, and it was highly unlikely that there'd be much bleeding involved, so he accepted Duke Bergalta's offer.

The one thing that perhaps more than any other had persuaded Commander Narasan to accept the offer was the fact that his gifted nephew Astal had recently been commissioned, and he was now a very junior officer in the ninth cohort. An easy campaign with little danger was quite probably the best way for the young fellow to get his feet wet. Astal was not the only recently commissioned officer in Narasan's army, so Narasan's decision to accept Duke Bergalta's offer would provide training for several other junior officers as well as for his nephew. Narasan had noticed that Astal's closest friend was the well-educated young Keselo, who indeed showed at least as much potential as Astal himself. There was another junior officer, however, who showed almost no promise whatsoever. His name was Jalkan, and he'd formerly been a priest in the Amarite church. That in itself should have immediately disqualified him. There was no question that the Empire was corrupt, but the Amarite church took corruption to its outer edges. After he'd somewhat reluctantly agreed to sell Jalkan a commission, Narasan almost immediately began to regret the decision. Jalkan proved to be lazy, stupid almost beyond belief, arrogant, and unnecessarily cruel to the men who served under him.

After Jalkan had made several serious blunders, Narasan began to draw up a list of the scrawny little officer's misdeeds. He was fairly certain that the time would come in the not-too-distant future when that list would be very useful. Jalkan was obviously convinced that his purchase of his commission protected his status. Narasan yearned for the day when he could disabuse Jalkan of *that* misconception.

Following a rather brief conference in the war-room, Narasan's army began the march toward the Duchy of Bergalta, moving south in easy stages. It was late summer now, and the weather was very pleasant. The slaves of the various landowners in the region were at work in the fields, lending an almost bucolic air to the march.

The army was not too far from Bergalta's northern border, and about noon on a sunny day, Sub-Commander Gunda returned from a scouting expedition to the south. 'There's a ridge-line about a half-day's march on ahead,' he reported. 'The road we're following goes on through a fairly narrow pass, and we might want to set up our night's camp before we reach that pass – just to be on the safe side. We haven't seen any signs of an opposing army, but why take chances? The road gets steeper anyway, and the troops can make better time if they start out fresh.'

'That's the way we'll do it then, Gunda,' Narasan agreed. 'Just as a favor, would you have a word with Morgas of the ninth cohort? Tell him that I'd like to have Astal lead the march. That should give his ego a bit of a boost. Sometimes that boy has a retiring sort of nature. If we put him out front, it might make him feel a bit important.'

'That's got a familiar sort of ring to it, Narasan,' Gunda said with a broad grin. 'Your uncle Kalan used to shove you out front just about every time we were on the march.'

'It worked out quite well, Gunda, and when something works, it doesn't make much sense to change it.'

As always, Narasan's army was roused by the sound of horns at first light the following morning, and immediately after breakfast they broke camp and began the march toward the pass which lay just ahead.

The ridge line could hardly be described as a mountain range, but was more in the nature of a string of relatively gentle hills rising up out of the flat plain of the southern reaches of the Empire. The soil appeared to be quite rocky, and the local nobility had evidently decided that trying to farm it would just be a waste of time and effort, so the hills were covered with fairly dense brush and clumps of stubby trees.

Narasan's nephew Astal marched at the front of the ninth cohort, leading the army up the slope toward the narrow pass at the top of the ridge. As was customary, the bearer of the army banner marched just behind the young officer. The army's reputation tended to make potential enemy armies a bit nervous, so Narasan always made a point of displaying the banner to ward off any misunderstandings.

Gunda was marching beside Commander Narasan to keep him advised of the terrain lying to the front.

'Just exactly how narrow is that pass up there?' Narasan asked Gunda.

'It's pretty skimpy, Narasan,' Gunda replied. 'I'd say maybe no more than fifteen men wide. If there was anything serious about this little outing, I'd probably recommend avoiding it altogether, but it'll probably be all right in a situation like this. Astal's going to have to break formation to get his men through. I *hate* these narrow places. It's probably going to take us until long past midnight to get the entire army on through to the other side.'

'Does the road widen out at all after it goes through the pass?'

'Not enough to make much difference. It's a good thing that the Duke of Tashan doesn't have much in the way of an army. If there were opposing troops with any kind of experience, that pass up there could give us a lot of trouble.'

Narasan shaded his eyes from the newly-risen sun and squinted up toward the pass. The morning sky was clear blue, untarnished by any clouds, and the thick brush on the steep side of the ridge lay almost like a green carpet. It was one of those very pretty days.

Astal called the ninth cohort to a halt near the pass and issued the order to re-form in a crisply military tone. His soldiers assembled in a narrow ten-man-wide column, and then Astal took his place at the head of the column and gave the order to march.

Narasan felt a certain family pride. Astal was handling things exactly as they should be handled, and his men marched very well behind the crimson and gold army banner.

'It's going to take us all day and half the night to get on through to flat ground, Narasan,' Gunda advised. 'That pass isn't really very steep, but that narrow section's definitely going to slow us down.' He vigorously rubbed at his receding hairline.

'It's not like we had some kind of appointment, Gunda,' Padan reminded his friend. 'We'll get there when we get there.'

'I know that,' Gunda replied. 'I just don't like the idea of being all strung out like this. If somebody happened to jump us, we could be in a lot of trouble. I *hate* mountains.'

Padan shrugged. 'Why don't you go up there and order them to lie down, then? I don't think they'll listen to you, but it'll give you something to do instead of standing around complaining about every little bump in the road.'

'Very funny, Padan,' Gunda growled. 'Ha. Ha. Ha.'

'You ought to work on your laugh just a bit, Gunda,' Padan teased his friend. 'It's not really very convincing.'

The tedious business of marching through the narrow pass continued as the sun rose higher in the morning sky, and it was somewhat past mid-morning by the time the twelfth cohort had marched on through the pass at the top of the ridge line.

Then there was suddenly a great deal of noise coming from beyond the pass, and Narasan came to his feet in alarm. 'Find out what's happening!' he shouted at Gunda.

'On the way!' Gunda replied sharply, running as fast as he could up the narrow road toward the pass. When he was about halfway up, a runner came down the road to meet him. They spoke for a few moments, and then Gunda spun about and ran back down, spouting sulphurous curses every step of the way. 'We've got trouble, Narasan!' he bellowed. 'There's an enemy force on the other side of that pass, and they're attacking our people!'

'Spread out!' Narasan barked at his men. 'Never mind the road! Move!'

The army fanned out and scrambled up the side of the ridge, but before the main force was even halfway up the north side, vast numbers of well-armed soldiers began to appear along the ridge-line on either side of the narrow pass.

'I make it to be three armies, Narasan,' Padan reported. 'I don't think we've got much chance of breaking through.'

'We've got twelve cohorts on the other side, Padan!'

'I don't think so,' Padan said bluntly. 'I don't hear any noise coming from over there, and that means that our cohorts are all dead.' He peered up the ridge. 'Those banners up there look very familiar, don't they?' he said from between clenched teeth. 'The green one's definitely the banner of Galdan's army, and the blue one looks to belong to Forgak. I can't quite make out that third one.'

'Tenkla,' Narasan said shortly.

'Isn't *that* interesting. We've defeated all three of those armies during the past year, and it looks like they've decided that it's payback time. They're probably working for short pay – just to get the chance to climb all over us. Do you want us to keep on charging?'

Narasan clenched his fists in a futile gesture of fury. 'No,' he replied in a choked voice. 'There's no point in that now. We've already lost twelve cohorts. This silly war wasn't worth that. Sound the retreat, Padan. Let's get the men out of here if we can.'

Narasan pushed his grief firmly behind him as he led his army in the retreat. It was obvious that his men had been very disappointed by his decision to fall back. They'd all had friends in the twelve lost cohorts, and the yearning for revenge hung over them as the army marched back to Imperial Kaldacin.

Narasan had lost friends and family members in previous wars, and he was certain that in time he'd be able to set his sorrow aside and go on with his life. What made his grief so sharp this time lay in the fact that the loss of Astal was his own fault. Had he not placed Astal at the head of the column, the boy would almost certainly still be alive. Under ordinary circumstances, the ninth cohort would *not* have led the march through the pass. Narasan painfully realized that many of his decisions had grown out of his own egotism. Astal had been the closest thing to a son Narasan would ever have, and he'd pushed the boy into situations he hadn't yet been ready for as a way to boost his *own* image.

That cut into Narasan like the edge of a very sharp knife.

'Absolutely not!' Narasan told the pale-faced Gunda. 'Just put it in a suitable container and bury it in the army cemetery. I *don't* want to see it!'

'I sort of thought you might feel that way, Narasan,' Gunda replied through his tightly clenched teeth, 'but it was my duty to ask. Quite a few things are starting to come out into the daylight now. Did you know that Duke Bergalta's related to Adnari Estarg?'

'No, actually, I didn't. How did you find that out?'

'That young officer Keselo tracked it down. He told me that Adnari Estarg and Duke Bergalta are cousins, and it *was* one of Bergalta's servants who delivered Astal's head here to the compound. As I remember, Estarg was very put out with you when you refused to fight those southern armies that came here and put that fellow Udar on the throne of the Naos, and I'm catching a very strong odor of church involvement in our recent defeat. I wouldn't be the least bit surprised to find out that the money that paid all those scoundrels came out of the church treasury, and the whole thing was nothing more than a trap.'

'And *I* was the one who was stupid enough to step into it,' Narasan added glumly.

'Don't beat yourself over the head with it, old friend,' Gunda advised bleakly. 'There's probably a big celebration going on down there, but I don't think it's going to last very much longer.'

'We aren't in any position to put a stop to it, Gunda. They tricked us, and then they killed a very large number of our men.'

'You might not approve of this, Narasan, but Padan and I recently had a little talk with some fellows you might have heard about. They're the ones who specialize in the business of providing the guests of honor at funerals. It won't be long before three armies won't have commanders any more and two ducal thrones will be empty.'

'That's hardly honorable, Gunda.'

'Well that's just too bad, Narasan. *Their* scheme went way past "honorable", and if that's the way they want to play, we'll take the game one step farther.' Then Gunda gave his commander a tight-lipped grin. 'We could send flowers to the funerals, if you'd like, though. There's a weed that grows along the coast near Castano that stinks to high heaven. That *might* just let everybody down there know exactly what we think of them.'

'You're a very nasty fellow, Gunda.'

'I know. It's a failing of mine.'

Narasan's satisfaction with the clever scheme of his friends didn't really last very long. Revenge didn't alter the cold hard facts about the disastrous war in the south. To some degree Narasan had accepted Duke Bergalta's offer because it had given him chance to put his nephew at the head of the army during the march through that mountain pass. On the surface, that had been a way to give Astal a greater degree of self-confidence, but the more Narasan thought about it, the more he came to realize that the foolish decision had grown out of his own egotism. He'd placed Astal in mortal danger as an act of stupid pride. His grief returned, and it was overlaid with a tremendous amount of shame. It had been *his* foolish decision that had killed Astal and twelve cohorts of his army, and no amount of squirming around could alter that painful truth. He was quite obviously no longer fit for command.

And so it was that on a bleak day in early winter he broke his sword across his knee like a stick of dry kindling, dressed himself in his most scruffy clothes, and set up shop as a beggar on the far side of Imperial Kaldacin.

Begging was a fairly simple occupation, and it gave Narasan a great deal of time for thought. His foolish decisions in the recent war were symptoms of the general deterioration of Trogite society.

Pride and greed had come to the fore, and honor had vanished. Narasan saw that as an obvious sign that the world itself was faltering and would soon pass out of existence.

Narasan took a certain comfort in that thought. If he *were* indeed living at the end of days, his grief and shame wouldn't last too much longer, and then he could gladly go to his final rest.

3

❖━━❖

The young foreigner was a very handsome man, and he passed
Narasan's place of business several times. His look of growing
frustration intrigued Narasan a bit. Finally on a blustery winter day
Narasan asked the young fellow what was troubling him.

'I've been trying to find somebody here who'll rent me an army,
but I can't find anybody who's willing to even discuss it.'

'Did you speak with the soldiers themselves?'

'I didn't think that was permitted.'

Narasan laughed. The young man appeared to be a hopeless
innocent, but very sincere. Narasan explained a few realities and
then asked him why he needed to hire an army.

'There's trouble in the wind at home, and it looks like we're
going to need professional soldiers to help us deal with it.'

Narasan found the notion of a war somewhere beyond the
borders of the Empire rather intriguing. Recent events had made
wars here at home seem extremely unpleasant.

Then Keselo came around the corner with yet another ploy to
try to persuade Narasan to return to the army. Narasan refused, of
course, and sent the young officer back home.

'He's a good boy,' Narasan told the stranger, 'and if he lives, he might go far.' It occurred to Narasan that he'd quite often said much the same thing about his nephew, and his sorrow returned to tear at him again.

The youthful foreigner named Veltan appeared to be quite perceptive, and he immediately saw that something was tearing at Narasan's heart. Without knowing exactly why, Narasan briefly explained why he'd chosen to abandon his military career. 'Time's running out anyway,' he gloomily concluded, 'so in a little while it won't make any difference *what* I do. The world's coming to an end, you know.'

'I think you've seen what very few others have,' Veltan told him, 'but you didn't go quite far enough. The world's approaching the end of a cycle, not the end of time itself. Don't despair, Narasan. Time has no end – or beginning either, if the truth were known.'

A sense of awe came over Narasan. This pleasant-faced young foreigner was not at all what he seemed to be, and the depth of his understanding staggered the imagination. Veltan rather deprecatingly shrugged off a number of his own peculiarities and got right down to the point. 'I need your army, Commander Narasan,' he said, 'and I'll pay gold for its services. If things go well, we'll win, and winning's all that really matters, whether it's war or dice.'

'That's a practical sort of approach,' Narasan replied, his sense of overwhelming grief and shame fading. He stood up. 'It looks like my holiday's over,' he said. 'It was sort of nice to sit around doing nothing, but it'll be good to get back into harness again.'

The notion of undertaking a war somewhere beyond the boundaries of the Empire disturbed several of Narasan's officers quite noticeably, but Narasan himself welcomed the idea. The

Empire contained too many painful memories, and he was more than ready to go abroad.

Since the army would be going north, the port of Castano was the logical point of departure, and after Veltan had left, Narasan decided that his best course of action would be to send Gunda, whose family had originated there, to that port to hire the fleet of ships the army would need to carry them to Veltan's homeland.

A few days after Narasan's force reached Castano, Veltan came sailing into the harbor in a rickety little fishing sloop and stunned Narasan by presenting him with ten blocks of pure gold. Narasan had never seen gold in that form before, but he was forced to admit that it was very pretty.

Veltan seemed to be very impatient, and he finally decided that the two of them should sail north toward the Land of Dhrall in his sloop so that Narasan and a Maag pirate by the name of Sorgan Hook-Beak could work out the strategy for their combined campaign in the Domain of Veltan's sister. Narasan had some doubts about the wisdom of that notion. He'd heard about the pirates of the Land of Maag, but he'd never actually met one. The term 'howling barbarians' had come up quite frequently in the descriptions of them he'd heard, and the terms 'barbarians' and 'strategy' seemed to Narasan to clash just a bit.

There was a large fleet of narrow ships in the harbor of Lattash, and Narasan immediately saw the advantage the Maags would have in any encounter with the broad-beamed Trogite vessels. Maag ships were obviously built for speed, not for capacity.

After Veltan beached his sloop, he led Narasan toward a dome-shaped hill to the south of the village. They went on through a crudely constructed shed past a fair number of burly Maags who were pounding on pieces of red-hot iron and then joined some leather-clad natives at the mouth of what appeared to be the entrance to a cave.

They entered a long passageway that finally opened out into a large chamber where a small fire was burning in a pit near the center, most probably to provide light. Then Veltan introduced him to his sister Zelana, who was certainly the most beautiful woman Narasan had ever seen, and then to a pretty little girl Narasan presumed to be Lady Zelana's daughter.

There were other people in the cave, but Narasan was primarily interested in meeting the Maag called Hook-Beak.

'He should be here soon, Commander Narasan,' Lady Zelana assured him.

Then a very small Maag called Rabbit came out of the passageway leading a hulking fellow with a bent nose. Narasan immediately saw how the man had come by the name 'Hook-Beak'.

Veltan introduced them and, somewhat to Narasan's surprise, Hook-Beak candidly admitted that he'd previously made his living as a pirate. That open admission elevated the Maag in Narasan's estimation. Strange though it seemed, evidently this fellow had a sense of honor. It was quite possible that they'd get along well together.

'What an unnatural sort of thing,' Narasan murmured to himself.

Narasan and Sorgan spent a great deal of time with Veltan's sketchy map of the ravine leading down to the village of Lattash, but when they'd shown it to the comical native Red-Beard, he'd dismissed it as worthless because of its lack of detail. Then the small Maag called Rabbit suggested a sculptured map rather than a flat drawing. Narasan was stunned by the sheer genius of that notion, and he rather painfully realized that if he'd been in possession of such a map during the disastrous campaign in the southern Empire, his nephew Astal might still be alive.

As they came to know each other better, Narasan and Hook-Beak frequently wandered away from the supposed purpose of their daily meetings in Lady Zelana's cave to share reminiscences of past wars. Narasan had observed over his years in the army that 'war stories' tended to bring men closer together, and given the current situation, these relaxed exchanges could be even more important than discussions of strategy. Although it seemed most unnatural, he found that he was growing to like this uncivilized pirate.

The weather cleared a few days later, and about mid-afternoon the fleet of ships that were carrying Narasan's advance force sailed into the harbor. Narasan went on down to the beach to speak with his men.

There was a certain wariness on both sides when Narasan introduced his officers to the Maags, and Sorgan rather wisely suggested that it might be better if their forces were separated by the river when they began their march up the ravine after the annual flood had subsided.

Then on a calm and cloudy day Lady Zelana summoned them to her cave to give them certain information about the enemies they'd be facing during the upcoming war. Longbow introduced them to an elderly native called One-Who-Heals, who immediately descended into the world of absurdity and superstition, describing their enemies as creatures who were an impossible mixture of insects, reptiles, and humans. Narasan managed to keep his composure enough to suppress an urge to laugh out loud, but he was more than a little startled when Veltan confirmed the old native's ridiculous assertions.

Then the archer Longbow described a process whereby he'd been able to extract venom from dead enemies and then use it against their living counterparts. Sorgan found that to be amusing for some reason Narasan couldn't quite understand. Sorgan appeared to have a rather warped sense of humor.

Then, even as the natives had predicted, a very warm wind swept in from the west, and not long thereafter, a solid wall of water burst out of the mouth of the ravine. Narasan hadn't really expected a flood of such magnitude, and he was stunned by the sheer volume of water rushing down to the bay.

The Trogites and Maags remained on board their ships waiting for the flood to subside, but Narasan *did* go ashore once to take a closer look at one of the drowned enemies. As it chanced to happen, the old shaman One-Who-Heals was on the berm that stood between the river and the village, and he pointed out the peculiarities of a drowned enemy. It wasn't much bigger than a half-grown child, and it was garbed in something resembling a hooded cloak woven from some sort of grey fabric. Then the old native pried the creature's mouth open with a stick to show Narasan its fangs. It was obvious that the long fangs were *not* the teeth of a human. The spines along the outside of the creature's forearms were also very unusual.

Narasan's doubts began to fade. 'If I'd known about *this*, I'd have held out for more gold,' he muttered to himself.

4

◆━◆━◆

The weather had turned warm as the flood subsided, and Narasan found it to be almost pleasant as he and his men began their march up the south bench of the ravine, despite the fact that things were very muddy.

As they neared the gap at the head of the ravine, the trees became less intimidating and the undergrowth diminished. The upper end of the ravine seemed almost to have a park-like quality with snow-covered mountains off in the distance and a tiny brook trickling over stones through a grassy little meadow surrounded by evergreen trees.

The archer Longbow was waiting for them, and he led Narasan, Gunda, Padan, and Jalkan up to the narrow gap to give them a chance to see the barren Wasteland lying far below. Then he drew their attention to a rocky ridge line a mile or so out in the desert. 'There they are,' he said.

Narasan stared in awe at the enemy force crowded along that ridge-line. So far as he could tell, they stretched from horizon to horizon.

Sorgan and his men arrived not long thereafter, and Sorgan also seemed to be a bit disturbed by the enormity of the approaching enemy force.

When the clever young Keselo discovered that the sandy slope was in actuality a stairway constructed of stone blocks, however, the situation changed radically. The stairway was a convenient source of building material, and the fortress Narasan's men could build with those blocks would be virtually impregnable.

Not long after daybreak the following morning, a hollow roar that could not possibly have come from a human throat came echoing out of the desert, and enemies by the thousands came charging across the desert and up the now useless stairway. Longbow's archers lined the battlements along the front wall of the fort, and when the enemy soldiers came into range, Longbow lifted his horn and sounded the death-knell for almost half of the attacking force. The cloud of arrows rising from the front wall of the fort nearly blotted out the sunrise, and it immediately set off an avalanche of dead enemies rolling back on down the stairway to confound the rear ranks. The mindless charge continued, however, until the last few enemy soldiers were killed before they ever reached the front wall of the fort.

Narasan smiled briefly. Things seemed to be going rather well this morning.

Veltan came by early that afternoon to speak with Longbow about the total lack of any encounters with the enemy during their trek up the ravine. Longbow gave him an explanation that chilled Narasan all the way down to the bone. It was fairly obvious now that they were trapped here at the head of the ravine with no possible means of escape.

Longbow, however, had already solved that problem – or so it appeared. As it turned out, however, their enemies were about two steps ahead of them. There were hidden burrows near the bench on the south side of the ravine, and their enemies swarmed out of those burrows and killed at least a quarter of the party of Maags who were coming down the ravine.

Narasan was certain that the time had come for a conference with his friend Sorgan, but Sorgan, it appeared was way ahead of him. The burly Maag came down to the bottom of the ravine and joined Narasan there. They agreed that the hidden burrows had quite obviously made their original plan obsolete, and now faced an entirely different situation.

They had just begun to come up with alternatives when a deep rumble preceded an earthquake so violent that they could barely stand up.

Then there was an almost deafening crash of thunder and a blinding flash of light as Veltan appeared out of nowhere. 'Run!' he shouted. 'Run for your lives! Get your people away from this cursed ravine!'

Then Red-Beard, who'd been staring at the upper end of the ravine, suddenly shouted, 'Fire Mountain!' and he turned and ran.

Red-Beard's somewhat distorted sense of humor deserted him at that point, Commander Narasan noted. Of course, with the twin volcanos at the head of the ravine spouting liquid lava-rock miles into the air, nobody in Narasan's army was laughing very much as they fled down the south rim of the ravine toward what they all fervently hoped was the safety of the bay of Lattash where their ships waited.

When they reached the vicinity of Skell's fort, Narasan paused. The fort had been built out of massive boulders, and the very narrow gap at the center that had been intended to let the river pass through wouldn't really allow very much lava to rush on down. The fort had been constructed to hold back an enemy, and it seemed that it might even do its job when the enemy happened to be liquid lava.

When the first trickles of lava hit the large pond on the upstream side of the fort, a vast cloud of steam came boiling up to block Narasan's view. Muttering a few choice curses, he moved on down to a point on the rim where he could see the downhill side of the fort. There was steam boiling out, but he didn't see any lava streaming through. The lava was quite obviously turning back into solid rock when it hit the water, and that rock was reinforcing what had started out as a fort, but was now a dam. Narasan had more than a few suspicions at that point. Given the heat of the liquid lava, the pond to the east of Skell's dam *should* have vanished in a cloud of steam, but it didn't. Evidently, somebody – or something – was replenishing the water as fast or faster than the lava could boil it away. Narasan was greatly relieved. Skell's dam, aided by that steady supply of water, would hold the lava back for long enough to give his men time to row on out to the fleet lying in the harbor. It appeared that he and his men would survive – even in the face of the natural disaster which had come boiling up out of the bowels of the earth.

5

❧

When the combined fleet passed through the narrow inlet at the mouth of the bay, Narasan realized that the waves of the open sea were quite a bit larger than the waves had been in the protected bay, and he found that to be quite exhilarating. There was a sense of freedom at sea that was absent in the lives of those who lived on land. That gave Narasan a somewhat better understanding of Sorgan Hook-Beak.

Of course, the design of the *Seagull* also played a part in Sorgan's personality. In many ways the *Seagull* was much like her namesake, swift, graceful – and usually hungry.

The Maags were polite enough not to dash off and leave the broad-beamed Trogite vessels wallowing far behind, and Sorgan stayed well within hailing distance as the fleet moved south along the west coast of Lady Zelana's Domain. At Veltan's request, his rather scruffy little fishing sloop was attached to one of the Trogite ships by a long rope. Veltan seemed quite fond of that sloop for some reason, and Sorgan had definitely approved of bringing it along. 'We'll be moving into strange waters, Narasan,' he'd explained, 'and that little tub can do the sounding for us any time we get close to a shoreline.'

'Sounding?' Narasan had asked, just a bit puzzled.

'Check the depth of the water – or locate any reefs or hidden boulders. A ship that's just had her bottom ripped out won't stay afloat for very long, and I haven't learned how to walk on water yet.'

The coast of Lady Zelana's Domain was heavily forested by huge trees that filled Narasan with awe. The forest in the lower reaches of the ravine had been clogged with dense brush, but out here on the coast the huge trees had evidently smothered out the bushes with a perpetual drizzle of falling needles, and they stood in solitary splendor, almost like some vast green temple. The air here along the coast was humid, of course, and the rays of the early summer sun slanted down among the column-like trees like shafts of gold. Narasan felt a strange sense of regret when the forest gave way to the farmland of Veltan's Domain.

Then, a few days after they'd set out, the mellow sound of a horn came from the *Seagull*, and Sorgan's longship pulled in closer. 'Ho, Narasan!' Sorgan bellowed.

'Is something amiss?' Narasan called back.

'Not that I know about. Lady Zelana wanted me to let you know that we'll be turning east before long – maybe sometime tomorrow. We'll go on around the southern end of her brother's country and then swing north. His house is on up the east coast a ways. From what she tells me, we're a week or ten days out yet.'

They rounded the lower end of a sizeable peninsula about midmorning the next day, and Gunda came back from the bow of the ship with his cousin, Captain Pantal. 'If you look off to the right, you'll see that island called Arash, Narasan,' Gunda advised. 'Maybe it might not be a bad idea for me to go on over to another ship and sail down through that channel to Castano and tell Andar to bring the main part of our army on up here. That way we'll be ready just in case the war starts sooner than we expect it to.'

'That's not a bad idea, Gunda,' Narasan agreed. 'I'll talk with Sorgan and let him know that you're not just running away.'

Gunda gave him a hard look, but he didn't say anything.

The *Seagull* drew closer in response to a brassy note from a standard Trogite trumpet. It occurred to Narasan that the horns of the Maags had a much more mellow sound to them. For some reason the sound of trumpets had always irritated Narasan.

Sorgan was standing at the rail as the *Seagull* came in closer. 'Problems, Narasan?' he called.

'Not that I've noticed so far,' Narasan replied. 'Of course it's still early, so there's plenty of time left for today to turn sour on us.'

'Why do you always look on the dark side, Narasan?'

'It's a failing of mine. We're fairly close to the channel that leads down through the ice zone to the north coast of the Empire. Gunda's going to sail on down there and gather up the rest of the army and bring them on up here.'

'That's not a bad idea, Narasan. It'll save some time, and we'll be ready if the snake-men try to sneak up on us again.'

'And you accuse *me* of being gloomy.'

'Always look on the dark side, Narasan. Then if things turn out all right, it's a pleasant surprise.'

They sailed on past two more of those protruding peninsulas on the south coast of the Land of Dhrall, and then the mixed fleet turned north to sail along behind the *Seagull* as Lady Zelana guided Sorgan toward the home of her younger brother.

The land along that eastern coast was much more flat than the western coast, and Narasan observed that the farmers of Veltan's domain had vast fields of grain stretching inland for as far as the eye could reach. Veltan hadn't gone into much detail when he'd described his Domain, but Narasan was quite certain that the class distinctions prevalent in the Empire simply did not exist here. The scrawny former priest Jalkan stubbornly refused to even consider that possibility, and his perpetual sneer irritated Narasan so much that he began to search for any possible excuse to dismiss the scoundrel and send him packing.

As they sailed along the coast, Sorgan Hook-Beak prudently sent Veltan's fishing sloop on ahead of the *Seagull* to test the waters for obstructions. Narasan smiled faintly. Sorgan quite obviously loved the *Seagull*, and he'd go to any lengths to protect her. In a peculiar sort of way, the *Seagull* was the equivalent of Sorgan's wife, and he'd sooner die than put her in any kind of danger.

They moved slowly on up the east coast for the next few days and then about mid-morning on the third day, the sloop turned sharply to the left and led them on toward the beach. Narasan shaded his eyes and saw Veltan and some others waiting.

Captain Pantal dropped anchor a short distance from the beach, and Narasan, Jalkan, and Padan took a small skiff the rest of the way in. Narasan noted that Sorgan was *also* in a skiff, along with Ox, Ham-Hand, Zelana, and the two children, but he seemed to be holding back just bit – obviously out of courtesy. That surprised Narasan a little. The notion of courtesy in a Maag seemed like a contradiction in terms.

Keselo and the others had already joined Veltan, and Keselo was talking with a serious-faced native who was holding a somewhat makeshift spear.

Keselo seemed to be quite impressed by the native's creativity, and he suggested a rather interesting possibility. If the clever little smith called Rabbit could provide all the natives with spear-points and shields, they could be trained to some degree to utilize the phalanx formation. They probably wouldn't be first-rate soldiers to begin with, but it wasn't as if the creatures of the Wasteland were tactical geniuses. Even if the natives were only partially trained, they could be very useful in the upcoming war. 'Do you think you could train them, Keselo?' Narasan asked the young officer.

'I'd be willing to give it a try, sir,' Keselo replied.

'Do it then, and keep me advised.'

'Yes, *sir*!' Keselo replied with a smart salute.

After Sorgan and his friends came ashore, Veltan led them all along a well-traveled path that led inland.

When Narasan saw Veltan's single-rock castle, it confirmed something he had suspected from the moment the two of them had first met. Veltan – and his brother and sisters as well – might *look* as if they were human, but it was quite obvious now that they'd gone so far *past* human that the term was almost laughable. Veltan's somewhat self-effacing manner had concealed some stunning realities, but the huge house brought reality out into the open with no possible way to deny it. The baffling part of what was now right out in the open was *why* a being with such unlimited power had come to Imperial Kaldacin to hire an army to deal with a sub-human enemy. Narasan was fairly certain that Veltan – or his sister – could have obliterated the creatures of the Wasteland with a single thought. 'We've got a very strange situation here,' he muttered to himself.

Veltan led them to what he referred to as his 'map-room', and Narasan immediately saw that it was a combination of the 'war-room' in the army compound back in Kaldacin and Red-Beard's sculptured map in Zelana's cave in Lattash. The addition of the balcony surrounding the miniaturized replica of the probable battlefield gave them the ability to see the entirety of the region in much greater detail than Narasan had ever previously encountered. The terrain in the vicinity of the waterfall was intimidating, but Narasan immediately saw that if they could reach the area around the geyser that was the source of that waterfall, they'd be able to hold off their enemy almost indefinitely with only minimal help from the local farmers. The important thing, of course, would be to get there first.

Then the stunningly beautiful wife of the farmer Omago came through the door to advise them that their supper was ready, and Veltan, with a note of pride in his voice, told them that the beautiful lady was quite probably the best cook in the world.

Then the scrawny halfwit Jalkan made some obscene remarks that nearly sent Narasan into total collapse. Fortunately, the lady's solidly-built husband took steps *before* Veltan could raise his hand and obliterate Narasan's entire army. Narasan found himself wishing that Omago had gone just a bit further, however. Omago *did* have that spear in his other hand, and he'd just wasted a wonderful opportunity to rid Narasan's army of a growing embarrassment.

Jalkan came up screaming, spitting blood, and jerking at the hilt of his sheathed dagger, but Keselo stopped the idiot dead in his tracks with a highly appropriate threat to kill him right there on the spot.

Narasan fervently hoped that Jalkan would make yet another blunder so that Keselo could go even further.

Unfortunately, Jalkan – as usual – failed.

As Narasan regained control of his temper, however, he realized that this embarrassing incident had been exactly what he'd been hoping for.

Jalkan was spluttering and screaming about his rank as an officer in Narasan's army, but Narasan abruptly – and publicly – revoked that commission and ordered Padan to chain the fool and take him back to the beach. Then, in what he felt to be an extremely appropriate public gesture, he offered the lady's husband the opportunity to deal with Jalkan personally – with spear, if he wished.

Omago seemed to be tempted, but he rather reluctantly declined.

Narasan was terribly disappointed, but in good time he'd come up with an appropriate punishment that would convince Veltan that he'd hired the right army.

Narasan and Sorgan spent much of their time in the map-room for the next few days. The river that ran down to the sea from the foot of the waterfall was quite some distance to the north of Veltan's house, so it was fairly obvious that sailing up to the river mouth would be the best course of action, since, even as had been the case in the previous war, there was only one possible invasion route their enemies could follow.

'We've got to get people up there in a hurry, Narasan,' Sorgan said quite firmly. 'Whoever gets there first is going to have an enormous advantage.'

'I can see that, old friend,' Narasan agreed.

'Old?' Sorgan protested.

'Sorry. Just a figure of speech.' Narasan frowned. 'I think we'd better have a chat with Veltan's friend – the fellow who specializes in knocking out the teeth of those who insult his wife.'

'You should have killed that fool right there on the spot, Narasan.'

'And get blood all over this map? Don't be silly, Hook-Beak. I'll deal with Jalkan all in good time. I'm busy right now. I've noticed that Rabbit and Keselo seem to be getting along quite well with the farmer who gave Jalkan a lesson in good manners.'

'I think the three of them might just be the same breed of cat,' Sorgan agreed. 'They all keep coming up with new ideas. You *did* know that your man Keselo's teaching Omago and the other farmers how to form up to make their spears more effective, didn't you?'

Narasan nodded. 'He told me that he's been teaching them the rudiments of the phalanx formation. If Keselo has enough time to polish them, they'll probably turn out to be quite useful during the upcoming war.'

'I'll take all the help I can get,' Sorgan agreed.

'Don't feel alone. Right now, though, we're going to need a guide to show our advance force how to get past that waterfall without getting washed back out to sea. They need to spend their time building forts, not practicing their swimming.'

The two strangers Veltan led into the map-room the following morning were a peculiar looking pair. Prince Ekial was fairly tall, and his face had obviously sustained some fairly serious wounds at some time in the past. The armed and obviously dangerous warrior queen called Trenicia was not the sort of person anyone with good sense would offend. The warrior queen was not *quite* as tall as Sorgan, but she came close. There were a few ancient myths in some of the more rural regions of the Empire about women warriors, and until now Narasan had never given them much credence, but Trenicia washed his doubts away just by her presence. Veltan advised Narasan and Sorgan that Prince Ekial and

Queen Trenicia were here as 'observers', largely because at some day in the not-too-distant future they'd be fighting the creatures of the Wasteland in different regions in the Land of Dhrall.

At supper that evening when they were all feasting on the wonderful meal Omago's wife had prepared, Sorgan raised the issue of bringing Longbow's archers to join them in the ongoing war with the creatures of the Wasteland, but Longbow dismissed the notion of coming by ship almost before it even came up. He'd obviously been measuring distances in the map-room, and he rather casually advised Narasan and Sorgan that the archers could come across country in about half the time it'd take if they came by sea.

The next morning Narasan and Sorgan were in the map-room closely examining the region around the waterfall. 'I don't see any possible way for us to get up there, Narasan,' Sorgan admitted. 'That's a straight rock wall with tons of water coming down from up above.'

'I can see that, Sorgan,' Narasan agreed, 'and that cliff doesn't seem to have any breaks anywhere near the falls. I suppose we could build a ramp, but that'd probably take us most of the summer.'

Veltan's friend Omago came through the doorway and joined them.

'You're just the man we needed to talk to, Omago,' Sorgan said. 'Are you at all familiar with the region around this blasted waterfall?'

'Not really, but I've sent word to Nanton. He's a shepherd, and he grazes his flock up there, so he probably knows every tree and bush in the area by its first name. I've asked him to meet your ships at the mouth of the river and then guide you up to the pasture-land above the falls.'

'You're way ahead of us, Omago,' Narasan noted. 'We'd more or less agreed that we should send a sizeable number of our men up there to build some fortifications to hold our enemy back until we could get our main force up there, but Veltan's map doesn't show any route those men could follow.'

'The map's fairly accurate,' Omago agreed, 'but when sheep are looking for grass, they'll find a way to reach it, and anywhere Nanton's sheep go, he'll go too. The paths you'll follow will be steep and narrow, but if sheep can make it to the top, so can your men.'

Sorgan squinted. 'Skell, I think,' he said.

'Run that past me again, Sorgan,' Narasan said. 'It went by a little fast.'

'I think maybe we should send Skell on up there with Omago's shepherd friend to look things over. Skell knows exactly what to look for, and he'll be able to pinpoint the best spots for our forts, and that could save us a lot of time. Then, too, if the snake-men are already up there, Skell's slippery enough to sneak past them and get on back down here to warn us.'

'I'm sure Veltan would have warned us if the enemy force is already up there, Sorgan,' Narasan told his friend. 'You worry too much. I think I'll send Padan along with Skell. Padan can put down markers that'll show my troops the way to get up there. Sorgan, my friend, this *might* just turn out to be an easier war than we'd anticipated.'

'I've always been sort of fond of easy wars, Narasan. As far as I've been able to determine, they're the best kind there ever is.'

6

Two Maag ships sailed north at sunrise the following morning carrying at most a couple hundred Maags. Narasan thought that might be just a little light, but Skell seemed to think it was all he really wanted.

'When you get right down to it, Narasan, all that Skell's really doing is marking the trail for us so that we'll know how to get up there,' Sorgan told him. 'He'll send out scouting parties to find suitable locations for forts but that's about as far as we need him to go. We'll only be a few days behind him, so it's not like he'll be alone up there for six months or so.'

'I suppose you're right,' Narasan conceded.

'You're a worrier, Narasan, did you know that?'

Narasan smiled slightly. 'Occupational hazard, I suppose,' he conceded. 'Over the years I've come to realize that if anything at all can possibly go wrong, it probably will.'

'Skell's got a couple of things working for him that'll give him an edge if something *does* go wrong.'

'Oh?'

'They're called Longbow and Red-Beard. I don't think either one of us would like to come against *those* two. Sometimes

Longbow sends chills up my back. Every time I turn around, he's at least three jumps ahead of me.'

'Did anybody remember to tell Lady Zelana that those two are going along with Skell?'

'Why don't we let Veltan take care of that?' Sorgan suggested with a sly smirk.

'What a wonderful idea, Sorgan,' Narasan replied with no hint of a smile.

'What do you think, Narasan? Do we want to take those farmers with us? They're not really very good, you know.'

'Maybe we should,' Narasan replied. 'I'm fairly sure that Veltan wants us to get them involved, and he's the one who's paying us. Keselo's been training them, and he tells me that they're getting better. They were a bit awkward right at first, but they seem to be improving. This *is* their homeland, after all, and they won't really inconvenience us *too* much.'

'I *hate* fighting alongside amateurs,' Sorgan complained. 'You never know when they're going to just jump up and run away.'

Narasan shrugged. 'We can keep them sort of off to one side until we're certain that they'll do what they're supposed to do. Then we can gradually move them into the main action. Nobody's really all that great during his first war, but we all got better at it as time went by, didn't we?'

'You're probably right, Narasan. I guess there's really no such thing as a natural-born warrior – except for maybe Longbow. I think that one may have cut his teeth on arrowheads when he was just a baby.'

'How's our supply of venom holding out? That definitely gave us an advantage in the last war.'

'We've got enough to get us by until we kill more snake-men.'

'That took a bit of getting used to, didn't it? You almost never come up against an enemy that supplies what you'll need to defeat him.'

'Not an *intelligent* enemy, that's for sure,' Sorgan agreed, 'but the snake-men wouldn't recognize intelligence if it walked up and bit them on the nose.'

All in all, Narasan was satisfied with their rather rudimentary plan. The war in Lady Zelana's Domain had taught him that setting anything in stone in a war with the creatures of the Wasteland could have disastrous results. As individuals, their enemies were stupid beyond belief, but Narasan had come to realize that their *real* enemy here in the Land of Dhrall was *not* a single individual. The concept of a group awareness was alien – even absurd – but Narasan had come to realize also that dismissing things on the basis of absurdity could have disastrous consequences.

Fortunately, they had help, but once again, Narasan was somewhat uncertain about just exactly *who* was helping them. The spring flood that had purged the ravine above Lattash of enemy invaders had *seemed* to be a natural event that occurred every year, but would the natives of Chief White-Braid's tribe have built the village of Lattash right in the path of a natural disaster of those proportions if they'd been aware that its occurrence was inevitable? Narasan was very dubious about that.

Veltan and his family definitely had abilities that no human could possibly possess, but when the twin volcanos at the head of the ravine had suddenly exploded, Veltan quite obviously hadn't known that it was going to happen. His shrill warning that had sent them all scrambling up the sides of the ravine had been filled with a kind of panic-stricken astonishment. *Something* was helping them in this war, but for the life of him, Narasan couldn't identify it. He was grateful for the help of this unknown friend, but he'd feel much more at ease if he knew just exactly who – or what – the friend was.

SKELL JODANSON
OF JORMO

1

Skell and his younger brother Torl had been born in the port city of Kormo on the west coast of the Land of Maag, and they were the sons of the famous Captain Jodan of Kormo. Captain Jodan's longship was the *Shark*, a name that struck terror into the heart of every Trogite who sailed the western sea. There had never been any doubt that Skell and Torl would grow up to be sailors, and their childhood was a time of impatience and yearning. As they grew older, it became common practice in the port of Kormo for every sea captain to order a thorough search of his ship before leaving the harbor, since there was a distinct possibility that one of Jodan's boys was hiding somewhere on board.

Skell and Torl became very good swimmers during that stage of their boyhood, largely because they'd been thrown over the side of at least two or three longships a week.

The complaints Captain Jodan kept receiving from other ship-captains finally irritated him enough that he decided that it was time for his boys to go to sea. Skell and Torl had always assumed that when their father finally relented and let them go to sea, they'd be sailing aboard *his* ship, the *Shark*, but Captain Jodan didn't see it that way. During his younger years, he'd occasionally had shipmates who were the sons of the captain, and he'd found them to be lazy, incompetent and generally despised by the rest of the crew. He'd long promised himself that when *his* sons went to sea, they'd have to work their way up from the bottom and earn every promotion in the same way that other sailors were obliged to do.

As it happened, Captain Jodan had sailed with the now-famous Dalto Big-Nose when they were both young, and the two shipmates had become lifelong friends. And so it was that when Captain Jodan decided that it was time for his boys to go to sea, he contacted his friend and handed the boys over to serve as deck-hands on board Dalto's ship, the *Swordfish*.

Skell and Torl were very excited as the *Swordfish* sailed out from the harbor at Kormo on a fine spring day, and they were standing at the bow looking out to sea in boyish anticipation when Captain Big-Nose found them.

It was at that point that the boys learned the first rule of sea-manship: 'Always look busy when the captain's on deck.'

They spent the next three days on their knees scrubbing the deck of the *Swordfish*, and things definitely went downhill from there. Any time that a task was difficult or unpleasant, Dalto auto-matically called for Skell and Torl. The boys soon agreed that they'd jump ship at their first opportunity, but the *Swordfish* had plenty of food and water on board, so she stayed out at sea for months on end, leaving Skell and Torl on their knees, scrubbing the deck.

In their spare moments – which were few and far between – they came to love the sea. She was forever changing, and at times she was so fair that the boys were almost stunned by the play of light and darkness sweeping majestically across the waves. It was usually at that point that Captain Big-Nose caught them idling and gave them a blistering reprimand.

Later – *much* later, actually – Skell reflected back on that first voyage, and he began to see the logic behind the Captain's behaviour. He had set out from the start to persuade the boys that their father's fame had nothing to do with *their* status. Big-Nose started them at the bottom because *every* apprentice seaman started there. After that it was up to them to prove that they were worthy of any task other than scrubbing the *Swordfish*'s deck or carrying buckets of rancid bilge-water up out of the hold.

By the time that the *Swordfish* returned to the port of Kormo, Skell and Torl had graduated to the posts of oarsmen, and they were beginning to feel like *real* sailors.

The *Swordfish* laid over in the port of Kormo, and before she went out to sea again, the boys' cousin Sorgan signed on as a top-man. Sorgan had sailed aboard a couple of other Maag longships, and he was a few years older than his cousins. He tended to take a superior attitude toward his younger relatives, and Skell decided at that stage of the relationship that it might be proper to point out that he and Torl were the *real* superiors in the family, since *they* were the sons of Captain Jodan, while Sorgan was merely the son of their father's sister.

That mightily offended Sorgan, so he 'whomped' on Skell for quite some time – to the vast amusement of the other crewmen. Skell did manage to give his cousin one good solid punch, however, and it was that single punch that gave Sorgan Hook-Beak his name.

The *Swordfish* continued to savage the wallowing Trogite ships in the waters off the coast of the Land of Maag, although she occasionally sailed off along the south coast, and then went as far as the coast of the Land of Shaan, where Dalto's crew raided Trogite encampments in search of gold. So it was that Skell, Torl, and Sorgan learned the rudiments of land warfare.

The gathering of gold *was*, of course, the main reason that Maag longships went out to sea, but as the years went by, Skell came to realize that it was the sea herself that had captured him. Gold was nice enough, but it could never match the beauty of the sea when columns of sunlight came down through the clouds to march across her glittering surface or when the moon rose to bathe her in pale light. She was forever changing, and, like every other Maag who chose a life at sea, Skell came to love her. Like every sailor, he enjoyed himself enormously when the *Swordfish* made port, but he knew that the sea was his real home.

After Skell had been at sea for about ten years, the *Swordfish* hauled into the port of Weros, and the crew went ashore in search of entertainment after Captain Big-Nose had sternly advised them that the *Swordfish* would be sailing out again in three days, and that he wouldn't wait for any of them who happened to be late. Skell and Torl returned just in time, but Sorgan didn't, so the *Swordfish* sailed off, leaving him behind. Skell and Sorgan had settled their differences by then, and Skell actually missed his cousin.

Then, on a rainy afternoon just after Skell had turned twenty-seven, the *Swordfish* hauled into the harbor of Kormo, and the *Shark* was anchored there. Captain Jodan rowed his skiff over, conferred briefly with Captain Big-Nose, and then he came back out on deck to advise his sons that they'd just been transferred to the *Shark* – as first and second mates. Their predecessors, it seemed, had been killed in a tavern brawl in the port of Gaiso a few weeks earlier.

Their father obviously wasn't happy about the situation, but he didn't really have much choice. When they were about halfway to the *Shark*, he stopped rowing and gave them a stern lecture on 'proper behavior'. They were now officers, so the other members of the *Shark's* crew would *not* be their close friends. 'Always be serious' had been at the core of his lecture. Laughing and grinning weren't permitted. He closed his lecture with, 'Don't *ever* call me "papa". I'm "Captain", and don't you forget it.'

The *Shark*, like the *Swordfish* and most other Maag vessels of that era, had preyed on the wallowing tubs of the Trogite Empire, although Captain Jodan, so far as Skell could remember, had never once used the word 'Trogite', preferring instead the word 'Trog'. Skell always had to cover his mouth when his father said that. For some reason, the word 'Trog' always struck him as hilarious.

After Captain Jodan's sons had served as officers on the *Shark* for a few years, the ship had hauled into the port of Weros to lay in a supply of fresh beans in the galley. Mildewed beans don't really taste very good, and the crew had been growing increasingly grouchy.

Skell cleverly foisted the task of buying fresh beans off on Torl, and then he went off along the scabby-looking waterfront for a tankard or six of strong ale. He was more than a little startled when he saw cousin Sorgan working on a battered-looking old ship tied up against one of the long wharves jutting out into the bay. 'Ho, Sorgan!' he called out. 'Have you decided to build them instead of sailing them now?'

'Very funny, Skell,' Sorgan growled, dropping the hammer he'd been using to pound caulking in between the obviously new boards that formed the deck. 'This ship will be the *Seagull* – if Ox, Ham-Hand and I can plug up all the leaks in her hull. She doesn't look too good yet, but give us a bit more time, and she'll be *mine*.' There was a definite note of pride in cousin Sorgan's voice.

'You actually broke down and bought your own ship, Sorgan?' Skell asked, walking out on the dock.

'I surely did, cousin,' Sorgan replied. 'From here on out, I'm going to be getting the captain's share of the loot when we rob a Trogite ship.'

Skell looked the tired old ship over. 'You've got quite a long way to go, cousin,' he said skeptically. 'Fixing her up is going to cost you a lot of money.'

Sorgan gave him a sly wink. 'Money's easy to come by here in Weros, Skell. A sailor who's been out at sea for six months works up quite a thirst, and by midnight, he's usually so far gone that he couldn't see lightning or hear thunder if his life depended on it. When we start running short of money, I just send Ox and Ham-Hand out along the waterfront to troll for sailors who still have money in their purses.'

'You're a thief, Sorgan,' Skell accused his cousin.

'*All* Maags are thieves, Skell. The Trogites don't just hand over their gold because they like our looks, you know. We have to threaten them to get what we want. Say hello to Torl and your papa for me, all right?'

'First chance I get, cousin,' Skell replied, giving Sorgan a brisk salute.

Sorgan thumbed his nose in reply, and they both laughed.

Business on board the *Shark* was very good for the next few years, and Skell observed that Captain Jodan was putting away sizeable chunks of his share of the booty. Then, shortly after Skell's thirty-first birthday, Captain Jodan abruptly called his sons into his cabin.

'I've had enough,' he announced. 'I've spent most of my life at sea, and I'm tired of it. I'm going to live on dry land, and that means that the *Shark* is yours now, Skell.'

Skell resisted a sudden impulse to jump up and dance on his father's tired-looking old table.

'There's one stipulation, Skell,' Captain Jodan advised his eldest son. 'From now on, I get one fifth of everything you steal, and don't try to cheat me. The first time you try something like that, I'll sell the *Shark* right out from under you, and you'll go back to being a common sailor.'

That ruined Skell's sense of jubilation quite noticeably.

The crew of the *Shark* relaxed more than a little after Captain Jodan's retirement, and Skell soon realized that he was going to have to quite firmly establish a few facts. First off, despite his youth, he *was* the captain of the *Shark*, and the crew *would* obey his orders. For some reason, the crew of the *Shark* didn't seem to take him seriously, and that soured Skell even more.

Finally, Skell's blond-haired brother Torl came into Skell's cluttered cabin late one evening. 'You're not doing it right, big brother,' Torl advised, seating himself at Skell's dirty table. 'You smile too much. The crew won't take you seriously as long as you've got that silly grin on your face. If you want the crew to pay any attention to you, you're going to have to try to look more like papa. He *never* smiled. Try to look grim and sour on the outside – even when you're laughing on the inside.'

'If I tried something like that, I'd explode, Torl.'

'I don't think you *really* will,' Torl disagreed. 'Just keep telling yourself that you're hiding your real feelings from the crew. Then you can sneak back to your cabin here and laugh all you want to.' Torl looked around the cabin. 'It'll give you something to do when you're cleaning this mess up. If papa happened to stop by and see what you've done to his cabin, he'd skin you alive.'

'I've been sort of busy here lately, Torl.'

'Trying to find a clean shirt, maybe? Now then, don't you think it's just about time for us to get *me* a ship?'

'What do you need a ship for?'

'Let me put it to you in a different sort of way, big brother. Did you *really* want me to stay here on board the *Shark*? When you get right down to the bottom of things, I'm at least as ambitious and greedy as you are, and if you keep me here on the *Shark*, I might just start getting certain ideas that won't make you the least bit happy. Do you get my drift?'

'That's *mutiny*, Torl!'

'I think that's the word people use sometimes, yes.'

'How can I possibly buy you a ship, Torl? Papa's taking one fifth of everything we steal right off the top.'

Torl shrugged. 'We'll have to *steal* my ship, then. Papa only wants gold. He wouldn't have much use for one fifth of a ship – even if we could find a saw big enough to cut off part of it.'

Skell scratched his chin, squinting through one of the portholes in his cabin. 'Gaiso, I think.'

'I didn't quite follow that.'

'The crew of every ship that sails into Gaiso goes directly to the taverns – probably because the tavern-keepers of Gaiso don't water down their grog like the keepers in other towns do. The few sailors who stay on board to guard the ship have barrels of that Gaiso grog on board to keep *them* pretty drunk as well. If we slip into the harbor of Gaiso along about midnight, you'll be able to pick which ship you want, and we'll steal it. If we put different colored sails on it and change a few other things as well, nobody'll ever know that we stole it, will they?'

'That's an awfully good idea, Skell.'

'Naturally,' Skell replied with a broad smirk. 'My ideas are always the best. I'll be able to give you a few men, but you'll have to hire more to fill out your crew. Don't start throwing your money away, though, because you'll be paying *me* a fifth of everything your ship brings in.'

'A *fifth*?' Torl protested.

'You get to help me support Papa. We wouldn't want him to starve, now would we?'

'That's not fair at all, Skell!'

'Fair doesn't have anything to do with it, baby brother. If you don't agree, you don't get a ship – and don't start waving "mutiny" in my face again – not unless you're ready to give up grog and ale. If you won't agree to help support Papa, I'll sail off and leave you behind the first time you get drunk. *Then* what are you going to do?'

'You're a cruel and hard man, Skell.'

'Naturally. I'm the Captain of the *Shark*. I'm *supposed* to be cruel and hard. Are we agreed, then?'

'What choice do I have?'

'None, little brother. I never give people choices.'

And so it was that the *Shark* sailed unobserved into the harbor of Gaiso in the middle of one dark, gloomy night, and Torl selected a ship that suited him. The *Shark* eased up beside that ship, and Torl led the boarding party that threw the few crewmen who'd remained on board over the side. Then Torl and his men hauled anchor and sailed along behind the *Shark* out of the harbor.

The brothers then pulled into a secluded cove and put the crew of the *Shark* to work modifying her until she no longer bore any outward resemblance to her former identity. For some reason, Torl decided to call his ship the *Lark*. Skell couldn't for the life of him understand exactly why. Maag ships usually had very threatening names, and '*Lark*' didn't seem to fit. Torl had a peculiar sense of humor sometimes.

After a bit of fairly difficult consideration, Skell decided that the grim-faced and somewhat older seaman Grock might be the best man to serve as the *Shark's* first mate. Grock was one of those 'serious' men who seldom smiled, but he'd been a crewman on the *Shark* for more than ten years, so he was very familiar with her quirks and peculiarities. He was also a very good judge of character, and it was at his suggestion that Skell chose Baldar Club-Foot as second mate. 'He's a good sailor, Cap'n,' Grock said. 'That bad foot of his makes him sorta gimpy, but he don't put up with no nonsense. Younger sailors are a bit silly sometimes, but Club-Foot knows how to jerk 'em up short when they need it.'

'He's our man, then,' Skell agreed. 'Now, then, I think we'd better sail on up the coast to Kormo. My brother's going to need a crew for the *Lark*, and I want *my* men back here on board the *Shark* before we go hunting Trogs again. The way things stand right now, we're both short-handed, and even those scows the Trogs call ships could probably outrun us.'

'Aye, Cap'n,' Grock agreed.

Once the two ships were fully manned, the brothers went back to work, robbing every Trog that came their way – just to keep Papa happy, of course.

Captain Jodan began to expand his simple seaside home as the seasons marched by, and before very long it more closely resembled a castle than the modest residence of a retired sailor.

Business was very good for the next several years, but then some disgustingly clever Trog came up with the idea of the 'ram', a thick pole firmly in place at the waterline at the bow of every Trog ship that passed the coast of Maag. Skell learned about that the hard way, and he'd only barely managed to get the *Shark* to the port at Kormo before she'd gone to the bottom.

His imitation grouchiness became very real for a while after *that* near disaster.

Skell heard some very interesting rumors in Kormo while the *Shark* was being repaired in the shipyard, and as soon as she was fit to sail again, he went on down the coast to see if he could catch up with the *Seagull*. If the rumors he'd picked up in the taverns of Kormo even came close to the truth, cousin Sorgan had just struck gold, and Skell thought it might be the polite thing to help his kinsman with the counting.

The fleet Sorgan had been gathering was in the harbor at Kweta when the *Shark* sailed into the bay, and Sorgan seemed quite happy to see his cousin. When he showed Skell all the gold blocks that were stacked up in the *Seagull's* hold, Skell became *very* enthusiastic.

There *were* a few disturbing things involved, however. Their employer was a woman, and that bothered Skell just a bit, and he was even *more* disturbed when he met her. Lady Zelana was quite probably the most beautiful woman he'd ever seen, but just below the surface of that stunning beauty she was harder than a rock. Then there was the native called Longbow, who was evidently her bodyguard. Longbow was the sort of man that anybody with half a brain would go *way* out of his way to avoid irritating. There was a bleakness about Longbow that sent chills up and down Skell's back. There was another native in Lady Zelana's party as well, and he was called Red-Beard. Red-Beard came very close to destroying the pose that Skell had spent years establishing. Every time Red-Beard opened his mouth, Skell had to steel himself to avoid laughing out loud.

After Skell and Sorgan discussed the matter at some length, they decided that Skell should lead an advance fleet to a place called Lattash on the west coast of the Land of Dhrall to protect Lady Zelana's Domain until such time as Sorgan arrived with the main fleet, and Torl would remain on the coast of Maag to gather up any latecomers. Skell wasn't *too* enthusiastic about the prospect of a land war, but the pay promised to be good, and that was all that really mattered.

The voyage from Kweta to the Land of Dhrall took quite a bit longer than Skell had thought it might. Evidently the sea spreading out from the east coast of the Land of Maag was much larger than Skell had ever imagined. The humorous native Red-Beard assured him that the Land of Dhrall was actually there – 'unless the gods got bored with it and made it vanish.' Red-Beard seemed to think that remark was very funny, but Skell wasn't in a laughing mood just then. They'd been two weeks at sea, and he was feeling very edgy.

In time, however, they made landfall and eventually sailed into the bay of Lattash. As soon as they landed, though, Skell began to have problems. The various ship captains had all piously promised Sorgan that they'd behave themselves when they reached the Land of Dhrall, but they'd lied through their teeth. The assumption that the primitives in the village of Lattash were weak and helpless and therefore prime targets for Maag freebooters turned out to be seriously flawed. Maag sailors in search of gold or entertainment began sprouting arrows, and Skell was obliged to come down on the offenders – hard. It took several floggings to get his point across, but it still seemed to him that getting the sailors out of the village would be his best course of action.

'It don't really matter *what* kind of excuse we come up with,

Cap'n,' Grock advised. 'All that's *really* important is getting those rowdies out of the village afore the natives kill ever'body in the fleet.'

'We *did* hire on to fight a war, didn't we, Cap'n?' Baldar Club-Foot suggested.

'That's what cousin Sorgan told me,' Skell agreed.

'Soljers as does their war-fighting on dry land almost always spend a whole lot of their time a-building forts or barricades, I've heard tell. Since the enemy's going to be coming this way from the east, and that river that comes down out of the mountings above town runs through a narrow ravine, we could tell all the other ship-cap'ns that your cousin Sorgan told you to go up a ways and build a fort to hold the enemy back.'

'He didn't really say anything like that, Club-Foot,' Skell objected.

'Lie to 'em, Cap'n,' Baldar suggested. 'What we're *really* trying to do is to keep them all from getting kilt, ain't it?'

'That comes close, yes.'

'Lying might not be very nice, but if it keeps 'em alive, it'll be worth the trouble.'

'*And*, if you tell the other ship Cap'ns that they won't get paid if the fort ain't good enough, they'll hustle right along, I'll bet,' Grock added.

'I guess it's worth a try,' Skell conceded a bit dubiously.

When Sorgan's fleet finally arrived, their employer, the beautiful Lady Zelana, evidently decided that a bit of honesty might be in order. First off, one of the old headmen of the assorted tribes described the annual spring flood. That *really* disturbed Skell, since most of his men were up in the ravine where they'd be trapped –

and drowned – if the old chief's description of the yearly disaster came anywhere close to being accurate.

Then there was the issue of venom. Skell had heard stories about poisonous snakes, but he'd never actually *seen* one – and he *really* wanted to keep it that way.

Lady Zelana's bleak-faced bodyguard, Longbow, put Skell somewhat at his ease, however, with his description of the process whereby he'd used the enemy's venom to kill other enemies. It seemed to Skell that there was a certain justice involved there.

Skell would be the first to admit that he hadn't once encountered one of what his cousin colorfully called 'the snake-men', largely because he'd spent most of his time in Zelana's Domain building an impregnable fort to prevent any intruding enemy force from reaching the village of Lattash. He'd *seen* a few of them, but when something's a half-mile away it doesn't usually pose much of a threat.

The thing that had *really* disturbed Skell during the war in Lady Zelana's Domain had been their alliance with the Trogs. There was no question about the fact that Commander Narasan's men were very good soldiers and that they'd been a great help, but it had just seemed so *unnatural* to Skell to have Trogs for allies.

The natives had warned them that the flood – which *had* been very useful – was an annual event in the region, so Skell had finally accepted it as a more or less natural phenomenon, but the sudden appearance of two volcanos at the head of the ravine – just when they'd *really* needed them – was an entirely different matter. The natives had hinted around the edges of some very unlikely explanations, but Skell had been fairly sure that Lady Zelana had been at the bottom of it. That raised a somewhat unsettling question, however. If Lady Zelana could make mountains explode whenever it suited her, why did she need an army?

By the time it was all over and the invaders had been obliterated, cousin Sorgan and the Trog commander had become close friends, and Sorgan offered his assistance in the war the Trogs had been hired to fight. Skell had been more than a little dubious about that – *until* Lady Zelana and her brother had made a very generous offer of even *more* gold.

Skell decided that he might as well go along at that point.

2

---◆---

It was early summer when the combined fleet of Maags and Trogs sailed south to the Domain of Lady Zelana's younger brother Veltan, and that made Skell a bit more comfortable. Bad weather was seldom a problem in the summertime.

After they'd passed a somewhat indeterminate boundary, Skell observed that Veltan's Domain was primarily farmland. There *did* appear to be mountains up near the northern part of the region, but they were quite a long ways off.

The fleet turned toward the east when it reached the southern coast of the Land of Dhrall, and then they swung north, following a rather irregular coast.

Veltan's scruffy-looking little fishing sloop was leading the fleet, and evidently the men on board the sloop – Longbow, Red-Beard, Rabbit, and Keselo – had been looking for a certain landmark, because the sloop abruptly turned shoreward, and she was beached without much warning. Skell muttered a few choice curses under his breath as the *Shark* heeled over very sharply when Grock jerked on the tiller.

The white sand beach seemed much cleaner than most of the beaches Skell had seen in his lifetime at sea, and the wheatfields on the gentle slope rising from the beach were an almost luminous green. There was no getting around the fact that this was beautiful country, but Skell still preferred the open sea. He prudently ordered his men to drop the anchor some distance out from the beach. The *Shark* drew more water than Veltan's sloop, and Skell wasn't in the mood to take any chances.

Commander Narasan and several other people went ashore to meet with Lady Zelana's younger brother, but for some reason, cousin Sorgan held back just a bit. That puzzled Skell, but then it occurred to him that Sorgan was trying to be polite. 'What an unnatural sort of thing,' he muttered to himself. Evidently Sorgan had been spending *far* too much time with the Trogs, and some of their customs had rubbed off on him.

After a while, Sorgan finally went ashore, and Skell left Grock in charge and rowed on into the beach to see if he could find out just exactly what was in the wind. He hung back a bit, quietly observing and listening. Sorgan and the Trogs seemed a bit surprised that a farmer named Omago had gathered up a sizeable number of other farmers to help in the defense of Veltan's Domain. Skell was a bit dubious about that. If the local people here in the Land of Dhrall could hold off the enemy all by themselves, why had Lady Zelana and her relatives gone to all the trouble and expense of hiring professionals from various other lands to do the fighting?

Then Veltan suggested that they should all go to his house to have a look at *his* 'lumpy map'. Evidently, the Trogs had found Red-Beard's miniature imitation of the ravine above Lattash very useful.

Sorgan let the others go on ahead and motioned to Skell. 'I think maybe you'd better stay here, cousin,' he said. 'I don't think it'd be a good idea for our people to start wandering around on the beach or running around in any nearby villages. We don't want the same sort of foolishness happening around here that you came up against when you first reached Lattash, do we?'

'Not even a little bit,' Skell agreed. 'I'll pass the word to the other Maag ship-captains that you want everybody to stay on board their ships for right now. We don't really know just exactly where we'll be fighting this war anyway, so there's a fair chance that we'll have to sail off to some other part of this region, and it'd take quite a while to drag the sailors back to their ships if we were to just turn them loose.'

'*That's* for certain sure,' Sorgan agreed.

Skell rowed his skiff back on out to the *Shark*, and then he sent Grock and Baldar out to advise the other Maag ship-captains that Sorgan had decided that the sailors should all remain on board their ships. Then he went on over to the *Lark* to advise his brother that they'd probably be moving before too long.

'Cousin Sorgan seems to be getting just a bit more clever,' Torl noted as the two of them stood at the stern of the *Lark* admiring the gentle sky of evening. 'We might not have to flog half the ship-captains in the fleet this time.'

'I didn't make too many friends that day,' Skell conceded, 'but if I *hadn't* flogged those idiots, the bowmen in that village would have killed everybody in the fleet.'

'Who's that coming back to the beach?' Torl asked, pointing at a black-leather-clad Trog who seemed to be dragging another Trog down the trail that led to the shore.

Skell peered through the fading light. 'I think that's Padan,' he said.

'Why's he dragging that other one behind him?'

'How should I know? Maybe one of the Trogs broke some of the rules.'

'You could be right about that, Skell. The Trogs have rules for just about everything – how many times your heart's supposed to beat, how often you're allowed to blink, when you're supposed to breathe – all those terribly important things that whoever's in charge decides for every soldier in the whole silly army.'

'They *are* just a bit picky about things, aren't they?' Skell agreed. 'It's probably nothing very important, but maybe we should row on over there and ask Padan what happened.'

Padan was just coming up out of the hold when Skell pulled his skiff up alongside of the wide-beamed Trog ship. 'Ho, Padan,' Skell called. 'Is there something afoot that we ought to know about?'

'We just had a stroke of good luck is about all, Skell,' Padan replied with a broad grin.

'We struck gold, maybe?' Torl asked.

'Well, sort of. Did you two get to know that arrogant ex-priest Jalkan at all during that war up in the ravine to the east of Lattash?'

'Well enough not to want to have anything more to do with him,' Torl replied.

'You know, I think just about everybody who's ever met that scrawny rascal feels exactly the same way about him. Anyway, Veltan's best friend in the wheat fields near his castle is that farmer called Omago, and he's married to a beautiful woman who's probably the best cook in the whole wide world. We were all studying Veltan's map when Omago's wife came into the map-room to tell us that supper was ready. Jalkan ogled her a bit, and then he made some off-color remarks that almost made Commander Narasan faint dead away. Omago the farmer flattened Jalkan with a good solid punch right straight in the mouth that scattered teeth all over the place.'

'I'm sorry we weren't there to see that,' Torl said.

'It gets better,' Padan said with a broad grin. 'Jalkan started screaming about punishing the farmer for his lack of respect for somebody who ranks just a step or two below God Himself, but then Commander Narasan jerked his divinity out from under him by revoking his commission right there on the spot. The commander ordered me to chain the little rascal and then kick him in the backside every step of the way back here to the beach.'

'If your foot gets tired, I'd be happy to take over for you, Padan,' Torl offered. 'Between the three of us, we could probably spend the next week or so kicking Jalkan back and forth between the castle and the beach.'

Skell pursed his lips. 'We could even make bets on something like that,' he suggested.

'I never pass up an opportunity to make a good bet,' Padan said. 'We'd probably have to set up a few rules, though – so much for the longest kick, and a side bet for the highest one.'

'It'd give us something to do beside standing around watching the tides rise and fall,' Torl added. 'When you get right down to it, though, it'll probably start to get tiresome after a while. When it stops being fun, we might want to consider just giving him a decent burial and let it go at that.'

'But he's not dead yet, Torl,' Padan objected.

'So?'

Sorgan called Skell into the round room where the map was to tell him that a shepherd called Nanton would show the way to get around the Falls of Vash. 'Narasan and I've decided that you'd probably be the best one to lead the scouting party, Skell,' he said.

'What else is new and different, cousin?' Skell grumbled.

'Don't be such a grouch, Skell. Just look the country up there over and see if you can spot the most likely invasion route. Then pick the best places for us to build forts to hold the enemies off.'

'And were you going to show me how to pull on my shirt as well, cousin?'

'Oh, quit!' Sorgan growled.

'Does this happen very often?' Narasan asked with an amused expression.

'All the time,' Sorgan replied, rolling his eyes upward. 'Skell thinks that he's funny, but I quit laughing a long time ago.'

'How long do you think it'll take Gunda to get here with the rest of your army?'

'It's a little hard to say for sure, Sorgan. I left a very reliable man in charge of the bulk of the army – Sub-Commander Andar. He'll know what needs to be done as soon as Gunda tells him that it's time to move out. I think his big problem will be finding enough ships to bring eighty thousand men up here. That sort of leaves things up in the air for right now. I'm sure that Gunda will find some way to get the information up here to us once he knows how much longer it's going to take.'

Sorgan shrugged. 'I'm sure we'll be able to keep busy in the meantime. Veltan's map is just a bit on the teenie-weenie side, so I'll feel a bit more confident after Skell's looked at the real thing.'

'Teenie-weenie?' Narasan sounded a bit amused.

'I think I might have spent too much time in the vicinity of Eleria up in the ravine,' Sorgan said, shaking his head.

'All right, then,' Skell said. 'We don't really have to wait for Gunda to get here. Torl and I'll go on ahead and scout things out. Give us a couple of days and we'll have a fair idea of where we should set up the forts. Then the rest of the men can come on up and start laying down the bases for those forts. By the time Gunda gets here, the bases will be in place and Gunda's men can take it from there.'

'What do you think, Narasan?' Sorgan asked.

'It sounds good to me,' Narasan agreed.

'You'll probably need about five ship-crews when you go on up there, wouldn't you say?' Sorgan asked Skell.

'Get serious, cousin,' Skell growled. 'Torl's crew and mine are already too many men. I'm not leading an invasion, you know. I'm just going up there to have a look around, and the fewer men I've got trailing behind me, the faster I'll be able to move. I know what needs to be done, Sorgan, so just stay out of my way and let me do it.'

Skell and Torl set sail at first light the following morning, primarily to get clear of the bay *before* cousin Sorgan woke up and started adding more and more ships to the advance party. For some reason, Sorgan always seemed to believe that 'more is better'. They'd argued about that quite often when they were younger men.

Skell and his brother thought that it would take about two days to reach the mouth of the River Vash, and Skell spent most of his time getting better acquainted with the archer called Longbow. A number of things had happened in the ravine leading down to the village of Lattash that had demonstrated that Longbow knew more about their enemies than anybody else, and that made him extremely valuable.

It was late in the afternoon on their first day out when Skell joined Longbow at the bow of the *Shark*. 'I spent most of my time building that fort when we were trying to block off that ravine,' Skell said, 'so I don't really know all that much about the people we're fighting. I've heard that you know more about them than anybody else, so I think you might be the one I should talk with. Is there anything I should know?'

'The most important thing you should know about the creatures of the Wasteland is that they have no sense of fear,' Longbow replied.

'They're brave, you mean?'

'I wouldn't think of it as "brave", Skell. "Stupid" might come closer, but that's not quite correct either. As individuals, they don't have anything at all that we'd call intelligence. They just do exactly what the Vlagh wants them to do – even if it's impossible.'

'I'd say that "stupid" comes pretty close, then.'

Longbow shrugged. 'Their minds don't work the way ours do – probably because they don't *have* separate minds. What one of them knows, they all know, and their decisions are made by that group awareness. The center of that awareness is "That-Called-the-Vlagh". The Vlagh makes the decisions, and a servant of the Vlagh will keep trying to carry out those decisions, even when it's the only one left alive.'

'That gets right back to "stupid", doesn't it?'

'*We* might look at it that way, but *they* don't. Of course, they don't know that they can die. As far as they know, they'll live forever, and nothing can possibly kill them.'

'How did you manage to figure all this out, Longbow?'

'I'm a hunter, Skell, and the first thing a hunter learns is to think the way whatever he's hunting thinks. If he can't, he doesn't eat very often.' Longbow looked out over the choppy water ahead of the *Shark's* bow. 'You spend most of your time out here on the face of Mother Sea, don't you?'

'That's what sailors do, Longbow.'

'Have you spent very much of your time fishing?'

'Some, yes. Why?'

'When you're fishing, you bait your fishhook with something you think the fish will want to eat, don't you?'

'If I want to catch any, yes.'

'Then a good fisherman has learned to think like a fish, wouldn't you say?'

'I'd never thought of it exactly like that, but you're probably right,' Skell conceded. 'What sort of bait works best when you're fishing for snake-men?'

'I've had fairly good luck with people,' Longbow replied with a faint smile.

'*People?*' Skell said sharply.

'Don't get excited, Skell. If you put people out in front of the creatures of the Wasteland, they'll rush out into the open to try to kill them, and that makes it easy to hit them with arrows. The servants of the Vlagh don't have any idea of what an arrow is, so they don't understand why all of their friends are falling down. There are other ways to do it, but using people for bait seems to work best. Floods and volcanos work fairly well, but waking them up can get a little complicated. It's better to keep things simple.'

They reached the mouth of the River Vash late in the afternoon of the following day, and Omago's bearded friend, Nanton, was waiting on the beach just to the north of the river mouth. Skell and Omago went ashore in one of the *Shark's* skiffs, and Omago introduced Skell to their guide.

'Are all the men on both boats going to come with us?' Nanton asked Skell.

'Ships,' Skell corrected absently.

'What?'

'We call them ships, not boats.'

'What's the difference?'

'I'm not really sure,' Skell admitted. 'I was sort of thinking about this when we were sailing up here from Veltan's place, and it seems to me that a dozen or so men might be enough for our first run on up to the top. All we're really going up there for is to take a quick look around. The thing that's *really* important will be marking the trail so that the armies that'll be coming along later will know how to get up there. Have you come across any enemies yet?'

'None so far this summer,' the shepherd said. 'There were some of them nosing around early last spring asking questions, but I haven't encountered any up on top yet.'

'Can they actually talk?' that surprised Skell a bit.

'The ones I came across could. They claimed that they were traders, but I didn't believe them. I think they were just snooping around.'

Skell squinted at the river. 'How far upstream is that waterfall?' he asked.

'About twice as far as it is from here to the house of Veltan. We won't be going that far upriver from the streambed that leads up to the top, but the river calms down after she gets out of the mountains.'

'Good. We'll be able to row my ship and my brother's on up to that streambed, and I'll take ten or fifteen men on up to the top. We'll look around a bit, and then I'll send somebody back down to lead the rest of the men on up there to join us.'

'It'll probably work out better that way,' Nanton agreed.

'Is your flock up there, Nanton?' Omago asked.

'For the time being, yes. If there's going to be a war up there, though, I'll move them to a safer meadow.'

'It sounds to me like you're very familiar with those mountains,' Skell said.

'I've spent most of my life up there – at least in the summer. I bring my flock back down in the autumn.'

'Wouldn't it be easier if you just kept them down here in the lowland?' Skell asked him.

'Maybe, but the grass up in the mountains is better, and I don't have to spend all my time chasing the sheep away from farmland. Farmers always seem to get very worried when they see a few hundred hungry sheep coming over the hill.'

'I wonder why,' Skell said with no hint of a smile.

3

❧

It took them a couple of days to row the two ships up the gently flowing River Vash to the place where Nanton's little stream came down out of the mountains. Skell anchored the *Shark* on the upriver side of the stream and then rowed his skiff over to the *Lark* to confer with his brother. 'I'm catching a strong feeling that Omago's friend doesn't really want a crowd trailing along behind when he leads us on up to the area we need to scout, so I think I'd better keep things fairly tight. Nanton knows the lay of the land up there, so he can save me a lot of time if I stay on the good side of him.'

'We're going back to "don't offend the natives", I take it,' Torl noted.

'Let's keep things quiet as long as we can. Why don't you stay here? Put the men to work building docks along the bank of the river here. There'll be a lot of ships coming upriver before long, and they'll be unloading sizeable numbers of men. Let's make it easy enough so that we don't have Trog ships backed up all the way down to the river mouth.'

'Who all are you going to take with you?'

'Nanton, of course, and Omago,' Skell replied, squinting at the narrow little stream, 'and I definitely want Longbow and Red-Beard. Narasan wants Padan to mark the trail, so he'll go along, too.'

'That's all? Aren't you cutting it just a little fine, Skell?'

Skell shrugged. 'We're just going up there to look, little brother,' he said. 'I'll take Grock as well – just in case I need to get word back down here to you if things start getting wormy up there, and we'll round it out with Rabbit and Keselo. Those two work with Longbow very well, so they might be useful. I want to move fast and quiet, and I think that'll be as many men as I'll need.'

'That's pretty skimpy, Skell.'

'It's enough to get the job done, little brother. Let's not clutter things up if we don't have to.'

Skell and his small party started up the narrow gorge at first light the following morning and it soon became quite obvious that this would *not* be just a casual stroll. The brush along the sides of the little brook was dense, and the tall evergreen trees blocked out the sunshine to the point that Skell's party moved in what was almost a perpetual twilight. Grock, the *Shark*'s first mate, had been clever enough to bring along a coil of rope, and they'd gone no more than a quarter of a mile before it became quite obvious that they'd be using it frequently, since the brook tumbled rather than flowed. It seemed to Skell that there was a frothy little waterfall every fifty feet or so. Fortunately, Rabbit was a very agile little fellow, and he could scramble up those rocky spots with Grock's rope coil slung over his shoulder, tie the end to a large tree and then drop the rope to the men behind him. It seemed to Skell that by midday he'd spent more time going up the rope hand over hand than he'd spent walking. 'How in the world can you drive a herd of sheep up through all of this?' he asked the shepherd.

The bearded Nanton smiled faintly. 'When a sheep *really* wants something – fresh grass, or a female sheep who's lonesome for company – he can come very close to climbing up a sheer rock face. Of course, he's got four feet and very sharp hooves.'

'You like your sheep, don't you?'

'Tending sheep is much easier than digging and planting, and I've always felt that "easy" is nicer than "hard". Wouldn't you agree?'

'I'd go along with you on that,' Skell agreed, 'but it seems to me that all this clambering over rocks and climbing up a rope goes off in the direction of "hard", don't you think?'

'It's better than doing honest work, wouldn't you say?' Nanton replied mildly.

The sun started to move on down toward the western horizon a few hours later, and Skell called a halt at that point. 'Let's call it a day,' he said. 'I don't think crashing around in the bushes would be a very good idea after dark. There *might* not be any bug-people in the vicinity, but let's not take any chances.'

'Good thinking,' Rabbit agreed.

The small group of scouts rose early the following morning, and after they'd eaten, they continued the tiresome business of going hand over hand up Grock's coil of rope. Padan occasionally looped bits of yellow twine around the limbs of various trees and bushes to mark the path for Nanton's army that'd soon be coming this way.

'This is just a suggestion, Captain Skell,' the young Trog called Keselo said about mid-morning, 'but I think Commander Narasan's army could move up through this gorge more quickly if we were to string ropes up along the steeper places. That coil of rope Grock brought along has been very useful.'

'Grock knows what he's doing, that's for sure,' Skell agreed. He looked around. 'Where is he, by the way?'

'He told Omago that he was going to see if he could find a more open way for us to follow on up to the top. I take it that he doesn't particularly like bushes.'

'I'm not all that fond of them myself.'

'They provide a good place to hide if you want to ambush an enemy,' Keselo said, 'but that's about all they're good for.'

'Which side is Grock looking at?'

'He jumped across the creek and went up toward the wall of the gorge on the other side. I don't really think he'll have much luck, though. There seems to be a lot of loose stones at the foot of that wall over there.'

'He might get lucky,' Skell said. 'We can hope, I guess. My hands are starting to get just a little tender from all this going hand over hand up that rope of his.'

'I think he's coming back right now, Captain Skell,' Keselo said, shading his eyes. 'He's running!' the young Trog exclaimed. 'If he happens to trip and fall, he'll bounce most of the way down to the river!'

Skell glared up the steep slope. 'That idiot!' he exclaimed. 'Grock!' he shouted. 'Slow down! You'll break your neck!'

'I just found gold, Cap'n!' Grock shouted back. '*Gold!* There's tons of it up there in that rock wall!'

'Stay right where you are!' Skell commanded. 'I'm coming up!' He motioned to Keselo. 'Let's go up and have a look,' he said.

'Aye, Cap'n,' Keselo replied in a fair imitation of an ordinary Maag seaman's customary response.

They both pushed their way through the dense brush, waded across the brook and went up the other side.

Grock was trembling violently, and he was licking a dark stone with his tongue.

'Let me have a look,' Skell told him.

'Aye,' Grock replied, handing Skell the dark-colored rock fragment. 'It's right here, Cap'n,' he said pointing at a gleaming yellow fleck in the surface of the rock. 'I'd a-walked right on past it, but a little gust of wind set one of them fir-trees t' wavin' back and forth, and the sunlight came a flashin' off this speck like you wouldn't believe. Then I backed off just a bit and took a good look. That rock wall up there's got bright yellow specks flashin' all over it. It might take a bit of work t' chop all of them outta that wall, but it'd shore be worth the trouble.'

Skell hadn't realized that he'd been holding his breath, and he let it out almost explosively.

'Ah – Captain Skell,' the young Trog said. 'I think that maybe we should have Rabbit take a look at this. He knows more about metal than anybody I've ever met, so I'm sure he'll be able to tell us if this is *really* gold.'

'What else *could* it be?' Grock demanded. 'It's yellow, and that means gold, doesn't it?'

'Rabbit!' Skell bellowed. 'I need you! Come here!'

The small, wiry smith from the *Seagull* came running up the steep slope. 'Have we got trouble of some kind?' he asked.

'Maybe,' Skell replied, 'or maybe not.' He held out the stone Grock had given him. 'Take a look at this and tell us what you think. Is that yellow speck gold, maybe? Or is it something else?'

'It's easy enough to verify,' Rabbit said. He took his knife out of its sheath and lightly flicked the point across the yellow spot, sending out a bright spark. 'I'm sorry, Cap'n Skell, but it's *not* gold. It's pretty enough, I guess, but gold doesn't spark like that when you scrape it with a knife. I've heard about this, but it's the first time I've ever seen any of it.'

'Are you absolutely certain sure?' Grock asked with a note of bitter disappointment in his voice.

'There's a quick way to find out,' Rabbit said. 'Has anybody got a gold coin in his purse?'

Keselo handed the little smith a fair-sized coin.

Rabbit flicked the point of his knife across the edge of the coin. 'No sparks, Cap'n Skell,' Rabbit pointed out. 'From what I've heard, that yellow fleck Grock found is a kind of iron ore that's been contaminated with something that's got a yellow cast to it. There's a story that's been going around Weros for years about a fellow who found a large deposit of this particular ore. He spent about ten years hacking it out of a stone face, and he was absolutely positive that he was getting richer every day. When he finally found out that it wasn't really gold, he went down to the bay and drowned himself.'

Skell gave the young Trog Keselo a hard look. 'You knew right off that this wasn't gold, didn't you?'

'I was fairly sure that it wasn't, Captain Skell,' Keselo admitted. 'But I thought that Rabbit here was the man best qualified to decide one way or the other. I think this is what's called "iron pyrite". It's basically iron, but it's been contaminated with sulphur. I've heard that people in some places use it instead of flint when they want to start a fire.'

'It's worthless, then?' Skell asked, growing even more disappointed.

'Maybe not completely worthless. It *is* basically iron, and iron's worth *something*, and you *can* start fires with it.'

'Oh, well,' Skell sighed. 'I guess we'll have to go back to doing honest work, then. I'm sorry, Grock, but it looks to me like we didn't get rich today.'

As they started back down the hill to the brook, Skell seemed to feel a slight prickly sensation on the back of his neck, and he looked around sharply. He was almost positive that somebody was watching them, but there was nobody out in plain sight, so he shrugged it off.

'They aren't the brightest animals in the world,' Nanton admitted to Longbow as the pair of them followed the steep, twisting stream-bed up into the mountains with Skell close behind them, 'but they're very affectionate, and their wool's quite valuable.'

'Doesn't it get just a bit boring sitting on a hill and spending whole days watching them eat grass?'

'Boring's the pleasant part of the life of a shepherd, Longbow,' Nanton replied. 'It's when things get *un*-boring that I start to wish that I'd gone into a different line of work. Dealing with a pack of hungry wolves can get *very* exciting.'

'Isn't it just a bit difficult to aim a sling?'

'Not if you practice every day. After a while, the sling almost becomes an extension of your hand.'

'Ah,' Longbow said, 'and you never miss when you send a rock out to touch a wolf or a deer, do you?'

'Not that I can recall, no. How did you know that, Longbow?'

'I have much the same link with my bow. It's a bit difficult to explain that to people, isn't it?'

'I stopped trying to explain it years ago,' Nanton replied. 'Of course, it doesn't come up very often. The life of a shepherd is fairly solitary, so I don't have people standing around watching me when I chase off a pack of wolves.'

'Don't you just kill them when they start to pester your sheep?'

'Not too often. Usually I hit a wolf in the haunch. That sends him off through the tall grass yelping and bawling. That frightens the other wolves, and they all run off. There are five or six wolf-packs in that basin up on top, and I've taught them all to stay away from my sheep. Wolves are very clever animals, and it doesn't take them very long to learn that some things are dangerous.'

'Are there any other animals in that area?'

Nanton spread his hands. 'Just the usual ones – deer, birds, rabbits and squirrels, and then there are the bats that come out in the evenings to eat bugs.'

'Now there's a thought,' Longbow said with a broad grin. 'Bats eat bugs, don't they? Since our enemies are at least part bug, maybe we should have a talk with the bats and advise them that supper's coming up out of the Wasteland.'

'I don't know that I've ever seen a bat quite that big, Longbow,' Nanton replied, 'and I don't speak fluent batish, do you?'

'Maybe we should have a word with Veltan about that. If he were to fly around with the bats for a week or so, maybe he'd be able to pick up their language and form an alliance with them.'

'It might be worth a try,' the shepherd agreed. 'I'll take all the help I can get.'

Skell dropped back a bit. It appeared that Longbow wasn't *quite* as icy as everybody seemed to believe he was. The casual conversation between the shepherd and the archer had been very revealing. Skell knew that Longbow and Red-Beard were close friends, and he was also aware of the friendship that existed between Longbow, Rabbit, and Keselo. Evidently, Longbow was now opening a door to the shepherd as well. Skell wasn't quite certain just exactly why, but the icy archer apparently felt that the shepherd might be very valuable during the current war. It was something to think about, Skell admitted.

4

◆━◆━◆

They reached the top of the narrow stream-bed about noon on the following day, and Skell was a bit surprised when he saw the pleasant-looking basin that lay there. Nanton the shepherd had spoken of a 'meadow' up here, but Skell had never before seen a meadow quite so large. It was easily ten miles from the southern end of the basin to the northern ridge. The grass was lush and green and there were a few clumps of trees here and there. Skell hadn't completely understood what Veltan had described as 'the geyser' that was the main source of the River Vash, so he was awed by the tremendous amount of water spurting almost a hundred feet up into the air. Evidently, there were some very interesting things going on under the ground.

The basin was surrounded on three sides by rugged mountain ridges. There was a sharp depression in the south ridge where the suddenly released water from the geyser plunged on down as the Falls of Vash.

The ridge to the north had a much wider gap in the middle, and Skell was fairly certain that the break in that ridge would be very significant. Veltan's map had indicated that the Wasteland lay to the north of this basin, and that break would almost certainly be the invasion route.

'Pretty, isn't it?' Padan said, looking out across the meadow.

'Not bad, I guess,' Skell agreed. Then he pointed toward the break in the north ridge. 'We might want to look around this basin just a bit, but I think we'd better concentrate on that area up to the north. Our enemies will be coming from that direction anyway, and that break in the ridge looks to me to be about a mile wide. Cousin Sorgan and your commander should be coming along in a few days, but I don't think we'll have enough people up here to block that break off until your friend Gunda gets here with the bulk of your army. If the enemy doesn't come charging up out of that desert until next month, we might be all right, but if it just happens to be next week, we could be in a lot of trouble.'

The break in the ridge-line appeared to have been the result of some fairly recent event, since the sheared-off rock faces still in place showed little or no signs of weathering. The slope leading up to the break from the desert below was cluttered with rubble, which hinted strongly that some sort of natural disaster had demolished the ridge-line.

'Do you get many earthquakes up here, Nanton?' Longbow asked the shepherd as they all stood looking down toward the Wasteland.

'Every now and then, yes,' Nanton replied. 'Usually, they aren't severe enough to break down these ridge-lines, though.'

Skell was squinting down the slope. 'It's sort of a shame that all those rocks rolled down the north side,' he observed. 'They'd be a lot more useful if they'd stayed closer.'

'I wouldn't give up on them yet, Skell,' Padan said thoughtfully.

'When Commander Narasan and your cousin Sorgan get up here with their men, they *could* build a series of breast-works across that slope, you know. That'd definitely slow our enemies down, and that'd give our people time to build a more substantial wall up here. Then we'll have a much better chance of holding the enemy back until Gunda gets here.'

'That reminds me of something I'd almost forgotten,' Skell said. 'Ho, Grock!' he called.

'Aye, Cap'n?' Grock replied.

'I want you to go on back down that creek-bed and tell my brother that I want him to put the men coming up here through that steep gorge before long, and they'll be able to come up a lot faster if we've got ropes in place – the way we did with that coil of rope you brought along when *we* came up. Tell my brother to set up several separate trails. If Narasan's army comes up through that gorge one man at a time, it'll take them all summer to get up here.'

'We'll do 'er that way, Cap'n,' Grock replied. Then he turned and went back across the meadow toward the creek-bed.

'There's something else we might want to think about Cap'n Skell,' Rabbit said. 'Longbow's archers are coming through the mountains to join up with us here, and once they're in place, the enemies won't pester the men working on the wall, because they'll be too busy dying.'

'He's got a point there, Skell,' Padan agreed. 'About the best we can do with spears and swords is bring things to a standstill. It'll take the archers to turn the tide.' He looked at Longbow. 'Can you give us some kind of idea of just when your friends will get here?'

Longbow scratched his cheek. 'Probably a couple of weeks,' he speculated. 'They're coming through the mountains, and that can make for slow going.'

'If cousin Sorgan and Commander Narasan sailed north when they *said* they were going to, they're probably anchored down at the mouth of that little creek already,' Skell said, 'so as soon as Grock gets down there and tells them the way things stand up here now, they'll start coming up. I'd say that they'll be here inside two days, and then they can get started on our main fort here. A lot of things are still up in the air, but if everybody's doing what he's *supposed* to be doing, we'll be in fair shape in two or three more days.'

The sun was going down behind the ragged mountain ridge to the west of the basin as they walked back toward the still-spouting geyser. Mountain sunsets were sort of pretty, maybe, but as far as Skell was concerned they were no match at all for sunsets out on the face of the rolling sea.

They built a fire some distance off from the geyser and Rabbit cooked a large pot of beans. The Omago stood up to put more wood on the fire, but he instinctively ducked as a bat came swooping in out of the twilight. 'I *wish* they'd stop doing that!' he complained.

'It's the fire, Omago,' Nanton explained. 'Firelight attracts bugs, and the bats are hungry.'

Longbow's head came up sharply, and he reached for his bow.

'Is something wrong?' Rabbit asked, rising to his feet.

'I'm not sure,' Longbow replied. 'There's something that isn't quite right.' He looked around, his face suddenly bleak. 'I think it might be time to take a closer look at the neighbors.' He drew an arrow out of the quiver slanting up over his shoulder, set the arrow in place, drew his bow and released it. The arrow went straight and true, and a dead bat fell to the ground some distance from the fire.

Longbow went over and picked the dead bat up by its wingtips and held it up to take a closer look. 'You'd better come here, friend Red-Beard,' he said in a grim tone of voice.

'Trouble?' Red-Beard asked, standing up.

'Look for yourself.' Longbow held out the dead bat.

Red-Beard flinched back. 'I think I'd better go see if I can find the archers,' he said tersely.

'What's the trouble?' Skell demanded.

'This is,' Longbow replied, turning to show Skell the dead bat.

Skell instinctively jerked back from the hideous creature. It had the wings of a bat, the usual fur-covered body and clawed feet, but its head was the head of a bee – or possibly an ant – with protruding mandibles jutting from its lower face. It also had bulging eyes and odd-looking feelers growing out of the top of its head.

'Don't touch it, friend Skell,' Red-Beard cautioned. 'I'm catching a faint smell of venom.'

'Fangs and stingers again? Like the snake-men?'

'I'm not really sure,' Red-Beard replied, 'but I don't think it'd be a good idea to probe around with your bare hands.' He looked at his friend. 'It looks to me like they've beaten us to the battlefield again, doesn't it, Longbow? I was sure we were ahead of them this time. What did they do that made you realize that they weren't just ordinary bats?'

'They weren't really flying all that well, friend Red-Beard, and I saw a couple of them fly right past several flying bugs. A real bat wouldn't have done that.'

'How can we fight off a flying enemy?' Padan exclaimed.

'Longbow can shoot them right out of the sky,' Rabbit told the frightened Trog. 'I saw him shoot down a whole flock of geese once.'

'I wouldn't waste any time, friend Red-Beard,' Longbow said. 'It's fairly obvious that the Vlagh's been tampering with the natural order of things again, so we might need the archers *here* and not back in the mountains before long.' He paused briefly, and a faint frown touched his face. 'Now that I've had a moment or two to give this a bit of thought, things might not be as bad as they seemed at first. We didn't see any of these particular creatures during the war in Zelana's Domain, and that suggests that they're a new experiment. If that's true, they're most likely still groping around, trying to discover why they're here and what they're supposed to do.'

'Wouldn't that also mean that they don't know anything about fighting wars?' Rabbit asked.

'They won't know how *we* fight wars,' Longbow agreed. 'If this is really a new life-form, it's going to take it at least twenty hatches before it fully understands what it's capable of doing. They don't live long enough to reach that level of understanding in one generation. I'd say that about all they're capable of during the *current* hatch will be flying around and watching us.'

'Scouts, you mean?' Skell asked.

'Exactly. They won't live long enough to go much farther. Our shaman, One-Who-Heals, explained some things about the servants of the Vlagh to me quite a long time ago. They only live for about six weeks after they reach their final form – not long enough to learn very much. Their knowledge accumulates over the generations, so the ones we'll encounter later will be much more clever than the ones we've seen so far.'

'Maybe we should hide this dead one, then,' Rabbit suggested, looking around quickly.

'I didn't quite follow you there, Rabbit,' Keselo said.

'If they don't know what arrows can do to them, they'll start making a lot of mistakes, won't they? If they think a bow is just a stick, they won't pay much attention when a couple hundred archers stand up and draw their bows. We could have dead bats raining down out of the sky for a week or two if they don't understand what's *really* happening.'

'Good point,' Skell said. 'Let's pile some brush on top of this dead one and then act like nothing important just happened.'

'I'm not sure if this would work, Cap'n Skell,' Rabbit said, 'but it just came to me that maybe fish net would keep those bat-things from getting close enough to bite us, and if they get all tangled up in the net, we could go around when the sun comes up and give each one a poke with our poisoned spears. That should thin them out at least a little bit, wouldn't you say?'

'Nice idea, Rabbit,' Padan said, 'but where are we going to get that much fish net?'

'That's not really much of a problem, Padan,' Skell said. 'Every Maag longship has fish-netting on board. If we can catch fish, we don't have to sail back to port to buy more beans. I'll talk it over with cousin Sorgan when he gets up here, but after he sees that dead bug-bat, I'm sure he'll go along with Rabbit's idea. The notion of a flying enemy probably won't sit any better with him than it does with me.'

Skell's brother came up out of the narrow creek bed about midmorning the following day and joined Skell's scouting party near the geyser. 'Now *that's* something you don't see very often,' he said, pointing at the geyser. 'I can't *remember* the last time I saw a waterspout on dry land.'

'Strange things happen in strange country, Torl,' Skell said. 'Are your men stringing ropes up along that creek?'

'They're only about an hour behind me, and cousin Sorgan and the Trogs aren't very far behind *them*.'

'Good. We're probably going to need some forts in place before too much longer.'

'Have you spotted any enemies yet?'

'Oh, yes. We didn't *know* that they were enemies right at first, but they're out there.'

'Boring holes through the ground again?'

'Not that we know about. I suppose it's possible, but the only ones we've seen so far have been flying.'

'You're not serious!'

'I'm afraid so, Torl. That Vlagh thing's been experimenting again, and now we've got bats watching everything we do.'

'*Bats?*' Torl said incredulously.

'It didn't make *me* very happy either, Torl. We might just have to hole up until the archers get here – at least after the sun goes down. We haven't seen any of them in the daytime yet.'

'Are they poisonous – like those snake-men we came up against back in the ravine?'

'Red-Beard says they are. Longbow killed one of them so we could take a look at it, and Red-Beard told me he was catching the smell of venom when he got close to it.'

'How can we possibly hide from them after the sun goes down?' Torl's voice was just a bit shrill.

'Calm down, Torl,' Skell told him. 'That clever little smith from the *Seagull* has already come up with an easy answer. All we're really going to need is fish net, and every Maag ship in the fleet's got about a half mile of fishnet stored in the hold. When one of those bat-bugs gets all tangled up in the netting, he won't be a problem any more.'

'Sometimes that little Rabbit fellow's so smart that he makes me sick.'

'Just be glad that he's on our side, little brother,' Skell said.

5

❧

Cousin Sorgan and Narasan the Trog came up out of the narrow gorge about noon that day and joined Skell's small group of scouts near the geyser. 'Ho, Skell!' Sorgan shouted, 'have you seen any snake-men up here yet?'

'Not a one, cousin,' Skell replied.

'We got up here before they did, then,' Sorgan said.

'I wouldn't start celebrating just yet, Sorgan,' Skell said. 'I think we might end up missing those snake-men before this is all over.'

'What's that supposed to mean?'

'We've got a whole new breed of enemies this time, Sorgan. These enemies know how to fly.'

'That's not funny, Skell.'

'Do you see me laughing, cousin?'

'You're just making this up.'

'Not even a little bit. We've got a dead one under that brush pile over by that waterspout. It's got bat wings and a bug head. Come and look for yourself. There were dozens of bats flapping around one night, and Longbow had one of those hunches he gets all the time, and he picked one of the bats out of the sky with an arrow. As it turned out, that hunch of his probably saved a lot of lives. When it's flapping around in the dark, it looks pretty much like an ordinary bat, but when you take a closer look, "ordinary" goes right out the window. It's a bat with a bug's head, and just to add to the fun, it's got a strong smell of that venom the snake-men in the ravine had during the war we fought last spring. We kept the carcass, so you can look for yourself.'

Skell led them to the temporary camp near the geyser and uncovered the bug-bat's carcass. It was starting to get just a bit ripe, so Skell moved around to the upwind side. 'As you can see,' he told them, 'It looks like an ordinary bat – or a mouse with wings – right up until you get to its head. That's when "bug" takes over.'

'Are you certain that it's venomous?' Narasan asked dubiously.

'Red-Beard told us that he could smell the venom,' Skell replied. 'I'll take his word for it. I'm *not* going to touch the silly thing with my bare hands just to make sure.'

'Have they killed any of your men?' Narasan asked.

'Not so far. Longbow thinks that these bug-bats are just scouting for the time being. Bats *would* make good scouts, wouldn't they? I'm *definitely* hoping that scouting around is all our enemy uses these things for. If the whole enemy army's nothing but bug-bats, we're in a lot of trouble. Just the thought of an enemy that knows how to fly makes my blood run cold. Rabbit came up with an idea that *might* work. He suggested that we might want to bring all of our fish nets up here and tent over any place where we'll be after the sun goes down with netting.'

'Maybe,' Narasan said a bit dubiously. 'How far is it to the most likely invasion route?'

'Just a few miles off to the north,' Skell replied. 'I think it might cause some problems, though. There *used* to be a ridge-line that had pretty much blocked off that slope that leads down to the

Wasteland, but quite a while back it seems that there was an earth-quake that opened a gap about a mile wide in the ridge. It'll take us a long time to build a wall that long, so things won't be nearly as easy as they were back in the ravine.'

'Let's go take a look,' Sorgan growled.

The Trog commander stood looking down at the littered slope leading down to the barren desert of the Wasteland. 'Depending on how much time we've got, we could use all that loose stone to build barriers that'd hold the enemy back long enough for us to build breast-works across this gap,' he suggested.

'Only if the enemies have to walk,' Sorgan replied. 'If they're snake men like the ones we came up against in the ravine, it might work, but if they can fly over the barriers, they'll be on top of us before we can even blink.' He looked around. 'Where *is* Longbow?' he demanded irritably.

'He told me this morning that he wanted to take a look at the ridge-line off to the west, Cap'n,' Rabbit said. 'I think he wants to make sure that the enemies can't slip around behind us like they did back in the ravine.'

Sorgan grunted. 'Did Red-Beard give you any kind of idea about how long it's likely to be until the archers get here?'

'Right after he saw the bug-bat, he took off running, Cap'n,' Rabbit said. 'He's going to hurry them along.'

'Good. We're going to need them, I think. Swords and spears won't be much good this time, I'm afraid.'

'The Trogs are better at building walls and forts than we are,' Skell told the scar-faced horseman Ekial. 'From what I've heard, they've got walls all over down there in the Land of Trog.'

'I thought they were called "Trogites". Why do you shorten it down to "Trog"?' Ekial asked.

'It's something my brother and I picked up from our papa. He seemed to think that "Trogite" was a term they'd invented to make themselves sound important. Papa didn't think much of the Trogs. What they call ships are a lot like floating washtubs. That made things a lot easier for us, though, since we could chase down any Trog ship afloat in about a half a day.'

'Why would you want to do that?'

'So that we could rob them of the gold they'd stolen from some people off to the west.'

'How is it that you're both on the same side in *this* war then?'

'Lady Zelana hired my cousin Sorgan to gather up a fleet and come here to the Land of Dhrall to fight a war for her.'

'She's Dahlaine's sister, isn't she?'

'That's what I've heard, yes.'

'What's it like spending all your time out there on the water?' Ekial asked.

'It's the best kind of life there is,' Skell told him. 'When you've got a good ship and a good following wind, it's almost the same as flying. The air's clean, and the waves sparkle in the sun like jewels.'

'You're starting to sound poetic, Skell,' Ekial said with a faint smile.

'Life at sea tends to do that to people.'

'What made you decide to come here to a place where you'd have to fight a war on dry land, then?'

'Money, Ekial. Lady Zelana's got more gold than she can even count, and cousin Sorgan brought about a hundred blocks of it to the Land of Maag to hire an army.'

'That sounds sort of familiar,' Ekial said. 'Dahlaine did much the same thing when he came to Malavi to hire horsemen.'

'I don't think I've ever seen a horse,' Skell admitted. 'I've heard that they're a lot like cows – except that they don't have horns.'

'There are quite a few other differences,' Ekial said. 'Horses love to run, and a good horse can run all day if you ask him to. The Land of Malavi doesn't have very many trees, so it's all grassland that goes on for hundreds of miles in every direction. In a peculiar way, I suppose we feel much the same about the meadowland as you Maags feel about the sea.'

'Except that you don't get wet when you fall off your horse, do you?'

'Not very often, no.'

Then there was a sudden blinding flash of light and a shattering crash of thunder, and Veltan was there. 'Where's Narasan?' he demanded.

'The last time I saw him, he and Sorgan were looking around down there on the slope.' Skell turned and shouted at one of the men building the breastwork. 'You there! Go find Narasan and tell him that Veltan wants to see him!'

'Aye, Cap'n,' the sailor called back, running off down the slope.

'Is something wrong?' Ekial asked Veltan.

'We've got trouble on down south,' Veltan said tersely. 'There's a whole fleet of Trogite ships landing on the southern beaches, and I don't think they're friendly.'

Skell dispatched runners to bring most of the significant people to the gap overlooking the Wasteland, while Veltan paced back and forth muttering curses under his breath.

'What's this all about, Skell?' Sorgan demanded when he arrived.

'There's trouble in the wind, cousin,' Skell replied tersely.

'What else is new and different?'

'Don't try to be funny, Sorgan,' Skell snapped. 'This is serious business. Now we've got *two* invasions to deal with instead of just one.'

'That went by a little fast, Skell. Why don't you give me some details?'

'Veltan just got here, and he wants to talk to all of us. I'll let him describe what's happening. *He* saw what was going on, but *I* didn't. Let's get it right the first time, for a change.'

By the time the others had all reached Skell's temporary camp, Veltan had managed to get his temper under control. 'All right, gentlemen,' he began, 'after you'd all left to come up here, I received some very disturbing news from the south coast of my Domain, and I went on down there to have a look for myself. Evidently, there are some people down in the Trogite Empire who are very interested in the Land of Dhrall, and they've come here to investigate. A huge fleet of Trogite ships is anchored in the large bay between two of the peninsulas on the south coast, and the men from that fleet have occupied several coastal villages and captured almost all of the inhabitants. Most of the men from those fleets appear to be soldiers wearing red uniforms, but there are others who evidently *aren't* soldiers, because they're dressed in black robes, and they aren't carrying weapons of any kind.'

'Priests,' Narasan said in a bleak tone of voice, 'and the soldiers in red uniforms are members of church armies.'

'That explains a few things I didn't quite understand,' Veltan said. 'Anyway, the soldiers have built a number of fenced-in compounds and herded all of their captives into them. The ones in black robes have been going into those compounds to make speeches to my people.'

'That has a familiar sort of ring to it,' Padan said. 'Let me guess. The priests want to tell your people fairy tales about Amar – how wonderful he is and how everybody who doesn't fall down on his face every time he hears somebody mention Amar's name won't go to paradise after he dies. Is that pretty much the way it goes?'

'It's happened before, I gather,' Veltan said.

'It's been going around, yes,' Padan replied.

'As I recall, I mentioned the corruption of the Amarite church to you when you persuaded me to stop begging and go back to work, Veltan,' Narasan said. 'The church has turned corruption into an art form based entirely on raw greed. The thought that so much as a single penny might somehow get away from him sends a member of the clergy into deep mourning.'

'Excuse me, Commander,' the young Keselo said, 'but isn't it peculiar that the church fleet managed to find the passageway through the zone of floating ice not long after Jalkan – a former priest – escaped and stole Veltan's sloop?'

'Not really all *that* peculiar, Keselo,' Narasan replied bleakly.

'You should have killed *that* one when you had the chance, Narasan,' Skell said. 'My brother Torl had an interesting idea not long after you'd put Jalkan in chains. We'd been sort of joking around about taking turns kicking Jalkan up and down the beach. But after we decided that it might get tiresome after a while, Torl suggested that we could just go ahead and give him a decent burial – whether he was dead or not.'

'Interesting notion,' Narasan agreed. 'I *really* blundered that time. He looked at Veltan. 'Have the slave-ships arrived down there yet?'

'My brother told me about that,' Veltan replied. 'Right at first I thought he was joking.'

'I'm afraid not, Veltan,' Narasan replied. 'It's fairly traditional in these situations. The soldiers round up the native people, the priests tell the natives that the Trogite god will punish them if they resist, and then the slave-ships come by to pick up the people, take them back to the Empire and sell them to assorted Trogites who are too lazy to do their own work. That's been going on for centuries.'

'It's not going to happen that way *this* time,' Skell's cousin Sorgan said firmly. 'I just happen to have a large fleet of longships down on the coast, and as soon as I get back down there, I think I'll gather up that fleet and run on down to that big bay. The Trogites might have come here by ship, but I think I know of a way to arrange things so that they'll have to walk home.'

'Oh?' Narasan asked.

'It's called fire, Narasan,' Sorgan said with a wicked grin. 'I'll burn every Trogite ship in that bay right down to the waterline, and then I'll go on out and sink all those slave-ships.' He gave Veltan a slightly suspicious look. 'You knew this was going to happen all along, didn't you, Veltan?' he suggested. 'The fact that you've got the right man in the right place at the right time goes a long way past coincidence, it seems.'

'Well—' Veltan said, sounding a bit defensive.

'I thought so,' Sorgan said. 'I'm awfully sorry, Narasan,' he continued, 'but it sort of looks like I won't be able to help you very much in the war up here, because I've got a different war to fight on down along the south coast. I'll see to it that our second enemy won't come sneaking up behind you while you're busy up here, though.'

'Ah, well,' Narasan replied with mock regret. 'I think I'll be able to manage, Sorgan, but it just won't be the same without you.'

Then they both laughed.

All in all, Skell wasn't *too* disappointed that he wouldn't be allowed to fight the creatures of the Wasteland this time. He'd be going back down the gorge with cousin Sorgan and then sailing the *Shark* on down to the southern reaches of Veltan's Domain to fight a war at sea. Skell knew *how* to fight a land war if it was absolutely necessary, but he much preferred fighting at sea, and the prospect of burning an entire Trog fleet filled him with a warm little glow.

Then he felt another of those prickly twinges, and he was almost positive that somebody he couldn't see was watching him very closely. That took a lot of the fun out of his day.

THE SOUTH COAST

1

❧—◆—☙

Torl Jodanson of Kormo was somewhat relieved when cousin Sorgan volunteered to fight this particular war at sea. The mountains were pretty to look at, but Torl didn't really enjoy fighting wars in places where the enemies could hide behind trees or jump on him from behind. He much preferred open spaces where he could see just exactly what the enemy was doing. Then too, he was almost positive that the *Lark* would start feeling sulky if she wasn't allowed to join in the fun.

Some ships are like that.

After they'd eaten supper and strung out the fish nets to keep the bug-bats away, Skell raised a point that cousin Sorgan had possibly overlooked. 'I think we might have a problem, Sorgan,' he said.

'Oh? What's that?'

'That little creek-bed that comes up here from the river isn't very wide, and right now it's filled with Narasan's soldiers. They're coming up, and we want to go down. I suppose we *could* fight our way back down to the river, but that might irritate your friend Narasan just a bit.'

Sorgan frowned. 'You could be right, Skell,' he conceded.

'I'll go have a talk with that sheep-herder who showed us how to get up here,' Torl volunteered. 'He knows this country better than anybody else, so if there *is* some other way for us to get back down to the river, he'd be the one who'd know about it.'

'It makes sense, Sorgan,' Skell agreed with his brother.

Sorgan nodded. 'Why don't you go see what he has to say, Torl?' he agreed. 'We've got work to do down south, and we won't get much done sitting around twiddling our thumbs.'

'You know, cousin,' Torl said, 'I can't *remember* the last time I twiddled.'

'Go, Torl,' Sorgan told him wearily.

Omago's friend, Nanton the shepherd, had moved his flock to the southern end of the grassy plain, probably to keep the various soldiers up near the north end from poaching his sheep when suppertime rolled around, and Torl found him sitting beside a small fire and looking up at the starry sky.

'Doesn't it get awfully lonesome when you're the only person around for miles and miles?' Torl asked. 'I mean, there's nobody around to talk with, is there?'

'I can always talk to my sheep,' Nanton replied. 'They don't answer very often, but they listen fairly well. Is there something wrong?'

'Well,' Torl said, sitting down beside the fire, 'that little creek of yours was quite handy, but right now it's running bank full with Trog soldiers. Cousin Sorgan and the rest of us from the Land of Maag need to get back down to the river in a hurry.'

'The waterfall would get you back down in the blink of an eye,' the shepherd replied with no hint of a smile, 'but that might not be the best idea in the world.' He frowned slightly. 'There *is* a stream-bed a mile or so north of that one I showed your brother. I don't think anyone would want to come *up* that way, but if a man had enough rope, he could go down easy enough. It's not *quite* a sheer cliff, but it comes fairly close. Would climbing down a rope bother you and your crew very much?'

'We're sailors, Nanton. We spend at least half of our time climbing up and down ropes. How long do you think it might take us to get back down to the river?'

'Not much more than half a day. Downhill's always been faster than uphill.'

'Why, I *do* believe you're right, Nanton!' Torl exclaimed in mock surprise. 'Now why didn't *I* think of that?'

The seemingly humorless native actually laughed, and that brightened Torl's day. Making people laugh always made him feel very good.

Torl was about halfway back to the Maag encampment when he realized that just getting back down to the riverbank wouldn't solve *all* the problems they were likely to encounter, so he went looking for Commander Narasan.

The Trogite encampment was quite a bit more orderly than cousin Sorgan's disorganized cluster of tents and barricades. Trogs seemed to be obsessed with straight lines, for some reason. After Torl had asked a few soldiers where he might find Commander Narasan, he finally found the somewhat larger tent of cousin Sorgan's friend.

'We've got a bit of a problem, Commander,' Torl said after he'd entered the tent.

'Oh? What's troubling you, Captain Torl?'

'I hope this won't offend you,' Torl said, 'but your ships are cluttering up that river down below so much that cousin Sorgan's fleet won't be able to get close enough for us to get on board our ships once we get back down there. If we're going to block off that second invasion, we'll have to get on down south in a hurry. Is there some way you could order your ships to move aside so that we can get through?'

'Not personally, Torl,' Narasan replied, 'but I know of a way that *you'll* be able to take care of it.'

'You're going to promote me to the rank of a general in your army, Narasan?' Torl asked. 'I'm very flattered, of course, but won't that make the captains of your ships down there just a little suspicious?'

'Very funny, Torl,' Narasan said. 'All I really have to do is write down some orders, sign the piece of paper, and then give it to you. When you get down to the river, wave the paper around, and my ships will get out of your way.'

'What a brilliant idea!' Torl exclaimed. 'Now why didn't *I* think of that?'

'Do you *really* have to try to make a joke out of everything, Torl?' Commander Narasan said. 'Sometimes you're as bad as Red-Beard.'

'Laughter's good for people, Commander. I owe it to all my friends to make them laugh as much as I possibly can.'

'Why don't you go make Sorgan laugh for a while, then – or maybe your brother. I don't think Skell even knows *how* to laugh.'

'Oh, he knows *how*, Commander, but he doesn't like it. Our papa ordered him not to ever laugh, and Skell always does what papa tells him to – or *not* to do, in this case. I can make Skell laugh if I really have to, but I have to take off one of his boots first.'

'That went by just a little fast, Torl.'

'It's terribly hard to tickle the bottom of a man's foot when he's wearing boots, commander.'

* * *

Cousin Sorgan was talking with Veltan when Torl found him. 'I think I'll need to visit your map-room when we get back down to your house,' Sorgan said. 'We weren't paying very much attention to the southern part of your territory when we were studying your map before we came up here. We weren't expecting any trouble down there, since the snake-men would almost certainly be coming at us from the north. Do you have the doors of your house locked or anything?'

'We don't lock doors here in the Land of Dhrall, Sorgan.'

'How do you keep people from stealing everything you own, then?'

Veltan smiled, but he didn't answer.

'Oh,' Sorgan said, looking slightly embarrassed. 'Your people wouldn't do that, would they?'

'No, Captain. We don't steal from each other around here. We leave stealing things to the Vlagh and its underlings. The map-room's there. Look at it all you want to.'

The Maags of cousin Sorgan's fleet had found that the standard rope ladders had been very useful during the war in the ravine above Lattash, so they'd brought dozens of them along when they'd come up to the basin above the Falls of Vash. Nanton's description of the alternate route had been quite accurate, Torl noted, and the rope ladders turned out to be an almost perfect solution to what might have been a serious problem. It took Sorgan, Skell, and Torl less than half a day to reach the bottom of the almost perpendicular creek-bed.

Then they went along the riverbank looking for Padan's friend, Brigadier Danal.

'Absolutely not!' the lean, dark-haired officer replied when cousin Sorgan bluntly told him to get his ships out of the way.

'Ah – why don't you let me deal with this, cousin?' Torl suggested.

'He won't listen to you any more than he'll listen to me, Torl.'

'I just have to speak to him in a different voice, cousin Sorgan,' Torl replied mildly, handing Narasan's note to the stubborn Trog.

Danal read Narasan's written command twice, and then he gave up. 'It'll take about an hour to get all of our ships over to the other side of the river,' he said. 'Will that cause you any serious problems?'

'Not really,' Torl replied. 'Our men are still climbing down that steep stream-bed, but we'll need to have our ships up here so that we can get everybody on board. We'll probably be out of your way by mid-morning tomorrow.'

'I'd appreciate that, Captain Torl,' Danal said. He hesitated slightly. 'Is the commander absolutely certain that this second invasion will involve Trogites?' he asked.

'Our information came from a very reliable source, Brigadier. Evidently, the Trogite church is *very* interested in the Land of Dhrall.'

'The *church*?' Danal exclaimed.

'That's what our source told us.'

'Would you like some help?'

Torl grinned. 'I think we can handle it, my friend,' he replied. 'I gather that you're none too fond of church people?'

'Try the other side of "fond", Captain Torl. I *hate* the Amarite church!'

'We'll go on down there and spank them for you, then – and probably send them to their rooms without any supper.'

'I was thinking of something just a little more severe.'

'So was I, Danal. "Spank" doesn't even come close to what we're going to do to those rascals.'

'Good. I'll go get my ships out of your way.' Danal turned and went on down to the riverbank.

'What was that piece of paper all about, Torl?' Sorgan asked.

'It was an order from Commander Narasan, cousin. Did I forget to tell you that I had it tucked up my sleeve? I've *really* got to start paying closer attention to all these picky little details. It must have just slipped my mind.'

2

'You've got to pull the bow-string all the way back, Iron-Fist,' Torl chided his first mate. 'We'll be a good hundred paces away from those Trog ships when we go past them, and I want our burning arrows to hit the ships, not to come down in the water. Water doesn't burn very well.'

'Where in the world did you come up with this here idear, Cap'n?' Iron-Fist demanded.

'Have you ever seen the native called Longbow skewer a snake-man, Iron-Fist?'

'I was lucky enough t' be stuck here on board the *Lark* when ever'body went a-runnin' on up the ravine, Cap'n.'

'I wouldn't exactly call a broken leg a stroke of luck, old friend,' Torl disagreed.

'It kept me off the beach, Cap'n, an' around here that's about as lucky as a man's a-goin' t' get. Is this Longbow ever'body keeps a-talkin' about really *that* good?'

'He's probably the best in the whole wide world. Anyway, I'm sure that cousin Sorgan and big brother Skell will fall back on the idea of throwing torches at those Trog ships we want to destroy, but I got to thinking that a bow could shoot a burning arrow five or six times farther than anybody in the whole world can throw a burning torch, and if I've got a dozen or so men with bows and bundles of arrows, they'd be able to rain burning arrows down on the Trog ships in no time at all. That way, we won't have to swing in and slow down every time we see one of them. If you and the other men can do this right, we'll just fly past those scows and leave every one of them looking like a floating bonfire after we've gone by.'

Iron-Fist grinned broadly. 'Somethin' like that would purty much roon the day for any Trogs a-standin' on the beach, wouldn't it, Cap'n?'

'That was the whole idea. Ruining the day for Trogs is almost as much fun as having a winning number come up on your dice.'

Iron-Fist squinted out across the choppy waves at the other longships nearby. 'Didn't you say that your cousin wants to go ashore when we get down to the beach near Veltan's house?' he asked.

'That's what he told me. Why do you ask?'

'I think that maybe I might want to drift around a bit when we get there and find out if anybody just happens t' be in a bettin' frame of mind – with the bets based on some sort of number.'

'Something on the order of "I'll bet that *we* can set more Trog ships on fire than *you* can"?' Torl asked.

'That's purty much the way I'd put it, Cap'n.'

'How are you fixed for money, Iron-Fist?'

'I ain't quite all bent over by the weight of my purse, Cap'n.'

'I think I might be able to help you out a bit if you start to run short.'

'Share and share alike?'

'Sounds fair to me.'

'I'll put the other men as knows a bit about shootin' arrows t' practicin', Cap'n. I think we'll want 'em all t' be a-rarin' t' go when we start a-burnin' ever' Trog ship in sight – particularly if'n we happen t' have money a-ridin' on it.'

Torl scratched his chin. 'I think maybe I might want to see how my cousin and my big brother feel about some of those same kind of bets,' he mused.

'If they've got money a-ridin' on it, I don't think they'll be just *too* happy when they see us a-buildin' floatin' bonfires all along that south coast, Cap'n.'

'What a shame,' Torl said with mock regret.

The beach near Veltan's house came into view about noon on the following day, and cousin Sorgan led Skell and Torl on inland to take a long look at Veltan's map. There were several peninsulas jutting out into the sea down there, and the peninsulas formed bays. 'I thought so,' Sorgan mused. 'The best way to do this will be to block off the mouth of each bay and then sweep on in and set fire to every Trogite ship anchored in that bay. Then we'll move on to the next one. We don't want a single one of them to get away from us. If even one gets clear, it's altogether possible that it'll sail back down to the Trogite coast and gather up more ships and men. What we *really* want to do is make sure that the ones who are already here are trapped so that the only way they'll be able to go for more help will be to walk.'

Skell was leaning over the rail of the balcony above the map squinting down at the replica of the south coast. 'I don't see any towns of much size down there,' he noted. 'It sort of looks to me like there are a lot of small villages along that coast. If the Trog church-men are trying to round up all the natives so that they can sell them to the slavers, there'll only be four or five ships anchored just out from each village. That should make things a lot easier for us. We'll never come up against a massed fleet, so all we'll have to do is just sweep in and set fire to every Trog ship we come across. One sweep along that coast will eliminate their whole fleet.'

'That sounds about right to me, Skell,' Sorgan agreed. 'Then we can go on out to sea a ways, spread out, and make sure that no more Trog ships ever reach that coast. The ones who are already there will be trapped with no hope of reinforcements ever reaching them. Once their fleet's been destroyed, I don't think they'll try to go on up toward the mountains. Without those ships, they won't have any way to fall back if they meet an overwhelming enemy force. Only an idiot would take that kind of a chance. First we burn, and then we blockade. That second invasion stops right there.'

'Sounds good to me, cousin,' Skell agreed.

Torl had a few doubts, though, but he kept them to himself.

'I think tar would work better, Cap'n,' Buck-Teeth, the second mate of the *Lark* said. 'When you set fire to tar, it sticks to anything it touches, and it spreads fire a lot better than oily rags.'

'He might have a point there, Cap'n,' Iron-Fist agreed. 'And we could have a big pot filled with boilin' tar right on the deck where the arrow shooters are workin'. We could have a whole lot more burnin' arrows a-stickin' outta them Trog ships if we did 'er that way.'

'It's worth a try, I guess,' Torl agreed. 'We've got a lot of money riding on this, so let's not pass up any opportunities to make things turn out the way we want them to.'

'We got us some time t' play with, Cap'n,' Iron-Fist said. 'Sooner or later we'll come up with the best way t' do this.'

'Have you come up with a way to keep the men on the other ships from seeing what we're doing? If they start imitating us, our bets might just start falling apart.'

'We got all our arrow-shooters a-practicin' down below deck, Cap'n,' Iron-First answered. 'It's a little dark down there, but we put a lantern over the target so's the shooters can see where their arrows are a-goin'. It ain't *quite* as far as we'll be a-shootin' when we're a-doin' it fer real, but it's prolly close enough. Trog ships are mighty big, so they'll be awful hard t' miss.'

'Maybe we might want to swing in just a little closer when we first come across the Trog scows. We'll come up with egg all over our faces if our first wave of burning arrows hits the water instead of those ships.'

'And we'll lose our shirts as well,' Buck-Teeth added.

'You just *had* to go and say that, didn't you?' Torl said. 'I don't think I'll sleep very well until we find out if our scheme's going to turn out the way we want it to.'

'Don't worry, Cap'n,' Iron-Fist said. 'We'll *make* it work. When y' git right down to 'er, it *has* to work. We've got just about every penny on the *Lark* a-ridin' on this scheme of our'n, an' iffen it don't turn out like we want it to, the crew might just decide t' th'ow us all overboard.'

'Thanks, Iron-Fist,' Torl replied in a flat voice.

Sorgan's fleet was nearing the southern tip of the eastern-most peninsula jutting out from the south coast when a huge fleet of wallowing Trogite ships came sailing up toward them.

Things were more than a little tense until a small sloop came across to the *Seagull*. As it turned out, the Trog fleet was *not* the fleet of church invaders, but rather it was the remainder of Narasan's army.

Gunda spoke for a short while with cousin Sorgan, and then he returned to his own fleet to continue on up the coast. Sorgan sent out several skiffs to advise everybody to stay out of Gunda's way, and after the Trogite ships had passed, cousin Sorgan ordered his men to raise the sail on the *Seagull* and proceed along the coast.

When the fleet reached the southern-most end of the first peninsula, cousin Sorgan signaled for a stop. Back during the war in the ravine above Lattash, they'd all learned how valuable the flag-waving means of communication was, and cousin Sorgan had come up with a rudimentary imitation of the much more complex Trogite version. Sorgan's code only had four commands – 'Stop', 'Hurry up', 'Run away', and 'Let's talk' – but it was enough for right now.

Torl rowed his skiff over to the *Seagull* to find out if the general plan had been changed.

'Are we all ready?' Sorgan asked when Torl and brother Skell joined him in the cabin at the stern of the *Seagull*.

'We know what we're supposed to be doing, cousin,' Skell said. 'Let's get on with it.'

'I don't think so. Let's sit here out of sight until first light tomorrow morning. Give the oarsmen some time to rest up. We've got to move just as fast as we can once we start.'

'I don't think "fast" is likely to be involved all that much, Sorgan,' Skell said doubtfully. 'We'll have to slow down each time we come to a Trog ship. Since we'll be throwing torches, we'll have to wait a while to make sure that each Trog ship's on fire and that the fire's out of control. If some Trog on one of those ships is more than half-awake, all he'll have to do is grab up our torches and throw them over the side, and that particular Trog ship won't be on fire no more.'

'He's got a point there, cousin Sorgan,' Torl grudgingly admitted. 'If this is going to work the way we want it to, we should probably do our very best to set fire to every Trog ship along this coast in one single day.'

'I don't see how that's possible, Torl,' Skell protested. 'It takes a while to get a good fire going on a ship. It's not like we could just sail by and shout "fire" you know.'

Torl started muttering curses under his breath as his dream of winning a fortune in bets flew out the window. 'All right, cousin,' he said to Sorgan, 'if you'll pass the word to the other ships in the fleet that all bets are off, I'll tell you just exactly how we can burn every Trog ship along this coast in a single day.'

'I was sort of wondering just what you had up your sleeve,' Cousin Sorgan said. 'Let's have it, Torl.'

'Not until you give me your word that the bets have been cancelled, cousin. If my crew gets skinned alive when we lose all of our bets, they'll throw me overboard as soon as we're out of sight of land.'

'All right, I promise that I'll let everybody in the fleet know that your bets are cancelled. Now, what do we use to set fire to all the Trog ships in a single day?'

'Bows, arrows, and tar,' Torl replied glumly.

'Tar?' Skell demanded. 'How do you set fire to tar?'

'We've had a fair amount of success putting a torch to it, big brother. If you stick twenty or thirty burning arrows into the side of a Trog ship, it *will* burn – even on a rainy day.'

'I don't know if I've got that many men on board the *Shark* who know very much about bows and arrows,' Skell admitted.

'Go back to using torches then. That's up to you. Now, if you gentlemen will excuse me, I'll go burn Trog ships – just for fun, unfortunately. I think "profit" just got away from me.'

3

Torl took a certain amount of satisfaction in the business of setting fire to the Trogite ships anchored near the small villages along the south coast of Veltan's Domain. There was a rather arrogant quality about most Trogites that he'd always found offensive. Then too, the crew of the *Lark* had spent a good deal of time preparing for this mission, and, although they were obviously not nearly as skilled as Longbow, they *did* manage to plant their burning arrows in the sides of the oversized scows along the beach. The results even surprised Torl just a bit. A ship that has just been showered with several dozen flaming arrows will inevitably burst into flame in a fair imitation of Torl's own description of 'floating bonfires'. The panicky abandonment of the flaming ships by the crews was entertaining, but Torl still felt that he and his crew had been cheated out of their rightful winnings.

'Iron-Fist,' he called out to his first mate.

'Aye, Cap'n?'

'I think we can pick up the speed just a bit. I don't see very many of our arrows going into the water, so we seem to be doing this right. Our bets have been pushed aside, but I'd still like to rub cousin Sorgan's nose in the fact that we're the best ship-burners in the whole wide world.'

'We'll shorely do 'er, Cap'n,' Iron-First chortled.

The *Lark* leaped ahead and raced out in front of the other longships in Sorgan's fleet. The men on the other ships weren't very skilled with bows, and many of their burning arrows went into the water, and that made it necessary for the ships to slow down and fall farther and farther behind the *Lark*. It seemed to Torl that he could almost *hear* Sorgan's teeth grinding together as he watched the *Lark* racing on ahead to set fire to every single Trog ship in the entire bay.

When they reached the mouth of that first bay, Torl ordered his crew to pull in their oars and drop anchor.

The *Seagull* pulled in closer a while later. 'What are you doing. Torl?' Sorgan shouted. 'There's more bays and more Trogite ships ahead. Why are you stopping?'

'I think I've earned my keep today, cousin, and I certainly wouldn't want to cheat you and the other ship captains out of all the fun. Now that I've shown you how it's supposed to be done, I'm sure you'll be able to take care of the rest of the Trog ships without any help from me.'

'Very funny, Torl,' Sorgan growled. 'And just how did you plan to spend the rest of your day?'

'I thought I might find out if the fish are biting today.' Torl turned and walked along the deck of the *Lark* toward his cabin. 'You have a nice day now, cousin,' he called, 'and when you finish up, swing on by and I'll tell you what kind of bait works best in these waters.'

Cousin Sorgan was inventing new swear words as the *Seagull* moved away.

* * *

Torl had a nagging feeling that something wasn't right, but he couldn't quite put his finger on just exactly what it was. He paced up and down the deck of the *Lark* staring at the beach.

'It looks t' me like we scared all them Trogs real bad, Cap'n,' Iron-Fist said. 'I don't think I've seen more'n about three or four of 'em on that beach all day. Ain't they supposed t' have a great big ormy down here?'

Torl blinked. *That* was what was wrong! The beach should be covered with crowds of Trogs watching in horror as the only way they could ever return home went up in flames.

'I think I'd better go ashore and find out what's going on,' he said bleakly.

'Not all by yerself, Cap'n,' Iron-Fist said very firmly. 'Me an' the crew ain't *about* t' take no chances of a-losin' you. You ain't a hard-nose like most ship-captains, an' yer about five times smarter'n any Cap'n I've ever seen. Good Cap'ns is real hard t' come by.'

'I'm touched, Iron-Fist,' Torl said with a certain surprise.

'Don't git all gushy, Cap'n,' Iron-Fist said in a grouchy tone.

'All right, then. If I take a dozen men with me when I go ashore, will that make you feel better?'

'If'n y' let *me* pick the men, it will, Cap'n.'

The beach was deserted when Torl and his men went ashore, so they carefully went on up to the nearby village. They didn't encounter any Trogs, but the villagers all seemed quite happy to see them.

'Was there something you wanted?' a round-faced villager asked Torl.

'A few answers is about all,' Torl replied. 'What happened to all the Trogs? We've heard that there were thousands of them down here in the southern part of Veltan's Domain, but aside from the crews on those ships out in the bay, we haven't seen a single one.'

'They all ran off a while back,' the villager replied. 'I don't think we'll miss them very much. They weren't really very nice to us when they first came here. They came dashing up the beach waving weapons, and then herded us all into a pen that *I* wouldn't even have used for pigs. After a while, though, they got all excited about something that didn't seem to make any sense, and then, they all ran off toward the north.'

'Strange,' Torl said.

'If they decide to come back, I don't think they're going to like you very much. Why did you set fire to all their boats the way you did?'

'Veltan didn't want them to take you people off to be slaves, so we came down here and burned their ships. Did any of them ever say anything about just *why* they all ran off like that?'

'Nothing that made any sense to me,' the villager replied. 'Of course, a *lot* of things have been happening here lately that haven't made any sense. As closely as I could tell, they all got very excited about something going on up to the north.'

'There's not very much on up to the north of here but farmland,' Torl said. 'If you go on up farther, though, you'll reach the mountains.' Torl frowned. 'Did you happen to hear any of them talking about gold?'

The villager's face went sort of blank. Then he began to speak in a peculiar way as if he was reciting something that he'd memorized a long time in the past. 'It was long, long ago when a man of our village grew weary of farming,' he began, 'and he went up into the mountains far to the north to look at a different land. He came at last to a mighty waterfall that plunged down from out of the mountains to the farmland below. Then he found a narrow trail that led him up into the mountain-land, and there he beheld a wonder such as he had never seen before. It was beyond the mountains that he saw a vast area where there were no trees or grass, for the land beyond the mountains was nothing but sand, and that sand was *not* the white sand of the beaches when Mother Sea touches Father Earth. The sand beyond the mountains was bright and yellow and it glittered in the Wasteland with great beauty, and now all men in the Land of Dhrall know full-well that the sand of the Wasteland is pure gold, and it reaches far beyond the distance that the eyes can reach.

'And having seen what was there, the adventurous farmer returned to his home and never again went forth to look for strange new things, for he had seen what lay beyond the mountains, and his curiosity had been satisfied.' Then the villager stopped, and his face seemed sort of puzzled. 'I don't think I know what you were talking about, stranger,' he said.

'It's not really all that important, I guess,' Torl replied as if he wasn't very interested. 'Thanks for the information, friend. Whatever it was that got the Trogs all excited probably isn't very significant – except that it made them pack up and leave.'

'That's all that really matters, I guess,' the villager agreed.

Something very peculiar had just happened. It seemed that the villager didn't even know that he'd just recited a story that was really coming from somebody else's mouth, but what exactly had set him off? 'It must have been something I said,' Torl muttered, 'but as near as I can remember, all I asked him had to do with gold.' Then he blinked. 'Of *course*!' he exclaimed, 'it was the word "gold" that blanked out his mind and set him off.'

There was another villager standing not far away, so Torl walked over to the man. 'Hello, there, stranger,' he said. 'Why don't we talk about gold?'

The villager's face immediately went blank. 'It was long, long ago when a man of our village grew weary of farming,' he began.

Torl walked away and left the villager talking to himself.

Another villager came out of one of the makeshift huts.

'Gold,' Torl said.

'It was long, long ago—' the villager began.

Torl went on back down to the beach chuckling to himself. He privately admitted that it had been nothing but pure luck, but he'd just stumbled over the reason for the sudden departure of the Trogs.

'I wonder—' Torl mused. He looked on down the beach. There was another village no more than a mile away. 'Let's try it and find out,' he said to himself.

The sun was going down when Torl and his men returned to the *Lark*.

'Well, Cap'n,' Iron-Fist said, 'did y' find out what happened t' all them there Trogs?'

Torl shrugged. 'They went north,' he replied, 'and I was lucky enough to find out *why* they did that. We might want to drop by a few more villages, but I don't think it'll be necessary. *Somebody* – and I don't have any idea of just exactly who – did something very strange to the people in five different villages that I visited today. Just as soon as I mentioned the word "gold" every single villager I met today started to tell me exactly the same story – and they all used exactly the same words. I've heard it so many times now that I could probably recite it myself – and I wouldn't make a single mistake.'

'Now that's what I'd call *real* strange, Cap'n,' Iron-Fist said, a bit dubiously.

'"Strange" only begins to describe it,' Torl said. 'I wish I knew just who's behind this. I *think* whoever did it is on our side, but I wouldn't want to swear to it. I *hope* he's on our side, because he can do things that I've never even heard of before. We definitely don't want to cross *that* one.' Then Torl laughed. 'I'm fairly sure that this'll drive cousin Sorgan right straight up the wall, and I don't think Veltan's going to be very happy about it either. I'd say that this game just got very interesting.'

'You're just making this up, Torl,' cousin Sorgan said a day or so later when the *Seagull* returned to the bay where Torl was waiting.

'If you don't believe me, go try it yourself. All you have to do is say "gold" to any villager anywhere along the coast of this bay, and he'll tell you exactly the same story – *and* he won't even remember that he said anything at all.'

'That's ridiculous!'

'Go try it.'

'I've never *heard* such nonsense before.'

'Go try it.'

'You're just clowning around, Torl.'

'Go try it.'

'All right, I will, and when it turns out that you've been lying through your teeth, I'll whomp all over you.'

'I'm not even a little bit worried, cousin. I know exactly what you're going to hear every time you say "gold", because I've tried it myself a few dozen times.'

Sorgan snorted and went on out of Torl's cabin on the *Lark*, slamming the door behind him.

He came back several hours later with a stunned sort of expression. 'That's the strangest thing I've ever come across,' he declared.

'I told you that was what was going to happen, cousin,' Torl said smugly.

'Don't get *too* happy about it, Torl,' Sorgan said. 'You *do* know that the Trogs are marching north and that they didn't pay any attention at all to what we did to their ships, don't you? That means that we just failed. We were all positive that burning their ships would stop them right in their tracks, but that idea just fell apart on us. I don't think we can even catch up to those Trogs now. They're too far ahead of us.'

'I sort of thought so myself, cousin,' Torl agreed. 'What do we do now?'

'*You*, Torl, not "we",' Sorgan said quite firmly. 'Somebody's going to have to go back up to that basin and tell Narasan – and Veltan – that we just failed. Burning all their ships didn't mean a thing to the invaders. Then I want you to tell Veltan that *somebody's* been tampering with these farmers. For all I know, he might even have done it himself, but that doesn't make any sense at all, does it?'

'Not to *me*, it doesn't,' Torl agreed.

'I want you to put on full sail, Torl, and get up there just as fast as you can. Like it or not, we *do* have two invasions, and there's nothing I can do to stop the one that'll be coming at Narasan before many more days have passed.'

'I'll get the word to him just as quick as I can, cousin,' Torl promised.

'Even quicker would be better.'

4

As luck had it, there was a good following wind as the *Lark* sailed up along the east coast of the Land of Dhrall, but Torl was fairly sure that luck probably had very little to do with it. *Somebody* in this part of the world had been doing a lot of tampering here lately. A fair number of events during the war in Lady Zelana's Domain had made it quite clear that tampering was quite common in this part of the world, but Torl couldn't for the life of him see just where this unknown tamperer was going. If he was on *their* side, he should have been trying to *stop* the second invasion, but it seemed that he was encouraging it instead. Nothing that'd happened down on the south coast made any sense.

On the off chance that Veltan might be in his house, Torl anchored the *Lark* just off the familiar beach a few days after he'd left the south coast, and walked on up to that peculiar building. When he reached it, the wife of Veltan's friend Omago was waiting for him almost as if she had known that he was coming. Ara, the farmer's wife, was almost certainly the most beautiful woman Torl had ever seen, and he could not for the life of him understand just why she'd chosen to marry the rather stodgy farmer, Omago. He was certain that she'd have had much better options.

'I don't suppose that Veltan's here right now, is he?' Torl asked her.

'I'm afraid not,' she replied in that rich voice of hers. 'Did you want to see him?'

'There's something he needs to know, ma'am,' Torl replied. 'I was sort of hoping that I might be able to catch him here. My luck's been running very well lately, but it looks like it might have gone sour on me.' He shrugged. 'It was worth a try, I guess. Have you heard anything about what's going on up in the mountains?'

'Nothing very specific. I don't think the servants of the Vlagh have begun their attack yet.'

'That's something, I suppose. Narasan's people need to finish building their wall to hold off the enemy, and building a wall a mile or so long is likely to take them a while.'

'What was it that you thought Veltan should know about?' she asked. 'If he happens to stop by after you've moved on, I could pass it on to him. Did it have something to do with that invasion of the southern part of his Domain?'

'It did indeed,' Torl replied glumly. 'Cousin Sorgan was positive that we'd be able to deal with it, but our scheme fell apart on us.'

'Oh?'

'We burned every Trogite ship down there,' Torl said, 'and that *should* have stopped the invasion dead cold, but it didn't turn out that way at all.'

'What happened?'

'*Somebody* jerked our grand plan right out from under us. I know that Veltan, Lady Zelana, and their relatives can do all sorts of things that nobody else can do, but it seems that there's somebody *else* running around here in the Land of Dhrall who can do even stranger things. That other somebody did something that I don't think even Veltan could have pulled off.'

'Really?'

'The other somebody stuffed a ridiculous fairy tale into the mind of every single native down along the south coast, and they'll all repeat that fairy story in exactly the same way any time they hear the word "gold".'

'How did you find out about this, Torl?' Ara asked him rather sharply.

'I was talking to one of the natives down there – Bolen, I think his name was – and I just happened to mention gold during our conversation. As soon as I said "gold", his eyes glazed over and he told me this old story as if he was reciting something. I thought he'd just gone crazy, but after he'd finished, he seemed to wake up and go on as if nothing at all had happened.'

'How curious,' Ara said.

'It gets even *more* curious. Right at first, it didn't make any sense, but then I had a peculiar notion, and I walked around through several of those villages and said the word "gold" to every single native I met, and would you *believe* that every one of them did exactly the same thing Bolen had done. Their eyes went blank and each one told me exactly the same story. *Somebody* – or maybe some *thing* – is playing a very complicated game down there, and the fairy tale makes the Trogs go even crazier than the word "gold" makes the natives. They all started running off to the north as if somebody had just set fire to their tail feathers.'

She laughed then. 'What an amusing way to put it,' she said with a sly smile.

The majority of Commander Narasan's ships were anchored in the bay at the mouth of the River Vash, so the river itself wasn't as cluttered as it had been when cousin Sorgan's men had come down out of the mountains. Torl left Iron-Fist in charge of the *Lark*, and hurried up Nanton's stream-bed to advise Veltan that things in the south hadn't turned out as they'd hoped.

It was about noon of the next day when Torl reached the top, and he saw that the Trogites had been busy at the north end of the basin building wall rather than a fort, and their growing wall was already more than ten feet high.

It took him a while to locate Narasan and Gunda, since they were about halfway down the slope that led up out of the Wasteland.

'Back so soon, Torl?' Narasan remarked as Torl joined them. 'Things must have gone better than we'd anticipated.'

'I don't think "better" is the right word, Commander,' Torl replied. 'We burned all those Trogite ships, of course. That only took us a day or so, but the church soldiers, the priests, and even the slavers had already left by then.'

'Left? Are you saying that they're marching this way?'

'I wouldn't exactly call it a "march", Commander. "Run" would come a lot closer.'

'I don't quite get your point, Torl,' Gunda said.

'I think we'd better find Veltan,' Torl suggested. 'Something very strange happened down on the south coast, and Veltan's the expert on "strange", isn't he? To put this in the simplest way, the invaders are completely disorganized, and they're all just blindly running toward these mountains as if their lives depended on it. *Somebody* has been playing games down there, and they're the kind of games that only Veltan and his family could understand.'

'I think he might be down near the geyser,' Narasan said. 'Let's go find him.' Narasan's eyes were bleak, and his expression was grim.

* * *

'I tried it myself,' Torl told Lady Zelana and her younger brother. 'Every time I said "gold" to any native down there on the south coast, his eyes went blank and he recited that same silly story. I listened to the whole thing the first few times, but after that, I just walked away and left the native talking to himself.'

Veltan squinted at Torl. 'Did the story stir any odd feelings in you?' he asked.

'Boredom, before long. After you've heard the same story five times in a row, it's not really very interesting.'

'I'd say that we're looking at a selective infection, baby brother,' Lady Zelana said. 'The story excites the Trogites, but it doesn't have any effect on the Maags.'

'It might even go a bit further, sister mine,' Veltan suggested. He looked speculatively at Torl. 'Do you think you remember the story well enough to be able to recite it for us?' he asked.

'Probably upside down and backwards if you really want me to,' Torl replied.

'Let's hear it, then.'

'Did you want me to blank out my eyes as well?'

'No, that won't be necessary. Just recite the story.'

Torl cleared his throat. 'It was long, long ago when a man of our village grew weary of farming, and he went up into the mountains far to the north to look at a different land.' As he continued, he noticed that Veltan was watching Commander Narasan very closely.

'. . . And having seen what was there, the adventurous farmer returned to his home and never again went forth to look for strange new things, for he had seen what lay beyond the mountains, and his curiosity had been satisfied,' Torl concluded.

'Did that story effect you in any particular way?' Veltan asked Narasan.

'It was rather colorful, I suppose, but I don't know that I'd want to hear more like it.'

'That's probably because you're not a priest, Commander,' Torl suggested. 'Isn't it one of the rules of the Trogite church that all the gold in the world belongs to them?'

'He's quick isn't he, Veltan?' Lady Zelana said. 'It seems that this "infection" is even more selective than I'd originally thought. It seems to be aimed directly at the members of the Trogite clergy – and their hirelings.'

'Why did it point them all at the mountains then?' Veltan protested. 'Why didn't it send them running across the face of Mother Sea?'

'Evidently, whoever came up with this clever idea had something else in mind,' Lady Zelana replied.

The longer Veltan, Lady Zelana, and Narasan discussed the matter, the more exotic their notions became. So far as Torl could see, they were just scraping things off the wall. Quite obviously he'd chosen the wrong people here. He needed somebody with a more practical approach, and Torl knew exactly *who* he should be talking with, but he was quite sure that Veltan and Lady Zelana would be offended if he just turned around and walked away.

It was late afternoon before the supposed 'experts' had finally exhausted all possible – and several *im*possible – explanations and gave up.

Torl politely thanked them and casually sauntered away as if there was nothing pressing on his mind. As soon as he was out of sight, however, he went directly to Longbow's separate camp back in the forest beyond the geyser. It had been quite obvious during the war in Lady Zelana's Domain that the continual chatter of the

Trogites – and even the Maags – irritated Longbow, since he much preferred quiet. When Torl reached Longbow's campfire, however, the young Trogite called Keselo was there, and so was Rabbit, the smith of cousin Sorgan's *Seagull*.

'We've got a problem,' Torl announced as he joined them.

'We'd heard about that, Captain Torl,' Keselo said. 'I thought your cousin Sorgan had volunteered to take care of it.'

'Sorgan's answer didn't quite solve the problem,' Torl said rather ruefully. 'We *did* burn every Trogite ship that was anchored along the south coast, but I don't think the Trogs even know that their ships are gone. It seems that somebody is playing some very exotic games down there.'

'Games?' Rabbit asked.

'"Tricks" might come closer. When the church Trogs first came ashore, they rounded up all the people who lived in the villages down there and herded them into pens. Then some other Trogs who were dressed in black uniforms began to threaten their prisoners with all sorts of hair-raising things if the prisoners wouldn't tell them where all the gold in the entire Land of Dhrall was hidden.'

'Regulators,' Keselo said grimly. 'They're experts in the fine art of torture.'

'They didn't have to use it *this* time,' Torl declared. 'Every time a Trog – or anybody else – said the word "gold" to a native, the native sort of went into a trance and recited a fairy tale kind of story about some farmer who'd gone up into the mountains and found a place that was covered with gold instead of dirt. As soon as any Trog down there heard that story, he took off toward the north like a scared rabbit – no offense intended there,' Torl apologized to the little smith.

'It doesn't bother me all that much, Cap'n Torl,' Rabbit replied. 'I've heard it a thousand times.'

'Anyway,' Torl continued, 'as more and more Trogs heard that story, the priests who were supposed to be in command suddenly found out that they didn't have any armies any more, because the soldiers who were supposed to protect them had decided that they didn't want to *be* soldiers any more, and they were running in this direction just as fast as they could. Then, since there weren't any soldiers there to guard those slave-pens, the natives kicked down the fences and ran away.'

Keselo suddenly started to laugh.

'It gets better,' Torl told him. 'Just before we got down there, a fair number of black ships hauled into the bay and the slavers came ashore to buy all the natives from the fat priests, but the natives had already left. That's when *we* arrived and set fire to all their ships, and that didn't make them very happy at all – particularly when they realized that the natives were probably sharpening knives and spears and axes and planning to stop by to show them just how unpopular they were – and by then there wasn't anybody around to protect them. The assorted priests and slavers didn't have very many options at that point, so they all ran north out of those villages, hoping against hope that if they happened to be lucky enough to catch up with the soldiers, they *might* even live long enough to see the sun go down.'

'He tells funnier stories than Red-Beard, doesn't he?' Keselo said.

'As soon as you finish laughing, we'll get into the ugly part,' Torl said. 'Given the number of ships we burned along that coast, I'd say that there are about a half a million crazy Trogs running in our general direction right now. I think we'd better come up with a way to head them off, or we'll have bug-men coming at us from one direction and Trog-men coming at us from the other.'

He squinted at Longbow's campfire. 'I'll admit that right at first I thought that whoever had come up with that wild story was trying to help us, but now I'm not so sure. Those Trog soldiers went out of their minds when they heard the story, so they aren't even thinking coherently any more. Doesn't that mean that they won't take orders from anybody now?'

'Probably not,' Keselo agreed. 'Any sort of discipline has vanished, I'd imagine.'

Longbow was squinting bleakly at the sunset. 'I don't like the smell of this at all,' he said. 'I'd say that right now those soldiers are thinking at about the same level as the servants of the Vlagh think. I'm fairly sure that the Vlagh wasn't at all happy about what happened to all its servants in the ravine above Lattash. The over-mind was probably even *less* happy since the death of thousands of the servants almost certainly reduced the ability of that group awareness to solve problems. Right now, I'd say that protecting the lives of the remaining servants *might* be more important than moving into new territory.'

'That makes sense, I guess,' Rabbit admitted. 'Where are you going with this, Longbow?'

'I'm not quite sure,' Longbow replied. Then he blinked. 'Sheep!' he exclaimed. 'It was right there in front of me, but I didn't see it!'

'You lost me there, I think,' Rabbit said.

'I'm sure there was a time when sheep were wild animals – sort of like deer. Then men came along and tamed them.'

'I still don't get your point.'

'People aren't the *only* creatures who tame other creatures for their own purposes. Ants tame sow-bugs, and other insects do much the same thing. The Vlagh needed soldiers to do the fighting – and the dying – to protect the overmind. If we kill *too* many of the servants of the Vlagh, the overmind will fall apart. The Vlagh needed slaves, and it enslaved the church soldiers off to the south with the word "gold."'

'Is that silly thing really *that* clever?' Torl demanded incredulously.

'It's not really a single thing, Torl. What one sees, they've all seen, and after they've seen it, the overmind comes up with ways to *use* what they've seen. I hate to admit this, but it seems to be working very well right now.'

'That's terrible!' Torl exclaimed. 'How can we possibly win in a situation like this?'

'Don't rush me,' Longbow said in an obvious imitation of cousin Sorgan's rough voice. 'I'm working on it.'

THE TREASURED ONE

1

The scent of the roast lamb that was currently baking in one of Ara's brick ovens suggested that it needed perhaps just a touch more garlic to fill out the flavor. Spices had always lain at the core of fine cooking, and Ara's nose had led her down the proper path for as long as she could remember, and that was much, much longer than anyone around her realized. She carefully sprinkled the roast with grated garlic and then pushed the pot back into the brick oven reserved for the baking of meat.

The continual murmur of the thoughts of those around Ara seemed perhaps a bit quieter this afternoon than was usual. She could hear Omago, of course, but there was nothing particularly unusual about that. She was quite sure that she'd be able to hear Omago's thoughts from half a world away. There was an almost poetic beauty to her mate's thinking, and it had been that beauty which had drawn her to him in the first place.

The dream of Dahlaine's little boy had troubled Ara very much. At the outset, everything in Ashad's dream had gone exactly as she'd intended, but then Ashad had wandered off on his own. Now they all faced the distinct possibility of a second invasion of Veltan's Domain coming from somewhere off to the south. The motives of the Vlagh were very clear, but Ara could not for the life of her understand why the outlanders to the south would have any reason whatsoever to invade the Land of Dhrall.

Dahlaine's original scheme had been adequate, but only barely. It *had* stepped around the wall that stood before *both* generations of gods – the wall that forbade the taking of *any* kind of life – but at that point, Dahlaine had seriously blundered by unleashing the Dreamers with absolutely no control whatsoever over what forces the dreams might turn loose. Ara had shuddered back from a number of ghastly disasters that had been entirely possible. At that point she'd had no choice. Always in the past she'd just been an observer, but Dahlaine's idiotic decision had forced her to step in and take control. In a very real sense, Dahlaine had provided the Dreamers, but Ara provided the dreams.

Sometimes, though, the Dreamers had run off on their own, and that irritated Ara to no end.

Then she remembered something that had happened in the Land of the Maags. Eleria's dream in the harbor of Kweta had been more in the nature of a warning than an announcement of an absolute certainty, and that warning had given Zelana's archer all that he'd needed to meet the threat of an unscrupulous Maag named Kajak. Could it possibly be that Ashad's dream of a second invasion of Veltan's Domain had *also* been a warning? If that were the case, the second invasion might never come to pass in the real world.

For right now, Ara needed much more information about the people of the land to the south. Once she understood them, she might very well be able to stop that second invasion before it ever took place.

* * *

It was on a beautiful morning in early summer when Veltan advised Omago and Ara that the hired armies would be arriving that very day, *and* that Yaltar was still very disturbed by the disastrous results of his dream about exploding mountains. Ara was quite sure she'd be able to ease the little boy's sense of guilt, so she decided to go on down to the beach with Veltan and her mate.

Even before the outlander ships reached the shore, Ara felt suddenly awash with the jumbled thoughts of the various men who were on board those ships. Curiosity was foremost in their thoughts, of course. The outlanders had been totally unaware of the existence of the Land of Dhrall before the previous winter, so it was only natural for them to be curious. There was also a certain amount of apprehension. The creatures of the Wasteland had been so altered by the Vlagh that they were unlike anything else in all the world, and that disturbed the outlanders to no small degree.

The name of Zelana's archer Longbow kept cropping up. With only a few exceptions, the outlanders had been awed by that icy man. Ara tentatively reached out and touched the mind of the archer, and she found that he was *not*, as many on the ships believed, some kind of inhuman monster. He was coldly practical when a situation required that of him, but he *did* have normal emotions.

Then she very briefly brushed across an awareness so foul that she shuddered back in horror and disgust. One of the soldiers in the Trogite army was the most corrupt man Ara had ever encountered, and he was driven by a towering greed. So far as *that* particular soldier was concerned, the war with the servants of the Vlagh was of no particular significance. What he *really* wanted was every speck of gold in the entirety of the Land of Dhrall. Then several things came together all at once, and Ara realized that she'd just found the source of the second part of the dream of Ashad. 'Well, now,' she murmured, 'isn't *that* interesting?'

'What was that again, Ara?' Omago asked her.

'Nothing, dear heart,' she replied. 'Just thinking out loud is all.'

Ara braced herself and reached out to touch the filthy mind of the outlander called Jalkan, and she found nothing even remotely redeeming there. There was arrogance aplenty, and greed, cruelty, cowardice, and, perhaps more important, a towering lust.

'Now *that* might be the answer to the whole problem,' Ara mused. 'If this beast isn't around any more, Ashad's second invasion won't happen at all.'

A number of very interesting possibilities came to Ara at that point. If she could stir Jalkan's lust enough to push him over certain lines, she was almost positive that dear Omago would respond appropriately. She'd be obliged to take things down to the most primitive level, of course, and that troubled her more than a little. The end result, however, would fully justify what she'd have to do.

After a brief discussion on the beach, Veltan took a goodly number of the outlanders and a couple of the hunters from Zelana's Domain to his house to show them a room where he'd set up a miniaturized duplicate of the terrain in the vicinity of the Falls of Vash. Ara began to prepare dinner for Veltan's guests while Zelana, Eleria, and Yaltar watched. Ara was not really concentrating on the cooking however. Pushing her sense of revulsion aside, she turned her senses backward in time to the point where she could unleash the overwhelming urge to mate in any living male, and, as was the case in all warm-blooded creatures, that involved a specific scent. The scent would unleash Jalkan's lust most certainly, but it should *also* drive Omago into raw violence, and that would immediately eliminate Ashad's second invasion.

When Ara went to Veltan's map-room to tell the men assembled there that dinner was ready, she was exuding that most primitive of scents, and Jalkan, as she'd anticipated, responded with a few off-color remarks that clearly indicated that he expected things to go much further. Omago responded to those comments quite appropriately, but unfortunately didn't take it quite far enough. At the last moment, his innate decency pulled him back. Despite the urges of his primal instincts, Omago did *not* kill their enemy.

Ara suppressed her own primitive urge to scream at that point. She'd just discovered that raw instincts are almost impossible to control, and in a situation where the desired result did *not* come to pass, screaming would be instinctive.

Veltan's Trogite friend, Commander Narasan, had been stunned by Jalkan's remarks, and Ara hoped that *he'd* take the appropriate steps, but for some reason he did *not* reach for his sword.

What was the *matter* with these people? At great personal expense, Ara had given *everybody* in that round room all the excuse they'd ever need to exterminate the filthy Jalkan, but they'd all just passed it up. Why wouldn't *anybody* do what he was supposed to do?

Narasan ordered the Trogite Padan to put Jalkan in chains and imprison him in one of the Trogite ships standing just off the beach. That was *something*, Ara conceded, but for some reason, nobody seemed to realize that there'd been a much simpler answer.

It took Ara the rest of the day and most of the night to clear away the last of her primeval instincts and she felt a bit wrung-out the following day. Instincts sometimes accomplished things when nothing else would work, but they were absolutely exhausting – particularly when they didn't achieve the desired goal.

It came as no real surprise a week or so later that word of Jalkan's escape reached the house of Veltan. It seemed to Ara that every time she turned around, Ashad's silly dream was ahead of her. No matter what she tried to do to prevent the second invasion, the dream thwarted her. For some reason that she could not even begin to understand, that second invasion was absolutely necessary. 'I give up,' she said, throwing her hands in the air.

Since it was quite clear that Omago would be very much involved in the up-coming war, Ara listened carefully to the discussions in Veltan's map-room and – as she probably should have known that he would – Omago volunteered to go up along the coast to the mouth of the River Vash with the scouting party of Sorgan Hook-Beak's cousins, Skell and Torl.

As sometimes happened, Ara had a strong premonition that something very significant would turn up as her mate and a small party explored a trail that Nanton the shepherd knew quite well. Ara had learned in times long gone that she should never ignore one of those premonitions, so she decided to accompany the scouting party – inconspicuously of course.

As the two Maag longships sailed north along the eastern coast of Veltan's Domain, Ara's thought followed them curiously, and when Skell and a few friends left the ships to follow the shepherd up the steep course of the small tributary of the River Vash, Ara's thought followed them with that premonition growing stronger and stronger with every mile.

It was about mid-morning on the small party's second day of

struggling up the narrow streambed when a burly Maag called Grock made a startling discovery. 'I just found gold, Cap'n!' he shouted. '*Gold!* There's tons of it up there in that rock wall!'

It was Keselo, the young Trogite soldier, who suggested that the little smith from Sorgan's longship might be the logical one to verify the nature of the yellow flake.

Ara sensed the enormous disappointment of Skell and the rest of the little group when Rabbit proved to them that the bright yellow flake was *not* gold.

It was fairly obvious that Keselo had known from the very start that what Grock had discovered was not what it appeared to be, and Ara probed the young man's mind and discovered that what Grock had found was a peculiar combination of iron ore and sulphur.

Ara realized that *this* was what had aroused that premonition in the first place. If Jalkan's greed for gold was going to be the reason for Ashad's second invasion, this false gold might turn out to be very useful.

Ara withdrew her thought from Skell's scouting party and went into her kitchen to examine some very interesting possibilities.

It required a bit of experimentation for Ara to get the proper mix, but her kitchen was the natural home of experimentation, so on her third try, she produced a sizeable amount of bright yellow flakes that were identical to the one Grock had found in the mountains.

She was very pleased with the results of her experiment – until she saw the heaps of glittering sand lying all over her kitchen floor. Muttering to herself, she went to fetch her broom.

2

———✦———

The small group of men Nanton the shepherd had led up to the grassy plain above the Falls of Vash were busy exploring the region. It was more open than the ravine above the village of Lattash had been, and that seemed to concern the seafarers quite a bit. Given the number of servants the Vlagh could send charging up out of the Wasteland, Ara could understand that concern.

As evening was settling over the little camp near the geyser, the bats came out, and Longbow the archer quite suddenly came up with a notion that chilled Ara down to her very bones. A single arrow proved that Longbow's notion had been very correct. The bats were not at all what they had appeared to be, and Ara had a sudden urge to take up her beloved mate and go directly back home.

After a bit of discussion, though, the clever little smith called Rabbit came up with the notion of using fishnets to protect them from the flying enemies, and that eased the tension to some degree.

Then Longbow spoke briefly with the burly Red-Beard. It was fairly obvious that arrows would be the best solution to the problem of flying enemies, and Red-Beard went off to the west to hurry along the archers coming down from Zelana's Domain. Then

Skell sent the gold-hunter Grock back on down to bring more men – and fish nets – up to the basin.

The hard practicality of these men helped Ara to control her sudden panic, and she decided to wait a bit before she grabbed her mate by the arm and ran away with him.

Skell's brother Torl reached the basin the following day, and Narasan and Sorgan were only a few hours behind him. Skell led them up to the gap at the north end of the basin to show them the most probable route the servants of the Vlagh would follow when they came south.

Then Veltan came crashing in on his pet thunderbolt and advised his friends that the second invasion Ashad's dream had mentioned was coming up from the south. He went on and on about the incursion into the southern part of his Domain, but Ara pulled her awareness back to her kitchen and then sent her thought south to have a look for herself.

There were several large peninsulas jutting out into Mother Sea on the south coast of Veltan's Domain, and they formed large, protected bays. There were quite a few farming villages along the shores of those bays, and the wheat fields stretched inland for several miles.

It was not the wheat fields that attracted Ara's immediate attention, however. There were a large number of bulky Trogite ships with red sails anchored in the bay, and the armed soldiers from those ships were going ashore in the vicinity of every village. The soldiers were busily gathering up all the residents of those villages and herding them at sword-point into crudely constructed pens just outside each village as if they were no more than cattle.

It took Ara several minutes to get her sudden rage under control, and it didn't get any better when unarmed Trogites in flowing black robes entered each pen to harangue the terrified villagers about 'the only true god in all the world'.

When one of the villagers in the pen near the largest village on the shore of that particular bay politely advised a fat Trogite who'd just made that announcement that the god of *this* particular region was named Veltan, two of the red-uniformed outlanders clubbed him into unconsciousness. They might have even gone further, but Ara smoothly deflected one outlander's club, and he very nearly brained his companion.

Since the origin of this invasion was obviously the filthy-minded Trogite called Jalkan, Ara sent her thought out in search of him, and he wasn't all that hard to find. There was a farming village on the shore near the central bay here on the south coast, and there were several red-sailed Trogite ships anchored just off the coast. The natives were all penned up, and the Trogite priests and their soldiers had stolen the huts of those natives. Jalkan was in a fairly central hut, and he was not alone. He was speaking with a grossly fat man dressed in an ornate yellow robe.

'Nobody was ever very specific about just where the mines were located, Adnari Estarg,' Jalkan was saying. 'I'd imagine that they're up in the mountains, though.'

'We're going to need more specific information than just "up in the mountains", Jalkan,' the fat man said. 'There *might* be gold in this primitive part of the world, but if we can't get anything more specific than that, it might just as well be on the back side of the moon.'

'That's why we brought those Regulators along, Your Grace. The Regulators have ways to make *anybody* talk. We know for certain that there's gold here. You saw those gold blocks I showed you back in Kaldacin. They prove that there *is* gold in this part of the world, and all we have to do to locate it is turn the Regulators loose on the natives. After the natives see a few of their friends die while the Regulators are questioning them, I'm sure they'll start to be very cooperative. How long do you think it's going to take for the slave-ships to get here?'

'A week, at least. The slavers buy; they don't catch.'

'Things should work out very well, then. It won't take the Regulators very long to get the information we need out of the natives, and once we have that information, we can sell the natives to the slavers and get them out of our way. There's a distinct possibility that we'll make almost as much gold selling the natives to the slavers as we'll make in the gold mines.'

'I never pass up gold, Jalkan,' the fat man said with a broad grin.

Ara drew back just a bit. The discussion between those two had chilled her to the bone. These people were absolute monsters. Their willingness to wring information out of people with torture raised a very serious problem, though. The people of the Land of Dhrall had never been very interested in gold, so the farmers here in the south probably didn't even know what the word meant.

Then something came to her out of nowhere. If the Trogites so desperately wanted to hear about gold, Ara was quite sure she could arrange things so that they'd hear enough stories about it to drive them wild.

She directed her thought to the crude pens where the Trogite soldiers had confined the villagers and conjured up an 'ancient myth' which she then planted in the minds of everyone in that pen. From here on, every time one of the villagers heard somebody say 'gold', he'd automatically recite Ara's absurd story word for word.

Then with a faint smile, she sat back and waited for the fun to begin.

*   *   *

The Trogites that Jalkan called Regulators now guarded the natives, and they were a harsh, brutal group of men who wore black uniforms, apparently to distinguish them from the soldiers, who wore red. The one Jalkan and his fat friend relied upon was called Konag, and Ara didn't like him at all. She thought it might be sort of nice if *he* were the one who carried the story she'd conjured up to Jalkan and Estarg.

It was about mid-morning when Konag went through the gate of the compound where the villagers were confined and approached a rather frightened farmer. 'We need to know a few things about the mountains to the north,' Konag said. 'If you're the one who tells us what we want to know, I'll see to it that you get more to eat and a more comfortable place to sleep.'

'I'd be happy to tell you, stranger,' the farmer replied, 'but I don't really know very much about those mountains. I've always stayed pretty close to home. What was it that you wanted to know about?'

'Where's the gold?' Konag demanded.

The farmer's eyes brightened. 'Ah,' he said. 'You should have told me what you wanted earlier. *Everybody* around here knows about gold.'

'Oh? How's that?'

'It was long, long ago when a man of our village grew weary of farming and went up into the mountains far to the north to look at a different land. He came at last to a mighty waterfall that plunged down from out of the mountains to the farmland below. Then he found a narrow trail that led him up into the mountain-land, and there he beheld a wonder such as he had never seen before. It was beyond the mountains that he saw a vast area where there were no trees or grass, for the land beyond the mountains was nothing but sand, and that sand was *not* the white sand of the beaches where Mother Sea touches Father Earth. The sand beyond the mountains was bright and yellow and it glittered in the Wasteland with great beauty, and now all men in the Land of Dhrall know full-well that the sand of the Wasteland is pure gold, and it reaches far beyond the distance that the eyes can reach.

'And having seen what was there, the adventurous farmer returned to his home and never again went forth to look for strange new things, for he had seen what lay beyond the mountains, and his curiosity had been satisfied.'

All in all, Ara was quite pleased with the myth she'd implanted in the minds of the villagers the Trogites had penned up. There was adventure, mystery, and an ending that involved a huge treasure. It was all an out-and-out lie, of course, but it was a very *good* lie.

Konag seemed stunned by the farmer's recitation, and he abruptly turned and ran off in search of Jalkan.

The farmer who had just recited Ara's myth looked quite puzzled – which wasn't at all remarkable, since he had no memory at all of his performance.

'That's impossible, Regulator Konag!' the fat priest called Estarg exclaimed when the black-uniformed Trogite told him what the farmer had said. 'There isn't that much gold in the whole *world*.'

'I wouldn't be all that sure, Adnari,' Jalkan disagreed. 'Veltan gave Commander Narasan ten blocks of pure gold in the harbor of Castano, and he was treating those gold blocks as if they didn't mean a thing.'

Ara gently increased the level of avarice in the minds of the three Trogites by placing an image of gold in their minds.

'I'll go on up there and take a look, Adnari,' Konag volunteered eagerly.

'How did you plan to even *find* the place that peasant told you about?' Jalkan demanded.

'I'll take a party of Regulators along. They'll be able to chase down peasants to get information.'

'Don't steal any of my gold when you get up there, Konag,' the fat priest said in a threatening voice.

'*Our* gold, Adnari,' Jalkan corrected. 'A goodly part of that gold up there is *mine*.'

The fat man glared at him.

'Let's be sure it's there before we start arguing about it, gentlemen,' Regulator Konag said firmly. 'It might just be some local fairy tale.'

'If that peasant was lying, I'll rip him up the middle with a dull knife,' Jalkan declared.

'The peasant told you that everybody around here knows the story about the fellow who found the gold,' fat Estarg said, his eyes squinting shrewdly. 'Before you go running off into the wilderness why don't you ask some of the others if they've ever heard it. If they haven't, then the first peasant was lying through his teeth, and we can *all* join hands and rip him up the middle.'

The penned-up farmers all confirmed Ara's myth, of course, and after a day or so, Regulator Konag gathered up a dozen of his black-uniformed men and led them up through the farmland toward the mountains lying across the northern boundary of Veltan's Domain. Their route lay somewhat to the west of the more populated coastline, so they encountered very few *real* farmers along the way, but Ara provided several *imaginary* farmers to fill in the gaps – and to repeat her myth.

The more she thought about that, the more Ara came to realize that it was not absolutely essential for Konag and his men to actually climb up into the mountains and look out at some vast stretch of imitation gold. All that was really necessary would be to make them *believe* that they'd seen it.

It would most definitely solve a problem that had been nagging at her since she'd first come up with her scheme. There *were* a large number of Sorgan's sailors and Narasan's soldiers in the basin above the Falls of Vash, and Ara *definitely* didn't want Konag and his men to know that they were there.

Konag and his men dreamed that they were breathing very hard when they reached the top of the imaginary pass that opened out into the basin above the Falls of Vash, but – in their dream, at least – they hurried on toward the wide gap in the ridge-line at the north of the basin.

And there they stopped, astonished and awed by the wonder stretching off to the northern horizon. The sea of gold sparkled in the morning sun, and several of Konag's hard-bitten Regulators actually wept at the sight.

Ara held the dream image before them for perhaps an hour, and then she turned them around and pointed them toward the south.

They were all positive that they were totally exhausted by the time they reached the foot of the vast waterfall, so they decided to stop for the day when they reached their previous camp site – which in fact, they had never left. This merged dream with reality to the point that Konag and his men were absolutely convinced that what they had dreamed was hard truth. Ara was quite pleased by how well it had turned out.

Then she implanted a sense of urgency in the minds of Konag and his fellow Regulators, so they arose early the following morning and set out toward the south before the sun was even over the horizon.

Jalkan and Adnari Estarg would have much preferred to keep a tight level of secrecy on the matter, but Ara had already bypassed them. Konag's Regulators were all possessed by an overpowering urge to tell everyone they met about the wonder they had seen, so at least half of the church soldiers in the encampment on the southern coast of Veltan's Domain knew about the field of gold before Konag reported it to his superiors.

Konag went directly to the crude hut that Jalkan and Estarg had appropriated upon their arrival.

'Well?' Jalkan demanded when Konag entered. 'Was that idiot actually telling you the truth?'

'No,' Konag replied with an absolutely straight face.

The fat church man groaned. 'I knew it was too good to be true,' he grieved.

'No, Your Grace,' Konag disagreed. 'When you get right down to it, the native's story didn't *begin* to tell us just how *much* gold was out there. The golden sand that blankets that desert beyond the mountain goes all the way out to the horizon. My men and I were fairly high up in the mountains, so I'd say that it was at least fifty miles to the horizon, and I have no idea at all of just how wide it was.'

'Did you bring any back with you?' Jalkan asked eagerly.

'Adnari Estarg ordered us not to,' Konag replied. 'We were supposed to verify that foolish story and then come right back.'

'I'd *really* like to see some of it, Konag,' Jalkan whined in a voice filled with disappointment.

'It's not really all that far north, Jalkan,' Konag told him. 'You can go up there and look at it all you want if it means that much to you.'

3

Ara's thought surveyed the south coast of Veltan's Domain to get a better idea of just how many Trogites were now in the region. There were villages all along the coast, of course, and by now each village had been appropriated by church soldiers, and there was now a slave-pen attached to each village.

As the days passed and word of Konag's discovery reached those other villages, an increasing number of church soldiers decided that army life no longer suited them.

At first, the desertions were almost always made under the cover of darkness, but then Ara implanted a growing anxiety in the minds of the soldiers who had remained behind. Her message got right to the point. 'If you wait too long, those who have already deserted will get all the gold, and there won't be any left for you,' seemed to work quite well.

The soldiers began deserting their posts in broad daylight at that point, and after a few days, the priests who were theoretically in charge of the scattered villages began to send urgent messages to Adnari Estarg, begging him to send them more soldiers.

But by then, of course, there *were* no more soldiers, since they were now deserting in battalions.

The messengers stopped coming to Adnari Estarg's door a few days later, and then the priests began to arrive, pleading for help.

Adnari Estarg ordered the priests to return to the villages to which they had been originally assigned, and a few of them even obeyed his orders – but not really very many. Ara extended her warning to include the priests, and very soon, most of the priests had joined the ranks of the deserters.

Ara's thought lingered in the vicinity of the village where Jalkan and Adnari Estarg were growing increasingly distraught. She found that there was a certain charm in their growing sense of panic.

Ara was rather fond of the farmer known as Bolan, since it had been his recitation of her 'myth of gold' that had neatly snared Konag, so she briefly touched him to point out the fact that since there weren't any soldiers guarding the slave-pen any more, there wasn't really any reason to remain there. Bolan got her point almost immediately, so after the few priests remaining in the village had gone to bed that evening, Bolan and his friends tore down the western wall of the slave-pen and vanished into the night.

Seven Trogite ships, all painted dead black, came into view early the following morning, and Ara was fairly sure she knew exactly who – and what – the men on those ships were. If she was right, Bolan and the other villagers had left just in time.

A fair number of bleak-faced men came ashore, and one of the few priests who still remained in the village went down to the beach to meet them. 'I'll go tell Adnari Estarg that you're here, Captain Brulda,' the young priest said to the one who appeared to be the leader of the strangers.

The grim fellow laughed. 'I wouldn't do that if I were you,

young man,' he advised. 'If you wake Estarg up before noon, he'll find all sorts of unpleasant things for you to do. Where are the slave-pens? We'd like to take a look at the merchandise *before* Estarg starts telling us fairy tales about these new slaves.'

'The Adnari wouldn't *lie* to you, Captain,' the young priest declared.

'Oh, really?' Brulda said sarcastically. 'And will the sun come up in the west tomorrow as well? Estarg wouldn't know the truth if it walked up and bit him right on the nose. We want to see the slaves, boy. Lead the way.'

'Are you sure these slaves are healthy?' one of the other strangers asked the priest as he led them toward the slave-pen. 'We bought five shiploads of slaves down the coast of Tanshall last year, and more than half of them died of some kind of disease before we were six days out.'

'Oh, they're very healthy,' the priest assured him, 'and they're farmers already, so their new owners in the Empire won't have to waste all that time teaching them what they're supposed to do.'

'That *might* even raise the price we'll get for them,' the slaver agreed.

The empty slave-pen with its broken-down wall upset the visitors more than a little, and they rushed into the village to discuss the matter with Adnari Estarg.

'You idiot!' the one called Brulda bellowed at the fat churchman. 'Why didn't you have any guards around that rickety pen?'

'What are you talking about, Brulda?' Estarg, who seemed to be still about half-asleep, demanded.

'Your slaves broke out during the night, you fool! Your slave-pen's empty!'

'That's impossible!'

'Go look for yourself, you dunce!'

Jalkan rushed out of the hut, and he came back swearing after a little while. 'They're gone, Adnari,' he declared. 'They broke down that rickety wall on the west side of the pen sometime during the night and ran away.'

'Go chase them down!' Estarg shouted.

'All by myself? Don't be ridiculous!'

'But all of my money is escaping! Help him, Brulda!'

'Not on your life, Estarg,' the slaver said. 'I came here to *buy* slaves, not to capture them.'

The bickering and screaming continued for quite some time, and Ara found it all rather entertaining.

Then she saw something that promised to brighten her day even more.

Several dozen Maag longships, led by Sorgan Hook-Beak's *Seagull*, were coming into the large bay.

'The ships are burning, Adnari!' The young priest who'd met the slavers on the beach screamed, bursting into the crude hut in a state of sheer panic

'What are you talking about?' the slaver Brulda roared.

'Some pirate ships just swept in, and they set fire to every ship in the bay!'

Ara found the reaction of the assorted scoundrels in the hut quite satisfying. When six men all try to go through a doorway at the same time, things start to get quite physical. Eventually, the slaver Brulda managed to bash his way through the others with the stout club he had hanging from his belt.

'My ships!' he cried out in anguish. 'My ships are on fire! Somebody do something! Save my ships!'

There was nothing that any of the Trogites on the beach could do to save any of the ships in the bay, and the men still on board those ships were forced to swim ashore to keep from being burned alive. The Maags quite obviously knew exactly what they were doing, and by now nothing short of torrential rain would even slow the fires, and the sky was clear and blue, with no rain in sight.

The Trogites on the beach watched in horror as their only means of returning home went up in smoke and flame. They had come as conquerors, but now they were trapped.

'Ah, me,' Ara murmured with mock sympathy. 'What a shame.'

And then she laughed. There were several ways she could have made her mocking laughter audible to the panic-stricken Trogites, but she decided against it. Her little scheme still had many more twists and turns to entertain these scoundrels, and she was sure she'd enjoy them more if the Trogites didn't expect them.

'You're exaggerating, Jalkan,' Adnari Estarg declared. 'These natives are little more than sheep. They wouldn't *dare* to do something like that.'

'I wouldn't want to bet my life on that,' Jalkan replied bluntly. 'We didn't really treat these people very well when we came ashore, so I wouldn't be a bit surprised to find out that they're making plans right now to come back here and kill every one of us.'

'Amar wouldn't permit that!' the young priest who'd met the slavers on the beach protested.

'Grow up, boy,' Brulda the slaver said. 'Amar's nothing but a myth, and this is the *real* world.' He turned to Jalkan. 'Do these natives have weapons of any kind at all?'

'I saw an archer during the first war who could kill people from a quarter of a mile away, Brulda. These natives *do* know how to kill an enemy, and right now the word "enemy" means *us*. If we still had those five armies we had when we came here, we *might* be all right, but they all deserted when they heard about the gold in the mountains, so we're all alone and totally unprotected. If we stay here, I don't think any of us will still be alive next week.'

'That gets right to the point, I guess,' Brulda admitted. 'I don't see that we've got much choice. If we want to keep breathing, we'll have to go north and see if we can catch up with the deserters.'

Ara smiled. She hadn't really left these rascals many options, and the slaver Brulda had chosen the correct one right at the start.

'I'll need some of your men, Brulda,' the fat priest declared, 'probably twenty or so.'

'What for?'

'They'll have to build a sedan chair for me to ride in if you're sure we'll have to try to catch up with the deserters.'

Brulda laughed at that point.

'What's so funny?' Estarg demanded.

'You didn't *really* think that my men would pick you up and carry you, did you, Estarg?'

'I'm an Adnari in the Church of Amar, Brulda,' Estarg proclaimed in a haughty tone of voice. 'Your men have a religious obligation to serve me in any way I think is proper. It's beneath me to walk as a commoner would.'

'Stay here, then. It doesn't matter to me. I'm going north, though – just as fast as I possibly can.'

'I forbid it!' Estarg shouted.

'Forbid all you want, fat man,' Brulda replied, 'but I stopped taking orders from you when my ships were all burned. The way things stand right now, it's every man for himself. If you want to go north with the rest of us, you're going to have to walk – with your very own feet.'

'That's outrageous!'

'You *do* remember how to walk, don't you, Estarg?' Brulda asked with an evil grin.

'But—' Estarg put both hands under his belly.

'It's walk or die, Estarg, and it's entirely up to you.'

Ara despised the slaver Brulda, but she was forced to admit that he *did* have a way with words.

All in all, Ara was quite pleased with the way this had turned out. There were now two enemy armies in Veltan's Domain, but they were not *really* armies in the conventional sense of that word. The servants of the Vlagh were driven by the need for more land and more food, and so they would mindlessly rush south, no matter what – or who – stood in their path. The servants of Jalkan – or Estarg, actually – were driven by their hunger for gold, and they would just as mindlessly rush north, no matter what stood in *their* path.

At some time in the far-distant past, Ara had heard someone speak of 'a war of mutual extinction'. It was a rather stuffy sort of term, but in this situation it seemed to come very close to what was really going to happen.

THE GREAT WALL

1

❱━❰

Sub-Commander Gunda had sailed south to the seaport of Castano on board the *Ascendant*, the ship of a distant cousin, and when they reached their destination, Gunda realized that his ancestral home was not nearly as attractive as he remembered. The harbor itself was littered with floating garbage, and the stone columns that supported the piers extending out into the harbor were covered with slimy green algae. The 'magnificent' buildings had all been turned a dirty grey by the perpetual cloud of smoke that came belching out of every chimney in town.

Gunda set aside the more comfortable clothes he'd worn on the voyage south and pulled on his black leather uniform, his polished breastplate and helmet, and belted on his sword. This *was* something in the nature of an official call, so it was appropriate for him to wear his uniform.

The waterfront of Castano was laced with stone piers, and it had that distinctive odor of rotting fish that quite probably hung over every seaport in the entire world. The streets of the town were narrow and dirty, and most of the people Gunda encountered had that lofty expression that virtually every Trogite in the empire seemed to be born with. The Land of Dhrall was very primitive, but it *was* clean – cleaner by far than the birthplace of civilization. Gunda sighed and went on through the port city to the south gate.

It was early summer now, and Gunda was quite sure that the gently rolling hills to the south of Castano would push his disappointment aside, but the hills were not nearly as impressive as he'd remembered them to be. His memories of the western part of the Land of Dhrall, where towering mountains ran down to the sea and gigantic trees reached up toward the sky kept intruding, and Gunda found the hill-country to the south of Castano rather skimpy by comparison.

The temporary encampment of the bulk of Commander Narasan's army lay just to the south of Castano, and it was more or less a canvas-tent duplicate of the army compound back in Kaldacin. That similarity made entering the camp almost like coming home for Gunda.

He walked through the open gateway in the log palisade surrounding the camp, sharply returning the salutes of the pair of guards, and went directly to the only building in the compound. Tents were adequate for sleeping, but army headquarters required something just a bit more substantial.

The clerks and various administrators in the large central room of the headquarters building all rose and came to attention as Gunda entered.

'Relax, gentlemen,' Gunda told them. Strict military courtesy had always irritated Gunda for some reason. 'Where's Andar's office?'

'Back through that hallway, Sub-Commander,' a very young officer replied, pointing toward the rear of the central room.

Gunda nodded and went on through the office.

Sub-Commander Andar was a bit taller than the average

Trogite, and, like most of the higher-ranking officers of Narasan's army, his hair was touched at the temples with silver. He was a solid, dependable man, and Narasan had left him in charge of the bulk of the army that was still here in the Empire.

Andar was dressing down a very junior officer for some blunder when Gunda entered the office. Andar had a deep, rolling voice, and he could turn oratorical at the drop of a hat. When he saw Gunda enter the office, though, he abruptly dismissed the young soldier.

'Did that boy make a serious mistake?' Gunda asked.

'Not really,' Andar replied. 'He's been getting just a bit full of himself here lately, is all, so I thought it was just about time to take him down a peg or two. How did things go up north, Gunda? We haven't heard a thing since the advance force left Castano.'

'Well, I guess we won the war in the western part of Dhrall – sort of,' Gunda replied a bit dubiously. He took off his helmet and absently brushed his hair forward to cover his receding hairline. 'There were a lot of things going on there that I didn't entirely understand.' He looked around at Andar's office. 'Are the walls here fairly solid?' he asked his friend. 'Some things happened up there in Dhrall that we probably wouldn't want to get spread around.'

'It's secure, Gunda,' Andar assured him, '—as long as you don't shout.'

'Good.' Gunda sat down in the chair beside Andar's desk.

'You encountered a few problems, I take it,' Andar rumbled.

'More than just a few, old friend,' Gunda replied. 'You probably won't believe this, but our revered Commander has come down with a bad case of friendship for a Maag pirate who goes by the name of Sorgan Hook-Beak.'

'You're not serious!'

'I'm afraid so. The peculiar thing is that it worked out quite well. The Maags are undisciplined, but they're very good fighters.'

'They're monsters, Gunda!'

'Maybe, but they're not nearly as monstrous as the things we were fighting.'

'Barbarians, I take it?'

'Several steps below barbarians, Andar. I don't think they even qualified as animals.'

'Could you be a bit more specific, Gunda? I want to know just exactly what we're likely to be coming up against.'

'You're not going to like it much,' Gunda said glumly. 'I think Narasan should have held out for more gold.'

'That bad?'

'Even worse, I think. If I understood what I was told correctly, the things we were fighting were only *part* human. The rest was a mixture of bugs and snakes.'

'I think your load's starting to shift,' Andar scoffed.

'*Everybody's* load shifts up in that part of the world, Andar. We kept coming up against a nightmare while we were still awake. One little nip from those bug-snakes will put you in your grave right there on the spot.'

'That's not the least bit funny, Gunda.'

'Do you see me laughing? I'm not making this up, Andar. You'd better take everything I tell you seriously, because your life could depend on it.'

'Are the natives up there as helpless as our employer suggested?' Andar asked.

'The natives of Veltan's Domain might be, but there's an archer up in Zelana's Domain who doesn't seem to know how to miss. *He* was the one who told us how to use the enemy's own venom to kill other enemies.'

'Is that really ethical, Gunda?'

'We were fighting *bugs*, Andar, not people. Ethics aren't relevant when your enemy isn't human.' Gunda paused. 'It's going to take you a while to hire enough ships to carry all of our men on up to Veltan's Domain, wouldn't you say?'

'*Quite* a while, I'm afraid. Sea-captains *love* to haggle, for some reason, and sometimes it takes half a day to hire just one ship. Were you planning an extensive visit to the local taverns to celebrate your homecoming?'

'Not really,' Gunda replied. 'I'm fairly certain that I know approximately where the Commander and the rest of the advance force is likely to be bound for, but I'm not sure that's where we'll be fighting the next war. I think I might want to drift around the waterfront just a bit and find one of those dinky little fishing-sloops – like the one Veltan used to take Narasan on up to the Land of Dhrall before the rest of us in the advance force went on up there. I'll have one of the clerks draw you a copy of my map so that you'll be able to find your way through the channel to the southern part of the Land of Dhrall. Then I'll go on ahead and talk with Narasan and find out just exactly where he wants us to go ashore. Then I'll come on back. I'll probably meet you somewhere in that channel through the ice, and I'll be able to guide you to the place where Narasan wants us to land.'

'That probably *would* save us quite a bit of time, Gunda.' Andar squinted slightly. 'Did we lose very many men up there?'

'Several thousand at least.'

'I don't suppose that Jalkan happened to be one of the casualties,' Andar said rather hopefully.

'I'm afraid not. The Commander had to reprimand him a few times, but that's about as far as it went.'

'What a shame,' Andar said regretfully.

'Don't give up hope, my friend,' Gunda said with a tight grin. 'It's only a question of time. Sooner or later, *somebody* will kill Jalkan, and then we'll be able to mark the date on our calendars.'

'What for?'

'I was thinking along the lines of something in the nature of a national holiday.'

'I'd be more than happy to celebrate *that* one, my friend,' Andar agreed.

Gunda moved around the seedy-looking waterfront of Castano looking for a reasonably priced fishing sloop for the next few days while Andar went through the tedious business of hiring enough merchant ships to carry the bulk of the army up to Veltan's Domain. Although Andar had access to the army treasury, Gunda was fairly certain that his friend would go up in flames if his sloop cost the army *too* much.

Gunda finally located a yawl that seemed to suit his purpose, and then he introduced Andar to the scruffy old fisherman who wanted to sell it. The two of them were haggling spiritedly when Gunda left the shabby waterfront tavern to have a word with his distant cousin, the captain of the *Ascendant*, about the rudiments of steering a boat. Despite his family background, Gunda knew next to nothing about boats.

The sun rose bright the following morning, and there was not a cloud in the sky, so Gunda went down to the harbor of Castano to play with his new toy.

He was moderately inept right at first, and he stirred up quite a few curses from other ships as he floundered around in the harbor, but after a few days he grew more practiced. He was quite certain now that, barring some natural disaster, he'd be all right at sea.

Then he went back to the army compound to see how Andar was coming along.

'I've still got a ways to go,' Andar admitted. 'I'm having a bit of trouble finding enough ships.'

'How many more do you think you'll need?'

'At least a hundred. You're not going to move eighty thousand men on a handful of ships.'

'I'll take the *Albatross* and go on ahead then.'

'*Albatross?*'

'It's a nice, seagoing sort of name, wouldn't you say? I mean, an albatross is a sort of second cousin to a seagull, isn't it?'

'I don't know if I'd use *that* name, Gunda. I've heard that sailors aren't really very fond of those particular birds. They seem to think that the presence of an albatross is bad luck, or something like that.'

'That's just a superstition, Andar.'

Andar hesitated slightly. 'Has Narasan finally got his head back on straight?' he asked quite seriously. 'He sort of went all to pieces after his nephew was killed in that war on down to the south.'

'He seems to be pretty much all right now. I think taking on this war in a different part of the world has helped him get over what happened to his nephew. Padan's keeping an eye on him, and he'll let us know if our glorious leader's still all in one piece. I'll go on up there and find out where Narasan wants us to put the army ashore, and then I'll come on back to lead you on in.'

'That's assuming that I can find enough ships to get everybody up there all at the same time,' Andar rumbled. 'I *might* have to make two trips, though. Ships of any kind are getting very scarce here in Castano, for some reason.'

'Do the best you can, old friend,' Gunda said. 'I'll see you in a couple weeks anyway.'

'You don't have to rush on my account, Gunda. I'm getting paid no matter what I do.'

Gunda set sail from Castano at first light the next morning, and when the *Albatross* moved out of the choppy water in the harbor and reached the open sea, she opened many new doors for him. He found that once he'd adjusted the set of the sail just right, she'd cut through the waves like a well-sharpened knife. The ropes creaked pleasantly, and the sharp bow seemed to hiss as the *Albatross* raced north. After an hour or so, Gunda realized that he could actually *feel* her reaction to the waves as she sliced through them.

The sun was going down when Gunda decided to put out a sea anchor to hold the *Albatross* in more or less the same location until morning, and then he bailed out most of the water that'd come seeping in during the day. She was a nice enough boat, but it seemed that she had a few leaks that really needed some attention.

He sailed on the next morning and by late afternoon the southern edge of the ice-zone came into sight. The *Albatross* obviously moved much faster than the wallowing Trogite merchant ships that had carried the advance army to the Land of Dhrall. 'Aren't you the little darling?' he said to her quite fondly.

As the sun was going down, Gunda entered the southern end of the channel through the ice zone and prudently moored the *Albatross* to a towering ice floe. This wouldn't be a good time to start taking chances.

He slept well that night as the *Albatross* rocked in the gentle waves almost like a baby's cradle. He awoke at first light, raised his sail again and cautiously moved on up through the mile-wide channel as the sun rose to greet him.

It was about noon on the following day when the *Albatross* reached the northern end of the channel, and Gunda relaxed a bit as he came out. There hadn't been any real danger involved in sailing up through the channel, but the towering ice floes *had* made him a bit edgy.

Once he'd cleared the ice-zone, a good following breeze came up, and the *Albatross* leaped ahead with unbridled enthusiasm. Gunda tried to shake off all of his almost poetic responses to things that he was fairly certain most sailors had learned to take in their stride, but he finally gave up. 'Oh, well,' he murmured, 'as long as we're enjoying ourselves, what difference does it make?'

It took him almost two days to reach the south coast of Veltan's Domain, and another day to reach the eastern-most peninsula. The south coast, he noticed, was primarily farmland, and the little villages along the coast seemed neat and orderly. Now that summer had arrived, the farmland that lay inland from the snowy-white sand beaches was bright green with newly sprouted wheat, and the blue summer sky was dotted with fleecy white clouds.

As he turned north to sail the *Albatross* up along the east coast of Veltan's Domain, Gunda came to realize just *why* he'd found Castano revisited so ugly. He was ruefully forced to admit that in comparison to the clean openness of the Land of Dhrall, the glorious Trogite Empire was cramped and dirty, and it reeked like an open sewer.

It was mid-afternoon of the following day when he saw the peculiarly mixed fleet of broad-beamed Trogite tubs and narrow

Maag longships anchored just off a white sandy beach. He approached the *Victory*, the ship of his cousin, Pantal, and he saw that his friend Padan was watching him very closely.

'Ho, Padan,' Gunda called.

'Is that you, Gunda?' Padan demanded, seeming just a little surprised. 'Where's the rest of the army?'

'Probably still back in Castano. Andar's having some trouble finding enough ships to carry all the men on up here. I'm not positive, but he *might* have to make two trips to get them all up here.' Gunda tied the bow of the *Albatross* to the anchor-chain of the *Victory*. 'I need to talk with Narasan. If he's found out where we'll encounter the enemy, I'll need to know the exact location so that I can put the army ashore there.'

'Not a bad idea,' Padan admitted. 'Come on board. There are a few things you should know.'

Gunda climbed up the rope ladder to the deck of the *Victory*, and he and his boyhood friend clasped hands. 'We've missed you, Gunda,' Padan said. 'You really startled me with that little fishing-boat. It looks a lot like the one that belongs to Veltan, and I wasn't really expecting to ever see *that* one again.'

'Oh? Has Veltan sailed away?'

'It wasn't Veltan who sailed off in that sloop. Scrawny Jalkan finally made the mistake we've all been waiting for. Narasan revoked his commission right there on the spot, and I dragged him down here to the beach in chains.'

'That's the best news I've heard in years,' Gunda said, grinning broadly. 'What did the little scumbag do that our glorious leader found so offensive?'

'He insulted the wife of one of Veltan's close friends.'

'That must have been *some* insult.'

'It was enough. Narasan almost fainted dead away when he heard it, and he revoked Jalkan's commission.'

'That sort of makes this whole war one of the nicer things in life, doesn't it? What's Veltan's sloop got to do with all this, though?'

'I was just getting to that. I brought the rascal down here to the beach and locked him in what I *thought* was a secure compartment down in the hold of the *Victory* here. He was chained to the wall, and the compartment door was barred from the outside. I was absolutely positive that there was no way he could escape, but I found out this morning just how wrong I was. Somehow, he managed to wriggle out of the chains, push the bar away from the door, and slip over the side of the ship. Veltan's sloop was anchored not far away, and when I woke up this morning, Jalkan – and sloop – were both missing.'

'Man, are *you* going to get yelled at!' Gunda exclaimed.

'I know,' Padan replied glumly. 'It won't be the first time, but I'm fairly sure that Narasan's going to rake me over the coals until the cows come home *this* time. I *really* blundered, Gunda, and Narasan will probably come down on me with both feet.'

'Poor baby,' Gunda said with mock sympathy. 'Where do I go to find our glorious leader?'

'He's probably still in Veltan's castle – in the map-room, most likely.' Padan paused. 'I don't suppose I could persuade you to keep what I just told you to yourself, could I?'

'That wouldn't be at all proper, Padan,' Gunda replied, 'and I've always been big on propriety.'

Commander Narasan was seriously discontented when Gunda told him that Jalkan had escaped. 'Why didn't Padan post guards on that slimy little rascal?' he demanded.

'You'll have to ask Padan about that, Narasan,' Gunda replied. 'Right now, I need to know just exactly where we want Andar to put the army on shore. They've probably left Castano by now, so it's likely that I'll meet him somewhere in the channel that comes up through the ice-zone.'

'Let's go to Veltan's map-room,' Narasan suggested. 'There's a sizeable river mouth a few days to the north of here, and we'll want the army to come ashore quite a ways up that river.' He paused. 'How did you manage to get so far ahead of the main fleet, Gunda?' he asked.

Gunda shrugged. 'I picked up a nice little fishing yawl down in Castano,' he replied. 'Her name's the *Albatross*, and she can go almost twice as fast as any other Trogite ship I've ever seen.'

Narasan winced. 'How much did you pay for her?'

'Couldn't really say, old boy,' Gunda replied in an offensively lofty tone. 'Andar's got the key to the army treasury, so I left all the haggling to him, while I went down to the harbor to persuade the *Albatross* that she was supposed to sail along in the water and not try to get up and fly.'

'Very funny, Gunda.'

'I'm glad you liked it, old friend.'

'You've got a bit of a problem, cousin,' Pantal said the next morning when Gunda rowed out to the *Victory*.

'Oh?'

'I hope you weren't planning to leave here this morning.'

'That's sort of what I had in mind,' Gunda replied.

'Right now, about the only thing that's keeping your yawl off the bottom of the harbor is that rope you tied to the *Victory's* anchor chain.'

'What are you talking about?'

'Come and look for yourself,' Pantal said, pushing a rope ladder over the side of his ship.

Gunda climbed up the ladder and followed his cousin over to the other side of the *Victory*.

He stopped and stared in utter disbelief at the *Victory's* anchor-chain. As Pantal had said, the rope from the bow of the *Albatross* was tautly hanging straight down, and Gunda could see the hazy outline of his yawl under the water.

'What happened to her?' he exclaimed.

'I think the word most people use is "sank",' Pantal replied.

'Did some rascal sneak out here and chop a hole in her bottom?'

Pantal shook his head. 'I had men on watch last night. Nobody came near the *Victory*. Who sold that tub to you?'

'An old fisherman in Castano.'

'Let me guess. He was more than a bit crippled, and even more drunk.'

'You know him?'

'Not by name, but there are a lot of people like him in Castano. He was getting along in years, and he had all those aches and pains that old men are always complaining about. Have you ever heard the word "caulk", Gunda?'

'Not that I remember. What does it mean?'

'Quite a bit of unpleasant work, cousin. Ships of any size are built out of boards. Have you noticed that?'

'Don't try to be funny, Pantal.'

'No matter how tight the shipbuilders jam the boards that form the hull of a ship together, water *will* start to seep through after a while. Sailors deal with that problem with a hammer, a chisel, and several bales of hemp. You ram the hemp between the boards and then poke and hammer it until it's well seated. The water will still try to seep in, but you *want* it to. When the hemp gets wet, it swells, and *that's* what seals up the hull. After you've caulked her hull, the *Albatross* will float like a well-sealed jug.'

'How often will I have to do that?'

'Every year, usually. If you happen to hit rough water fairly often, you might have to do it twice a year. Now you probably understand just why that old fisherman was willing to sell you his yawl. Just the thought of caulking her again probably gave him nightmares.'

'Cousin, I haven't got the faintest idea of how to go about doing something like that,' Gunda confessed.

'I didn't really think you would, cousin. I'll have my men take care of it for you – but it's going to cost you.'

'Somehow I knew that was coming,' Gunda said sourly.

'Nothing in the whole world comes free, cousin,' Pantal said. 'Why don't we go back to my cabin and talk about the price, shall we?'

Pantal's men raised the *Albatross* to the surface of the harbor, bailed her out and then hauled her on into the beach. Then they began the long, slow process of caulking up her hull.

'You're really quite lucky, Gunda,' Pantal said. 'Did you have to bail her out very many times when you were coming up here?'

Gunda shrugged. 'Two or three times, if I remember correctly. The old fisherman told me that she was sort of leaky, and that I should keep an eye on that. What was it that made her finally fill up with water and sink like she did?'

Pantal shrugged. 'It could have been any one of quite a few things – colder water, a large wave slapping into her on one side or the other, or a sizeable length of caulking giving away all at once. It's hard to say for sure. You could very well have drowned out there, you know.'

'When I get back to Castano, I think I'll look that old fisherman up and have a few words with him,' Gunda growled. 'How long's this likely to take?'

'Several days, anyway.'

'Couldn't you put more men to work on it? It's sort of important right now for the *Albatross* to be seaworthy again.'

'They'd just be getting in each other's way, Gunda. She's not all that big, so there isn't really enough room in her hull for two dozen men or more.'

The days seemed to drag on as Pantal's men re-caulked the *Albatross*, and Gunda spent most of his time in Veltan's map-room studying the region where the war here would most probably take place.

It was becoming increasingly obvious that Narasan would need the rest of his army here very soon. The *Albatross* had *seemed* to be the best answer, but Gunda was definitely starting to have second thoughts about that.

2

------◆------

'She's tight now, cousin,' Pantal advised Gunda late in the afternoon several days later, 'and I think she might surprise you. She hasn't been treated very well for several years, but now that she's been re-caulked, she'll go through the water like a hot knife through butter.'

'I *hope* so,' Gunda replied. 'I'd really like to get back to Castano like about four days ago.'

'I don't think she'll go quite *that* fast, Gunda, but you never know.'

'I'll do my best to find out. I've been watching the night sky for the last few days, and we've got a full moon now. If the sky stays clear, I won't have to drop anchor when the sun goes down.'

'That isn't the best idea in the world, cousin,' Pantal said a bit dubiously. 'If you're going to try sailing at night, stay a goodly distance away from any coast or islands. The *Albatross* doesn't draw much water, but still—'

'I'll be careful cousin,' Gunda assured him, 'but things are likely to start getting tight around here before too much longer, and Narasan's going to need the rest of his army *here*, not down in Castano.'

* * *

Pantal's assessment of the potential of the restored *Albatross* turned out to be a slight understatement. Sometimes it seemed that she almost flew as Gunda raced on down the east coast of Veltan's Domain. When he reached the tip of the peninsula jutting out from the south coast, however, he found that he had to fight the prevailing wind. Somewhat reluctantly, he lowered the sail and fell back on the oars.

Fortunately, the wind changed direction before the blisters on his hands started bleeding, and he raised the sail again.

Then he discovered that there was a steady current moving in a westerly direction along the north side of the ice zone, and he reached the channel that led south in just under two days. Of course, he was taking advantage of the full moon now, so the actual sailing time probably wasn't much different than it had been when he'd come up from Castano. He was more than a little sandy-eyed as he started down along the channel, but he'd discovered that he *could* get by on no more than four or five hours of sleep a night. He was always tired, of course, but he promised himself several good nights of sleep *after* he reached Castano.

It was late in the afternoon of his fourth day out from Veltan's harbor when he saw the north coast of the empire low on the southern horizon. 'Well, well,' he murmured to the *Albatross*, 'You done real good, baby. I'm proud of you. As soon as we reach the harbor, we'll be able to catch up on our sleep. Won't that be nice?'

Then Gunda laughed just a bit wryly. 'I think maybe my load's shifting again. I almost expected her to answer me. I *really* need some sleep.'

He was jarred back into complete wakefulness as soon as he entered the harbor of Castano, however. As closely as he could determine, every pier and wharf along the entire waterfront of the city had several broad-beamed ships tied to it, and the men on board those ships were all wearing the distinctive red uniforms of church soldiers.

'What are *they* doing here?' Gunda exclaimed. 'Those idiots!'

He beached the *Albatross* some distance up the coast from the central waterfront, chained her to a large tree, and then went around the city wall to the army encampment just to the south of the city. He went on through the gate and entered the headquarters building.

'Where have you been, Gunda?' Andar demanded in his deep, rumbling voice.

'I got held up for a while up in the Land of Dhrall,' Gunda replied. 'What's going on here in Castano? Every place I looked I saw a church ship.'

'They aren't talking to anybody, Gunda,' Andar replied. 'The church armies started marching in about three days ago, and then that church fleet sailed into the harbor. They've taken over the entire waterfront, so there's no way I can load our men on the ships I hired. I'm not sure just exactly where those church armies are going, but it looks to me like they're planning a major campaign somewhere.'

Gunda started to swear – extensively.

'Was it something I said?' Andar asked.

'Jalkan!' Gunda snapped.

'Please, Gunda, don't use that kind of language. There are children nearby.'

'It's about time for them to grow up, then.' Gunda managed to get his temper under control, and he told Andar about Narasan's revocation of Jalkan's commission and the little scoundrel's imprisonment in one of the Trogite ships.

'I'd say that it's time for a celebration, then.'

'Not really. Somehow, Jalkan managed to get loose, and then he stole Veltan's sloop and sailed away. We both know exactly where he went, don't we?'

'In the light of what's been going on here in Castano, I'd say that he most probably went to the central convenium in Kaldacin, and he was more than likely to have been spouting the word "gold" before he even got there, and it's quite obvious that *some* of the higher-ranking churchmen took him at his word. That *does* sort of explain just why the church has expropriated every single wharf here in Castano, wouldn't you say?'

'And there's not much we can do about it. Can you come up with any kind of estimate of just how many church soldiers are boarding those ships?'

'Church armies have distinctive banners, just like real armies do. I've had people watching, and so far there's evidence that there are five church armies being loaded on those ships in the harbor.'

Gunda winced. 'That's about a half-million men, Andar. We've already got *one* war on our hands, we definitely don't need another one. Have you caught any hints about just *when* that church fleet's likely to sail out of the harbor?'

'I'd say probably sometime in the next two days,' Andar replied. 'There's something else you should know about, Gunda. Yesterday, a couple of ships with black sails arrived, and the men on board those ships conferred at some length with the higher-ranking churchmen. We all know what *that* means, don't we?'

'Slavers?' Gunda said. 'What are they—?' He broke off. 'Of course!' he exclaimed. 'They're *not* planning to rush up the east coast to confront Narasan. Slaves are *almost* as valuable as gold, and the church armies won't have to fight anybody to gather up potential slaves – not in a region where all the tools and weapons are made of stone, anyway.'

'You could be right, Gunda. I'd say that it's too bad that the pretty-lady's husband didn't go a step or two further than just a punch in the mouth. A sword in the belly or an axe right between the eyes would have solved this problem before it even started, wouldn't you say?'

'I met him – briefly. He's one of those people who just ooze decency out of every pore. Evidently, a punch in the mouth was about as far as he felt he should go.'

'Decent people can be *so* inconvenient at times,' Andar complained.

As Andar had predicted, the church fleet began to leave the harbor of Castano two days later, and Gunda put his uniform aside, dressed himself in some scruffy clothes, laid some rolled-up fish-net across the bow of the *Albatross*, and sailed out of the harbor in a generally northern direction. He easily outdistanced the wallow-ing church ships, and reached the floating ice-zone not long after noon the following day. He put out his nets about a half-mile from the southern end of Veltan's channel, and then he waited.

It was almost dark when the first of the red-sailed church ships reached the mouth of the channel and dropped their anchors. 'What took them so long?' Gunda murmured to the *Albatross*.

As he'd been almost positive they would, the church ships hauled anchor as the sun rose and sailed on into the channel. 'Well,' Gunda muttered to the *Albatross*, 'that answers *that* question, doesn't it, baby?'

She didn't exactly answer him, but she *did* bob slightly in what *seemed* to him to be a sign of her agreement.

'It's time to go on back to Castano, baby. We'd better let Andar know what the church people are up to.'

Andar bent several rules as he loaded the soldiers of Narasan's army on board the ships he'd hired. There were a few shrill protests when he announced that there would be no separate quarters for the officers, and, since the weather was pleasant, there was no *real* reason for everybody in the army to have a roof over his head. The ships that sailed from the harbor were extremely crowded, but the entire army *was* going north, despite the fact that there weren't *really* enough ships to carry them all. Practicality was often necessary, but sometimes Andar carried it to extremes.

Gunda had attached a long rope to the bow of the *Albatross* and tied the other end to the stern of the lead-ship, the *Triumph*, and when the *Triumph* approached the channel through the ice-zone, he went to the cramped cabin that served as Andar's headquarters. 'I think we might want to be just a bit careful when we go out of the north end of the channel,' he suggested. 'It might be best if you stayed out of sight of the southern coast. If our count was right, there are probably five church armies camped along the southern shore, and it might be better if they don't know that we're here. I'll take the *Albatross* in a bit closer and see what the churchies are up to.'

'Don't take any chances, Gunda,' Andar cautioned. 'Narasan's likely to have me for lunch if I let you get killed.'

'I'll be careful, Andar. All I really need to know is whether the church ships are anchored along the coast. I'm almost positive that they are, but let's make certain. We don't want to have to go looking for them.'

A couple of sailors helped Gunda pull the *Albatross* up close behind the *Triumph*, and then Gunda slid down the rope and untied it from the bow of his little sloop. He quickly raised her sail, swooped on around the *Triumph*, and sailed on toward the north end of the channel.

It was almost dusk when the *Albatross* came out into open sea again, and Gunda sailed north toward the coast of the Land of Dhrall in fading light. The moon was still in her last quarter, and Gunda knew that he'd have plenty of light once she rose, so he anchored the *Albatross* some distance to the north of the ice-zone to wait for her.

It was quite probably almost midnight when the moon rose, and Gunda raised the anchor of the *Albatross* and rowed her on toward the coast, reasoning that if he left her sail down, she'd be almost invisible as he went along the south shore.

The villages along the coast were easy to locate because of the lantern-light coming from the crude houses, and Gunda rowed the *Albatross* slowly past each village he came to. There were several church ships anchored just out from each village. Gunda couldn't make out too many details, but it seemed that there were some kind of enclosures in the vicinity of each village, and they appeared to be well-guarded by red-uniformed church soldiers.

'It looks to me like we were right, baby,' he muttered to the *Albatross*. 'I think we've seen enough. Let's go back and talk with Andar.'

3

---❯◆❮---

The *Triumph* and the following fleet reached the eastern-most peninsula jutting out from the south coast of Veltan's Domain three days later, and Gunda was startled to see what appeared to be the whole fleet of Maag longships moving swiftly down from the north. Things were just a bit tense until Gunda managed to get Sorgan's attention. For some reason, the Maags seemed to be in a belligerent frame of mind. Gunda climbed down a rope ladder to the *Albatross* and rowed on over to the *Seagull*. 'What's afoot?' he called up to the burly Ox.

'It seems that we've got us another war on our hands,' Ox shouted back.

'How did *you* find out about it?' Gunda demanded. 'I thought *we* were the only ones who knew.'

'We were up in the mountains and Veltan came popping out of nowhere and told us that a whole fleet of Trogite ships had landed down here in the south. The cap'n told him that we'd take care of it for him.'

'That makes sense,' Gunda replied, pulling the *Albatross* in beside the *Seagull*. 'I think I'd better have a talk with Sorgan. I believe I've managed to come up with the answers to a few questions he might have.'

'Come on board, then.' Ox pushed a rope ladder over the rail, and Gunda climbed on up even as Sorgan came forward from the stern of the *Seagull*.

'What's going on down here, Gunda?' he demanded.

'I've got the rest of Commander Narasan's army on those ships over there, Sorgan,' Gunda replied. 'We're bound for the mouth of the River Vash, like the commander told me to back in Veltan's castle. Anyway, when I got back to Castano, the church had appropriated every pier and wharf in the entire harbor, and they were busy loading five church armies onto church ships. When that was all done, they sailed north. I followed them in that little fishing yawl of mine, and, sure enough, they sailed right into the mouth of the channel through the ice-zone. Isn't it peculiar that not too long after Jalkan had escaped and stole Veltan's sloop, a whole fleet of church ships loaded up five armies and came sailing up through that channel in the ice?'

'So *that's* what set this off!' Sorgan exclaimed. 'Were you able to find out just exactly where they were bound for?'

'I was indeed, Captain Sorgan,' Gunda replied with a broad grin. 'We kept our main fleet out of sight, but I rowed my little yawl on up to the south coast. There are four or five church ships anchored just off the beach any place where there happens to be a farming village, and there'll probably be slave-ships arriving before long.'

'We sort of expected that,' Ox said, his eyes narrowing.

'I thought you might have,' Gunda said. 'It's a very old church custom, I'm sorry to say. It's been contaminating the Empire for centuries now. The slave-ships have black sails, but the sails on the church ships are red. The Amarite church is very fond of the color red. It tells everybody who passes by just how terribly important the church is.'

Sorgan grinned suddenly. 'I think we've come up with a way to make them very unhappy about red things, Gunda,' he announced.

'Oh?'

'Fire's sort of red, wouldn't you say? After my people have set fire to every one of their ships, they'll probably wish that they'd never *heard* the word "red".'

'What a wonderful idea!' Gunda replied. 'Now why didn't I think of that?'

Sorgan laughed an evil sort of laugh. 'When you see Narasan, tell him that we're down here, and we'll do what we came to do.'

'I'll do that, Captain Sorgan. You have a nice day now.' Gunda grinned at the pirate and then climbed back down to the *Albatross*.

There were still a few ships anchored off the beach near Veltan's castle, but most of the fleet had already sailed off to the north, so Gunda didn't see any reason to stop.

The coast to the north of the castle was quite a bit more rugged than had been the case farther south, and there were mountains rearing up a few miles inland. 'Picturesque,' Andar observed, gesturing at the mountains.

'Enjoy them while you can, my friend,' Gunda replied. 'They stop being pretty when you start climbing. Narasan showed me a map of the region where we'll almost certainly encounter the enemy, and it didn't exactly brighten my day. There's a narrow sort of pass that'll take us on up to the top, and that'll slow us down quite a bit. I don't think we'll be able to go up through that pass any more than five men abreast, so it's going to take us quite a while to get the whole army up there.'

Andar sighed. 'Oh, well,' he said. 'Difficult wars pay better, I guess.'

'Only if you're still alive when payday rolls around,' Gunda reminded his friend.

It was late afternoon of the following day when they reached the mouth of the River Vash, and it appeared that most of the ships that had carried the advance force were anchored there. Gunda saw the *Victory*, the ship that belonged to his cousin Pantal, near the center of that fleet, and Gunda and Andar took the *Albatross* and rowed on over to find out just how things stood.

'We haven't heard very much yet, Gunda,' the stocky Pantal admitted. 'The troops that are going up that gulch – or whatever you want to call it – have it pretty well blocked off, so nobody's able to come back down and let us know what's afoot up there.'

'That happens a lot in hilly country,' Gunda said. 'How far upriver is this pass located?'

'About two days. Are you familiar with Brigadier Danal?'

Gunda nodded. 'He's been in Narasan's army for almost as long as Padan and I have.'

'He's more or less in charge at the mouth of the pass. He's been very useful. He had his men build quite a few piers along the north bank of the river, and when you've got a pier on both sides of a ship, you can unload your troops in a hurry. He's having a bit of a problem sending the supplies on up to the top, though. A man who's trying to carry a sack that weighs a hundred pounds doesn't move very fast.'

'Are we likely to hit any rapids on the way upriver?' Andar asked.

Pantal shook his head. 'It's fairly smooth going this far down-river,' he replied. 'The natives say that things get a little rough farther upstream, but that's not really any of our concern.'

'Good,' Andar said. 'We'll start upriver first thing in the morning, then. It's likely to take quite a while to unload all the troops, so we'd better get at it.'

The *Triumph* started upriver at first light the next morning, and Gunda's friend Andar seemed a bit awed by the size of the trees along the banks of the river. 'How long would you say it'd take a tree to grow to be that big?' he asked Gunda.

'I don't even want to guess,' Gunda replied. 'I wouldn't put it at much under five hundred years. Some of those really big ones have probably been there for at least a thousand years.'

'Can you imagine something that's been alive for a thousand years?'

'I don't think it's very exciting. You wouldn't be able to do much exploring if your roots kept you in the same place for all those years.'

'I had an idea last night before I went to sleep,' Andar said.

'Like whether you wanted to sleep on your back or your belly, maybe?'

'It went a bit further, Gunda. Your cousin told us that the men who are loaded down with supplies are slowing things down quite a bit.'

'I seem to remember that, yes.'

'A man could move quite a bit faster if he didn't have to carry so much weight, wouldn't you say?'

'I try not to say obvious things very often. It makes people think that you're dull when you do that.'

'Did you want to hear this, or would you rather make bad jokes?'

'Sorry. What's this grand plan of yours?'

'Twenty-five pounds wouldn't really slow a man down would it?'

'Not noticeably. Where are you going with this?'

'We've got eighty thousand men. If each man carried twenty-five pounds up that gully, we could put two million pounds of supplies in Narasan's hands when we reached the top.'

Gunda blinked. 'Did you work that out in your head when you were half-asleep, Andar?'

'No, not really. I had to do some figuring on a piece of paper. Two million pounds would be a thousand tons.'

'That *would* keep the army eating for a while, I suppose.'

'Our troops will be going up there anyway, and carrying supplies while they're climbing up would be more useful than looking at the scenery, don't you think?'

'Where did you find somebody clever enough to string all those ropes up through that pass, Danal?' Gunda asked, staring up the steep gully.

'It was a young fellow named Keselo, I think,' Brigadier Danal replied.

'I should have guessed that, I suppose,' Gunda admitted.

'Is he really *that* bright?' Andar asked.

'Sometimes he's almost bright enough to shine in the dark,' Gunda replied sourly. 'That irritates me, for some reason. Young soldiers are supposed to be stupid, and Keselo breaks *that* rule every time he turns around. "Wise" is supposed to belong to us older soldiers, but Keselo keeps poaching in our territory.' He straightened. 'I guess I'd better scamper on up there and let Narasan know that we've arrived with the rest of his men,' he said.

'Don't forget your pack, Gunda,' Andar reminded him.

'I *am* going to be in a bit of a hurry,' Gunda protested.

'It's one of the obligations of higher-ranking officers to set examples for the ordinary soldiers,' Andar reminded him.

'You *had* to go and say that, didn't you?'

'That's one of *my* obligations, Gunda,' Andar replied with a broad grin. 'I'm obliged to remind you of all the things *you're* obliged to do. It's a heavy burden, but I think I'm strong enough to carry it. Take the pack, Gunda. Don't argue with me.'

'What's in this pack that's supposed to fill our commander with delight?'

'Beans, isn't it, Danal?' Andar asked.

Danal nodded.

'*Beans?*' Gunda demanded. 'You're beating me over the head with a sack of *beans?*'

'Would you prefer rocks?'

The basin at the top of the narrow pass appeared to be primarily a meadow dotted here and there with clumps of trees. About the only unusual feature of that basin was the source of the River Vash. Gunda had heard about geysers before, but this was the first time he'd actually *seen* one. His mind shuddered away from the thought of the sort of underground pressure that could send water spurting a hundred or so feet into the air in such volume that it was the primary source of a river that was quite nearly a mile wide at the mouth.

There was an old sergeant lounging in the shade of a tree near the top of the pass, and he stood up and saluted when Gunda came out of the steep pass. 'The Commander's men have set up camp at the north end of the basin sir,' he supplied, pointing toward a broken-down ridge-line. 'From what I've heard, he's been waiting for you and the rest of the army.'

'Has the enemy made any attacks, yet?' Gunda asked.

'None that I've heard about, sir.'

'Well, that's something, I guess.' Gunda hitched up his pack and went on up to the north end of the basin to Narasan's camp.

The north ridge appeared to have been shattered by some sort of natural disaster, and the ruins looked almost like the walls of a city that had been battered by catapults for a year or more. It was most probably the peculiar rocks of the region that caused Gunda to compare a natural formation to a man-made one. The peaks which had formed the ridge were almost universally black, and when they'd shattered, they'd broken off into innumerable rocks with flat surfaces. Gunda even saw a sizeable number of black rocks littering the red-colored slope that led down toward a very large depression – also red – that extended out from the foot of the slope. Gunda was vaguely aware of the fact that red-colored rocks – or sand – were somehow related to iron. That was just a bit baffling. If there was so much iron ore in this region, why did the natives make all their tools and weapons out of stone?

He shrugged and went on into the army camp just to the south of the shattered ridge-line.

'You made good time, Gunda,' Narasan observed when Gunda reported in. 'We were more than a little worried that you might have encountered that church fleet on the south coast.'

'I think we might have got lucky,' Gunda replied. 'When I got back to Castano, the church had commandeered every wharf in the harbor. They sailed north, and I went on up to the channel to make sure that we were right about where they were going. We were, of course. Then I went on back to Castano, and Andar had been breaking rules for all he was worth – little things, like no separate quarters for officers, no roof over *everybody's* head, and a few others he didn't mention to me. He managed to get the entire army on board the ships we had, but several of them were low enough in the water that even a mild storm would have shoved them under.'

Narasan winced.

'It's summertime, old friend. The chance of a storm at sea is pretty slim right now. Anyway, we encountered Sorgan down near the south coast, and the notion of burning church ships has him all excited, doesn't it?'

'It thrills *me* more than just a little, as well,' Narasan admitted. 'The thought of having one enemy army attacking from the north and another from the south didn't make me very happy.'

'What's in that bag you've got tied to your back, Gunda?' Padan asked.

'We're not going to laugh about this are we, Padan?' Gunda demanded grimly.

'Why would I want to laugh?'

'It's an idea that Andar dreamed up one night. All of the army's food supplies are stacked up in big piles on the river bank. Danal had conscripted a fair number of burly soldiers to carry them up here, but the weight of the packs slowed them down to a crawl, and that was hindering the movement of the rest of the army. Andar suggested that reducing the weight might speed things up, so from here on, every soldier who comes up that pass will be carrying twenty-five pounds of food with him.'

'Now *that* would never have occurred to me,' Narasan admitted.

'What are *you* carrying, Gunda?' Padan pressed.

Gunda clenched his fist and held it up in front of Padan's face. 'Beans,' he said, 'just beans, and don't even *think* about laughing, Padan.'

'I wouldn't dream of it, old friend,' Padan replied with no hint of a smile.

'Good. You get to keep your teeth, then.' Gunda turned back to Commander Narasan. 'Has anybody seen any of the snake-men yet?' he asked.

'No,' Narasan replied, 'but the enemy knows that we're here. It appears that the thing all the natives call "the Vlagh" has been experimenting again. It has scouts watching us, but this time they're bats, not snakes. They've still got poisonous fangs, though.'

'Flying snakes?' Gunda exclaimed.

'It's not quite as bad as it sounds, Gunda,' Padan said. 'That clever little Maag who works for Hook-Beak suggested that fish nets might be the best answer to the problem, and it seems to be working quite well. None of our people have been bitten – yet.'

'Don't start tacking "yet"s onto everything you say, Padan,' Gunda growled. 'That's very irritating, you know.'

'Just trying to cover all the possibilities, old friend.'

'I'm glad you came on ahead, Gunda,' Narasan said. 'You're the expert when it comes to building forts, and we've got a bit of a problem staring us in the face this time.'

'Oh?'

'If you look around, you'll see that this basin up here's surrounded by fairly steep ridges – all except for this one on the north side – and that, naturally, is almost certainly the direction from which the enemy will attack. There's a gap about a mile wide in this ridge. I think it'd take almost all summer to build a fort that big. Padan's had men laying a base across that gap, but it's slow going, I'm afraid.'

'You must have slept through some of our classes when we were boys, Narasan,' Gunda said bluntly. 'When you want to block off something of that size, you build a wall, not a fort. After I'd heard about that, I made a special trip off to the area to the east of

Kaldacin to look at the wall that separates the cities of Falka and Chalan. The people of those two cities never really got along with each other for some reason, so the rulers sort of collaborated in the building of a wall that separates them.'

'Bugs – or snakes, for that matter – wouldn't find climbing a wall very difficult, Gunda,' Padan objected.

'They will if there are towers jutting out from the face of the wall every hundred feet or so, Padan – particularly if there are archers on top of the towers. Archers could peel them off that wall every time they started to crawl up, couldn't they?'

'You might be right, Gunda,' Padan conceded.

'Let's try it,' Narasan said. 'This problem's been keeping me awake for quite some time now.'

'You can go back to sleep now, glorious leader,' Gunda said smugly. 'Mighty Gunda has returned, and so all's well.'

'That's *very* irritating, Gunda,' Narasan said sourly.

'I'm glad you liked it, glorious leader. Now, then, what did you want me to do with these beans. I'm starting to get a little tired of carrying them around.'

'It's called "basalt", Sub-Commander Gunda,' Keselo explained. 'We almost never encounter it down in the Empire, but it's quite common in areas where there are volcanoes.'

'What makes it break off square like this?' Gunda demanded.

'I'm not really certain, sir. Our instructor at the University of Kaldacin didn't give us too many details when he was describing rocks that weren't common in the Empire.'

'Was there *anything* you didn't study when you were going to school, Keselo?' Gunda asked curiously.

'Not really, sir,' Keselo admitted. 'I was trying my best to avoid making decisions at that particular time. I *did* avoid theology, though. The teachers in the theology department were all Amarite priests, and the students in their classes were expected to pass around a collection plate during every session.'

'Those people will do almost *anything* to get their hands on all the money in the world, won't they?'

'They always seem to try, sir,' Keselo agreed.

'At least we *earn* our money. Let's go back to this rock. Is it strong enough to use for buildings – or forts?'

'It's a bit more brittle than granite, sir, but the enemy *this* time doesn't understand catapults or battering rams, so basalt should stand up.'

'That's all I really needed to know,' Gunda said. 'Flat rocks are easier to work with than round ones, and these flat black rocks are scattered around all over up here.'

'That's probably because we've got volcanoes all around us here.'

'Fire-mountains, you mean?' Gunda asked with a certain alarm.

'That's what Red-Beard called them. Not *every* volcano spits fire, though. Some of them just spew out ash instead of liquid rock.'

'Is there any kind of warning when something like that's about to happen?'

'There are usually a few earthquakes before the top of the mountain gets blown away.'

Gunda shuddered.

Keselo looked on out toward the grassy basin. 'Here comes Rabbit,' he said.

'Wasn't he supposed to go south with Sorgan?'

'Veltan borrowed him,' Keselo explained.

'What an interesting idea. I can't remember the last time I borrowed somebody.'

Rabbit came up from the grassy basin to join them on the shattered ridge-line. 'I hear tell that you're going to build a wall along here,' he said.

'That's the plan,' Gunda replied.

'Would it bother you if I made a suggestion?'

'Not really,' Gunda said. 'What did you have in mind?'

'Do you suppose that when you get up to the top you could add some poles about ten feet tall on the front side and the back?'

'That shouldn't be too hard. What are we going to use poles for?'

'To hold up the fish-netting.'

'I don't think we'll see very many fish trying to fly over the top of the wall, Rabbit.'

'Maybe not, but we probably *will* see the bug-bats. Longbow seems to think that they're just flying around to see what we're doing, but Red-Beard said that he could smell the venom on the one that Longbow killed. If they get all tangled up in the fish-netting, they probably won't be able to bite anybody.'

'That's not a bad idea, but I think the net might get in our way if we've got enemies climbing up our wall.'

'Bats only come out at night, I've heard,' Rabbit said. 'We can raise the nets up high enough to get them out of your way in the daytime, and then lower them again when the sun goes down.'

'That might work out fairly well,' Gunda conceded. 'Trying to fight a war at night wouldn't be very much fun, anyway.'

The flat black rocks Keselo had identified as 'basalt' worked very well, and, since Gunda had the majority of the men in Narasan's army at work building the wall, it was coming along even faster than they'd hoped. If the snake – bug – bat – whatevers held off for just a few more days, the wall – complete with the towers – would be finished, and the whatevers would be in deep trouble.

Narasan spent most of his time now observing the progress of Gunda's wall, but he also kept an eye on the progress of the breast-works Padan's men were building on down the slope that angled up from the floor of the vast desert the natives called 'the Wasteland'. The breast-works were being erected in the classic half-circles, butted up against the ridge on the right of Gunda's wall, circling down the slope and then coming back up to rejoin the ridge on the left side. The slope was littered with chunks of basalt, so there was plenty of building material available. The first breast-work was fairly close to Gunda's wall, and when that one was finished, Padan's men began to erect the second one. If Padan had enough time, he'd quite probably keep building those breast-works until he reached the desert floor. All in all the breast-works and Gunda's wall had reproduced a fairly standard defensive position. There were a few local peculiarities as well. Gunda had heard that *some* Trogite armies included sharpened stakes in front of each breast-work to hold off advancing armies, but Gunda was almost positive that the stakes back home had *not* been dipped in deadly venom. All in all, Gunda was quite pleased with their project. They had effectively replaced the shattered ridge-line, and they could almost certainly hold their fortifications in the face of whatever the enemy tried to throw at them for the rest of the summer.

Off to one side of the breast-works young Keselo was training the local farmers in the rudiments of the phalanx formation, and Gunda was forced to admit that the boy was really very good. The farmers he was training were almost as good as professional soldiers now. 'Have you been watching Keselo very closely, Narasan?' Gunda asked. 'That boy's coming right along.'

'I've been watching Keselo for quite some time now, Gunda,' Narasan replied.

'He's good, isn't he?'

'Indeed he is. If we can manage to keep him alive, he might go a long way in our army.'

'All the way to the top, maybe?'

'It's not entirely out of the question, Gunda. He's extremely intelligent, and he's an excellent teacher. I didn't really think those farmers would be of much use during this war, but Keselo's managed to make first-rate soldiers out of them in a very short period of time. Of course, they haven't actually encountered the enemy yet, but I'm fairly sure they'll hold their positions when the enemy attacks.'

'We'll see,' Gunda said. 'This isn't what I'd call an ordinary war. So I'm not about to make any bets.'

Gunda's wall was nearly finished when Veltan came up from his encampment near the geyser to advise Narasan that Longbow's humorous friend Red-Beard had just arrived with several thousand of the archers from the Domain of Lady Zelana. 'He met with Longbow over on the western ridge,' Veltan said, 'and he has quite a bit of information that you and your men should know about, Narasan.'

'Like just exactly where Longbow's been lately?' Padan suggested.

'He's been keeping busy,' Veltan replied.

Red-Beard was speaking with Lady Zelana when Narasan and his officers approached the camp.

'Just exactly what's Longbow been up to lately?' the little Maag called Rabbit asked Red-Beard. 'He's been running off into the mountains every time I turn around.'

'He's up near the top of the western ridge,' Red-Beard replied. 'At least that's where he was the last time I saw him. I understand that there's some trouble off to the south.'

'We're sort of hoping that Longbow's taking care of it,' Commander Narasan said. 'I detached all the archers in the army to help him hold back that second invasion.'

'He mentioned that,' Red-Beard replied. 'Things might go better for him now that he has archers who know which end of an arrow is which. I wouldn't offend you for the world, friend Narasan, but your army archers aren't really very good, you know. Don't they ever practice?'

'Army policy seems to get in the way, friend Red-Beard,' Padan said. 'Trogite soldiers are required to spend five hours a day marching, and another five hours practicing their swordsmanship. That doesn't leave them very much time to improve their skills as archers.'

'Why do they even *carry* swords?'

'Tradition,' Padan replied with a shrug. 'Army officers – and drill sergeants, of course – view traditions as something holy. Soldiers are supposed to kill each other with their swords. The bow is viewed as an abomination. Killing somebody who's more than five feet away just isn't proper.'

Red-Beard looked at Commander Narasan. 'He's just making this up, isn't he?' he demanded.

'Not really,' Narasan replied, sounding a bit embarrassed. 'Maybe it's time for us to give some thought to changing a few rules.'

'Won't that make the world come to an end?' Padan asked.

Narasan ignored that. 'Go on with your story, Red-Beard,' he said.

'Longbow told me that he'd had to do *most* of the work when the people in red clothes came running up one of the narrow gullies. I guess your archers can *see* the people in red clothes, even if they can't put an arrow anywhere close to them, so Longbow's got them watching every gully that comes up here from down below. Things will probably go much better now that he has people who know what they're doing. I don't think the people in red clothes will give us much trouble now.'

'We need those archers *here*, Red-Beard!' Gunda protested. 'Our entire defense here hinges on them.'

'I'd say that we've got an interesting problem, then. We can argue about it if you want, but Longbow's already got half of the archers I brought in over the mountains, and I don't think he's very likely to let them go.'

4

Gunda's men were putting the finishing touches to the wall a
few days later, and Gunda felt that it had turned out rather
well. The flat basalt rocks were solid, even though they were a bit
rough. He was sure that if he'd erected such a wall down in the
Empire, it would have generated quite a few sneers, but this *wasn't*
the Empire, and Gunda hadn't had time enough – nor the inclin-
ation – to sheathe his wall with polished marble slabs.

It was about noon that day when a large cloud of dust began to rise
up from the floor of the Wasteland far on below the slope. Gunda
immediately sent word back to Commander Narasan, and it wasn't
too long before the top of Gunda's wall was cluttered with
observers – including a couple who quite obviously came from alien
lands. The scar-faced Ekial didn't seem out of place, but Gunda was
a bit startled – and awed – by the warrior queen Trenicia.

'I'd say that we've got visitors on the way,' Andar rumbled.

'But I don't have a *thing* to wear!' Padan protested.

'Does he do that very often?' Andar asked Gunda.

'All the time,' Gunda replied. 'He thinks he's funny, but I
stopped laughing years ago.' He squinted on down the slope. Then

he looked at Veltan. 'I might be wrong,' he said, 'but it seems to me that the desert out there's quite a bit lower than it was when we were fighting the war in the ravine above Lattash.'

'This was the deepest part of the inland sea that covered the Wasteland in the distant past,' Veltan explained. 'I've never actually taken any measurements, but I rather think that depression out there's even lower than the floor of Mother Sea.'

'Maybe if you talked with Mommy real nice, she'd fill that sink-hole out there with water again,' Padan suggested.

'Mommy?' Veltan looked a bit confused by the word.

'Wouldn't that sort of get you on her good side?' Padan asked with a feigned look of wide-eyed innocence.

'I don't think our baby brother would want to take any chances there,' Lady Zelana advised. 'He made a mistake when he was talking with her once, and she sent him to the moon without any supper.'

'Are there *really* that many enemies down there?' Andar asked, staring at the dust cloud with awe.

'They're probably just kicking up dust to conceal their real numbers,' Danal suggested. 'That's not an uncommon practice, you know. If you don't have as many men as your enemy has, you don't want him to know it, and if you've got more, you want to hide that as well.'

'It's possible,' Lady Zelana said, 'but this is probably a new hatch. After what happened in the ravine above Lattash, the Vlagh didn't have many servants left, so it had to spawn more. It *might* just be that it's been experimenting again. The Vlagh's always coming up with different varieties of children.'

'I'm still having trouble with that,' Keselo admitted. 'Are we *really* being attacked by *women*?'

The burly warrior woman from the Isle of Akalla reached for her sword.

Veltan put a restraining hand on her arm. 'He wasn't trying to offend you, Queen Trenicia,' he said. 'It's just that he's not at all familiar with your culture.'

'Somebody should explain it to him,' the warrior queen declared.

'I wouldn't really think of the servants of the Vlagh as "women", Keselo,' Lady Zelana cautioned. 'They're females, of course, but the majority of *all* insects are female. The males only have one responsibility – which I don't think we need to discuss just now.'

Young Keselo suddenly blushed a bright red.

Lady Zelana laughed with delight. 'Isn't he just the dearest boy?' she said to the rest of them. 'Anyway,' she continued, 'when the Vlagh produces a hatch, it numbers in the tens of thousands.'

'But those would only be babies,' Andar protested.

'Very true,' Zelana agreed, 'but the childhood of an insect is only about a week long. After that, they're full-grown adults.'

'And females as well?'

'Exactly.'

'The life of a boy-bug might be very interesting,' Padan mused.

'It *does* have some drawbacks, young man,' Zelana warned him. 'After he's performed his duty, he's of no particular use any more, so the servants of the Vlagh – females, of course – bite off his head and throw him out with the rest of the garbage.'

'Does a career as a boy-bug still interest you, Padan?' Gunda asked rather blandly.

'I'm starting to have some second thoughts,' Padan admitted with a shudder.

* * *

A breeze came up an hour or so later, and it blew most of the dust cloud away, and the onlookers atop Gunda's wall were stunned by the sheer numbers of enemies they now saw moving purposefully across the ruddy desert far below. 'I think it's time for us to take up our positions, gentlemen,' Narasan said grimly to his officers.

'Is it my imagination, or are the ones down there quite a bit bigger than those we encountered in the ravine?' Padan asked.

Gunda squinted down the slope. 'It's sort of hard to tell for sure at this distance, but I think you might be right.' He turned to Veltan. 'Can that Vlagh thing do that? I mean, can it just double the size of its soldiers in no more than a month?'

'Probably,' Veltan replied. 'The Vlagh's an imitator. When it sees a certain characteristic that seems to be useful, it modifies the next hatch to include that peculiarity. The men of the Land of Maag are very tall, so I'd say that the Vlagh imitated that characteristic in this current hatch.'

'Why didn't it just build bigger warriors right from the start?' Rabbit asked.

'Bigger creatures need more food,' Veltan explained, 'and there's not really very much to eat out there in the Wasteland. There's been much more food available since the war in the ravine, so now the Vlagh can afford to spawn out bigger servants.'

'Trees and bushes, you mean?'

'Probably not,' Veltan replied. 'Wars produce dead people, and other dead things as well. There was plenty to eat after that war. The volcanos burned a lot of that food, but apparently the servants of the Vlagh managed to salvage enough to feed the larger warriors.'

'That's disgusting!' Keselo exclaimed.

Veltan shrugged. 'The Vlagh doesn't think the way we do,

Keselo,' he replied. 'It'll do whatever's necessary to get what it wants. Then too, there's never really been enough food out in the Wasteland to feed enough servants to achieve the Vlagh's ultimate goal. When you get right down to it, that might just be what this war's all about.'

'Gunda!' Andar shouted from the top of a nearby tower. 'Look on past the first rank of enemy soldiers. I think we've got an entirely different variety of enemies coming this way.'

Gunda peered through the dust rising from the lower end of the slope. At first he didn't see anything at all unusual, but then his eyes caught a peculiar movement low to the ground. Then a brief gust of wind cleared the air. '*Turtles?*' he said. 'Why on earth would the Vlagh want turtles?'

'They *are* about ten feet across, Gunda,' Padan noted, 'and if I'm counting right each one of them has eight legs.'

'Spiders?' Gunda demanded. 'Part turtle and part spider? That doesn't make any sense at all.'

'I'm afraid it does, Gunda,' Veltan disagreed. 'I think the Vlagh just stole a very good idea from our Trogite friends.' He reached out and tapped Gunda's metal breastplate. '*This* idea, actually,' he said. 'Now the Vlagh has soldiers that wear armor.'

'But why did it use spiders instead of reptiles?' Padan demanded.

Veltan shrugged. 'Spiders can move faster, and they can spin webs.' He frowned. 'I'm not entirely certain about this,' he admitted, 'but I *think* spider venom is even more deadly than reptile venom.'

'I think we're in a lot of trouble,' Padan said.

The larger variety of snake-men made a few probing attacks along the outermost breast-works, but fell back as the sun settled down towards the western horizon, and Commander Narasan sent out word that it was time for a conference.

'Definitely time,' Gunda muttered to himself as he went down the stairs on the backside of his wall to join the others.

'These ones are at least twice as large as those we encountered in the ravine,' Keselo reported, 'but it didn't seem to me that they were quite as quick or agile.'

'Bigger has always been clumsier,' Rabbit suggested. 'I learned that fairly early in life.'

'It's possible – even probable – that this is the first hatch of these larger snake-men,' Veltan disagreed. 'It's going to take them several generations to adjust to their altered size.'

'Doesn't that suggest that we'll win this war before they've learned how to deal with their new size?' Padan asked.

'I wouldn't make any large wagers on that, my friend,' Gunda disagreed. 'If what happened in the ravine is any indication of what they're capable of, they might just surprise us, and when you're fighting things with poisonous fangs, "surprise" usually means dead.'

'Did any of those larger ones come anywhere near your breastworks, Keselo?' Narasan asked.

'No, sir,' Keselo replied. 'It seemed to me that all they were doing was watching.'

'Were you able to get any idea of just how thick their shells are?' Red-Beard asked.

'Not really,' Keselo admitted. 'They were holding back.'

'An arrow with an iron tip *might* penetrate those shells, but I don't know that I'd want to bet my life on that.'

'We might want to give some thought to catapults, Commander,' Andar suggested. 'If "sharp" won't do the job on those beasts, then "heavy" leaps to mind.'

'It has some possibilities, sir,' Brigadier Danal agreed. 'A fifty-pound rock would almost certainly shatter those shells, wouldn't you say?'

'It's worth a try, I suppose,' Narasan agreed.

Then Sorgan Hook-Beak's younger cousin Torl joined them near the fire.

'How are things going on down south,' Veltan asked.

'Well,' Torl replied a bit dubiously, 'we burned all the ships the Trogs had anchored down there, but I'm not sure that did us all that much good. There were some very strange things going on down there.'

'Why don't you start at the beginning, Captain Torl?' Narasan suggested.

Torl shrugged. 'We burned every one of their ships, but it didn't mean a thing to them. They'd already left the region by the time we got there.'

'*Left?*' Gunda exclaimed. 'Where did they go?'

'I'd say that they're coming *here*,' Torl replied.

'Do you suppose you could start from the beginning, Captain?' Narasan asked again.

Torl described a number of peculiar events down on the south coast, and what he called a 'fairy tale' was the most peculiar. Gunda couldn't fully understand what Torl was describing, but Narasan seemed to think that it might be important, so he took Torl on down to where Veltan and his sister were staying. Gunda shrugged. He had other things on his mind just then.

There were several hundred of the enemy bug-bats tangled up in Rabbit's fish-nets the next morning. Longbow had told them that the flying enemies were in all probability serving only as scouts, but they were still venomous, and that made Gunda go cold all over. He sent a crew of his men armed with long, venom-tipped spears down along the wall to dispatch the helplessly fluttering creatures and another crew wearing thick leather gloves to untangle the dead enemy scouts from the nets and then to dispose of them.

The larger variety of the enemies Sorgan Hook-Beak had called 'the snake-men' made a few very tentative approaches to the breastworks on down the slope, but there was nothing even remotely resembling an all-out attack as yet. The huge ones with turtle-shell breastplates stayed quite some distance to the rear, which didn't bother Gunda all that much, since the crews that he'd put to work building catapults weren't quite ready yet.

It was about noon when the bleak-faced archer Longbow came up across the grassy basin to speak with Commander Narasan and Veltan. Gunda went on down the stairs at the rear of his wall to join the small group that met with the archer.

'Are those church soldiers still coming up through those gullies?' Padan asked.

'I think they've pretty much given up on the gullies,' Longbow replied. 'The shepherds showed us every single route that anybody could possibly follow to reach this basin, and there were archers covering them all. It took those soldiers quite some time to realize that they wouldn't stay alive if they tried to reach the top through those passes, so now they've all gathered at the foot of the waterfall.'

'They're going to try swimming instead?' Padan asked.

Longbow smiled faintly. 'Not that I've seen so far,' he replied. 'Apparently they've given up the notion of finding some easy way to get up here, so they've fallen back to "difficult".'

'Oh?' Padan said. 'Ladders, maybe?'

Longbow shook his head. 'Even fanatics wouldn't be stupid enough to think *that* would work. It looks like they've decided that they need a highway, so they're building one.'

'I'm not sure I follow you, Longbow,' Narasan said.

'They started quite some distance below the falls,' Longbow explained, 'and they're building a ramp along the side of the west wall of the gorge where the falls are.'

'Right out in the open?' Padan demanded. 'I wouldn't have thought that even church soldiers could be stupid enough to try something like that when your archers are lining the top of the gorge. They won't get very far up that side if it's raining arrows on them every minute of the day.'

'They've come up with a way to keep that particular rainstorm from making their lives difficult,' Longbow said.

'Oh?'

'I think it's called "a roof", Padan,' Longbow explained. 'It appears to be a very nice roof that's going to keep them from getting wet – or dead. I think a fairly large number of them *will* reach the top of that ramp when they finish building it. Whether we like it or not, it appears that we *will* have to deal with two separate enemies up here.'

THE SEA OF GOLD

1

It was about noon when Longbow decided that it might not be a bad idea to advise Zelana and her brother of the situation and to suggest something in the nature of a conference *before* their outlander friends started to make decisions that could quite possibly be disastrous.

As he walked on down into the grassy basin that surrounded the huge geyser, he let his mind wander back to that day in the deep forest that had always been his home when Zelana and Eleria had sought him out and persuaded him – or, more accurately, coerced him – into joining them and their family in this ongoing war. That particular day had changed his life forever.

In many ways, Longbow regretted that. Life alone in the forest had been very simple, since nothing had interfered with the hunt, and the hunt had been his sole purpose since the day when Misty-Water had died. He'd known exactly how to hunt down the brainless servants of the Vlagh and kill them, and he'd found great satisfaction in his ongoing retribution.

It was a warm day, and actually rather pleasant as Longbow went on down toward the geyser. Grassland was not really as nice as the forest, certainly, but there *was* a certain beauty there. Longbow could see much farther here, of course, but he missed the trees and the excitement of the hunt. Wars *did* kill more of the servants of the Vlagh, even as Eleria had said that it would on that day when he'd first met Zelana and the little girl, but wars were complicated, and they involved large numbers of people moving from this place to that, and endless, and tiresome, discussions and arguments.

That always seemed to come back to him in his dealings with the outlanders. They seemed to enjoy arguing with each other about things that weren't really significant. A solitary hunter could move faster and reach his goal much sooner than any army in the world could possibly match, probably because there was nobody around to argue with.

'I'm not really cut out for this,' Longbow conceded rather ruefully. 'Maybe I should have given the whole thing just a bit more thought.'

The geyser which was the source of the River Vash was really quite spectacular – something on the order of a large column of water reaching up for nearly a hundred feet before it flared out, almost like a blossoming flower.

Zelana and child Eleria had set up a rather rudimentary camp far enough away from the geyser to avoid the continual spray of water carried by even the slightest breeze. Longbow amended his notion that the place where they spent most of their time could be called 'a camp', since it consisted of little more than a crude bed where Eleria slept and a wooden pail half-filled with fruit for her to eat. Zelana, of course, did not need a bed, nor food, for she was complete, and needed nothing.

Eleria came to him with her arms out, as always, and when he picked her up, she said – also as always – 'kiss-kiss'.

Longbow smiled and then kissed the delightful child.

'Is it my turn now?' Zelana asked.

'All in good time,' Longbow replied. 'I thought it might be a good idea for you and your brother Veltan to pay our outlander friends a little visit. Some things have been happening here lately that have disturbed them quite a bit.'

'Oh?' Zelana asked.

'We have what appears to be a second invasion coming up from the south. Sorgan's cousin Torl told us a rather peculiar story about some things that happened when the armies of the Trogite church landed on the south coast of your brother's Domain. He said that every time a church soldier mentioned gold, the local farmers all recited a story about a huge amount of gold sand somewhere out in the Wasteland, and as soon as the soldier heard that story, he was driven to dash up this way to gather up as much as he could carry.'

'I've heard about that, Longbow,' Zelana replied.

'Right at first, I thought that the Vlagh might have created this hoax as a way to destroy Narasan's army, but now I'm starting to have second thoughts. Wouldn't that be just a bit too complicated for the Vlagh?'

'Not really,' Zelana replied. 'There *were* servants of the Vlagh involved in Kajak's attempted attack on the *Seagull* back in the harbor at Kweta, remember?'

'Yes, but that only involved a few Maags. This time, we're talking about half a million men – *and* Kajak had actually *seen* the gold Sorgan had stacked up in the hold of the *Seagull*. The only thing the Trogites off to the south have to go on is a rather vague folk tale, and why would that give them any reason to attack Narasan's army? It just doesn't make any sense.'

'Don't blame *me* for that, Longbow,' Zelana replied. 'Go shout at the Vlagh.'

'Sorry, Zelana. Irrational things irritate me, that's all. All I really came here for was to suggest that you and your brother should come by Gunda's wall and head off any wild ideas Narasan might devise. The notion of being attacked from two directions at the same time is starting to disturb him quite a bit, so we'd better see what we can do to settle him down.'

'It'll cost you a kiss-kiss, Longbow,' she said with a sly little smirk.

They gathered near the back side of Gunda's black basalt wall late that afternoon as the sun neared the ridge-line to the west. Narasan and most of his officers were there, and Rabbit and Torl sort of represented Sorgan.

'Just to make sure that we all know what this is all about, why don't you tell us what you saw near that waterfall, Longbow?'

'There's not really too much to tell, Narasan,' Longbow replied. 'The church armies seem to have finally realized that trying to come up here through those various stream-beds wasn't going to work for them, since we had archers in place to shower arrows on them every time they tried that. Now they're all gathered just below the falls, and they're building a ramp up along one side of that gorge.'

'That's stupid, Longbow,' Rabbit declared. 'Your bowmen can rain arrows down on them all day long if they do that.'

Longbow shook his head. 'They're roofing it over, little friend. From what I was able to see, the roof's not very substantial, but it's good enough to hide them, and an archer has to be able to see what he's shooting arrows at.' He paused, squinting off toward the rosy sunset. 'Their ramp isn't really all that wide, though,' he added. 'I suppose we *could* put a sizeable number of archers in place to kill them as they came out into the open. We'll need a lot of arrows, though.'

'You're on your own this time, Longbow,' Rabbit said with a sly grin. 'My forge and my anvil are still on board the *Seagull*, so I won't be able to help you very much.' Then he frowned. 'This is starting to have a very familiar smell, Longbow. The thought of all that gold on board the *Seagull* turned Kajak's head off back in the harbor at Kweta, and now we've got several Trogite armies that seem to be having the same problem.'

'That's something we might want to consider, Veltan,' Zelana said to her brother. 'When you came looking for me in the Land of Maag, you picked up a few hints in Weros that the Vlagh had servants in the Land of Maag, and they'd been tampering with Kajak.'

'Picking up a few Maag pirates is one thing, dear sister,' Veltan replied dubiously, 'but we're talking about five Trogite armies and half of the priesthood of the Amarite church here. I think you might be stretching things more than a little bit.'

'It's *not* impossible, little brother. The Vlagh had servants watching us – even when we were a long way from the Land of Dhrall – and that means that it's aware of just how big an impact gold has on the outlanders. In a very real sense, we've been using gold as bait. I caught Sorgan, and you caught Narasan. Wouldn't you say that the Vlagh might very well have realized just how good our bait really is? If it's had servants out there waving gold at those Amarite priests – and all those church armies – it's entirely possible that it's managed to catch more than a few of them, and now they're blindly rushing up from the south, overcome with greed and totally unaware of just exactly what will happen to them if they win.'

'And just what might that be?' Gunda asked her with a puzzled look on his face.

373

Longbow stepped in at that point. 'After they've rushed up here and destroyed you and all of our other Trogite friends, the Vlagh won't really need them any more,' he explained. 'If that's the case, it's quite possible that the servants of the Vlagh will invite their new-found friends to dinner, where the friends will be the main course.'

'That's terrible!' Gunda exclaimed in horror.

'Oh, I don't know, Gunda,' Andar said. 'When you've got two enemies and one of them eats the other one, it solves quite a few problems, wouldn't you say?'

'All right, then,' Narasan said in a crisp tone, 'we might not like this very much, but we *are* going to have to deal with it. If anybody has any ideas, now's the time to let the rest of us know about them.'

'We *do* have the advantage of higher ground,' Danal mused. 'That roof the church soldiers are building over their ramp might protect them from arrows, but I don't think it's sturdy enough to stay in place if we start dropping boulders on it.'

'Particularly when we're dropping them from two hundred feet up,' Andar added in his deep voice. 'That ramp of theirs is an interesting idea, but it's got a few holes in it – or it *will* have after we've dropped some five-ton boulders on it.' He frowned. 'They should have realized that, shouldn't they? The commanders of the church armies aren't really all that bright, but even an idiot would be able to see that, wouldn't he?'

'Their brains have gone to sleep,' Sorgan's cousin Torl said bluntly. 'That's what I was telling you before. Just as soon as one of the farmers down south recited that fairy tale about oceans of gold up here, the soldiers started to run in this direction as if their very lives depended on it. They aren't thinking any more, so they can't see any holes in a plan that some halfwit scrapes off the wall. *Somebody's* tampering with them somehow.'

'It *is* the sort of thing the Vlagh might try, little brother,' Zelana suggested to Veltan.

'I have to admit that it smells a bit Vlaghish,' Veltan agreed, 'but as closely as we've been able to determine, there are *five* church armies down there. That's a *half-million men*, Zelana! *Some* of those men should be at least partially awake, wouldn't you say?'

Zelana shook her head. 'The Vlagh's accustomed to dealing with large numbers of servants, and there's no such thing as independent thought among its creatures.' She paused. 'If the level of thought among those church soldiers has been reduced to that of insects, the only thing that concerns them right now is the possibility that others might reach the gold before *they* do.'

'You could be right, dear sister,' Veltan agreed glumly.

'They'll have to get up past the waterfall before they give us much trouble,' Narasan said firmly as he adjusted his iron breast-plate. Then he looked at Padan. 'Why don't you gather up a few thousand men and go on down to the south end of this basin, old friend? Let's find out how much church soldiers enjoy a sudden downpour of five-ton boulders.'

'Iff'n y' want 'er that way, that's the way we'll do 'er,' Padan declared in a clever imitation of the Maag dialect.

'Clown,' Narasan murmured with a faint smile.

It all sounded quite practical, but Longbow had a few doubts. Something very peculiar was happening, and Longbow was quite sure that he wouldn't rest easy until he managed to put his finger on just exactly what it was.

The discussion among the black leather-clad Trogites continued even after the sun had gone down, but Longbow didn't see that it was really getting anywhere. Zelana, clad in filmy gauze, was sitting beside a small fire some distance away from Veltan's hired soldiers with the sleeping child Eleria in her arms when Longbow quietly joined them. 'What does firelight taste like?' he asked curiously.

'Smoke,' she replied. 'It's not nearly as pleasant as the light in my grotto, but it's better than darkness. What are Veltan's soldiers doing?'

'Arguing,' Longbow said. 'There seems to be quite a few disagreements about just exactly how to proceed. If you'd like, I'll escort you two back to your little camp near the geyser, and we can put Eleria in a more comfortable bed.'

'I don't really mind holding her, Longbow,' Zelana said, looking fondly at the little girl's face, 'but you might be right. She'll probably sleep better in a regular bed.'

Longbow smiled and helped her to her feet. Then he took the sleeping child Eleria in his arms. 'This isn't going at all the way we'd expected, Zelana,' he said quietly as they walked on down toward the geyser. 'Gunda's fort and the barricades Padan and his men built on down the slope below the wall would have probably held the creatures of the Wasteland back – *if* the archers from your Domain hadn't been diverted to hold back that second invasion. To make things even worse, Narasan just had to send a goodly number of the men we'll need *here* to go on down to the falls to destroy the roof over that ramp. We need more men, but we don't have any.'

'Why don't you go on down to the southern part of your baby brother's Domain and tell Hook-Big to come back up here where he belongs, Beloved?' Eleria suggested in a sleepy sort of voice. 'The trouble's *here*, not down there.'

'Aren't you supposed to be asleep?' Zelana asked her.

'How can I sleep when you two keep talking?' Eleria replied in a peevish sort of tone. 'Since you're the one who's paying Hook-Big, he's supposed to do what you tell him to do, isn't he? Let *his* people drop rocks on the bad people from the south, and then bring the good people back here to do what your baby brother tells *them* to do.'

'I think she's right,' Longbow said a bit ruefully.

'Of course I'm right,' Eleria said. 'I'm *always* right. Now you owe me a kiss-kiss.'

'Just go back to sleep, little one,' Zelana told her. 'She *is* right, Longbow. I'll go on down to the south coast and tell Hook-Beak to stop playing and get back up here as fast as he can.' She paused then and gave Longbow a sly look. 'Then you'll owe *me* a kiss-kiss too, wouldn't you say?'

Longbow chose not to answer that.

At first light the following morning, Longbow joined Veltan and Narasan on the top of the central tower of Gunda's wall. 'Are they moving yet?' he quietly asked.

'Nothing so far,' Veltan replied. 'They'll probably wait until the sun comes up.' He peered down the slope. 'Exactly where did you put Omago's men, Commander?'

'Keselo's stationed them at the outer edges of the breast-works,' Narasan replied. 'If things here go pretty much the way they did back in the ravine, the main enemy attacks will hit the center of that outermost breast-works. Omago's men haven't been involved in any real conflict as yet, and over the years we've found that it's usually best to sort of ease new warriors into serious battles. I don't want to offend you, Veltan, but I'm fairly sure that a goodly number of your farmers won't really have the stomach for killing.'

'I think they might surprise you, Narasan. Omago can be very clever when the need arises, and he made quite an issue of the fact

377

that the creatures of the Wasteland are primarily bugs – no matter what they *appear* to be – and farmers absolutely *hate* bugs.'

'We'll see,' Narasan replied a bit dubiously.

Longbow was peering down the slope in the dim light of early morning. 'They're starting to move,' he said quietly, pointing out at the rocky Wasteland.

'I don't quite—' Veltan began. 'Oh, *now* I see them,' he said. 'They're quite some distance from the first barricade, aren't they?'

'We surprised them several times during the war in the ravine,' Longbow explained. 'Apparently, the Vlagh doesn't like surprises very much.'

'I'll have to admit that I don't really know all that much about them,' Veltan said a bit ruefully. 'The *real* expert in my family is Dahlaine. Before the emergence of people, Dahlaine spent eons studying insects. From what he told me once, the Vlagh is something on the order of a thief. When it sees a characteristic that might be useful, it attempts to duplicate it. I'm just guessing here, but I'd say that almost all of its experiments fail, and the altered creatures are dead before they even come out of the eggs. Every so often, though, one of them survives, and the Vlagh duplicates it by the thousand. Then it begins to experiment with the survivors.'

'That sort of explains all these new varieties of enemies, doesn't it?' Narasan mused. 'The tiny ones we encountered in your sister's Domain didn't turn out too well – particularly in the face of those natural disasters. *This* time we have enemies that fly, as well as enemies that wear armor.'

'Not to mention some *other* enemies who appear to be real people,' Longbow added. 'This might just turn out to be a very interesting war.'

'I'd really prefer one that was boring,' Narasan added. 'Interesting wars tend to set my teeth on edge.'

As had almost always been the case during the war in Zelana's Domain, the attack on the outer breast-works began with a hollow-sounding roar coming from somewhere off to the rear of the advancing force. Longbow noted that the larger servants of the Vlagh were not nearly as agile nor as quick as the smaller ones had been, and they proved to be easier targets for the Trogite archers Red-Beard had been training.

As the sun rose up over the ridge-line to the east, Rabbit came up the steps to the top of the wall. 'Can you see Keselo down there?' he asked. 'I don't really have very many Trogite friends, so I don't want to lose him.'

'He's over on the left side of what Narasan calls the "breast-works". Narasan says that it's fairly standard practice to sort of ease beginning soldiers into the main battle.'

'I don't think those farmers are going to work out all that well, Longbow,' the little Maag said dubiously. 'If you want to make a warrior out of somebody you need to start out when he's a lot younger than most of the people Omago gathered up are, and the pay needs to be better.'

'We'll see.'

There were more than a dozen of those chest-high barricades laid out across the slope that ran down to the Wasteland, and Narasan's soldiers – along with Veltan's farmers – were manning the farthest one away from Gunda's wall. Longbow and his little friend weren't able to see very many details, but it appeared that the Trogites weren't really having too much trouble holding the overgrown snake-men back.

Then, along about noon, another of those commanding roars

came from quite some distance back out in the Wasteland, and the surviving enemies turned and fled back out into the red-tinged desert.

'Now *that's* something we never saw back in the ravine,' Rabbit said. 'I thought that the bug-people were too stupid to even know *how* to turn and run.'

'Maybe they learned a few things in the ravine,' Longbow suggested.

'I thought you had to have brains to learn,' Rabbit scoffed, 'and bugs don't *have* brains, do they?'

'They *do* have a brain, little friend,' Longbow disagreed, 'but they don't carry it around with them. It's the Vlagh – or more probably the "overmind" – that does all the thinking. Maybe the "overmind" finally realized that throwing servants away isn't really a good way to win a war.'

The golden summer afternoon wore on, and there were no further attacks by the servants of the Vlagh. The somewhat tentative nature of this first attack seemed to make everyone atop Gunda's wall a bit edgy. It was increasingly obvious that most of Narasan's men shared Longbow's suspicion that their enemy had in some sense come to realize that sheer brute force had little chance of success.

'I don't like this at all, Narasan,' Gunda admitted. 'If that thing out there is starting to think – even a little bit – we could be in a lot of trouble here. The midget snake-men we came up against back in the ravine weren't really clever enough to be able to tell night from day, but these bigger ones? I don't know. If one of them just happens to pick up a rock and throw it at us, we're looking at an entirely different war.'

'You're being obvious, Gunda,' Narasan observed. 'For right now, about all we can do is remain flexible. If the enemy comes up with anything at all new and different, we'll have to come up with ways to deal with it – in a hurry, most likely.'

The sun was low over the western ridge when Keselo came on up to the wall. He quickly climbed up the rope ladder and joined Longbow and the others on top of the central tower.

'The enemies seem to be quite a bit bigger this time, Commander,' he reported to Narasan.

'We thought that was the case,' Narasan replied. 'Did you notice any other peculiarities?'

'They're just a little awkward, sir, and they can't move quite as fast as the smaller ones back in the ravine.'

'Do they still have the fangs and stingers?' Gunda asked.

Keselo nodded. 'That part hasn't changed. Their mouth-fangs are larger, and the stingers on their forearms are longer.'

'That would suggest that their venom sacks are larger, wouldn't it?' Rabbit asked.

'We didn't take one apart to verify that, friend Rabbit.'

'Just offhand, how many of them did the soldiers kill?' Gunda asked.

'Several hundred, anyway,' Keselo replied. 'I didn't walk along the breast-works and take a count. From what I saw, though, it appears that the venom on our spear-points is still strong enough to kill them. That had me just a bit worried, to be honest about it. If that venom we gathered at Lattash had lost its potency, we could have been in a lot of trouble. The reason I really came up here was to get permission to move Omago's farmers closer to the center of the breast-works. They seemed to feel just a bit left out because their positions were off to the sides where they were fairly safe.

Now that they've seen how *real* soldiers operate, they'd like to see a bit more action.'

'You're in charge of them, Keselo,' Narasan said. 'The decision is yours.'

'And so are any mistakes you happen to make,' Gunda added with a slight smirk.

'Thanks, Gunda,' Keselo replied sourly. Then he looked directly at Narasan. 'I had a notion just after the enemy pulled back, sir,' he said. 'If we were to wait until it gets dark and then pull back to the next line of breast-works and plant a good number of poisoned stakes in the open ground between the two, the enemy will probably be more than a little confused if they attack again tomorrow.'

'That's not a bad idea at all, Keselo,' Gunda said approvingly. 'And then you could move your men back to the outermost breast-works tomorrow night. If the enemy thinks you've deserted that first breast-works, he'll probably just try to romp on over it, and your people could destroy half an army without much trouble at all.'

'And then fall back to the *third* line during the second night?' Keselo suggested.

Gunda blinked. 'Now why didn't *I* think of that?' he said. 'You're a very nasty young man, Keselo. After a week or so of bouncing back and forth like that, the enemy's going to be so confused that he won't know which way to turn.'

As night fell, the Trogite soldiers atop Gunda's wall unrolled the fish-netting to hold back the bug-bats. Longbow was almost positive that the Vlagh's imitation bats were primarily scouts, but Narasan preferred not to take any chances.

Dahlaine, the grey-bearded eldest of Zelana's family joined them on the central tower. 'They don't seem to move after dark, do they?' he observed.

'There are plenty of bug-bats out tonight, big brother,' Veltan replied. 'They may not bite, but they *are* flying around out there in the dark.'

'You *did* give your men down on the slope enough of that netting to protect *them*, didn't you?'

'We gave them netting, Dahlaine, but I don't think they'll really need it. So far as we've been able to determine, the bug-bats never bite anybody. Their job seems to involve watching us and then carrying what they've seen back to the Vlagh.'

'You're wrong, Veltan. Once the actual fighting starts, *all* of the servants of the Vlagh turn belligerent. Right now, those fish-nets are the only thing that's keeping your soldiers alive.'

Longbow, however, had come up with an alternative. 'Night vision would be absolutely necessary for a creature of any kind to have if it was watching other creatures after the sun goes down, wouldn't it?' he asked Veltan's older brother.

'I'm sure it would,' Dahlaine agreed.

'And wouldn't a very bright light almost blind a creature that never comes out of its hiding place until after darkness sets in?'

Dahlaine blinked, and then he suddenly burst out laughing. 'Don't go away, Longbow,' he chortled. 'I'll be right back.'

There was a sudden flash of light and crack of thunder and Dahlaine was gone.

Moments later, there came another flash and a sharp crack. Dahlaine had returned, and he was holding a small glowing ball in his left hand. 'Don't look at her too closely, friends,' he cautioned. 'That's very bad for your eyes.' Then he opened his hand, and the small object rose up into the air, glowing brighter and brighter as it moved upward. Then, when it was perhaps a quarter of a mile above Gunda's wall, it stopped, and the light emanating from it grew so intense that it flooded the wall and the slope leading down to the Wasteland as if noon had suddenly appeared out of nowhere.

The bat-bugs in the vicinity shrieked in agony, and immediately fled from the light.

'What in the world *is* that little thing?' Gunda asked in an awed voice.

'Just one of my pets,' Dahlaine replied. 'If she were larger, we'd probably call her a sun.'

2

At first light the following morning, Longbow climbed down the rope ladder on the outer side of Gunda's black wall and went down the slope, easily leaping over the rough-stone barricades Padan's men had erected. Given the agility of the smaller servants of the Vlagh they'd encountered back in the ravine, it seemed to Longbow that the barricades might be more effective if they were higher, but he decided not to make an issue of it.

His primary reason for this early visit to the outermost barricade was to speak with the men who'd actually encountered the Vlagh's most recent experiments.

He found Brigadier Danal and Sub-Commander Andar, garbed in the standard Trogite black leather and bright-gleaming iron, talking quietly together near the center of the barricade.

'You're up early,' Danal said as Longbow joined them. 'Is there something afoot?'

'Not yet,' Longbow replied. 'I haven't seen any of the newer creatures up close, so I thought that I should talk with some people who'd actually encountered them. Did you notice any significant differences?'

'They're much more clumsy than the ones we fought back in the ravine were,' Danal said. 'Sometimes it almost looks like they're stumbling over their own feet.'

Longbow nodded. 'That's not uncommon,' he replied. 'If I remember correctly, when I was still growing I had the same problem. If your body grows so fast that your mind can't adjust to the new size, you'll probably trip over every blade of grass you come across. Were there any of the ones with turtle-shells involved in yesterday's attack?'

'None that *I* saw,' Sub-Commander Andar replied in his deep, rumbling voice. 'Did *you* happen to see any, Danal?'

'No,' Danal replied, 'and I think I'd rather keep it that way, too. A poison-fanged enemy is bad enough, but a poisonous one with armor added might just be a lot worse.'

'Did Keselo mention his notion of falling back to the next breast-works after nightfall?' Longbow asked them.

Andar nodded. 'It's an interesting idea, but I don't think it'll work very well unless somebody can come up with a way to put out that bright light hanging over this slope. We'll need darkness to hide what we're doing.'

'Smoke might work,' Danal suggested.

'Only if you can find enough firewood,' Andar disagreed.

'We won't have to come up with anything until this evening,' Longbow told them. 'How are your archers doing?'

'They're better than they were before,' Danal replied. 'They aren't as good as *your* people are yet, but they seem to be able to hit what they're aiming at about half the time.'

'They're probably letting their arrows fly too soon,' Longbow advised. 'You might want to lay out a line of some sort – twenty or thirty feet out to the front. Then tell them not to release any arrows until the enemy crosses that line.'

'We'll give it a try,' Andar rumbled.

Longbow drifted off to one side, and then he sent a silent thought out to Zelana.

'*Was* there something?' she asked in a lofty sounding voice that she knew very well irritated him.

'Your brother's little sun is very nice, Zelana,' he said, 'but if the men out here are going to try Keselo's deception, they'll need darkness to conceal what they're doing.'

'If Dahlaine puts his little sun away, the bats will probably come back out again, Longbow,' she reminded him. She paused. 'Wouldn't fog conceal them almost as well as darkness?' she asked. 'Dahlaine's little toy sun would still keep the bats away, and the fog would conceal the movements of Narasan's forces from the other servants of the Vlagh.'

'I hadn't even considered fog,' Longbow admitted, 'probably because fog's very rare in the mountains at this time of year. Could you really bring in a fog-bank along about sunset today?'

'Of course I can, Longbow. You should know that by now.' She paused. 'It'll cost you another kiss-kiss, though.'

Longbow was almost certain that Zelana's imitation of Eleria's favorite expression was nothing more than a form of teasing, but then again . . . ?

As the sun rose, the inhuman roar from out in the Wasteland announced the beginning of the second day of the war in the South. Longbow moved along behind the breast-works advising the marginally trained Trogite archers to wait until the enemy force was almost on top of them before they loosed their arrows.

'Is it really a good idea to let them get so close, sir?' One earnest young archer asked.

'It's better to wait than it is to waste arrows,' Longbow replied. 'If they're close enough, you can't miss. Then too, if there's a big pile of dead ones out in front of this barricade, it'll hinder the ones coming along behind. Look at it this way, young friend. What you're *really* doing with your bow is constructing another barricade, and you're using dead enemies as building blocks.'

The young Trogite laughed a bit nervously. 'I guess I hadn't really thought of it that way, sir,' he admitted. 'The nice part is that I won't even have to pick up any heavy blocks to build that wall, will I?'

'Always let your enemy do the hard work,' Longbow agreed.

'I'll remember that, sir, and I'll tell all my friends as well.'

'Good idea.'

'Sergeant Red-Beard should have told us to do it this way when we first started.'

'*Sergeant* Red-Beard?' Longbow demanded incredulously.

'That's what we all called him when he started training us. Do you think it might have offended him?'

'Oh,' Longbow replied, trying very hard to keep from laughing, 'probably not. Red-Beard's fairly relaxed.' Then he had a thought. 'If you want to be correct, though, his *real* title is "Chief".'

'I'll tell all my comrades about that. It's always best to use correct titles, don't you think?'

'I couldn't agree more, young friend,' Longbow replied with a perfectly straight face. Red-Beard was always waving his sense of humor in everyone's face, but Longbow was almost positive that his friend wouldn't laugh very much when the Trogite archers all began to address him by the title he'd desperately tried to avoid back in Lattash.

The recent experiment of the Vlagh had produced woefully inept warriors, Longbow concluded as he watched the attackers come lumbering up out of the Wasteland. His past experience made him quite certain that they would improve as newer hatches succeeded these early generations, however. The smaller version had almost certainly been lurking in the forests of Zelana's Domain for centuries, so they'd had plenty of time to correct most of the earlier defects. It had taken One-Who-Heals quite some time to explain this to his pupil, Longbow ruefully recalled. The individual servant of the Vlagh was incapable of learning anything. Modification of any kind came only with the passage of generations.

As time went on, this new modification would quite possibly improve and become more dangerous, but for right now it didn't pose much of a threat.

The mindless charge of the overgrown servants of the Vlagh continued until late afternoon, and by then the pile of dead ones some twenty feet to the front of the Trogite barricade was even higher than the barricade itself.

Then that hollow roar from out in the Wasteland halted the attack, and not long afterward, Zelana's fog bank came rolling in.

'Not a bad day, really,' Sub-Commander Andar growled. 'We're still here, and they're still out there, so I'd say that we won this one.'

'Let's take advantage of this fog while it's still here,' Brigadier Danal suggested. 'It's probably going to take most of the night to plant the poisoned stakes in the open ground between this breastworks and the one behind us.'

389

Andar shuddered. 'This business of using poison to fight a war makes me go cold all over,' he declared. 'Who came up with the idea anyway?'

'It was my teacher, One-Who-Heals,' Longbow explained. 'Our enemies are venomous, and the ones we killed today will provide the poison we'll use to kill the ones who'll attack us tomorrow.' Then he suddenly laughed.

'What's so funny?' Andar demanded.

'You've met Red-Beard, haven't you?'

'He's the one who trained our archers, isn't he?'

Longbow nodded. 'Red-Beard's got a very peculiar sense of humor. I'm quite sure he'd try to take what I just told you about one step further and suggest that since today's enemies will kill tomorrow's enemies, we could probably just go fishing and let our enemies fight this war all by themselves.'

'We should at least go through the motions here, Longbow,' Danal objected. 'If we don't *look* busy, our employer might decide that he doesn't need us, and we won't get paid.'

'Bite your tongue, Danal,' Andar said.

Zelana's fog bank, illuminated by her brother's bright little sun, not only concealed the activities of Narasan's men from the enemies out in the Wasteland, but also provided them with all the light they needed to plant the poisoned stakes between their outermost barricade and the one behind it. And so it was that they'd completed the task in about half the time it would have taken during an ordinary night.

'Now we get to wait,' Andar grumbled.

'You could always catch up on your sleep,' Danal suggested. 'I'm sure that big-mouth out here in the red desert will wake you up in time to watch the bug-people start trying to tiptoe through our stakes.'

'I'm an awfully sound sleeper, Danal.'

'I've noticed. The sound of your sleeping reaches for miles sometimes.'

'What's that supposed to mean?'

'You snore, Andar. Sometimes you snore so loud that the sound alone could shake down a stone fortress.'

Just then the familiar roar came from out of the Wasteland, and the new breed of snake-men shambled forward in the early morning light.

'So much for your nap, Andar,' Danal observed.

The awkward enemies clambered over their dead companions to reach the outermost barricade, and they seemed to be more than a little confused when they didn't encounter any resistance there.

'Let them know where we are, Danal,' Andar suggested.

'Right,' Danal agreed. 'Let's hear a battle-cry, gentlemen!' he commanded, and a great shout arose from behind the second barricade.

The enemies at the first barricade milled around in confusion for a while, and then another roar came from the Wasteland.

'That was quick,' Longbow said as the creatures of the Wasteland began to move up the slope toward the second barricade.

'I didn't quite catch that,' Andar said.

'Veltan advised us that the bug-people have what he called an "overmind",' Longbow explained. 'What *one* of them knows, they *all* know, and it appears that what *one* of them sees, the others *also* see.'

'Are you saying that they can pass their eyeballs around?' Andar demanded.

'Not quite,' Longbow said. 'I think that touch might be

involved. When they're spread out like they are here, they're always close enough to each other to pass information on back to the Vlagh in a very short time.'

'That would be a lot like that notion Rabbit came up with back in Lattash, wouldn't it?' Danal suggested.

'Very close,' Longbow agreed.

'I didn't exactly follow that,' Andar said.

'There was a lot of snow up in the mountains,' Danal explained, 'and the natives warned us about a seasonal peculiarity. As I understood it, every year a very warm wind blew in from the sea and melted the snow overnight. That caused a flood. There were Maags part way up the ravine above Lattash, and we had to warn them that the warm wind was coming their way. The clever little Maag called Rabbit suggested using horns to pass a warning to the Maags up in the ravine that it was time to head for higher ground. That warning moved from out in the bay to the Maags up in the ravine in just a few minutes. The Maags climbed up to safety, but the snake-men who were invading didn't get the point. You wouldn't *believe* how many enemies were drowned in that flood.'

'Good comparison, Danal,' Longbow said. 'The creatures of the Wasteland don't blow horns to pass things along, though. They use touch instead. The Vlagh almost certainly knows what's happening here within a few minutes. That shout we just heard was probably a command to continue the charge.'

'That suggests that they're more efficient than I'd been led to believe,' Sub-Commander Andar said. 'If they can pass information to each other instantly, they'll have quite an advantage, wouldn't you say?'

'They didn't do that during the war in the ravine,' Danal recalled.

'Not that I noticed, no,' Longbow agreed. 'I'd say that the Vlagh learned quite a bit more from that first war than we'd realized.'

'It looks to me like there's one thing they *didn't* learn,' Danal observed. 'They don't seem to realize that our stakes have been dipped in venom. They're dropping like flies out there.'

Longbow peered over the barricade and saw that the enemy charge was faltering as the front ranks began to topple over when they reached the poisoned stakes.

Then a somewhat sharper roar came from the Wasteland, and the more awkward enemies abruptly stopped their charge and stood in place.

Longbow muttered an oath.

'What's the problem?' Andar asked.

'Your poisoned stakes aren't going to help this time, I'm afraid,' Longbow replied. 'It appears that the Vlagh has finally realized how lethal they are, so it just ordered its army to stop the advance.'

'That's not really a bad thing, Longbow,' Danal noted. 'If the enemy army can't advance any farther than this, the war's over, and we just won. Our stakes stopped them dead in their tracks.'

'Not quite dead, Danal,' Andar disagreed. 'Most of them are still standing.'

'Maybe they'll get hungry after a while and go someplace else to find something to eat,' Danal suggested.

It was about mid-morning when the eight-legged turtles came scampering over the outermost barricade. The terms 'scamper' and 'turtle' seemed almost contradictory, but Longbow couldn't come up with any alternatives. With only a few exceptions, turtles were slow-moving reptiles whose body armor made anything faster than a slow creep almost impossible. The long, hard-coated spider-legs, however, lifted the shell-encased body above the ground, so the creature was able to move at a surprising rate.

The armored enemies moved out in front of the now-stationary bug-men and began to advance through the field of stakes, snapping them off as they came.

Danal swore. 'Isn't that cheating?' he demanded.

'I'd say that it's imitation,' Andar disagreed. 'The turtle-shells serve about the same purpose as our breastplates. Apparently the thing Longbow calls the "overmind" saw how useful armor could be, so it came up with a duplicate – except that this turtle-bug's got eight legs instead of four, so it can move faster than an ordinary turtle.'

'It's also immune to arrows, I'd imagine,' Longbow added, 'and if it can spin webs like ordinary spiders do, things might just start to get interesting before long.'

'They cleared away almost all of our stakes in less than half a day, Commander,' Andar reported that evening when they met again atop the center tower in Gunda's wall. 'Fortunately, they don't appear to be night creatures, so they all pulled back as the sun went down.'

'Did anybody at all manage to kill one of them?' Gunda demanded.

Andar shook his head. 'Arrows just bounce off of them, and they didn't *quite* reach the second breast-works, so none of us had the opportunity to try spears. I don't think spears would have punched through those shells, anyway.'

'I think we might be in trouble, Narasan,' Gunda declared. 'Our main enemy is still that Vlagh thing, and it's beginning to look like it learned a lot more than we thought during the war in the ravine.

Now it's got bigger soldiers – and armored ones as well. We'd better start coming up with some answers here, or the enemy's going to walk all over us.'

'I'll see if I can find my big brother,' Veltan said. 'He's the expert on insects, so he'll be able to give us much more specific information.'

Longbow briefly squinted up at Dahlaine's bright-shining imitation sun which appeared to still be joyously aflame. That raised a couple of questions. If Dahlaine's toy sun was bright enough to cause pain to the bug-bats, why did the other servants of the Vlagh stop advancing when the *real* sun went down? *This* war was turning out to be much more complicated than the previous one had been – quite probably because the Vlagh had learned many things during the conflict in Zelana's Domain, and 'learning' and 'bug' didn't really fit together at all.

Veltan, Dahlaine, and Zelana joined them on the tower after a short time had passed, and Narasan rather quickly described the larger enemy soldiers and the eight-legged turtles.

'*Those* are the ones you should try your best to avoid,' Dahlaine cautioned. 'Eight legs means spiders, young man, and spiders are even more dangerous than snakes.'

'I thought snakes were about as bad as it's likely to get,' Rabbit said.

Dahlaine shook his head. 'Snake-venom kills – usually very quickly. Spider-venom paralyzes its prey. Most spiders spin webs that capture the prey. Then the spider bites the captive to keep it in one place until the spider's ready to eat again. It's not uncommon for a spider to have four or five meals tangled in the web, waiting to be eaten.'

'That's terrible!' Rabbit exclaimed.

'It gets worse,' Dahlaine replied. 'A spider doesn't have jaws – or teeth – so it can't chew its food. A significant part of its venom is a powerful digestive fluid that liquefies the internal organs and flesh of any creature it attacks. Then the spider's able to suck that liquid out of whatever – or whoever – it's having for supper. All that's left when the spider finishes is skin and bones.'

'We'd better come up with some way to kill them, then,' Longbow said.

'Fire, maybe?' Keselo suggested.

'Fire might be the best answer,' Dahlaine agreed.

'Is there any part of a spider's body that's not protected by the outer shell?' Longbow asked.

Dahlaine thought about it. 'The eyes, possibly.' Then he smiled faintly. 'That *would* give you quite a few targets, Longbow.'

'Oh?'

'A spider has eight eyes, you know.'

'No,' Longbow replied, 'I didn't know that. There might be a few possibilities there, then. Maybe this isn't quite as hopeless as we first thought it was.'

3

Longbow hadn't slept much in the past few days and he was bone-tired. He went some distance on out into the grassy basin and bedded down in the forest to the west of the geyser. Dahlaine's suggestion that the turtle-shelled spiders might be an easy target for his arrows had lessened Longbow's sense of helplessness, and he fell into a deep sleep almost before he'd laid his head down.

It was much later when he seemed to hear a tantalizingly familiar woman's voice saying, 'Go away, brave warrior, go away.'

He sat up quickly and looked around, but there was nobody there. He was almost positive that he remembered that rich-sounding voice, but he couldn't quite put his finger on just whose voice it was.

He lay down again and went back to sleep almost immediately.

'Go away, Longbow, protector of Zelana, go away. Put not thyself in needless danger. Stand aside, brave Longbow, stand aside.'

He jerked himself up into a sitting position again, but there was still nobody there.

This was beginning to become very irritating. 'Don't pester me,' he grumbled, lying back down. 'I'm trying to get some sleep.'

But yet again the woman's voice came out of the night in an even more commanding tone. 'In the name of Misty-Water, I command thee to go from here. This war is *mine*, not thine, and I will give thee victory if thou wilt but stand aside.'

And then the voice of Longbow's dream was gone, and he sank once more into dreamless sleep.

'Were you trying to reach me last night?' he sent the soundless question out to Zelana as the sun rose the following morning.

'It wasn't me, Longbow,' her silent voice came back. 'Are you sure you weren't just dreaming?'

'I think I might be just a little too old to be one of the Dreamers, Zelana.'

'Doesn't that sort of depend on just exactly what you mean when you say "old", Longbow?' she asked archly.

'Don't do that,' he scolded. 'Whoever – or whatever – it was, it was trying very hard to persuade me to just pack up and go away.'

'It certainly wasn't *me*, then. I couldn't live without you, dear, dear Longbow.'

'Are we just about done playing?' he asked her.

'Sorry.' She paused. 'Do you think it might just have been the Vlagh – or one of its more intelligent servants?'

'I don't see how it *could* have been. Whoever it was gave me a command to go away in the name of Misty-Water, and there's no way the Vlagh could know about her or have even the faintest idea of her significance to me.'

'It *could* have been just a real dream, Longbow. I've occasionally had people tell me that there are times when dreams seem so real that the people who have *those* particular dreams can't tell where reality leaves off and the dream begins.'

'Well, maybe,' Longbow said dubiously.

* * *

During the night Sub-Commander Andar had pulled his forces back to the third barricade, and, though it was probably futile, they'd laced the intervening open space with the now-customary poisoned stakes.

Longbow and Rabbit went on down to join their friends just before the sun rose.

'You're late,' Andar rumbled in his deep voice.

'Overslept,' Longbow said with a shrug.

'There's something I've been meaning to ask you,' Andar said. 'From what I've been told, you know more about the bug-people than anyone else, so maybe you can explain just why they pull back every evening. Several hundred of their companions get killed every time they overrun one of our breast-works, but they just turn around and walk away when the sun goes down. Then they have to start over and recapture what they'd had right in their hands the previous day. Isn't that sort of stupid?'

'Stupid's part of the nature of the bug-men,' Rabbit told him. 'It *might* just be that they don't know that the sun's going to come back tomorrow. For all they know, the sun dies late in the afternoon, and it'll stay dark for the rest of eternity – it's either that, or maybe Big-Mama gets lonesome when the sun goes down.'

'Big-Mama?'

'The Vlagh. If I understand what Lady Zelana told us correctly, the Vlagh's the one who laid all the eggs that turned into the bug-people when they hatched. If she lays the eggs, doesn't that make her mommy?'

Longbow glanced over the top of the barricade. 'Good,' he said. 'I see that your men planted stakes out to the front. That should bring the spider-creatures here. We need a dead one – fairly soon, I think.'

'What for?'

'So that we can take it apart and see if we can find any other weaknesses. Your archers aren't *really* well-trained enough to drive arrows into a spider's eye from a hundred paces away, are they?'

'Not as far as I know, they aren't,' Andar agreed.

The introduction of fire-missiles hurled by Trogite catapults elevated the sometimes stodgy Trogites quite noticeably in Longbow's opinion. Naptha, pitch, and tar in the proper proportions most *definitely* disturbed not only the larger bug-men, but also the heavily-shelled spiders. So far as Longbow was able to determine, setting fire to *any* creature got its immediate attention. Being on fire probably *would* be just a little distracting.

The only problem lay in the indiscriminate launching of the fire-missiles into the ranks of the approaching enemies. Longbow dropped several dozen hard-shelled spiders with venom-tipped arrows planted in their eyes, but the bodies he wanted to retrieve in an intact condition inevitably were at least partially consumed by the indiscriminate distribution of fire.

'Andar!' he finally shouted. 'Would you *please* stop throwing fire out there? You're burning everything in sight.'

'That was sort of what we had in mind, Longbow. If something works, don't change it, I always say.'

'That's the problem. It *doesn't* work – not for me, anyway. I want a raw turtle, not a cooked one.'

'Oh, maybe I overlooked that. How long do you think it's going to take you to kill one of them and retrieve the carcass?'

Longbow swept his eyes across the stake-dotted slope between this third barricade and the one perhaps a hundred paces on down below. There were several hundred *dead* enemies – mostly already burned to a crisp – lying between the two barricades, but none that were intact. 'Why don't you tell your men to relax for a while?' he suggested. 'They're probably a bit tired after all this hard work, anyway. Let a few enemies get close to us. I'll decide which one I want, kill it, and retrieve the body. *Then* your men can go back to cooking everything in sight.'

He looked out over the top of the barrier and saw several of the oversized bug-men tentatively advancing, but the hard-shelled spiders seemed to be holding back. It was quite obvious that the Trogite fire-missiles were making the servants of the Vlagh a bit nervous.

When the advancing bug-men reached the center of the open space between the two barricades without being showered with fire, however, the spider servants grew more bold and began to come spilling over the barricade on down the slope.

'Not the best decision there,' Longbow muttered under his breath as he carefully drew another arrow from his quiver.

The newer servants of the Vlagh were obviously more intelligent than the ones Longbow and his friends had encountered in the Ravine above Lattash, but their expanded intelligence seemed to have been limited to the introduction of a certain amount of caution. Of course fire would get the immediate attention of almost any creature in the whole world.

Longbow waited until one of the hard-shelled spiders was no more than a few yards from the front of the barricade, and then he loosed his arrow directly at one of the large eyes at the front of the creature's head. The creature collapsed instantly, and several Trogite soldiers vaulted over the barricade and dragged the dead enemy back behind the protective wall.

'That's all we need, Andar!' Longbow shouted. 'Build up the fire again!'

'I thought you'd never ask,' Andar bellowed.

Then the catapults lashed forward again, raining fire down on the servants of the Vlagh once more.

Dahlaine spent most of that afternoon carefully examining the Vlagh's most recent experiment. 'That thing out there never ceases to amaze me,' he told Longbow, Veltan, and Zelana after he'd finished. 'This particular creation isn't what it seems to be. There's no hint of reptile here. This thing's nothing more than a modified spider.'

'That shell doesn't look very spider-like to me, big brother,' Veltan disagreed, as Rabbit and Narasan joined them.

'The shell's nothing more than a modification of an ordinary spider's outer skeleton, Veltan. Evidently, the Vlagh saw the value of the Trogite breastplate, and then it looked around in the animal world until it found something that closely resembled it – the turtle shell, of course. Then it altered a spider to add that defensive shell to ward off the arrows that eliminated so many of its servants during the war in our sister's Domain. The thing that troubles me the most here lies in the Vlagh's experimentation with spiders. There's no real connection between spiders and the Vlagh's usual servants. The average spider lives on a steady diet of creatures that closely resemble the standard servant of the Vlagh. What we've got here is something on the order of what you'd get if you crossed a cat with a mouse.'

'That's absurd, Dahlaine!' Zelana protested.

'The Vlagh *is* an absurdity, dear sister. Hadn't you noticed that? What baffles me the most here is just why the Vlagh chose spiders to serve as its armored servants. There are several varieties of beetles that would probably have worked just as well, and beetles are much closer to the Vlagh's species than spiders are. Spiders are solitary creatures, and the original servants of the Vlagh cluster up.'

'The world of bugs is awfully complicated, isn't it?' Rabbit observed.

'Indeed it is,' Dahlaine agreed.

'Wilt thou not hear me, brave warrior?' the soft voice half roused Longbow from his sleep. 'The victory is mine, if thou wilt but stand aside. Though they know it not, the armies that come up from the south are *mine*, and they come here at *my* bidding. I command thee to stand aside and impede them no more. Go from this place. Stand no more between me and my victory.'

Longbow came up with his eyes wide open as a number of things came together all at once. Torl's account of the ridiculous fairy tale the farmers far to the south in Veltan's Domain had automatically repeated each time they heard the word 'gold', and the Trogite soldiers' obsessive response to the tale suddenly began to make sense. Somebody – some woman, evidently – had picked up the idea of using gold for bait, and she'd just nearly caught about a half-million church soldiers.

But why?

The more Longbow thought about it, the more certain he became that the voice in his dream's continual repetition of 'get out of the way' meant exactly that. And the instruction was clearly not meant for Longbow alone. His friends were *also* supposed to stand aside so that the two distinctly separate enemies could fall upon each other in a war of mutual extinction.

'Good boy,' the now-familiar voice murmured fondly. 'I was sure that you'd get my point – eventually.'

* * *

'I need to talk with you, Zelana,' Longbow sent out his silent, urgent call the following morning.

'Some new disaster, perhaps?'

'I don't really think so. I think your brothers should sit in as well, and probably Narasan, too.'

'Is something bothering you, Longbow?'

'I'm not sure if "bother" is the right word. If I'm anywhere at all close to being right about this, we're getting help – from somebody we didn't even know was there.'

'That's very irritating, Longbow. Don't leave things hanging up in the air like that.'

'I'm sorry, but I'm still trying to sort this out. Maybe we should meet down near the geyser. I don't think we want to spread this around just yet – and we *definitely* don't want word of this to get back to the Vlagh.'

'This had better be good, Longbow.'

'If I'm anywhere close to being right, it goes a long way past good.'

Longbow went out of the forest where he usually slept and walked on down to the noisy geyser, trying to sort through his most peculiar experience.

When he reached the geyser that was the primary source of the River Vash, Zelana and her brothers were already there, along with Rabbit, Keselo, Gunda, Torl, and Narasan.

'What's this all about, Longbow?' Rabbit asked.

'Let's go back just a ways,' Longbow said. 'Ashad's dream told us that there was going to be a second invasion of Veltan's Domain, and, sure enough, five church armies showed up on the south coast almost before *we* reached Veltan's house.'

'This is all ancient history, Longbow,' Gunda protested.

'Perhaps, but I think we might want to take a second look at it. Now, then, the church soldiers rounded up all the local people down there and then sat around rubbing their hands together while they waited for the slave-ships to arrive.'

'We've heard about all this before,' Narasan said.

'I know, but perhaps we weren't listening quite hard enough. Before the slavers even made it to the beach, something very peculiar was going on. Torl tells us that every time one of those farmers heard somebody say "gold", he went into a kind of trance and recited an ancient fairy tale – which probably wasn't really all that ancient, since Omago had never heard of it. Then, after any one of the church soldiers heard the story, he immediately decided to give up army life and run north just as hard as he could. Then, after they discovered that trying to come up here through the various ravines, gullies, and passes was extremely dangerous, they gathered together to build that ramp, which isn't really in a very good place, and they've stayed at it with what seems to be mindless determination.' He looked at Narasan. 'You know much more about those church armies than I do. Does that sound at all like something they'd normally do?'

'Probably not,' Narasan conceded, 'but the thought of vast amounts of gold just lying on the ground waiting for them to come along and pick it up might have unhinged their minds just a bit.'

'*All* of their minds? Wouldn't at least a *few* of them want more proof?'

'I think I see what you're getting at, Longbow,' Narasan said. 'Those church soldiers *aren't* behaving normally, but that doesn't alter the fact that they're charging at my rear, and I can't hold *them* back and fight off the bug-people at the same time. What set you off on this?'

'Somebody – or some*thing*'s – been talking to me while I'm asleep. The language is quite formal, but what it all boils down to is "get out of the way". This whoever – or whatever – seems to believe that those church armies and the servants of the Vlagh will destroy each other *if* we'll just get out from between them and stop dropping boulders on that ramp the church armies are building.'

'When did *you* suddenly become one of the Dreamers, Longbow?' Dahlaine asked skeptically.

'It's not really the same sort of dream,' Longbow replied. 'The children *make* things happen with their dreams. I think that all *I'm* supposed to do is persuade you to step aside.'

'Whose voice is it that you're hearing?' Rabbit asked.

'I'm not really sure,' Longbow admitted. 'I know that I've heard it before, but I can't quite put my finger on just exactly who it is.'

'I think we're going to need something more in the way of proof before we abandon our defenses,' Gunda said with a note of skepticism. 'There are just a few too many "maybes" involved in your dream, Longbow.'

'I think that pretty much sums it up, Longbow,' Dahlaine said. 'If somebody – or something – has been tampering with the minds of the church soldiers, I'd say that it's more probably the Vlagh than some unknown friend. If we pull out and the church armies join forces with the servants of the Vlagh, we could very well lose the entirety of Veltan's Domain before summer's over. We'll keep our eyes open, but if we don't get something a bit more solid to work with, I don't think we'll dare to just pack up and leave.'

'They're sort of thick-headed, aren't they?' Torl said quietly to Longbow as the two of them stood atop the central tower of Gunda's wall. 'It might just be that they weren't down south to watch the grand plan of the Trogs go all to pieces when those farmers started reciting the fairytale.' Then the young Maag looked down at the Wasteland. '*That* might have something to do with it, you know. Your theory might have carried more weight if that sand down there was yellow instead of red.'

'I'm not sure if even *that* would have convinced them,' Longbow disagreed. 'They're a very stubborn people, Torl, and their ideas sometimes get locked in stone.'

'It looks like we might have weather coming,' Torl said, pointing at the ridge-line off to the west.

Longbow frowned slightly as he peered at the boiling cloud swirling higher and higher over the ridge. 'I don't think it's weather, Torl,' he disagreed. 'It looks more like a sandstorm to me.'

'I *hate* those,' Torl declared. 'Sand seems to creep under my clothes and slide down my throat when those silly things come boiling in like that.'

Longbow frowned slightly. 'It shouldn't be coming from that direction,' he said. 'The west side of that ridge is covered with trees and bushes. I don't think there's enough sand over there to form a cloud *that* big.'

'It's yellow, Longbow, and you don't come across very many yellow trees around here.'

The yellow cloud came rolling ponderously down the slope and then streamed on out over the barren Wasteland.

'Good baby!' Torl shouted up at the cloud. 'Go pester the bugmen and stay away from here!'

Then the yellow cloud seemed almost to coalesce, sinking rapidly down to cover the Wasteland with a dense shroud of dull yellow. Then it seemed almost to sink into the sand itself.

And then it was gone – almost as if it had been sucked into the very sand.

The sun came out into the open again, and Longbow stared in utter disbelief at what now lay spread out as far as the northern horizon.

'Good God!' Torl gasped. 'That's gold out there! I thought it was just iron ore, but it's *gold*!'

Longbow suddenly laughed. 'Not exactly, friend Torl,' he said. 'It might *look* like gold, but it's still iron. I'd say that our unknown friend has just baited her trap and she'll probably catch about a half-million Trogites with it. I think life just got a lot brighter, don't you?'

4

Narasan's soldiers were all standing along the top of Gunda's wall staring out at the glittering Wasteland in awed silence.

'I think that maybe you should wake your men up, Narasan,' Longbow suggested. 'The creatures of the Wasteland are still coming up that slope, and if your men don't hold them back, we'll have company right up here.'

Narasan pulled his eyes away from the vast ocean of glittering yellow sand and looked around. 'Get back to your posts!' he barked at his men. 'You're not getting paid to look at the scenery!' Then his expression became just a bit sheepish. 'I'm not sure that's going to work, Longbow. My *own* head's starting to come unraveled at the sight of all that glittering sand out there.'

'I think that's the idea, friend Narasan. It might help if you keep reminding yourself that what you see out there is imitation gold, not the real thing. A lot of things are starting to come together now. First the farmers recited the story about the fellow who came up here and saw what we're seeing right now. Then the church soldiers believed the story without any tangible proof, and came rushing up here to gather up something that didn't exist until about a half-hour ago. Somebody out there's tampering, and in spite of everything Zelana's told me, I'm almost positive that it's *not* the Vlagh.'

'I certainly *hope* not,' Narasan agreed. 'If the Vlagh can create the kind of illusion that just came popping out of nowhere out in that desert I'm likely to lose my whole army.'

'Commander Narasan!' a soldier called from one of the other towers atop Gunda's wall. 'We've got pirates coming up from behind us!'

Narasan and Longbow turned quickly to look off to the south. Narasan chuckled suddenly. 'I think some help just arrived. That looks to me to be Sorgan Hook-Beak. Am I right or not?'

Longbow nodded. 'He made good time getting back here. I'm just guessing, but I think Zelana's been tampering again.'

'There seems to be quite a lot of tampering going on around here, wouldn't you say?' Narasan suggested with a slight smile.

'Not out loud, I wouldn't,' Longbow replied.

Sorgan Hook-Beak froze in his tracks when he reached the top of Gunda's wall and caught his first glimpse of the vast 'sea of gold' lying off to the north. 'Dear gods!' he exclaimed, staring out over the glittering Wasteland.

'It's not real,' Longbow told him. 'It's just more of that imitation gold Grock found when we were coming up through Nanton's pass. Somebody out there's playing games.'

'I'm going to have to see some proof of that, Longbow,' Sorgan declared. 'It certainly looks like gold to me.'

'Longbow's certain that it's just a hoax, Hook-Beak,' Narasan explained, 'but I think I'll side with you this time. I want to see some proof that it's *not* gold before I just shrug it off.'

'Rabbit!' Longbow called, 'We need you!'

The little Maag came up the stairs to the central tower.

'Can you tell from here if that glittery sand out there is real gold or just more of that fake gold?' Sorgan demanded.

Rabbit squinted out at the Wasteland. 'Not for certain sure, Cap'n,' he replied. 'I'd need to get my hands on some to be able to tell one way or the other.'

'That might just be a little difficult right now,' Narasan said. 'We seem to have a very large number of unfriendly creatures standing in the way.'

Rabbit squinted out at the Wasteland lying below. 'I might just be able to drop a basket tied to the end of a rope down there from up on top of that west ridge, but I'm not sure just how much I'd be able to scoop up if I did that. What I'd really need is—' He stopped suddenly and smacked his forehead with his hand. 'I must be about half asleep,' he said. 'I've got something in my purse that'll prove one way or another just exactly what that sand out there really is.'

'Oh?' Sorgan asked. 'What's that?'

'I bought it from another smith once when we'd hauled into port at Kormo. He called it a "lodestone". I'd heard about them, and I thought it might be sort of interesting, but I've never used it for anything serious. Any time it gets close to something made out of iron, it reaches out and grabs it.'

'Have you ever seen that actually happen?' Sorgan asked skeptically.

Rabbit grinned at his leader. 'I surely have, Cap'n,' he said. 'When we're in port, and I'm running low on money, I can almost always win a few tankards of good strong ale if I can find somebody who's willing to bet that I don't have a rock that knows how to jump.' He untied his purse from his belt and fished around in it with his fingers. 'Here she is,' he said rather proudly, holding up a black lump of rock about the size of a man's thumb. Then he took his knife from its sheath and held it a few inches above the stone. The black lump leaped up and stuck to Rabbit's knife with a kind of clinking sound.

Sorgan blinked. 'Now *that's* something I've never seen before. I can see how you managed to win a lot of bets, Rabbit.'

'I've heard about them,' Narasan said, 'but I've never actually seen one.'

Rabbit ran his fingers over his lodestone. 'I think I'd better put her in a cloth pouch,' he mused. 'She's all sort of smooth and round, and just tying a rope around her might not work too well, and I definitely don't want to lose her. I'll make a sort of pouch out of cloth and put her in that. Then I'll tie the rope to the pouch.'

'Won't the pouch sort of block off whatever makes her jump at iron?' Sorgan asked.

Rabbit shook his head. 'She always jumps at iron, Cap'n – or iron jumps at her. She'll even reach out through leather to grab iron. She just *loves* iron for some reason. I'll put her in a cloth pouch, lower her down to that shining yellow sand and drag her back and forth a couple times. If that sand out there is really iron, the outside of the pouch will be covered with it when I haul her back in. If nothing sticks to the pouch, the sand isn't iron. It might not be gold, but it definitely won't be iron.'

'I think I've seen a good place for us to try that,' Longbow told his little friend. 'It's over on the other side of that west ridge. The rock face that goes down to the Wasteland isn't very high there, so we won't have to carry so much rope.'

'Let's go, then,' Rabbit said. 'I think that if we come up with the right answer, we've just won another war.'

* * *

'Whoever's doing this for us is very clever,' Torl said when he joined Rabbit and Longbow as they climbed up the ridge to the west of the basin. 'I'd say that this desert of imitation gold was what he had in mind right from the very start.'

'She,' Longbow corrected. 'It was a woman's voice that kept ordering me to get out of the way.'

'Do you suppose it might have been Lady Zelana's sister?' Rabbit asked, shifting the coil of rope he was carrying over his shoulder.

Longbow shook his head. 'I'm sure I'd have recognized her voice,' he said. 'The voice I heard wasn't Aracia's. It was a familiar voice, but I can't seem to remember where I've heard it before.'

'Well, whoever it is seems to have even more power than the people who hired us do,' Torl declared. 'She's probably the greatest swindler in the whole world.'

'*Swindler*?' Rabbit protested.

'Waving fake gold at people isn't exactly honest, Rabbit,' Torl said with a sudden grin, 'but it doesn't bother me one little bit. She just hired five armies to fight our war for us, and she paid them with imitation gold.'

'We *will* have to hold back the creatures of the Wasteland until our new friends finish building that ramp,' Longbow reminded him.

'That's true, I suppose, but cousin Sorgan's men are coming up that shepherd's pass to lend us a hand. We don't *really* have to kill off *all* of the bug-people now. All we have to do is hold them back until our new friends get here. Then we can step aside and cheer while the churchies and the bugs destroy each other.' He looked around at the rocky ridge. 'How much farther is this place we're looking for, Longbow?'

'Just on the other side of that large tree,' Longbow replied, pointing on ahead.

'Are you sure we've got enough rope?' Rabbit asked. 'The Cap'n won't be *too* happy if we can't get an answer for him until sometime tomorrow.'

'It's only about fifty feet high there, little friend,' Longbow replied.

'If it's *that* shallow, why aren't the bug-men coming up there instead of out on that slope?' Torl asked.

'It's too narrow,' Longbow explained. 'The Vlagh needs places that are fairly wide when it starts moving its servants.'

They passed the towering tree and went down into a narrow stream-bed that had cut its way down through the surrounding rocks.

Torl looked out across the Wasteland. 'It looks to me like your "sea of gold" ran dry a ways out there, Longbow,' he said. 'It goes back to being red near the far side of this ridge, and after a mile or so the red fades out and everything goes back to being plain old brown sand.'

'It's just bait, Torl,' Longbow explained. 'Our unknown friend's trying to lure the fish we want to catch *here*, not all over the Wasteland out there.'

Torl looked a bit sheepish. 'I guess I didn't think of that,' he admitted. 'All that imitation gold out there seems to be turning my head off for some reason.'

'Your mind should clear up as soon as we get the proof that the yellow sand cluttering the Wasteland is nothing but a fraud,' Longbow suggested.

'You wouldn't think that water – which isn't really very hard – could cut through solid rock like this, would you?' Rabbit suggested. 'Particularly since it only runs down through these gullies for a few weeks out of every year.'

'That sort of depends on how much time the water has to get the job done,' Longbow explained.

'Just how long would you say it took the water to cut out this little gulch?'

'Not too long – fifty thousand years, maybe.'

'*That's* your idea of a short time, Longbow?'

Longbow smiled. 'Water's very patient, my little friend,' he replied. 'All it really wants to do is go downhill.'

They moved cautiously down the now-dry streambed and stopped a few feet back from the abrupt break.

'There's a lot of the new sand right at the bottom of this cliff, Rabbit,' Torl said, carefully leaning out over the edge.

'How far down would you say it is?'

'Fifty – maybe sixty – feet is about all.'

'That had me just a bit worried,' Rabbit admitted. 'We'd have all looked a little foolish if this rope was about three feet too short.' He sat down and took a piece of loosely-woven cloth out from under his belt and gathered it up around his lodestone. Then he passed his knife over the makeshift bag.

The pouch jumped up and attached itself to the knife.

'It looks like we're in business,' Rabbit said, carefully tying the cloth into a tight sack. Then he tied the end of the rope coil he'd brought along to the pouch and carefully began to lower the bag to the sand below. When it reached the sand, he raised it and then lowered it several times to make certain that it would capture even more grains of the glittering sand. Then he carefully pulled the rope back up, took hold of the cloth sack and held it up for Longbow and Torl to see. The little pouch was almost completely covered with glittering yellow flakes.

'It looks to me like she's very hungry, Rabbit,' Torl said. 'You really ought to feed her more often, you know.'

Rabbit grinned broadly. 'She earned her keep today,' he said.

'When Narasan and Cap'n Sorgan see this, they'll know for certain that all that shiny yellow sand out there's nothing but imitation gold. I think Longbow's friend just won this war for us.'

It was about mid-afternoon when Longbow and his two friends came back down the steep west ridge into the grassy basin, and Zelana and Veltan were waiting for them near the geyser.

'Well?' Zelana asked.

Grinning broadly, Rabbit held up the pouch covered with flakes of imitation gold. 'Does this answer that question?' he asked. 'It's pretty enough, but it's sure not gold.'

'I think we'd better reconsider a few things, sister mine,' Veltan said. 'I don't see any advantage to the Vlagh in this hoax. If we stop pestering those church soldiers and let them finish their ramp, they'll go crazy when they see what appears to be gold stretching out as far as the eye can reach. They'll rush on down the slope and trample the servants of the Vlagh into the ground just to get to something that isn't really worth anything at all.'

Zelana's expression became sort of rueful. 'It seems that I'm trying to make a career out of jumping to conclusions,' she admitted. 'The Vlagh isn't the *only* deceiver in the world. This "imitation gold" might just turn out to be worth more than the real thing. I think you'd better go have a talk with Narasan, baby brother. Tell him to send word to Padan. We definitely don't want anybody to interfere with those church soldiers. We want them up *here*.'

'Right!' Veltan agreed enthusiastically.

The sun had gone down – the *real* sun, Longbow reminded himself as Dahlaine's toy sun grew brighter and brighter over the now glittering slope. Narasan had called them all together atop the central tower of Gunda's wall to consider some options.

'Are you absolutely certain sure that it's only iron, Rabbit?' Sorgan Hook-Beak asked in an almost plaintive tone.

'The lodestone sort of proved that, Cap'n,' Rabbit explained. 'It *loves* iron, but gold doesn't interest it one little bit.'

'It looks like I've blundered here, Veltan,' Narasan admitted. 'I was so certain that those church armies had come here to punish me that the notion that they might be here to help never occurred to me.'

'Punish?' Sorgan asked curiously.

'Some church armies tricked us once down in the southern part of the empire,' Gunda explained. 'One of the Commander's relatives was killed, and so he was very upset. Padan and I came up with a way to even things out, though, and the church didn't like it one little bit.'

'Just what was it that you did to make them willing to come *this* far to kick you around?'

Gunda shrugged. 'We hired several professional murderers, and they filled a few graveyards with high-ranking churchmen and assorted church army commanders.'

'Are there *really* people down in the Empire who make their living by killing people?' Sorgan seemed a bit surprised. 'We usually do our own killing in the Land of Maag.'

'Professionals are much neater,' Gunda said, 'and they'll kill the ones you want to get rid of any way you want them to – either quick and quiet, or slow and noisy. There's one murderer down in the Empire who'll guarantee that it'll take your enemy at least two days to finish dying. If the enemy dies any sooner, the murderer won't take your money.'

'Now that's what I'd call a *real* professional, cousin,' Torl said admiringly.

'I don't think I've ever disliked anybody quite *that* much,' Sorgan said.

'Anyway,' Narasan continued, 'whether they hate us or not, when they see all that imitation gold out there, that's the only thing they'll be able to think about.'

'I think the key word there is "when", Narasan,' Sorgan added. 'Dropping boulders on them definitely slowed them down to a crawl. It could take them *months* to finish that ramp, and we'll have to hold back the bug-people until the church armies get up here to take over for us.'

'I know,' Narasan replied glumly. 'I'd be more than happy to listen to any suggestions.'

'Maybe we should help them,' Omago the farmer said somewhat hesitantly.

'What exactly did you have in mind?' Veltan asked.

'Well, they'll need a lot of big rocks to finish that ramp, but there aren't really all that many boulders down there at the foot of the falls, because the river's worn most of them down over the years. If our people kept on pushing boulders off the cliff, those people down below would *think* that we were still trying to stop them, but what we'll *really* be doing will be providing them with exactly what they need to finish the job.'

'I *like* it!' Sorgan exclaimed. 'They don't know it, but those people down there are really our friends, and it's always nice to help a friend – particularly if he's going to do all the dying for us.'

'In line with that thought, I think we should modify Gunda's wall here just a bit,' Longbow added.

'It's a very *good* wall, Longbow,' Gunda protested.

'That's the trouble, friend Gunda. It's *too* good. When our friends from the south reach your wall, it'll take them quite some time to get over it in enough numbers to do us very much good. I'd say that we'll need a gap about a hundred feet wide for that many of them to charge through.'

'Why don't you gentlemen let *me* take care of that?' Veltan suggested. 'Leave Gunda's wall right where it is until our new-found friends come rushing up here to grab all of that imitation gold out there. Then I'll make a nice wide opening for them so that they can go on down and take over the dying for us.'

'And just how did you plan to do that, Veltan?' Gunda demanded.

'Are you sure you really want to know, Gunda?'

'Ah – now that you mention it, Veltan, I guess I really don't – not too much, anyway.'

'Are you quite certain that the bug-people will continue the foolish business of going back home every evening when the *real* sun goes down?' Narasan asked Veltan and Zelana a bit later.

'They're creatures of habit, Commander Narasan,' Zelana replied. 'If they do something one way today, they'll almost certainly repeat it tomorrow.'

'We saw that fairly often back in the ravine, Narasan,' Hook-Beak reminded his friend.

'They're perhaps a bit brighter *this* time,' Veltan added, 'but they still respond to the commands of the Vlagh, so if the Vlagh tells them to come home every evening, they'll keep on doing that until the Vlagh tells them otherwise. Blind obedience is part of their nature.'

'All right, then,' Narasan continued. 'We've come up with several ways to delay them to the point that they're not just dashing up here to start kicking at Gunda's wall. The bright light from Dahlaine's little toy has more or less eliminated the bug-bats. The breast-works and poisoned stakes pretty much stop the oversized snake-men, and our catapulted fire generally eliminates the imitation turtles. We've got thirteen lines of breast-works down the slope from Gunda's wall here. We don't really have to totally eliminate these enemies. All we have to do is slow them down. Since they all go home after work, we'll be able to rush on down and reoccupy the outermost breast-works tonight. Then, tomorrow night, we'll pull back to the next breast-works. Then, on the third night, we'll pull back one more again. That should give the church soldiers almost two weeks to finish their ramp and see all that imitation gold out there. At that point, we'll just politely tip our hats and walk away.'

'*You* can walk if you want to, Narasan,' Sorgan said, 'but I think *I'm* going to run, and you'd better not get in my way.'

Longbow found a certain hard practicality in Narasan's plan. If the servants of the Vlagh *seemed* to be making a certain amount of progress each day, the Vlagh quite probably would see no reason to dream up some new and unanticipated strategy. The servants of the Vlagh would continue to overrun one barricade each day, and if Omago's suggestion worked as well as it should, the church armies should finish their ramp at about the same time.

At least he'd finally managed to persuade Narasan and Sorgan that the voice which had haunted his sleep for the past several nights had been telling the truth. Of course, the sudden appearance of miles and miles of imitation gold had helped quite a bit.

'Maybe if I'm lucky, she'll go pester somebody else tonight,' he muttered as he walked on back to the forest a mile or so to the south of Gunda's wall. Although he now had several friends among the outlanders, Longbow still preferred solitude when the time came for him to sleep.

The trees in this forest were of an unfamiliar variety, quite probably because Veltan's Domain was much farther to the south than Longbow's original home, but they provided him shelter – although shelter wasn't that important in the summer.

He laid down on his bed of leaves and drifted off to sleep.

'Thou hast done well, brave hunter,' the now-familiar voice intruded into his mind. 'I shall trouble thee no more. Fare thee well, Longbow of Zelana's Domain. In times yet to come, we may meet again.'

THE BRIDGE

1

❯❯❯❯❯

Padan was more than a little dubious about Longbow's notion that some 'unknown friend' was sending help in the form of five church armies. The Amarite church *was* based upon raw greed, of course, but so far as Padan knew, none of the church soldiers, nor priests, nor even the brutal Regulators had seen the colorful alteration of the red sand stretching out over the Wasteland.

'It just doesn't float,' Padan muttered to himself as he went back down along the wide, turbulent river toward the waterfall where his men were still dropping boulders on the roof that had been cleverly designed to protect the church soldiers from the arrows of Longbow's archers.

Narasan had accepted the idea, however, so now Padan was obliged to go along despite his doubts. Padan had always felt that to be one of the drawbacks of army life. Once the commander made up his mind, the officers who served under him were required to obey. Back in the days when Padan, Gunda, and Narasan had been cadets in the army compound, the sergeants who had trained them had made a habit of beating them over the head with that every time they turned around. 'Just do as you're told' had seemed to pop up thirty or forty times a day. It made a certain amount of sense, of course, but if the commander happened to be wrong, half the army could wind up dead.

When he reached the brink of the gorge the river Vash had carved on down through the mountains to the south, Padan called his officers together. 'The plans have changed, gentlemen,' he told them. 'Something new has come up, so stop dropping rocks on that makeshift roof down there. Our glorious leader wants us to *help* those halfwit church soldiers down there instead of hindering them. From now on, roll the boulders off the edge so that they'll come down in *front* of that ramp instead of on top of it.'

'That doesn't make any sense, Padan,' one of the older officers protested.

'Narasan seems to like it,' Padan replied. He hesitated slightly, but then decided to let his officers know *why* they were changing the overall plan. 'It would seem that we've got a friend out here who's been playing some very interesting games,' he said. 'We all know how the Amarite church feels about gold, and this friend of ours is using imitation gold as bait. When those church armies finish their ramp and see miles and miles of what they *think* is the real thing, they'll go crazy, don't you think?'

'I know that it loosened *my* head up just a little when I first saw it,' another officer admitted.

'Let's just hope that the church-boys feel the same way,' Padan said. 'Our new "grand plan" is to help the dear old churchies get up here where they can see all that glittery dirt out there. Then we're supposed to just get out of the way and let them run on down the slope beyond Gunda's wall and tramp all over the bug-men.'

'While the bug-men are poisoning everybody who comes their way?' another officer added dubiously.

'That's sort of at the core of this new "grand plan",' Padan agreed.

'You don't really sound very convinced, Padan,' the first officer said.

'I don't really *have* to be convinced,' Padan declared. '*Narasan* bought the idea, and that's all we need to know. Get started, gentlemen. Move your men upriver a hundred yards or so and start dropping boulders *ahead* of that ramp instead of on top of it. Let's find out how long it's going to take those holy nit-wits down there to realize that *our* boulders are as useful as the ones out in the middle of the river.' He paused. 'If some of our boulders accidentally come down on top of a few dozen church soldiers, I won't be *too* upset,' he added.

Padan's men chuckled and grinned at him in a wicked sort of way.

It was about noon on the following day when the clever little smith Rabbit came down from the north. 'I'm supposed to tell you that there's going to be another one of those get-togethers up near that waterspout.'

'What *now*?' Padan replied irritably. 'I thought we'd pretty much covered everything yesterday.'

'They didn't come right out and tell me what this is all about,' Rabbit said, 'but I think Lady Zelana's big brother wants to know more about that church in your part of the world.' He hesitated, looking around to make sure that nobody was close enough to hear him. 'I think that what's *really* behind this has to do with just exactly *who* came up with this scheme. That ocean of fake gold that just popped out of nowhere has them all upset. I wouldn't want to swear to it, but I *think* that was something that nobody in Lady Zelana's family could have pulled off. Her older sister seems to be so upset about it that she could bite nails and spit rust.'

Padan laughed. 'That's a colorful way to put it, Rabbit.'

Rabbit shrugged and looked down into the gorge the waterfall had gouged out of the surrounding mountains. 'That's quite a drop,' he observed.

'You've got that right,' Padan agreed.

'It's likely to take those people down there a long time to get up here, wouldn't you say?'

'That's their problem, Rabbit, not mine. Let's go on up to the geyser and find out what's afoot.'

Rabbit shrugged. 'That's up to you, Padan. I just carry messages. I don't make decisions.'

The towering geyser which was the ultimate source of the River Vash was a noisy sort of thing, blasting high up into the air as it was driven by some incomprehensible force far down in the bowels of the earth. Padan conceded that it was a pretty thing, but the continual spray arcing out from the top of the geyser was very much like an endless spring shower.

Fortunately, Veltan's elder brother was wise enough to select an area some distance away from the geyser for them all to gather. At least they wouldn't get wet.

It seemed to Padan that almost everybody was there. 'Who's minding the store?' he quietly asked Narasan.

'The sergeants, mostly,' Narasan replied.

'Oh,' Padan said. 'Things should go more smoothly, then.'

'I wouldn't let that get out, Padan. If people find out who *really* runs the army, we might both have to go out and find honest work.'

'What's this all about, Narasan? Did we leave something out yesterday?'

Narasan glanced about and lowered his voice. 'Lady Zelana's big brother seems to be very curious about the Amarite church and those church armies,' he replied. 'Things seem to be much more relaxed here in the Land of Dhrall than they are down in the Empire.'

'What do you need *me* here for, then? I don't know beans about the church, and I think I'd rather keep it that way.'

'Wouldn't we all? I think our easiest answer to this would be to hand it off to Keselo.'

'I'll go along with you there,' Padan agreed. 'That young fellow's got more education than all of the rest of us put together.'

'Could I have your attention?' the grey-bearded Dahlaine asked. 'Our friends from the Trogite Empire are probably much more familiar with the religion of their part of the world than any of the rest of us are, so I thought it might be useful if they could give us some idea of what it's all about.' He looked inquiringly at Narasan.

'I'm not too well-versed in the peculiarities of the church, Lord Dahlaine,' Narasan replied modestly, 'but our young friend Keselo attended the University of Kaldacin, so he's probably the best qualified to answer any questions you might have. To be completely honest with you, I don't have much use for the church – or the arrogant people who run the stupid thing. Tell our friend here about the religion that contaminates our part of the world, Keselo.'

'If you wish, sir,' Keselo replied obediently. Then he paused, his expression growing quite troubled. 'The church of the Empire isn't really all that attractive, Lord Dahlaine,' he began. 'I'm fairly sure that at some time in the distant past it was more wholesome and pure than it is now, but over the years it's grown more and more corrupt.'

'Just how did it originate?' Dahlaine asked.

'That's not too clear, Lord Dahlaine,' Keselo replied. 'At some time in the distant past, a holy man named Amar, who may – or may not – have actually existed, came to the city of Kaldacin, which at that time was only a crude village, and he spoke to the people there about truth, charity, and morality. Nobody really paid too much attention to him at first, but then some rumors – that have never been confirmed – began to appear.'

'Exactly what sort of rumors?' Dahlaine asked.

'People said that they'd seen him flying – like a bird.'

'That's ridiculous, Keselo,' Gunda snorted.

'Not really, Gunda,' Red-Beard disagreed. 'Our Zelana can fly like an eagle, if she really wants to.'

'Not exactly, Red-Beard,' Lady Zelana corrected. 'I don't really need wings. Please go on, Keselo.'

'Yes, ma'am. I'm quite sure that most of those ancient stories were pure fabrications thought up by Amar's early followers to entice the non-believers into joining the faith. As the years passed, those fabrications grew wilder and wilder. Some said that Amar could remain under water for several days at a time. Others said that he could walk through a solid stone wall – without leaving a hole in that wall. Then there were stories about moving mountains, freezing entire oceans, and other absurdities. As the church grew larger, the stories grew more and more fantastic, and the gullible new converts came to accept almost anything. I think the real purpose of all those fabrications was to convince everybody that anything that's *im*possible *was* possible, if your name happened to be Amar. At that time, it was little more than a myth designed to bring in more and more converts every day.'

'Just exactly where is this mythic person supposed to be now?' Dahlaine asked.

'The current church doctrine's a bit vague, Lord Dahlaine,'

Keselo replied. 'The last I heard, the church maintains that he left the world behind and now wanders out among the stars, preaching to *them*.'

'I tried that one time,' Veltan said, 'but the stars didn't pay the least bit of attention to me.'

Keselo blinked and then he stared at Veltan in awe.

'That was quite a long time ago, Keselo,' Lady Zelana explained. 'Our baby brother offended Mother Sea, and she sent him off to the moon to learn better manners.'

'I was only teasing her, Zelana,' Veltan protested.

'We're straying here,' Dahlaine said firmly. 'From what you've told us so far, Keselo, I'd say that the early church of Amar was fairly simple and basically designed to make people feel more comfortable. What went wrong?'

'I don't think I could actually pinpoint the time – or the event that altered the Amarite church, Lord Dahlaine,' Keselo replied. 'I'd say that it was most likely a gradual change. The early priests of the faith were primarily paupers whose lives depended on the charity of the faithful. As time went on, though, contributions became increasingly mandatory, and the clergy more greedy. The way things stand right now, the higher-ranking members of the clergy are the wealthiest men in the Empire, but they still want more.' He smiled faintly. 'There's a tired old joke in the Empire that says that church doctrine requires everybody in the Empire to contribute everything – and then some – every time the collection plate goes by.'

'Well, hallelujah, Jalkan!' Gunda said with a broad grin.

Padan laughed. 'Nicely put there, old friend,' he said.

Keselo smiled. 'Sub-Commander Gunda was just joking, I think, but what he just said comes very close to being an accurate description of the current clergy of the Amarite church. Jalkan is probably the greediest man in the whole world – right up until you take a look at the higher members of the clergy. They take greed out to the far edge. They believe that *everything* in the entire world belongs to them – even the people.'

'And that brings us face to face with slavery, Lord Dahlaine,' Narasan added grimly.

'I was just about to raise that question,' Dahlaine said in a bleak tone. 'Was slavery a part of the original Amarite doctrine?' he asked Keselo.

'Most certainly not!' Keselo exclaimed. 'The original church denounced slavery as an abomination.'

'It would seem, then, that holy old Jalkan and his friends have strayed from the path just a bit,' Padan suggested.

'Maybe we should correct that,' Sorgan Hook-Beak declared. Then he grinned wickedly. 'I've always enjoyed correcting people when they're wrong.'

'It's our duty, friend Sorgan,' Narasan said blandly.

'You're going to be busy with the bug-people, Narasan. I'll take on the chore of whomping the church people.' He put on a woeful face. 'It's a dirty job, but somebody's going to have to do it.'

'Do those idiots in the Trogite church actually *believe* that they can own people?' Dahlaine demanded.

'I'm afraid so, Lord Dahlaine,' Keselo replied, 'but the church very seldom *keeps* the slaves. They sell them to the slave-dealers, who turn around and sell them to people who own vast amounts of territory but would sooner die than farm it themselves. Over the centuries an occasional emperor felt much as you do about slavery, and he issued an imperial proclamation abolishing the institution, but he almost never lived for very long *after* that proclamation, since if the church didn't kill him, the rich landowners did. There's a lot of money to be made from slavery, and the people who deal in slaves and the people who buy them aren't about to let anybody interfere.'

'I think we might have a bit of a problem here,' Dahlaine said then. 'If the church is corrupt, doesn't that mean that the church soldiers are as well? How can we trust people like that to do what we want them to do?'

'Who said anything about trusting them, big brother?' Zelana retorted. '*Somebody*, whom I dearly love, has taken the matter completely out of our hands by turning vast amounts of ordinary sand into something that looks like gold.'

'*I* think you're just making this up,' Zelana's sister declared, sounding more than a little offended. '*Nobody* could have done that.'

'You're wrong, sister,' Lady Zelana disagreed. 'Somebody *did*. I don't know *who* – or *how* – but she's obviously trying to help us, and we *need* that help.'

Aracia glared at Lady Zelana and then abruptly turned and stalked away.

'What's your sister's problem, Lady Zelana?' Sorgan Hook-Beak asked bluntly.

'She's just been outdone,' Zelana replied with a faint smile, 'and Aracia can't believe that *anybody's* capable of that. She's also having trouble with Keselo's description of the Amarite church. There's a goodly number of fat, lazy people in *her* Domain who spend hours every day telling her that she's beautiful and all-powerful. Aracia *loves* to be adored, but Keselo's story just raised the possibility that *her* priests are glorifying her just to keep their positions in what they call "the Church of Holy Aracia", so that they can avoid honest work.'

'Isn't that all sort of silly?' Sorgan asked.

'"Silly" comes fairly close, wouldn't you say, Dahlaine?' Lady Zelana asked her older brother.

'Not right in front of Aracia, I wouldn't,' Dahlaine replied with a faint smile. Then he straightened. 'Let's get back to business here,' he said firmly. '*If* those church armies *are*, in fact, coming here to help us – even though they don't know it – I think we'd better do all we can to help *them*.' He looked at Padan. 'How are they progressing?' he asked.

'They're doing a little better now that we're providing them with building materials. They've still got some distance to go, though. I think our major problem's going to be the width of that ramp they're building. It's only about ten feet wide, and that's not wide enough to get a significant force up here in a short time.'

'*And*,' Torl added, 'as soon as any of them get up here and see all that pretty sand, they'll start running toward it just as fast as they can. If they dribble on down to the Wasteland in twos and threes, the bug-people will have them for lunch.'

'That's where *we* come in, cousin Torl,' Sorgan said. 'Our trenches and barricades will definitely slow them down until their friends can catch up with them.'

'Did you by any chance recognize the voice of this lady who spoke to you while you were dreaming, Longbow?' Dahlaine asked.

'I'm positive that I've heard the voice before, Dahlaine,' Longbow replied, 'but I can't quite put my finger on just who she is.'

'She was undoubtedly concealing her identity from you,' Dahlaine said thoughtfully, 'and that sort of suggests that she's somebody we all know. Did she just talk to you, or did she show you anything?'

'She was never visible in the dreams,' Longbow said. Then he frowned slightly. 'Her language seemed to be quite archaic – almost as if she were speaking to me from the past.'

'That might have had something to do with her attempt to conceal her identity from you,' Dahlaine mused. 'It's not really important right now, though. She's managed to manipulate the thinking of about a half-million Trogites, and even though they don't know it, they're coming north to help us. We'll worry about who she is some other time. Right now we'd better do anything we can to help her. If this turns out the way I *think* it will, she's probably already won this war for us.'

Early the following morning Padan was standing near the river-bank above the thundering waterfall watching as his men, grunting and sweating, were rolling boulders down toward the brink of the gorge from about a quarter of a mile up the slope. 'It looks like we're about to run out of boulders up here,' he muttered. Then he peered down at the river below the falls. 'They must be sleeping on the job down there,' he added. 'They're definitely slowing down.' He looked around. 'Sergeant Marpek!' he shouted. 'Could you come here for a minute?'

Marpek was a solidly built fellow, which was only natural, perhaps, because he'd made a career out of solid building as one of the best engineers in Narasan's army.

'Is there some kind of problem, sir?' he asked as he joined Padan at the edge of the gorge.

'Is it my imagination or have those idiots down there slowed down quite a bit?'

Marpek squinted down into the gorge. 'They're still doing the best they can, sir,' he replied. 'They seem to be working as hard as they have for the last several days.'

'The ramp they're building hasn't come up more than a yard or so,' Padan protested.

'I'd be very surprised if it had, sir.'

'Could you explain that to me – in nice, simple, one-syllable words?' Padan asked. 'Try to keep it in mind that I'm not too fluent in the language of engineers.'

Marpek smiled. 'They need more rubble now, sir. The farther up the wall of that gorge they come, the more dirt, gravel, boulders and such they're going to need. If it was flat, they'd move at the same speed, but it comes up at about a thirty-degree angle, so it takes a lot more rubble to come one foot ahead than it did a few days ago.' He held out his hand and squinted at the space between his thumb and forefinger. 'I'd say that they've got about three hundred feet – or a hundred yards – to go.' He looked off into the distance, tapping one finger against his iron breastplate. Then he looked just a bit startled. 'I hadn't really given this much thought, sir, but now that I've put a few numbers together, I'd say that we've got quite a long time to wait before they finish.'

'Throw some kind of number at me, sergeant,' Padan said.

'At thirty degrees, ten feet wide, and two hundred feet high, I'd say that they'll need about sixty thousand cubic yards of rubble, sir,' Marpek said.

'*Sixty thousand.*'

'If they'd made it steeper, they wouldn't have needed so much,' Marpek mused, 'but it's too late to do anything about that now, I'm afraid.'

'That's going to take them most of the rest of the summer, Marpek!' Padan exclaimed.

'That's fairly close, I'd say.'

* * *

It was shortly after noon when Sorgan, Torl and Rabbit joined Padan at the rim of the gorge. 'What's got you so worked up, Padan?' Sorgan asked.

'Numbers, my friend,' Padan replied. 'I just received a fairly abrupt lesson in multiplication. Does the term "cubic yard" mean anything to you?'

Sorgan shrugged. 'Three feet by three feet by three feet, isn't it?'

'Unfortunately, there's still another number involved,' Padan added sourly. 'How does sixty thousand sound to you?'

'Just exactly what are we talking about here, Padan?' Torl asked.

'The amount of rocks and whatnot those people down there will need to finish that ramp.'

'Where did you come up with a number like that, Padan?' Sorgan demanded.

'Sergeant Marpek dropped it on me,' Padan replied glumly, 'and he's probably the best engineer in Narasan's army.'

'I think you'd better look somebody else up, Padan. That's not possible.'

'I'm afraid that it's *very* possible, cousin,' Torl disagreed. 'The higher up they build that ramp, the more rubble they'll have to pile up under it.'

'What if we gave them logs to play with instead of rocks?' Rabbit suggested.

'Rocks, logs, what's the difference?' Torl scoffed.

'If they've got logs, they won't have to pile garbage under them,' Rabbit replied. 'If they happen to get our point, they won't keep on saying "ramp". They'll say "bridge" instead, won't they?'

2

'The only problem I can see with the idea is that we don't really have very many axes or saws, sir,' Sergeant Marpek said. 'There are plenty of trees on the slope that comes down to the riverbank, and we've got plenty of men, but we just don't have enough tools to get the job done.'

Padan looked at Rabbit. 'Any ideas?' he asked.

'I don't have my forge or anvil here,' Rabbit reminded him, 'so I don't think I'll be of much use.' He hesitated. 'Your men *could* chop trees down with their swords, you know.'

Padan feigned a look of unspeakable shock. 'Blasphemy!' he gasped.

'I've got a fairly reliable whetstone, Padan,' Rabbit added, 'so your men *should* be able to polish the nicks and dents out of their swords if it bothers you so much. Then, too, if using their swords is going to offend them so much, they could always use their teeth, I suppose.'

'Their *teeth*?'

'Beavers chew trees down all the time, Padan,' Rabbit said, grinning broadly. 'And there's a bright side to that as well.'

'Oh?'

'If they've been chewing on trees all day, their teeth will probably be so sore that they won't want any dinner after the sun goes down. Look at all the money you'll save if you don't have to feed them.'

There were some violent protests when Padan ordered his men to start chopping down trees with their swords, but that came to an abrupt halt after Padan had given them an alternative. 'Report back to Commander Narasan. I'm sure you'll find chopping at turtle shells with your swords much more entertaining and a lot less boring than hacking down trees with them.'

Padan's men used the simplest means of delivering the trees they'd cut down to the church armies below. They simply pulled them down the slope and rolled them into the River Vash. The two-hundred-foot-high waterfall effectively put the trees fairly close to the church soldiers.

It took the armies below a while to come up with the concept of a bridge, and their first attempt was woefully unstable.

'If those amateurs down there try to roll one more log out on the ones they've already got in place, the entire thing will tumble down into the gorge and the whole crew will get killed,' Sergeant Marpek predicted.

'Oh,' Sorgan said with mock concern, 'what a shame.'

The always serious Marpek actually broke down and laughed along about then.

There were several minor disasters during the next few days as the church soldiers kept trying various short cuts to avoid building a bridge in the standard manner. Padan found the blunders moderately amusing, but the despairing screams of soldiers falling toward their deaths on the rocks far below started to get on his nerves after a while.

Sorgan dropped back from the region just upstream where his men were digging deep, twenty-foot-wide trenches and erecting rudimentary barricades on the far sides of each trench to check on the progress of the church soldiers. He arrived at the edge of the gorge just as another bridge collapsed, carrying yet another bridge crew plunging to their deaths.

'How many times has that happened so far,' Sorgan asked Padan.

'I think I've lost count,' Padan replied. He looked over at Rabbit. 'Is that the sixth failure or the seventh?' he asked.

'I make it seven,' Rabbit replied.

'They're just wasting time,' Sorgan fumed. 'Maybe we should stop giving them all those trees and build a bridge for them ourselves. Lowering the south end of the silly thing down to the upper edge of their ramp would be quite a bit easier than trying to lift the upper end here to the brink of the gorge. Lowering is always easier than lifting.'

'It might come to that,' Padan conceded. 'How are your trenches and barricades coming along?'

'The first three are all complete,' Sorgan declared, 'all except for the final decoration.'

'Decoration?'

'Ox came up with the notion, and I think it'll work out just fine.'

'What is it, Sorgan?'

'We go back to using those poisoned stakes,' Sorgan replied. 'We want them to slow down, don't we? After a dozen or so of a man's close friends fall over dead when they've stepped on those poisoned stakes, that man will start to be *very* careful where he puts his feet down. The ones who come across that bridge later will see all that imitation gold out there and start running as fast as they can, but when a man comes to a ditch that's about half full of his dead friends, he'll stop running right there, wouldn't you say? And the more they slow down, the more of their friends will catch up to them. If they dawdle around building that bridge right, they'll give my men enough time to dig two more trenches, and that'll probably fix it so that their whole army is up here before *any* of them come out of that last trench. Then we'll warn Narasan that they're coming and run off to the west just as fast as we can.'

'Slick, Sorgan,' Padan complemented the burly Maag. Then he paused. 'Don't you mean east?' he asked. 'That's where Nanton's pass is located.'

'I know,' Sorgan replied, 'but the river runs along the east side of those trenches and barricades. I swim fairly well, but the current in that river is fierce. I don't think I'd care to get swept over those falls, would you?'

'Not one little bit,' Padan agreed.

It was early the following morning when Narasan came down to Padan's temporary camp on the west side of the River Vash. Padan had just awakened and he was kneeling by the river splashing icy water on his face to push away the usual grogginess that clouded his mind every time he woke up.

'I thought you quit doing that a long time ago, Padan,' Narasan said.

'Not too likely, Narasan,' Padan replied. 'I need to be alert.'

'The world always needs more lerts,' Narasan repeated the tired old joke. 'How are the church armies doing now that they've decided to build a bridge instead of a ramp?'

'Quite a bit better than they were right at first,' Padan replied. 'They were in such a hurry to get to the land of gold that their first eight or ten bridges were awfully sketchy – like three trees tied together end to end with chunks of twine. After a goodly number of soldiers, priests and Regulators took up high-diving for a hobby, though, the rest of them started to wake up. A man who's just been splattered all over a few hundred feet of river beach after he's fallen about a hundred and fifty feet is a fairly convincing object lesson, wouldn't you say?'

Narasan winced.

'Their latest bridge – which isn't finished yet – looks to be strong enough to stay in place even if a thousand men try to come across all at the same time. They've got braces jammed up against the underside of their new bridge every few inches, I'd swear.'

'How much longer do you think it's going to take them to finish?'

'A couple more days is about all. Then they'll all dash north, shouting "Gold! gold! gold!" right up until they reach Sorgan's trenches and those poisoned stakes.'

'He told me about them when I passed through his camp. He can be a very evil man when he sets his mind to something, can't he?'

'Fun, though,' Padan replied with a broad grin. 'Those poisoned stakes at the bottom of this trench will make it almost certain that the entire five church armies will be coming up to Gunda's wall *all at the same time*, and that's all we've ever wanted.'

'I think I'll need to reconsider my original plan, though,' Narasan said glumly. 'I thought that falling back to the next breastworks every night would give the church armies enough time to get up there – in small groups, anyway. Sorgan's stakes will delay them, I'm afraid. We *will* get more men up there, but it's going to take them longer. I think I'll revise the plan and tell the men to hold each breast-works for *two* days instead of only one.'

'Whatever works the best, old friend,' Padan agreed.

Narasan looked off to the north. 'It's just a bit skimpy, I'm afraid,' he said with a slight frown.

'You missed me there, Narasan.'

'There are a couple of crags and such sticking up out of the Wasteland out there, and that's about all that those church soldiers will be able to see when they get up here. Those crags have a sprinkling of the imitation gold on them, but they aren't *nearly* as impressive as the flatter, sandy areas are.'

'If Sorgan's cousin Torl was anywhere close to being correct about what brought the churchies running up here, a few sprinkles should be all it's going to take,' Padan disagreed. 'It's what they'll see when they reach Gunda's wall that's important. *That's* when we'll want their minds to shut down to the point that it won't matter *what* sort of monsters are running up the slope toward them. We want greed to overcome terror at that point.'

'We can hope, I guess,' Narasan said.

MANY VOICES

1

Andar of Kaldacin was standing behind the eighth breast-works on the slope that ran down from the north of Gunda's wall, and he was seriously discontented. He kept encountering things here in the Land of Dhrall that seemed to be absurdities. Andar had fought in many wars during his career in Commander Narasan's army, but the enemies in those past wars had always been human.

Gunda and Padan had been given some time to adjust to the enemy's peculiarities during the previous war, but Andar had been left behind in the army encampment near the port city of Castano. He'd felt a bit flattered by Narasan's decision to place him in command of the bulk of the army that had remained behind, but that had also left *him* behind, and he resented that.

In a certain sense, Narasan's habit of always pushing Andar aside had probably been the result of the fact that Andar's father had been housed in a different building from Narasan's when the current officers were all children. Narasan's almost automatic reliance on Gunda and Padan had obviously derived from early childhood. Narasan trusted Gunda and Padan more than he trusted other officers of equal ability because he knew them better.

Andar ruefully admitted to himself that he would most certainly have relied on his boyhood friend Danal in much the same way he had *he* become the Army Commander.

The early light along the eastern horizon began to climb higher and higher, tinting the few clouds in that area a glorious pink.

'Any activity out there?' Danal asked as he joined Andar behind the crudely built breast-works.

'Nothing yet,' Andar replied in a hushed voice.

'At least we won't have to worry about those cursed burrows that kept cropping up back in the ravine during that last war,' Danal said.

'I never *did* get the straight of that,' Andar admitted.

'It's one of those things that people don't like to talk about,' Danal said with a shudder. 'The bug-things had most probably been planning that attack for a long, long time. First they bored holes through the mountains, and the holes came out high up on the sides of the ravine. We didn't know about them, so we just marched on up to the head of the ravine, built a nice sturdy fort, and waited for the bug-things to attack us. They wasted quite a few of their fellow bugs to keep us occupied while their friends crept through those burrows and came out behind us. That pretty much trapped us, because there was no place for us to go.'

'I never really understood that very clearly. How could bugs chop holes through solid rock?'

'Chew, not chop, Andar,' Danal corrected. 'From what the natives up there told us, the thing they always called "the Vlagh" had been preparing for that invasion for centuries.'

'Bugs don't live that long, Danal,' Andar scoffed.

'We're not in the land of reality any more, Andar. Things happen here that couldn't possibly happen anywhere else in the whole wide world. We had floods and volcanos working for us during that last war, and you don't see things like that out in the real world.'

Andar peered down the slope in the growing light of dawn. 'It looks to me like a few things have changed, Danal,' he said.

'Oh?'

'It would appear that the bug-people don't go back out into the desert when the sun goes down like they used to. It looks like they've set up camp in those two outermost breast-works. I think that the Vlagh thing's still back out in the desert, though. I've heard it bellow a few times since its soldiers – or whatever you want to call them – occupied those last two breast-works, and the bellow was still coming from a long way off.'

'The bug-people protect the Vlagh with everything they've got, Andar,' Danal said, 'which *does* make some sense, I suppose. It *is* the mother of every single bug out there, and children really should protect dear old mommy, wouldn't you say?'

'That's going to take a bit of getting used to,' Andar said, shaking his head. 'I've never had occasion to fight a woman's army before.'

'We were on the receiving end of several lectures that dealt with the creatures of the Wasteland when we were back in Lattash waiting for the snow to melt,' Danal told his friend. 'There was a very skinny old man – who I was told educated that archer named Longbow. He told us that almost *all* of the bug-people are females, but only the Vlagh lays the eggs that produce new variations of the original bug-people. The old man told us that the Vlagh steals characteristics from other insects – and even animals. The tiny ones we met in the ravine had snake-fangs – complete with venom – but after we'd whomped all over them, I guess the Vlagh decided that it was going to need big ones.'

'Whomped?' Andar asked curiously.

Danal shrugged. 'The Maags use that word all the time,' he said. 'It's sort of colorful, so most of the younger soldiers in Narasan's advance army started to talk about "whomping" other creatures – or each other, for that matter. If you listen carefully, you'll probably hear those young men threatening to "whomp" just about anybody who walks past. It's the newest "stylish" word, so they'll all keep repeating it until they've worn it out. Then they'll find another word to play with.'

Andar smiled. 'It's just a symptom of a fairly common disease, Danal. It's called "youth". They'll all get over it – eventually.'

'You're a cynic, Andar.'

'I know. It's quite possible that's a symptom of still another disease, the one that's called "old". Unfortunately, people *don't* get over that one.'

It was early that afternoon when the buckskin-clad archer Longbow led a sizeable party of native bowmen down the slope to join Narasan's force in the breast-works, and that quite obviously brightened Commander Narasan's day. Despite the training Longbow's friend Red-Beard had given the amateur Trogite archers, they were still fairly inept. From what Andar had heard, the native bowmen were much more skilled.

'Have those church armies finished building that bridge yet?' Narasan asked the tall archer.

'They're fairly close, I think,' Longbow replied. 'Sorgan's finished his trenches and barricades, so we're ready for those church armies. I think you should probably follow that plan you came up with earlier, though. We can't be completely sure how long it's going to take the church armies to get through Sorgan's defenses, so you'd probably better continue to delay the creatures of the Wasteland until we're more certain just exactly when our friends – who don't *know* that they're our friends – are going to reach Gunda's wall.'

'We're in a position to be fairly flexible here, Commander,' Andar said. 'We *can* continue to hold each breast-work for two days, if it's absolutely necessary, but if it starts to look like the church armies are going to arrive early, we can skip over a couple of our defense lines to make our time match theirs.'

'You could be right there, Andar,' Narasan agreed.

'Our army and theirs need to be closely coordinated,' Andar added, 'but, since their people are a little distracted right now, we can take care of the coordination for them, and they'll be able to concentrate on how they're going to spend all that gold they'll have in their purses before very much longer.'

'I like the way this man thinks,' Longbow said with a broad smile.

'So do I, now that you mention it,' Nasrasan agreed, giving Andar a speculative sort of look.

At sunrise – as always – the voice of the Vlagh roared its command, and the lumbering, awkward new breed of bug-warriors came mindlessly shambling across the open spaces lying between the several now-abandoned breast-works. The amateur Trogite archers held back, but the far more skilled native bowmen unleashed their arrows with a stunning accuracy, and the plodding, mindless attack faltered as the clumsy bug-men were suddenly obliged to clamber over heaps of their dead companions.

'That's pure idiocy!' Andar declared in disgust.

'Actually, it's about ten steps *below* idiocy, my friend,' Danal corrected. 'In the world of bugs, an idiot would be a genius.'

'Here come the turtles!' a soldier standing on top of the breast-works shouted.

'That's odd,' Danal noted. 'We didn't bother with those poisoned stakes this time, and I was fairly sure that the main job of the spidery turtles involved breaking off the stakes.'

'Not entirely, Danal,' Andar disagreed. 'Their shells *also* protect them from arrows. It's quite possible that the Vlagh might have graduated from idiot to imbecile. Go tell the catapult crews to get ready. I'd say that it's just about time to reintroduce the servants of the Vlagh to the wonderful world of fire.'

'If that's how y' want 'er, Cap'n, that's how we'll do 'er,' Danal replied.

'I think you've been spending far too much time with Padan here lately, old friend,' Andar observed.

A bank of clouds had built up along the western horizon that day, and the sunset was glorious. The Land of Dhrall had many faults, Andar felt, but the beauty of the place was almost heart-stopping. Civilization was all right, perhaps, but it fouled the air to the point that sometimes it was nearly impossible to see across the street.

The sun was still painting the sky a glorious red when the earnest young Keselo came down to the breast-works. 'Good evening, Sub-Commander,' he greeted Andar rather formally. 'Commander Narasan suggested that you might want to consider pulling back to the seventh breast-works tonight.'

'Suggested?' Andar asked.

'Well . . .' Keselo replied, 'actually he was issuing a command, but commands aren't really very polite, so I almost always modify them a bit before I pass them on.'

'This young fellow's the only man I know who apologizes to an enemy before he kills him,' Danal said, laughing.

'I do *not*, Brigadier Danal,' Keselo protested. 'I just try to be polite, that's all.'

'What's the polite way to kill somebody?'

'You're supposed to tip your hat first, Brigadier,' Keselo replied with no hint of a smile.

'I think he just got you, Danal,' Andar noted. Then he looked at Keselo again. 'I want a straight answer here, Keselo,' he said. 'Things might start getting a bit complicated from here on. Do you think Omago's men are ready to respond – even if they don't know exactly what's going on?'

'Omago himself will know exactly what to do,' Keselo replied, 'and his men have learned to respond to his commands without so much as blinking an eye.'

'That takes them even beyond professional soldiers,' Danal declared. 'How did he manage that?'

'The farmers all believe – with a certain amount of accuracy – that Omago speaks for Veltan.'

'And they're afraid of Veltan?'

'Not one bit,' Keselo replied firmly. 'The only ones who fear Veltan are our enemies.' He paused. 'Oh, before I forget, Sub-Commander,' he said to Andar, 'I'm told that there *will* be fog again, just like there was the last several times your men have pulled back. That's Lady Zelana's contribution during this current unpleasantness.'

'Maybe you should ask her not to waste it,' Danal said with a slight frown. 'I'm not exactly sure how she manages to fog things over every time we pull back, but if her supply of fog happens to run dry when we decide to run away, the bug-people or the church soldiers *might* realize what we're doing, and that could cause some serious problems.'

'She won't run out, Brigadier,' Keselo assured Andar's friend. 'If she wants something to happen, it *will* happen – even if it's impossible.'

'As long as we're discussing impossibilities, just who – or what – is going to open a large hole in Gunda's wall?' Andar asked.

'As far as I know, Veltan's going to attend to it, sir.'

'All by *himself*?' Andar exclaimed.

'I'd imagine that his tame thunderbolt will probably take care of it, sir.'

'How does *anybody* tame a thunderbolt?'

'I really wouldn't know, sir, but I have it on the very best authority that it was Veltan's thunderbolt that blasted out that channel through the ice-zone that gave us access to the Land of Dhrall in about one single day. Gunda's wall's very strong, but I'm quite sure it's not strong enough to stand up in the face of *that* kind of power.'

'I'm *never* going to get used to some of the things that happen in this part of the world,' Andar complained.

'You worry too much, Andar,' Danal noted. 'Miracles are just fine – as long as they're helping *us*. It's when they start helping our enemies that you might want to consider a petition of protest.'

Just after sunset when the servants of the Vlagh fell back to the two outermost breast-works, Lady Zelana's fog bank came rolling in to conceal the retreat of the Trogites and their local associates. As the fog came rolling in, Commander Narasan came down to the breast-works to confer with Andar. 'Using those catapults to set fire to the bug-people turned out to be very effective, Andar,' he said, 'but it's seriously reduced the amount of venom we've been able to gather. We really have no way to know just exactly when those church armies will break through Sorgan's defenses, so there's a distinct possibility that we'll need that venom to help us hold the bug-people back until those five armies arrive.'

'It's not really that much of a problem, Narasan,' Andar replied. 'Like you said, the native archers are more than capable of stopping the enemies right in their tracks.'

'You've adjusted to the situation here in the Land of Dhrall much more quickly than *I* did when I first arrived, Andar. When the native people told us what we'd probably encounter up in that ravine, I started having nightmares.'

'I have a certain advantage, Narasan,' Andar replied. 'I don't have to make those major decisions like you do. All I have to do is assume that you know what we should do to defeat the enemy. Any mistakes will be *your* fault, not mine.'

'Thanks a lot, Andar.'

'Don't mention it,' Andar replied blandly. Then he squinted on down the slope. 'I'd say that the fog bank's got us pretty well concealed now, Narasan. Why don't you go on back to Gunda's wall while I pull my men back? I know what I'm supposed to do, and you're just getting in my way.'

'Well, *pardon* me,' Narasan said, sounding slightly offended.

'I'll think about it,' Andar replied. 'Drop back sometime when I'm not so busy.'

Danal supervised the emplacement of the catapults early the next morning, and then he reported in. 'We're as ready as we'll ever be, Andar,' he reported. 'I'll keep an eye on things here. Why don't you get some sleep?'

'I'm wound just a little tight for that, Danal,' Andar admitted, 'but maybe you'd better tell the men to bed down. I don't *think* anything new and different's going to show up tomorrow, but around here, you never know, so let's make sure that the men are all sharp.'

'Right,' Danal agreed, moving off into the foggy darkness.

The night plodded on with the dense fog dimly illuminated by Lord Dahlaine's little false sun, and along toward morning Lady Zelana's little fog bank dissipated. Andar briefly considered the distinct possibility that the fog was nothing more than an illusion, but he firmly pushed *that* notion aside. Things were already complicated enough.

Then a faint line of light appeared along the eastern horizon, and Danal came back along the breast-works. 'Time to go to work,' he said quietly. 'I don't *think* the bug-people are awake yet, but around here, you never know.'

'Were there ever any night attacks back during the war in the ravine?' Andar asked his friend.

'None that I heard about. I wouldn't swear to it, but I don't think this particular breed of bugs can see very well in the dark. That's probably why the Vlagh decided to experiment with those bat-bugs. If Lord Dahlaine hadn't had that little toy of his available, things could have gotten a little wormy along about now.'

It seemed to Andar that it took hours for the sun to finally rise above the eastern horizon, but eventually she came sliding up into sight, and exactly when the bottom edge of the sun cleared the ridge off to the east, the now familiar roar from out in the glittering Wasteland unleashed the oversized bug-people.

'Enemy to the front,' a veteran sergeant bellowed in a loud voice, and the men all moved into position.

'I told the archers to hold off,' Danal said. 'I'm fairly sure that those bug-people won't quite realize that we've abandoned our previous position. Let's add as much confusion as we possibly can.'

'Can you actually confuse a bug?' Andar asked curiously.

'I'm not really sure,' Danal replied, shrugging. 'This might be a good time to find out, though.'

The clumsy creatures reached the now abandoned breast-works and began to mill about, evidently looking for someone to bite.

'They look confused to *me*, Andar,' Danal said with a tight grin. 'Now, if they were people-people, *one* of them at least would wake up enough to realize that we aren't there any more. Since they're only bug-people, though, they might just start biting the rocks in the breast-works.'

'That's absurd, Danal,' Andar scoffed.

'I wouldn't be too sure, my friend. That voice out there in the Wasteland ordered them to go bite *something*, and since we pulled all of our people back last night, there's nothing left there except rocks.' He stopped abruptly. 'You know, Andar, that *might* just be a distinct possibility, and if they start biting rocks, they'll break off their teeth. That could win this whole silly war for us.'

'I wouldn't make any large bets, Danal,' Andar replied. 'As soon as the Vlagh gets word that we aren't there any more, it'll start bellowing orders again – and from what I've heard, information reaches the Vlagh almost immediately.'

Then, almost as if it was confirming Andar's speculation, the voice of the Vlagh roared again, and the clumsy bug-men turned to advance across the open space between the abandoned breast-work and the now-occupied one.

'Archers to the front!' Danal commanded.

The more or less inept Trogite trainees *and* the highly skilled native bowmen took their positions, set arrows in place, and drew back their bows.

'Shoot!' Danal shouted.

The arrows flew forward in a nearly solid wave, and the enemy charge collapsed in the lethal shower.

The few remaining bug-people plodded forward, climbing over the heaps of their now-dead companions as the highly skilled native archers sent new arrow-storms out to meet them.

Then there was yet another roar with more than a slight touch of fury in it, and the hard-shelled spider creatures came over the now-unmanned breast-works to scamper across the open field littered with the dead.

'Catapults ready!' Danal bellowed.

'May I?' Andar asked.

'Be my guest,' Danal replied with a broad grin.

'Catapults launch!' Andar barked.

The wave of fire rose up from behind the breastworks, arched up and out, and then fell upon the charging enemies, engulfing them in fire.

2

✦━━✦━━✦

In a certain sense, Rabbit found the war here in Veltan's Domain much more interesting than the war in the ravine had been. He was more or less obliged to admit privately that the unexpected appearance of those five church armies had added a great deal of excitement, and Longbow's dreams had added even more. Rabbit had sensed a great reluctance on the part of Zelana's family to accept Longbow's firm belief that the church armies had been deceived to the point that they had unknowingly become allies in the war with the creatures of the Wasteland. That reluctance, it seemed to Rabbit, had grown out of a certain resentment. Zelana and her family were apparently very put out by the suggestion that Longbow's dream visitor could do things that were beyond *their* capabilities. That seemed almost stupid to Rabbit. Quite obviously, they were going to need help in this war, and refusing to accept help because Longbow's dream visitor was more gifted was ridiculous.

The bridge the Trogite armies were building was approaching completion, and Padan had pulled his people back into the forest on the west side of the basin to keep them out of sight. 'They don't need to know that we're still here,' Padan declared. 'They're busy doing exactly what we want them to do, so let's stay out of their way.'

Longbow's friend Red-Beard, however, thought that it might be wise to keep an eye on the 'friendly enemies'. Sometimes Red-Beard's clever remarks irritated Rabbit a bit, but if Longbow had been anywhere at all close to being correct, 'friendly enemies' might just be quite accurate.

It was late in the afternoon on a day a week or so after the church Trogites had started building their bridge when Rabbit joined Red-Beard and Sorgan's cousin Torl in a fairly dense clump of bushes on the west rim of the gorge the waterfall had gouged out of the mountains off to the south. 'Are they making any progress?' He asked quietly.

Torl covered his mouth to muffle a laugh. 'They seem to be having some trouble with the question of balance,' he said.

'Balance?' Rabbit asked, a bit puzzled.

'When you've got a log that's about a hundred feet long and you want to slide it across an open space that's eighty feet wide, the log starts to get a bit wobbly after fifty feet. But when it gets out to about seventy feet, it doesn't wobble any more. It just plunges on down into that gorge. Those nitwits over there have already sent four logs tumbling on down, and they've just started on log number five.'

'You're not serious!'

'Serious, no,' Red-Beard said with a broad grin. 'Accurate, yes. Eventually – sometime next week, maybe – *somebody* over there will realize that they'll have to put something heavy on *their* end of a log to keep it up *here* instead of down *there*.' He pointed down at the gorge.

'We *do* sort of want them to finish, you know,' Rabbit reminded them in a slightly worried tone.

'They'll manage,' Torl replied with a shrug.

'I think somebody over there just woke up,' Red-Beard said. 'It might take several more logs and a few hundred more men to sit on the short end of the log, but they're getting closer, I'd say.'

The three of them peered out at the busy Trogites.

'Using people for counterweights isn't the best idea they might have come up with,' Rabbit said dubiously.

'They've got lots of people, Rabbit,' Torl said. 'Sooner or later they'll get it right.'

The red-uniformed soldiers pushed the now-teetering log out a bit farther, and more and more of them laid across it to hold it in place. Then, when it had perhaps a foot more to go, the Trogites rammed it onto the rim.

'Just how long did it take them to get that one log in place?' Rabbit asked curiously.

'They started about noon, didn't they, Red-Beard?' Torl asked.

'A little earlier, maybe,' Red-Beard replied.

'If two logs a day is the best they can manage, they'll be at it for quite a while,' Rabbit said.

'They've got the first log across,' Torl said. 'Things should go faster now.' Then he suddenly grinned. 'If it wasn't that we really need them, the three of us could wait until about midnight and push their log clear of the rim and let it fall. Can you imagine the screaming we'd hear when the sun comes up tomorrow?'

Dusk was settling rapidly by now, and the Trogites had fallen back to their ramp and built several cooking fires. 'That pretty much does it for today,' Torl said. 'Let's go see what's for supper this evening.'

'Not quite yet,' Red-Beard replied. 'There are a few people coming up along the rim.'

'How did they get up *here*?' Torl demanded.

'Ladders, probably,' Rabbit suggested. 'I suppose when you get right down to it, ladders might have been even a better idea than the bridge.'

'Let's sit tight,' Red-Beard said. 'Those people are being very careful to stay out of sight of their friends down on the ramp.'

'I thought those church soldiers were supposed to wear red uniforms,' Rabbit said. 'The ones sneaking along the rim are dressed in black.'

'Regulators,' Torl explained. 'I heard about them down on the south coast. They're sort of like police, and everybody in those church armies – and even the priests – are afraid of them.'

'Maybe they just decided to go into business for themselves,' Rabbit suggested. 'If they run fast, they'll reach that ocean of imitation gold long before the red-shirts do.'

'It's possible, I guess,' Torl said a bit dubiously.

'I think the answer's creeping across that log they put in place just before sunset,' Red-Beard said.

Rabbit peered down through the gathering darkness and finally caught sight of several shadowy figures creeping slowly along the log that was now in place. When they finally reached the rim, Rabbit could hear them whispering urgently to each other. 'If we hurry, we'll be able to reach the area where all the gold sand's laying. Then we can scoop up several bags of gold and get back to the camp before anybody misses us,' one of them said.

'We'll have to hide the gold someplace,' another urgent voice came out of the darkness. 'If those greedy priests catch even a hint that we've got it, they'll turn the Regulators loose on us to torture answers out of us.'

'This might be a good time for us to get rid of those greedy priests, and the Regulators as well,' the first voice added.

'We can't kill priests!' Another voice gasped.

'We won't *have* to kill them,' the other voice replied. 'Priests are so holy that they can probably fly, so all that we'll be doing will be testing all of them. If we just throw them into that gorge, the holy ones will fly, right? The only ones who'll fall into the gorge and go splat when they reach the bottom will be the *un*holy ones, wouldn't you say? All we'll be doing is testing the priests for holiness, but if every single one of them goes splat – ah, well.'

The others all laughed raucously.

Then the black uniformed Regulators came out of the darkness – with clubs – and they beat the deserters into submission in only a few minutes.

'What should we do with them now, Konag?'

The bleak-faced man who'd led the Regulators along the rim smiled faintly. 'Why don't you just give them the "holiness test"?' he replied.

'I don't quite follow you, Konag,' the first Regulator said.

'You must have been too far away to hear them talking,' Konag said. 'When you want to test a man for holiness, all you have to do is throw him off some high place. If he flies, he's holy. If he falls, he's *un*holy.'

'Toss them all into the gorge, you mean?'

'What a brilliant idea!' Konag replied sardonically.

The following morning Rabbit decided that he should finish something he'd been tinkering with for the past few weeks. He took up the curved limb he'd chopped from a hardwood tree up on the west ridge and continued the tedious business of shaving it into shape with this knife.

'Whittling, Rabbit?' Torl asked him. 'Are you *that* bored?'

'Not really,' Rabbit replied. 'It came to me last week that I've been making arrows for Longbow and his people since last winter, but I've never once pulled a bow.'

'Isn't it just a little short?' Torl suggested.

'If I happened to make *my* bow as long as the bows of Zelana's people, I'd have to stand on a ladder to shoot the silly thing.'

Torl smiled faintly. 'I'm sure that our enemies will all run away in terror when they see Longbow and Shortbow coming their way.'

Rabbit gave him a flat, unfriendly look. 'I'll tell you what, Torl,' he said. 'As soon as I finish my bow, I'll need a target to practice my shooting. You could walk off a ways, and we'll find out if I know what I'm doing. I probably won't be very good, so you won't be in *too* much danger.'

'Maybe some other time, Rabbit,' Torl replied. 'I'm just a little busy right now.'

'Any time you start getting bored, my friend, I think that might be a way to liven up your day.'

'I'll keep it in mind, Rabbit,' Torl said, and then he walked off, shaking his head.

When he'd finished shaping his bow, Rabbit went looking for Red-Beard. 'What do your people use for bow-strings?' he asked after he'd showed his experiment to his friend.

'Dried gut, usually,' Red-Beard replied. 'Some archers use animal tendons, but I've always had better luck with gut. I've got a couple of spares, so I'll give you one of mine.' He took Rabbit's bow up, holding an end of it in each of his hands. Then he bent the bow.

'Nice and limber,' he noted. 'This might work fairly well for you.'

'We'll never know until I try.'

After Rabbit had strung his new bow, he took a handful of arrows and went on up into the woods on the west slope. He'd never shot an arrow at anything in his whole life, so he didn't really want an audience when he started to practice.

Longbow had made quite an issue of what he called 'unification' – something that sort of linked the archer, his bow, and the target. Rabbit gave that a bit of thought as he went up among the trees on the west slope. 'Maybe it's something on the order of what happens when I see that the chunk of metal I'm heating in the forge is exactly the right color,' he mused.

He looked around and saw a patch of green moss growing on a tree trunk about fifty paces on up the hill. He set the notch of an arrow on his bowstring without taking his eyes off that patch of moss. Then he raised the bow, drawing back the string as he did. Then, not even squinting along the arrow shaft, he let it fly.

He was actually startled when his arrow went straight and true directly to the center of the target.

'I must be better than I thought,' he murmured with a broad grin. 'I've never missed a target in my life.'

With growing curiosity, he notched another arrow and let it fly.

Now there were two arrows protruding side by side from the patch of moss.

After he'd loosed his last arrow, he walked on up to the tree to take a closer look.

His arrows were clustered together so tightly that he could cover their notched ends with the palm of his hand. 'That's impossible!' he exclaimed. Then he looked around rather suspiciously as it came to him that maybe Zelana was somewhere nearby playing games.

Then he realized that he probably wouldn't be able to see her even if she was.

It took quite a bit of effort to pull his arrows out of the tree trunk, and he broke two of them in the process. Then he went on back down the hill and put his bow under his blankets. 'I think maybe I should just keep this to myself,' he mused. 'Nobody's going to believe me anyway, so let's not make an issue of it. A man should never miss an opportunity to keep his mouth shut.'

'They're almost finished, Padan,' Torl reported late in the afternoon two days later. 'And it looks to me like those church Regulators are doing most of our work for us. They've managed to persuade all those church soldiers to stay where they're supposed to instead of running off toward goldie out there.'

'Goldie?' Padan asked with a light smile.

'She's one of my favorite pets,' Torl explained. 'I just *love* pets who do all the work, don't you?'

Padan scratched the side of his jaw. 'I'm not sure, but it *might* just be that those Regulators have changed things just a bit. It's possible that terror can overwhelm greed, I suppose.'

'It might not be a bad idea to let cousin Sorgan *and* Commander Narasan know about this,' Torl suggested. 'If the Regulators can hold all those church soldiers right here instead of letting them dribble off toward old goldie in twos and threes, a certain change of plans might be in order along about now.'

'You could be right, Torl,' Padan agreed. He looked at Rabbit. 'How are your legs holding out, little friend?' he asked.

'I still know how to run,' Rabbit said. 'I take it that you'd like to have me spread the news?'

'If it isn't too much trouble,' Padan replied.

'And maybe even if it is,' Torl added quite firmly.

'It sounds like those Regulator people might have made all our work here unnecessary, cousin,' Skell said after Rabbit had told them what had been happening.

'Maybe,' Sorgan said a bit dubiously. 'I still think we'd be better off if those idiots were still running this way like their lives depended on it. If they slow down a bit, they might decide to take another route to get to that gold desert out there.'

'I don't think so, Cap'n,' Rabbit disagreed. 'When Longbow, Torl and I went up onto that west ridge to find out if the yellow sand wasn't what it seemed to be, we were able to see a lot more of that desert out there. The sand that looks like gold but isn't peters out a couple miles off to the west. Longbow says that the dream-lady's using it to bait those church armies, so she put it just exactly where we need it to be.'

'I'd surely like to meet this lady,' Skell said. 'I think we might owe her about a thousand pounds of thank-yous.'

'*If* it turns out the way she seems to want it to, Skell,' Sorgan said a bit dubiously. 'But if something goes wrong, things around here could get *real* wormy in a hurry.'

3

Aracia and her brothers and sister, as well as the children, gathered near the geyser at the center of the basin late in the evening not long after the church soldiers from the south had finally completed the bridge that everybody thought was important, and it seemed to the warrior queen Trenicia that the sole purpose of this gathering had been to watch the little girl Lillabeth sleep. Trenicia was fairly certain that Lillabeth could sleep without an audience, but Aracia's family seemed to be very interested for some reason.

Queen Trenicia of the Isle of Akalla had been much confused from the very beginning by the male-dominated cultures of all these other lands. On the isle Trenicia ruled, men were little more than house pets who spent most of their time trying to make themselves look beautiful. They even painted their faces on special occasions.

There *were* some ancient tales – quite probably pure invention – that stoutly maintained the absurdity that at some time in the distant past *men* had been dominant, and that they'd treated women as mere chattels. The tales went on to describe in some detail the events of a certain day when a large group of women in search of firewood on a southern beach had come across the wreckage of what appeared to have been a large raft – or something that went beyond a raft – from some far distant land, and in various places in the wreckage, the women found weapons that had been made of some material that quite obviously was *not* stone.

Had the women who'd made this discovery been docile, Queen Trenicia was fairly certain that the history of the Isle of Akalla would have been much different. The women, however, had been anything *but* docile. After many centuries of being treated as property only, the resentment of the women had been enormous, and a goodly number of the discoverers of those metal weapons returned home with the weapons in their hands and firmly demonstrated their discontent.

The males of the isle were horrified. Quite suddenly, the women of Akalla were total savages who refused any and all commands and responded to the faintest hints of disapproval with brutal efficiency.

The men fled at that point, but the women weren't satisfied by mere flight. They wanted blood.

Trenicia was almost certain that the stories from the past had been exaggerated, but there might have been some justification for the behavior of those ancient women. At any rate, the wanton slaughter of the men of the isle finally alarmed the older and wiser women, and they reminded their savage younger sisters that if there were no men, there would be no children, and in a little while there would be no people on the isle.

The random killings had slowed at that point, and the women began to herd the surviving males into log pens. Then they brought the men out – one by one – and offered them to the other women. If a man was old or ugly or happened to have a bad reputation among the women, all the women rejected him, and he was killed right on the spot.

The practice of killing unwanted males had slowly disappeared in the society now dominated by women, but the males still believed that their very lives might depend upon looking desirable.

And so it was that the men of Akalla now spent every waking minute searching for ways to make themselves pretty. That, of course, made it totally impossible for the men to take on any chores whatsoever, so it fell to the women to plant, cook, harvest, govern, and fight any war that came along.

All in all, Queen Trenicia saw nothing really wrong with the current arrangement, and she was completely baffled by the peculiar arrangements in other societies.

Trenicia still could not understand why all the local gods – and their pet children – were so interested in Aracia's pet, so she turned to the beautiful child Eleria, who was sitting some distance apart from the others with a peculiar expression on her lovely face. 'Why is everybody so curious about Lillabeth?' she asked.

'She's dreaming,' Eleria replied. 'That's what we're supposed to do. We make things happen with our dreams – things that those who care for us aren't permitted to do.'

'But aren't your elders gods?'

'In a sense, yes they are.'

'But gods can do anything, can't they?'

'Not really,' Eleria replied in a somewhat obscure manner. 'They can't destroy life – of any kind.'

'Not even enemies who want to kill them?' Trenicia was made aghast by this limitation.

'That's why those of us who look like children are here. We destroy the enemies with our dreams. Back in the Beloved's Domain, I had a dream about a huge flood, and my flood drowned thousands of our enemies. Then, a bit later, Vash had his volcano dream, and he killed even more than I did.'

Trenicia looked at Lillabeth with a certain awe, and as she looked more closely she saw something in the air directly above the sleeping child, and the object had shifting colors that looked almost like fire. 'What's that pretty thing just above her?' she asked.

Eleria glanced at the sleeping child. 'It's a seashell,' she replied. 'Abalone, I think. It's kind of pretty, but I think my pearl's even prettier. Our jewels are the things that give us our dreams. They're the voice of the One Who Guides Us. She uses the jewels to tell us what we're supposed to dream.'

'Who is she?' Trenicia asked.

'I'm not really sure,' Eleria replied. 'I've known her since time began.' Then the little girl laughed a bit ruefully. 'The only problem there is that I can't quite remember when that was. I was there, of course, but it was so long ago that I can't put any kind of number to it. As I remember, we were all very busy back then.'

'Busy?'

'We were making things. Our elders had been doing that for a long, long time, and they were growing very, very tired, so we told them to rest, and we took up the burden for them. We've just about reached the point where we'll have to do it again, I think. The Beloved's starting to get just a bit strange. She's very, very tired, and she needs to go to sleep. I've been slipping around behind her back taking care of things for her, but that's all right. I've done that many times in the past.' Eleria glanced at the sleeping child. 'I think Enalla's just about to wake up now. She's probably already put her dream in motion, and her dream will probably win *this* war.' She pursed her lips. 'Dakas *might* have to help her – sort of like Vash helped me last time,' she added in a speculative tone.

'Do you children *all* have different names?' Trenicia asked. 'I thought Aracia's little girl was named Lillabeth.'

'That's what Aracia calls her, but her real name is Enalla.'

'What's *your* real name then?'

'Balacenia, of course. When Dahlaine came up with this idea, he decided not to use our *real* names. That was part of his deception. The other part involved pushing us all the way back to infancy so that our elders wouldn't realize just exactly who we *really* are.'

'When Aracia came to the Isle of Akalla, she didn't say a thing about this,' Trenicia said, feeling a bit offended.

'Aracia's like that sometimes.' The child laughed. 'She really irritates Dahlaine sometimes. He knows that she really wants to be the dominant one during their next cycle, and he doesn't like the idea.'

'Why are you telling me about all of this?' Trenicia demanded. 'If it's anything even close to being the truth, shouldn't you be trying to conceal it from me?'

'We're not *all* like Aracia, dear,' the child replied. 'I've always felt that being honest works a lot better than deception. I'm sure that the time will come when it'll be very important for you to know the truth, so I just took you for a little stroll down the path of truth. After a while, when you've had time to think it over, we might want to go a little farther down that path.' She paused, and then she gave Trenicia a childish little grin. 'Won't that be fun?' she asked with exaggerated enthusiasm, clapping her hands together.

4

Sorgan Hook-Beak, his cousin Skell, and First Mate Ox were standing on the south-side of the first trench peering into the darkness.

'I think you worry too much, cousin,' Skell said. 'From what I saw during that last war, Trogite armies don't fight wars very good after the sun goes down.'

'That might be true when you're talking about a real army, Skell,' Sorgan replied, 'but if Torl was anywhere close to being right about what happened down there on the south coast, we're talking about a mob, not an army. If they've seen all that false gold out there, their brains have shut down, and they won't think – or behave – like soldiers any more.'

'I'd say that might depend on whether they've finished their bridge or not, Cap'n,' Ox added. 'If they haven't managed to get up here yet, all *we're* doing is wasting sleep-time.'

'Not entirely, Ox,' Sorgan disagreed. 'Padan said that he'd send somebody up here to let us know when that bridge is finished, and if his messenger doesn't know where the trail through the poisoned stakes is, he'll probably die before he reaches us.'

'Somebody's coming, cousin,' Skell hissed, pointing off to the south.

'I make it to be Rabbit, Cap'n,' Ox added, 'or somebody who's almost a small as he is, and Rabbit knows the way through the stakes.'

'It's about time,' Sorgan said with a sense of relief.

'Is that you, Cap'n?' Rabbit's voice came out of the darkness.

'Who were you expecting?' Sorgan replied. 'What's happening down there?'

'Those soldiers in red clothes finally finished their bridge, Cap'n,' Rabbit said as he joined them, 'but things aren't going exactly like we thought they would.'

'Problems of some kind?' Skell demanded.

'Maybe so, or maybe not,' Rabbit replied. 'Everything was going pretty much like we expected. The soldiers in red clothes finally managed to get one log across that last gap, and when they saw the peaks with imitation gold on them out there, they got all excited. After the sun went down, eight or ten of them came sneaking across that log – probably trying to get a head start on all their friends.'

'We were fairly sure things were going to work out that way, Rabbit,' Ox said.

'They hit a snag, though,' Rabbit announced. 'Some other men dressed in black clothes had used ladders to get up to the rim, and they were waiting when the red-suits came across the log. The ones in black suits grabbed the red-suits and threw 'em off that rim. From what Torl and Padan told us, I guess the black-suits are the ones who make sure that the red-suits do what they're supposed to do, and they make sure that the red-suits get the point by killing anybody who tries to break the rules.'

Sorgan winced. 'How far down would you say it is from the rim to the rocks down below?' he asked.

'Two hundred feet at least, Cap'n,' Rabbit replied. 'I wouldn't say that very many red-suits walked away after a fall like that.' He shuddered. 'Anyway, Padan sent me up here to let you know that the bridge is finished and that the red-suits won't just come dribbling in up here. They'll come here by the hundreds at least.' He paused. 'Oh, one other thing, Cap'n. Padan and his people are about an hour behind me, and he said he'd *really* appreciate it if there was somebody here to show him how to get to your barricade without having to tiptoe through those poison stakes.'

'We'll see to it, Rabbit,' Sorgan said. 'Now why don't you hustle on up to Gunda's wall and let Narasan know what's afoot?'

'I'll do 'er, Cap'n – just as soon as somebody shows *me* how to get through the poison stakes in the other trenches without coming down with a bad case of dead.'

Padan and Torl reached Sorgan's first trench before first light and they were some distance ahead of their men.

'Rabbit stopped by and told us that things have changed just a bit,' Skell advised them. 'He wasn't just making things up, was he? Are those men dressed in black really *that* brutal?'

'Worse, probably, big brother,' Torl replied. 'Padan here sort of filled me in on the organization of those church armies, and if I understood it right, the Trogite church tends to take brutality out to the far end. The ones they call "Regulators" keep the soldiers – *and* the priests themselves – in line by using pure terror. I guess their standard approach goes something along the lines of "if you don't do what we tell you to do, we'll kill you". Then they prove that they mean just what they say by killing a few right there on the spot.'

'Is he making this up, Padan?' Sorgan asked skeptically.

'No, Captain Hook-Beak. That's pretty much how the Regulators operate,' Padan said. 'The church is out to get the money, and any kind of decency went out the window a long time ago.' He peered out into the darkness on either side of Sorgan's trench. 'I gather that the east sides of these trenches lie along the riverbank,' he noted. 'How have you managed to block off the west side?'

'We got lucky,' Sorgan replied. 'There's a rock face that runs for about a mile along the west ridge. I suppose that a man *could* climb up that face if he really wanted to, but it'd probably take quite a while. If those church soldiers are all excited about the imitation gold out there in the desert, they wouldn't want to waste that much time. Our poisoned stakes at the bottom of these trenches aren't very long and we scattered tree leaves over the top of them to keep them pretty much out of sight.'

'Are you sure that they'll penetrate the soles of those soldier-boots?'

'I wouldn't want to try to run across the trench to find out. How much longer would you say it's likely to take all of those church soldiers to get up here?'

'As near as I've been able to determine, they'll be at it for about two and a half days, captain. Now, whether they'll wait until all of their men are up here before they start, or march this way a battalion or so at a time, I couldn't say.'

Sorgan and Padan were standing atop the barricade farthest to the south at first light the following morning, and so far as Sorgan was able to determine, the church armies had not as yet begun their march. 'No visitors yet,' he said to Padan. 'Are you positive that those church soldiers won't recognize our yellow ribbons as markers?'

'Not very likely, Captain,' Padan replied. 'Gunda and I came up with *that* notion when we were still children, and we kept it pretty much to ourselves. *We* know what they mean, but nobody else does.'

'What about that one called Jalkan? If I understood what Narasan told me, that scrawny rascal was a member of your army for quite a long time, but now he's a part of the enemy army.'

Padan shook his head. 'Gunda, Narasan and I kept the idea strictly to ourselves,' he said. Then he smiled faintly. 'If you wanted to get right down to the bottom of it, we *were* being just a bit childish about it. The yellow ribbons were *our* idea, so we kept them entirely to ourselves. We don't use large strips of yellow fabric, and most of the time they're nothing but yellow string. How did *you* manage to sneak in and steal our secret?'

'Narasan was more or less obliged to tell me about it after he sent you along with Skell's scouting party. Skell would probably have thought you'd just gone crazy when you started tying yellow ribbons to bushes and trees along the way.'

'Here comes Longbow,' Padan said, pointing off toward the north, 'and it looks to me like Rabbit's showing him the way.'

'Good. We *definitely* don't want to lose Longbow. Lady Zelana would skin me alive if I let anything happen to him.'

'Any sign yet of those "friendly enemies"?' Longbow asked.

'Not yet,' Sorgan replied. 'Of course, it's still early. The sun isn't even up yet. How did Narasan take our news, Rabbit?'

'He claimed that it was awful unnatural for him to approve of *anything* those church armies came up with, but that deep down, he really approved of what those Regulators did to persuade the soldiers *not* to run on ahead so that they could get more gold. I think he's looking forward to what's going to happen when the church armies come face to face with the bug-people.'

Sorgan grinned. 'That's our Narasan for you,' he said, 'but to tell the truth, I'm sort of looking forward to it myself.'

'Enemy to the front,' Padan announced in an almost bored tone of voice.

Sorgan turned quickly to look off toward the south. 'Now *that's* what I'd call an army,' he said. 'I was still just a bit nervous about the "sneak ahead and get more" crowd, but I'd say that the Regulators got their point across.'

The massive army of men in red uniforms were marching in what Narasan called 'quick step', and it seemed to Sorgan that they were making good time – until they reached the edge of Sorgan's first trench. The front rank looked dubiously at the ten-foot drop to the bottom of the trench, and then they began to melt back in among the following ranks.

'I seem to be catching a certain lack of enthusiasm,' Padan said with a grin.

'If a man's not careful, he can break both of his legs in a jump like that,' Sorgan said. 'I'd imagine that I'd be a bit edgy about it myself.'

A lean man with an ugly face and wearing a black uniform conferred briefly with other men in similar uniforms, and his underlings – if that's what they were – moved rapidly along behind the now-hesitant red-uniformed men, pushing them off the edge of the trench.

'Efficient, maybe,' Padan observed, 'but just a bit extreme, perhaps.' Then he peered into the trench. 'Just how close to the other side of the trench did your people plant those stakes, Sorgan?'

'*Real* close.'

'The venom seems to be as strong as it was before,' Padan noted. 'It looks to me like everybody who went down over there is dead.'

Sorgan grinned at him. 'That was the whole idea, Padan. Now that those men in red have seen what's waiting for them, they'll have to slow down and very carefully start digging up the stakes. I'd say that it's likely to take them about two days to clear the bottom of the trench. By then, there'll be twice as many soldiers standing on the far side waiting to come this way.'

'Shrewd,' Padan said. 'After two or three more trenches, I'd say that all five church armies will be up here jumping up and down and waiting for the time when they can run out into the desert to gather up as much imitation gold as they can carry.'

But it didn't turn out that way, Sorgan was forced to admit. There was another get-together of the Regulators, and the one who was apparently their leader snapped out some fairly blunt instructions. Then the Regulators moved out again grabbing hold of more soldiers. This time, however, the Regulators didn't just push the soldiers over the edge of the trench.

They threw them instead – just as far as they could – and the pile of dead soldiers began to stretch farther and farther out into the trench as the Regulators carpeted Sorgan's trench with people.

'*That* does it!' Rabbit exclaimed in a voice that didn't have the slightest trace of his usual timidity. He raised that short bow that Sorgan had assumed was little more than a decoration and drew an arrow from the quiver belted to his back. 'Which way did that one called Konag go?' the little man asked Torl.

'Ah . . .' Torl's eyes swept across the far side of the trench. 'I think he's that one standing off to the right side, Rabbit,' he said. 'Do you think you can take him from here?'

'I'm definitely going to try,' Rabbit announced, drawing his bow and sighting along the arrow shaft.

His bowstring sang when he released it, and his arrow arched slightly as it flew over the trench.

The black uniformed man who'd ordered his subordinates to throw live soldiers out into the trench to carpet over Sorgan's stakes had been watching with an expression of bleak satisfaction, but that expression faded as he stiffened with Rabbit's arrow protruding from the middle of his forehead. Then he fell on his back with his blank eyes staring at the sky.

'How did you *do* that?' Sorgan demanded of his little smith.

'We call this a "bow", Cap'n,' Rabbit explained, 'and the thing that's sticking out of that fellow's head over on the other side of the trench is called an "arrow". If you put them together just right, they'll do all sorts of nice things to people who aren't nice.'

'That's not what I meant, Rabbit,' Sorgan said. He turned to look at Longbow. 'Have you been giving him lessons on the sly, maybe.'

'Not me, Hook-Beak,' Longbow replied. 'It's quite possible that he just picked it up himself after he watched *us* shoot arrows into the creatures of the Wasteland back in the ravine.'

'That comes fairly close, Cap'n,' Rabbit conceded.

'You must have spent hours and hours practicing, Rabbit,' Torl said.

Rabbit shrugged. 'It doesn't really take all *that* long, Torl – especially if the only thing you practice is hitting. I didn't waste any time practicing missing.' He frowned slightly. 'I suppose I *could* teach myself how to miss,' he said, 'but it might take me quite a while to learn how. Maybe if I work on it a bit, I *will* learn how to miss.' And then he laughed with an almost childish delight.

* * *

Sorgan was fairly sure that Longbow had trained Rabbit in the secrets of fine archery. 'We'll worry about that some other time,' he muttered.

'What was that?' Padan asked him.

'Just thinking out loud,' Sorgan replied, staring across the trench. 'I think that one arrow might have changed a few things,' he said.

'I've heard a few stories about that Konag,' Padan replied. 'I've heard that even the highest-ranking churchmen are afraid of him.'

'*Were* afraid,' Sorgan corrected. 'Now that he's dead, I don't think anybody's afraid of him any more.'

'Maybe,' Padan said, still looking across the wide trench. 'It looks to me like those church soldiers are starting to shed some of their timidity. One of the Regulators just got a sword in the belly.'

'What a shame,' Sorgan replied sardonically.

'There goes another one,' Padan reported. 'Things seem to be getting a bit exciting over there.'

'Don't start cheering yet, Padan,' Sorgan growled. 'If those soldiers over there work up enough nerve, they'll kill *all* of the Regulators, and then they'll go right back to "I can run faster than you can" and they'll all start dribbling down the north slope in twos and threes, and the bug-people will have them for lunch.'

'Not as long as your poisoned stakes are in place, they won't. They'll have to crawl along on their hands and knees pulling those stakes out one at a time. That should slow them enough for the rest of their forces to catch up with them.'

'We can hope, I guess,' Sorgan dubiously replied.

It was not long after noon when there was a sudden flash of intense light and a shattering crash of thunder.

'Do you *have* to do that, Veltan?' Sorgan demanded irritably.

'She gets me where I need to go in a hurry, Sorgan,' Veltan explained. 'Please don't irritate her. I need her right now.'

'What's happening, Lord Veltan?' Padan asked Zelana's younger brother. It seemed to Sorgan that Padan sometimes overdid his pretended politeness.

'My big sister's Dreamer just solved a number of problems for us, gentlemen,' Veltan replied. 'If you look off to the west, you'll see her solution boiling this way.'

Sorgan jerked his head around and saw a seething yellow cloud streaming over the ridge-top. 'What *is* that?' he demanded.

'It's called a "sandstorm", Captain Hook-Beak. You probably don't see very many of those out on the face of Mother Sea.'

'Almost never,' Sorgan agreed.

'I don't think that's a very good idea, Lord Veltan,' Padan objected. 'Won't that pretty much stop the church soldiers still coming up that ramp dead in their tracks?'

'The sandstorm's out *here*, Sub-Commander; not down *there*,' Veltan replied with a broad grin. 'The soldiers who are already here will have to take cover, but the ones coming up that ramp and crossing that bridge won't even know what's happening up here.' Then he suddenly laughed. 'And it gets even better.'

'Oh?'

'The sandstorm's blowing in from the south-west, and after it sweeps past Gunda's wall, it'll almost certainly roll on down the slope leading up from the Wasteland.'

'That might just disturb the bug-people a bit,' Padan suggested with a broad grin.

'Quite a bit more than just "disturb", Padan,' Veltan replied. 'The servants of the Vlagh will need shelter even more than these church soldiers will. That lovely sandstorm's going to freeze everything in place – *except* for those church armies that're still coming up out of the gorge. *They'll* keep moving, but nobody *else* will.'

'Not even *us*,' Sorgan reminded him.

'Don't rush me, Sorgan,' Veltan said. 'I'm still working on that part.'

5

———✦———

Keselo was very close to exhaustion. It made sense, certainly, to do these periodic retreats under the cover of darkness and Lady Zelana's helpful fog banks, but a night without sleep came very close to cutting Keselo all the way down to the bone. He stood wearily with his new friend Omago near the center of the sixth breast-work pushing out from Gunda's wall as the first light of morning stained the edge of the eastern sky.

'Why don't you try to catch a few winks, Keselo,' Omago suggested. 'I can keep an eye on things, but I don't think any of those bug-people will start to move before sunlight.'

Keselo shook his head. 'I couldn't sleep right now, Omago,' he said. 'I'm positive that our enemies will be coming up the slope before long, so I'm wound just a little tight.'

Though it seemed a bit unnatural in the light of the differences in their cultures, Keselo had developed a strong friendship with Omago. They got along very well, but Keselo had frequently been startled by the frequent leaps in Omago's thinking. 'Have you come up with any new ideas, my friend?' he asked.

'Nothing that might be useful,' Omago confessed. 'I'm just a bit tired too.'

'That's been going around here lately,' Keselo said. 'Andar's a very good officer, but he pushes his men a bit harder than necessary. There's an idea. Maybe if we sang lullabies to him for a couple of hours, he'd drift off to sleep and we could *all* get some rest.'

'I sort of think that your Commander Narasan would jump all over him for that,' Omago suggested.

'Probably so,' Keselo agreed. 'It was just a thought. Why don't you see if you can keep me awake by telling me stories about Veltan? I never got to know him very well back in the ravine in Lady Zelana's Domain.'

Omago smiled faintly. 'I could tell you stories about Veltan all day if you wanted to hear them. He used to spend a lot of his time in my father's orchard when I was just a boy.'

'Stealing apples?' Keselo asked.

'No, it was usually in the springtime when the trees were in bloom. An orchard in the spring is more beautiful than any flower garden, and Veltan always spends several weeks in that orchard when the trees are in bloom. We'd sit there and talk – well, *he* would. I just listened. There are things about Veltan that only the people of his Domain know about.'

'Really? Such as what?'

'He offended Mother Sea once, and she banished him to the moon.'

Keselo's eyes had almost closed, but they popped wide open. 'Did I hear what you just said right?' he demanded. 'Did you say that Veltan's been to the *moon*?'

Omago laughed. 'Oh, yes. Mother Sea was *very* irritated. Veltan had to stay on the moon for thousands of years. That was the moon's idea, actually. She enjoyed his company, so she lied to him and told him that Mother Sea was still angry about something he'd said. Veltan was *really* put out when Mother Sea told him that he could have come back home after a month or so.'

'You're just making this up, Omago,' Keselo accused.

'I'm just passing on what Veltan told me,' Omago said. Then he paused. 'I notice that it *did* wake you up a bit,' he added. He glanced off to the east. 'We're getting closer to sunrise, I'd say. Unless the bug-people have changed the rules, they should be coming back up the hill before too much longer.'

'You don't have to answer this if you don't want to,' Keselo said then, 'but how is it that an ordinary farmer like you managed to snare a beauty like your wife.'

'I didn't,' Omago replied. 'She snared *me*. She came past my orchard once in the early summer when I was thinning out my apples, and she wanted to know what I was doing. I explained thinning to her, and then she went off down the road. I couldn't think of anything but her for weeks after that. Then she came there again and made the bluntest announcement I've ever heard in my whole life.'

'Oh? What did she say? – If you can remember.'

'Oh, I can remember it all right. She said, "My name is Ara. I'm sixteen years old, and I *want* you."'

'That gets right to the point,' Keselo said. He was just a bit surprised that Omago's story had pushed his weariness aside. He was wide awake now, for some reason.

'There *is* something I should really tell you, Keselo,' Omago continued. 'I don't want to offend you, but I don't really like this soldiering very much. I don't like to tell others what to do, and the idea of killing things that *look* like people – even though they aren't – makes me sick at my stomach.' He shrugged. 'I guess *somebody* had to do it, though, and Veltan sort of depends on me. I just hope I don't make *too* many mistakes.'

'I'd say that you're doing very well, Omago,' Keselo replied. 'You invented the spear. If my history professor back at the university knew what he was talking about, you compressed about a thousand years of human history into a couple of weeks.'

Omago looked just a bit embarrassed and he glanced off to the east again. 'The tip of the sun just came up above the horizon,' he reported. 'I expect that the bug-people will be coming up the hill before long.'

From out in the Wasteland there came that now-familiar roar that echoed back from the nearby cliffs, and once again the lumbering, oversized (and, Keselo believed, under brained) new breed of bug-people came shambling up the glittering slope toward the now-empty breast-works which had been abandoned by Narasan's forces the previous night. As had happened several times before, the empty-headed servants of the Vlagh were completely baffled by the absence of soldiers behind the now vacant breast-works.

'Bugs aren't too intelligent, are they?' Omago suggested.

'Rocks are probably more intelligent,' Keselo replied, carefully feeling for the pulse in his left wrist with the fingers of his right hand.

'Are you hurt, Keselo?' Omago asked with some concern.

Keselo shook his head. 'Just counting,' he replied. 'If I'm right, we'll hear another roar from out there in just about fifty-seven heartbeats.'

'*Your* heart, maybe,' Omago disagreed. 'Mine seems to be beating just a little faster.'

They waited, and sure enough, the voice of the Vlagh roared forth the command to charge yet again.

'Fifty-three,' Keselo reported. 'Something out there appears to be a little faster than the others.'

'Where did you come up with that idea?'

'It was one of the things we were trained to do when we were student soldiers,' Keselo explained. 'Precise timing can be crucial in certain situations. It doesn't work too well if you've been running, but I've been standing in one place since first light.' He nodded toward the now-occupied breast-works they'd abandoned the previous night. 'Here they come,' he said.

'And there they go,' Omago added as the attaching force encountered the reintroduced poisoned stakes. Keselo had been very relieved when Commander Narasan had rescinded his earlier command and allowed his men to go back to the previous practice of planting those stakes to slow the attacks of the bug-people. If things went the way they were *supposed* to, the church armies would soon arrive to take over for Narasan's army, and Gunda had bluntly advised his friend that keeping as many of his men alive as possible was far more important than maintaining their supply of snake venom.

'It'll take a bit longer for the word to get back to the Vlagh this time,' Keselo predicted. 'The stakes always confuse them, and it takes them more time to send the report back.'

'And then the Vlagh will shout again and the ones wearing armor will rush up here and start rolling over the stakes?'

'Exactly. Then, as soon as the turtle-people get close enough, the archers will start shooting arrows at their eyes, and that should just about end this particular attack.' Keselo yawned at that point. 'Then we'll all be able to get some sleep,' he added.

'What if they charge us again?'

'Not very likely, my friend,' Keselo said. 'They never have before. It takes a very long time for this particular enemy to modify its tactics – months usually – maybe years, for all I know. Wake me if anything interesting happens.' Then he found a relatively comfortable corner in the breast-works, settled down, and promptly fell asleep.

It was early in the afternoon when Brigadier Danal woke them. 'Andar wants to know if you can come up with some kind of explanation for something that's a bit peculiar, Keselo,' he said.

'Oh?' Keselo said, struggling to shake off his sleep. 'What's that?'

'Take a look at Gunda's wall – assuming that you can still see it.'

Keselo rose and looked on up the slope at the yellow cloud billowing over Gunda's wall. 'I think that's what's called a "sand-storm", Brigadier Danal – or possibly a duststorm. As I understand it, they're fairly common in desert country.'

'You'd better let Andar know that it's something ordinary, Keselo. That thing up there's making him just a bit edgy. A lot of strange things keep popping up here in the Land of Dhrall, and they're making Andar sort of jumpy.'

The three of them went on along the breast-works to join Sub-Commander Andar.

'Keselo says that it's only what's called a "sandstorm", Andar. The world didn't just split open or something like that.'

'Could you give me a bit more in the way of an explanation, Keselo?' Andar asked.

'I've never actually seen one before, sir,' Keselo replied, 'but one of the professors at the university told us that in the dryer parts of the world where there aren't very many trees or much grass, a strong wind can pick up dust or sand and send it billowing along the ground for miles and miles. When the wind dies down, every-thing settles back to earth again.'

489

'How long do they usually last?'

'As long as the wind keeps blowing, sir.'

'That's not very precise, Keselo,' Andar complained.

'That's always a problem when you're dealing with the weather, sir,' Keselo replied. 'The study of weather involves a lot of things that we don't understand very well yet. We know that winters are cold and summers are hot, but that's about as far as we've been able to go with any degree of certainty. You might want to tell the men to cover their noses and mouths with cloth, though. I don't think breathing in sand would be very good for them.'

They all stood watching as the yellow cloud began to roll down the slope.

'I'd say that we aren't the only ones having trouble with this,' Danal said, looking on down the slope. 'The bug-people are streaming out of the breast-works we abandoned last night like something awful was about to happen to them.'

Keselo frowned, probing through the memories of the various courses he'd taken at the University of Kaldacin. Then he remembered something. 'I think it might have something to do with the way bugs breathe, Brigadier,' he said.

'Breathing is breathing, isn't it?'

'Not exactly, sir. Bugs, insects – whatever we call them – don't have noses like people or animals do. They breathe through a series of holes down their sides instead. A small, ordinary bug wouldn't really have many problems with a sandstorm because those holes along their sides are very thin. These giant bugs we've encountered here, though, would have much larger breathing holes. If one of them happens to take a deep breath in the middle of a sandstorm, there's a very good chance that it'd suck in enough sand to clog up the breathing holes. If that happens, it's entirely possible that the bug will die of suffocation.'

'Aw,' Danal said in mock regret, 'what a shame.'

'Is it at all possible that this silly sandstorm will kill them *all*, Keselo?' Andar asked.

'I don't really think so, sir,' Keselo replied. 'That Wasteland out there is pretty much all desert, so sandstorms are probably very common. I'm sure that the bug-people have come up with many ways to protect themselves – burrowing down into the ground, maybe, or even piling dead friends up in heaps and then crawling under them. The fact that they're running away suggests that they know just how dangerous a sandstorm can be, and I'm sure that they instinctively know how to protect themselves.'

Then from far out in the Wasteland there came a shrill scream that seemed to fade as it came from farther and farther out in the glittering yellow desert.

'Could that possibly be the Vlagh itself making all that noise?' Omago asked.

'It's possible, I suppose,' Keselo replied. 'Then again, though, it probably wasn't. The Vlagh has many servants whose only purpose in life is to protect their queen. They won't let anything happen to her.'

'I don't think I'm *ever* going to get used to that,' Andar declared. 'Fighting wars against females is *so* unnatural.'

'That particular female thinks that all *we* are is something to eat, Andar,' Danal disagreed. 'Ordinary courtesies go right out the window in a situation like that, wouldn't you say? Let's face it, my friend. If the Vlagh happens to invite you to dinner, *you're* likely to be the main course.'

THE INLAND SEA

1

Veltan, like the others, had been more than a little dubious about Longbow's assertion that the church armies were unknowingly coming to aid them in their struggle with the servants of the Vlagh, but the sudden appearance of that 'sea of gold' – which *wasn't* gold – and the almost hysterical reaction of the assorted Trogites coming up from the south had convinced him that the voice which had come to Longbow had spoken truly.

The more troubling question gnawing at Veltan now was just exactly *who* this unknown friend was, and *how* she had managed to pull off such a colossal deception. It was quite obvious by now that their 'unknown friend' had been operating at a level of sophistication far beyond anything Veltan or his brother and sisters could possibly have managed.

Right now, however, Veltan had more important things to attend to. He sent out his thought to his pet thunderbolt, and somewhat to his surprise, she didn't grumble or complain as she almost always did, but came to him immediately.

'Good baby,' he said to her. 'We need to go on down to the Falls of Vash and have a look at some people down there.' He hesitated slightly. 'I don't want to hurt your feelings or anything, but do you suppose you could be just a bit quieter than usual?'

She flickered questioningly.

'I guess it's not really all that important, dear,' he said. 'There's been quite a bit of peculiar weather around lately, so those strangers won't be *too* surprised – no matter what happens.' He mounted and settled himself. 'Let's go, baby,' he said, glancing at the slowly settling sandstorm.

He was more than a little surprised when they reached the huge waterfall and his pet rumbled faintly instead of producing that deafening crash.

'Good girl,' he said. 'That was just fine. Wait here. I'll only be a few minutes.'

He dismounted and drifted on down through the air toward the crudely constructed bridge that connected the Trogite ramp with the rim of the gorge that lay to the south.

The red-uniformed soldiers of the Amarite church were plodding up the ramp, and there were very few of them still waiting down below.

'Well, good enough,' Veltan murmured. 'From the look of things, I'd say that this is the tail-end of the column. Give them another half-day, and they'll all be up here.'

Then he saw a familiar face among the Trogites coming up from below.

'I guess that answers *that* particular question,' Veltan murmured as he watched the scrawny former soldier Jalkan limping up the ramp, accompanied by a grossly fat clergyman stumbling along beside him, wheezing and sweating gallons as he came. The two of them were surrounded by bleak-faced guards wearing the black uniforms of the Regulators.

Veltan reached out with his ears to see if the two enemies might possibly reveal anything useful.

'It's only a little farther, Adnari,' Jalkan said in that nasally whining voice that Veltan had always found so irritating.

'Let me catch my breath, Jalkan,' the fat man wheezed, stopping and wiping the sweat off his face.

'No,' Jalkan said firmly. 'We can't block off the ramp. The last brigade's still behind us, and we can't delay them.'

'I don't give a hoot about the soldiers, Jalkan!' The fat man flared. 'Their only purpose in life is to serve the church, and in this part of the world, *I* am the church.'

'Not in a war, Adnari Estarg,' Jalkan disagreed. 'Not unless you'd like to take up falling and dying as a hobby. The soldiers in that brigade know that there's gold just ahead, and if you delay them *too* much, they might very well decide to dispose of you by shoving you off the side of the ramp, and it's a long way down from here.'

'They wouldn't dare!'

'Would you really like to bet your life on that, Adnari?'

The fat man looked back over his shoulder at the impatient men in red uniforms who were glaring at him. 'The Regulators will protect me, Jalkan,' he declared.

'Did you want to bet your life on *that* as well?' Jalkan demanded. 'Now that Konag's not with us any more, we can't really trust anybody. Konag was the one with the iron fist, and the other Regulators obeyed him out of terror, and then *they* terrorized the soldiers in our five armies. Konag was our key, but he's gone now, so we can't lock doors anymore.'

Veltan scratched his cheek thoughtfully as a distinct possibility came to him unbidden. Something – or more probably, *somebody* –

had moved the clever little Rabbit to do something very uncharacteristic. First he'd carved out a bow, and the Maags had never been very interested in archery. Then the little man had been stirred to violence by Konag's brutal slaughter of any and all church soldiers who broke ranks and tried to run on ahead of the armies to reach the imitation gold before their comrades did. And *then* Rabbit, who should at best have been a rank amateur as an archer, dropped Konag dead in his tracks with a single arrow.

'I'd say that we've *definitely* got some serious tampering going on here lately,' Veltan mused.

There was a bit of shouting coming up to Veltan from the red-uniformed soldiers who'd just crossed the bridge and reached the rim of the gorge, and the word that rang out the loudest was 'gold!'

Veltan glanced to the north across the grassy basin. There were a few yellow-speckled crags jutting up out of the Wasteland, but the *real* 'sea of gold' lay some distance *below* the north ridge and Gunda's wall. It should *not* be visible from here, but there it was, bright and gleaming, and out in plain view.

There were a couple of very unlikely possibilities that *might* explain just how something that *should* be completely out of sight was right there to be seen. On a few occasions, Veltan had encountered mirages, those inverted reflections of far distant things, but always in the past, they'd been limited to water.

'It would seem that Longbow's friend is very creative,' Veltan mused. 'Good, though,' he added with a grin.

'I *really* wish you wouldn't do that, Veltan,' Sorgan Hook-Beak complained when Veltan's pet deposited him no more than a few feet away from the pirate. 'It almost scares me out of my skin.'

'I'll mention that to my pet, Sorgan,' Veltan promised, 'but I don't think she'll listen. She *loves* to startle people.' He looked down into Sorgan's third trench. 'I see that you're still planting stakes,' he noted.

'It works out pretty well, Veltan,' Sorgan said. 'The whole idea here is to slow down the church Trogs, and it takes them quite a while to dig the stakes up.' Then he chuckled. 'We've been cheating just a bit, though.'

'Cheating?'

'We don't waste venom any more. The church Trogs creep across the trenches on their hands and knees, very carefully digging up stakes that aren't really anything but bare wood-sticks. As long as they *believe* that the stakes will kill them, their advance is dead slow.'

'I think we might want to change the rules, Sorgan,' Veltan suggested. 'The last church army has finally made it up to the rim. Now that they're all up here where they're supposed to be, it's time for us to get out of their way so that they can go say hello to the bug-people.'

'I hope Longbow knows what he's talking about,' Sorgan said a bit dubiously. 'Are you certain sure that those church Trogs will do what they're supposed to do?'

Veltan nodded. 'Longbow's friend pulled off another of her deceptions. There were a few crags sticking up out of the Wasteland, but when the bulk of that last church army reached the rim, she gave them something much prettier to look at. They saw the entire Wasteland – *and* all the pretty sand she'd put out there for their entertainment. Now they're just dying to get out there and claim it.'

'How did she *do* that?'

'How would I know? She's so far ahead of me that I can't really understand anything she does. Pull back, Sorgan. It's time for us to get out of the way.'

'It's going to take a while, Veltan,' Sorgan said. 'My men are going to have to pull those stakes if we want the Trogs to move any faster than a slow crawl.'

'Why don't you let *me* take care of that, Sorgan?' Veltan asked with a broad grin. 'My pet needs a little entertainment anyway. I'm fairly sure she'll enjoy blasting all your stakes into splinters, so why don't we let *her* have all the fun?'

'What's happening on down there, Veltan?' Commander Narasan asked when Veltan's pet deposited him on the central tower of Gunda's wall.

'Everything's going like it's supposed to, my friend. Lillabeth's sandstorm made things much easier for us. That fifth church army has finally reached the rim, so they're all up here now. I just advised Sorgan that it's time for him to get out of the way and let those greedy churchies come on up here.'

'Padan passed through Sorgan's barricades and trenches when he pulled his men back after the churchies started building that bridge,' Narasan said then. 'From what he told me, the River Vash will have Sorgan and his men blocked off if they decide to go east. He'll have to go on up that west ridge, won't he?'

Veltan shook his head. 'He told me that he'd leave a small force behind his last barricade to delay the church armies, and then his main force will come north to the geyser and then go on off to the east.'

'What's going to happen to those men he'll leave behind?'

Veltan smiled. 'Sorgan told me that *those* men are the fastest runners in his entire army. He's quite positive that they'll be able to outrun the churchies without even working up a sweat.' He paused. 'I almost forgot something that might brighten your day.'

'Oh?'

'Scrawny Jalkan – along with a very fat Estarg – are coming to call. It's a shame that we won't be here to greet them, but we'll be terribly busy getting out of their way.'

'I don't suppose you'd consider a brief delay, would you, Veltan?' Narasan asked.

'What did you have in mind, Narasan?'

'Something sort of slow – and extremely painful.'

'Why don't we let the servants of the Vlagh have him, Narasan?' Veltan suggested. 'They have ways of inflicting pain that go far, far beyond anything you could possibly dream up.' Veltan paused. 'This is suddenly turning into a very unusual sort of war, wouldn't you say? We're just standing off to one side cheering enthusiastically while two of our deadliest enemies exterminate each other.'

'I have it on the very best authority that wars like that are the very, very best that any army ever has,' Narasan replied.

2

Red-Beard was quite pleased with the way things were going here in the Domain of Zelana's brother. He'd rather hoped that things might move more slowly, but winning *was* the goal, after all, and fast or slow was secondary. As soon as this war ended, it was almost certain that a new one would begin, and, of course, he'd be obliged to take part in that one as well. Out beyond that one, there'd be yet another. Red-Beard was almost positive that these wars would plod on along until the people of his tribe decided that somebody else might be more suitable to take up the burden of being the chief, and right now that was Red-Beard's main goal in life.

When Padan pulled his men back away from the Falls of Vash after the church armies had completed the bridge that linked their ramp to the rim of the basin, Red-Beard had decided to stay behind. Things were more interesting here in the grassy basin, and friend Longbow *might* need some help.

The two of them joined up with Sorgan Hook-Beak as the Maags pulled back from the series of barricades on the west side of the upper River Vash.

'Veltan seems quite happy about the way things are going,'

Sorgan told them as they went upstream toward that colossal geyser that was the source of the River Vash.

'We haven't made *too* many mistakes yet,' Longbow observed.

'Do you *always* have to look on the dark side, Longbow?' Sorgan demanded.

Longbow shrugged. 'Habit, I suppose,' he said. 'If you expect the worst, anything that's not terrible comes as a pleasant surprise.'

'I've been meaning to ask you something, Longbow,' Sorgan said. 'As far as I can tell, you haven't had the time to train Rabbit with that bow of his, but suddenly he's an archer who's almost as good as you are. How did you manage that?'

'I didn't,' Longbow replied. 'Apparently, he picked it up on his own.'

'Rabbit's clever enough, I suppose,' Sorgan said sceptically, 'but doesn't it take a lot of training and years of practice to get *that* good with a bow?'

Longbow squinted at the horizon. 'When he was spending most of his time hammering out those iron arrowheads for me, he and I talked about putting arrows where you want them to go. I suppose it's possible that he remembered some of the things I told him.'

'All that mysticism about "unification"?' Red-Beard asked. 'I never *did* get your point when you told me about it.'

'I don't really think it's all that complicated, Red-Beard,' Longbow said. 'I've given it some thought, and I'm almost sure that the idea of being unified with the target has to be there when the bowman unlooses his first arrow. If it's there right then, it'll always be there. If it isn't, it'll never show up.'

'Thanks a lot, Longbow,' Red-Beard said sarcastically.

'I wasn't trying to offend you, friend Red-Beard,' Longbow said. 'I was probably just lucky the first time I drew *my* bow. Our shaman, One-Who-Heals, used to talk about the unification of the bowman, his arrow, and the target quite often when the boys of our tribe began practicing with their bows, and some of us tried it to see if it worked the way he'd told us it would. As it turned out, it did, and the other boys got all sulky about it, because they'd never be able to do it after they'd shot off their first arrow. If Rabbit just *happened* to be thinking along those lines when he tried his bow the first time, it's *there*, and he'll never lose it.'

'That sounds just a bit far-fetched to me, Longbow,' Sorgan said. 'The thing that puzzles me even more, though, is what was it that got Rabbit all steamed up about that fellow called Konag? He went wild about that fellow for some reason.'

'I'm not really sure, Sorgan,' Longbow said. 'It *might* just have been a decision by that unknown lady who's helping us. If Konag was disrupting her plan, she needed to get rid of him. Since Rabbit was right there, she used *him* to dispose of an inconvenience.'

Then, even as they marched north toward the geyser, Red-Beard heard a deep rumble coming up from far below, and he looked around with a certain apprehension as he vividly remembered the twin fire-mountains that had ultimately destroyed the village of Lattash and clamped the unwanted chieftainship around his neck.

Red-Beard and Longbow were somewhat behind Sorgan's men as they moved quite rapidly up the west side of the River Vash toward the geyser. The church soldiers had moved north rather cautiously at first, but when they realized that the trenches were no longer filled with poisoned stakes, they began to move more rapidly, tearing down the barricades as they came.

'How much farther north do Sorgan's men have to go to reach the geyser?' Red-Beard asked his friend.

'A couple of miles is about all,' Longbow replied.

'Maybe we should tell them to hustle right along,' Red-Beard suggested. 'Those red-suited soldiers will be climbing up their backs if they just dawdle along.'

'Sorgan's going to turn toward the east after he passes the geyser,' Longbow said. 'He's far enough ahead of those Trogites to get clear before they catch up with him.'

Then there came another of those rumbles from deep below, and the ground trembled under their feet.

'That's starting to make me just a bit edgy,' Red-Beard said. 'It's not a good sign when the earth starts to wobble like that.'

'You could ask it to quit, I suppose,' Longbow replied. 'I don't know if it'll listen, but it wouldn't hurt to ask.'

'Very funny, Longbow,' Red-Beard said.

Then there came a sudden flash of light, a sharp crack of thunder, and grey-bearded Dahlaine was there. 'You'd better tell sister Zelana's Maags to get out of this basin as fast as they can,' he said. 'Ashad just had another one of *those* dreams, and I'm almost certain that something fairly awful is about to happen in this area.'

'Fire-mountains again?' Red-Beard asked with a sinking feeling in the pit of his stomach.

'I'm not completely sure,' Dahlaine replied. 'Ashad wasn't very specific. *Something's* going on down below, but that's about all we can say for sure. Tell Sorgan to hustle right along, and I'll go warn Narasan.'

Sorgan, Torl, and Rabbit were standing around the sizeable fissure in the ground where the geyser that had been the source of the River Vash for the past twenty-five eons had been spurting high up into the air, and the three of them seemed to be more than a little astonished by the fact that the geyser wasn't there any more.

'What's going on here?' Sorgan demanded, gesturing at the fissure.

'I wouldn't stand around waiting to find out if I were you, Sorgan,' Longbow replied. 'Dahlaine came by just a while ago and told us to advise you that something fairly awful's likely to come along soon.'

'Just exactly what do you mean by "awful", Longbow?' Rabbit asked as the earth began to shudder again.

'Does that answer your question, Rabbit?' Red-Beard asked the little smith. 'In this part of the world we've learned *not* to ask questions when the ground starts to wobble. The best thing to do when that happens is to run away.'

'Which way should we go?' Sorgan asked Longbow, his eyes gone wide.

'The east ridge is quite a bit closer, Sorgan,' Longbow replied, 'and in this sort of situation, closer is better, and running is much better than walking.'

'Do you think your unknown friend might be playing games again, Longbow?' Torl asked.

'Why don't we run for right now?' Longbow suggested. 'We can ask questions later.'

'And running fast is probably much better than running slow,' Red-Beard added. '*Real* fast, if you get my drift.'

'Pass the word, cousin,' Sorgan told Torl. 'Tell the men to run toward the east just as fast as they can – and let them know that their lives probably depend on it.'

3

Ashad had behaved as if his dream that night in the basin above the Falls of Vash had been more than just a little different from the dream he'd had in our cave under Mount Shrak when this had all begun. There was an urgency in his voice that hadn't been there in our cave. He didn't give me very many details, but I got the feeling that what was about to happen frightened him more than a little.

I realized that this wasn't really the time for reflection, so I advised Veltan and my sisters that it was time for us to take our Dreamers and leave this basin. If Ashad had given me more in the way of details I might have been able to be more precise, but after Yaltar's twin volcanos had engulfed the ravine above Lattash, we'd all learned that getting out of the way in the face of the natural disasters the Dreamers jerked out of nowhere was the best course of action.

Then I rode my thunderbolt on down to warn Sorgan, Longbow, and Red-Beard, and turned to give Narasan a similar warning.

'Are we looking at something on the order of those twin volcanos that saved the day for us back in the ravine?' Narasan asked rather tensely.

'I can't be entirely sure, Commander,' I admitted. 'Let's stay on the safe side, though. I think it might be best for you to get all of your men clear of this basin. Did your friend Padan join you here after he'd abandoned his position down by the Falls of Vash, or did he go on over to the east rim?'

'He came here. He's commanding the men off to the west.'

'You'd better get word to him,' I suggested. 'Let's not take any chances right now.' I glanced down the slope at the barricades Narasan's men had erected to delay the invasion of the servants of the Vlagh. 'Have the insect-people shaken off the effects of Lillabeth's sandstorm yet?' I asked.

'Not entirely, I don't think. Their attacks on the third breast-works down there have been sort of tenuous. We don't really know just how many bug-people the Vlagh had at its disposal, but I'm quite sure that a sizeable number of them were suffocated during that storm. It might take the Vlagh quite a while to bring in replacements.'

'I don't really think the Vlagh has that much time, Narasan,' I told him. 'The church armies are on the move again, and it won't be long before they'll reach your wall here. I think you'd better pull your men back from the slope and send them off to the east as well. Let's get all of our people out of harm's way.'

'Right,' the commander agreed. Then he turned. 'Gunda!' he shouted. 'I need you here – right now!'

Narasan's balding friend came running along the wall. 'Have we got trouble of some kind?' he demanded.

'I'm not sure if "trouble" is the right word, Gunda. Send a runner off to the west to tell Padan that I want him and his men to abandon their positions and come here just as fast as they can run. And send word on down to Andar as well. I want *his* people up here too.'

'We'll have bug-people all over us before the sun goes down if we do that, Narasan,' Gunda protested.

'Not if we aren't here anymore, we won't. Our grand plan has changed just a bit, Gunda. I think we might want to move on to "run away". Lord Dahlaine just advised me that the children have been playing again, and we don't want to get in their way.' Narasan paused, and then he turned back to look at me. 'Veltan told us that he and his toy were going to open a passageway through Gunda's wall here so that the church armies would be able to get through to greet the bug-people. Can you get word to him that we'll need that opening fairly soon?'

I smiled. 'My pet's just as efficient as Veltan's is, Commander. If Veltan's busy someplace else, *my* pet will get to have the fun *this* time. There *will* be a highway waiting here when the church armies arrive.'

The assorted officers in Narasan's army all seemed to be very fond of the term 'logistics', which I took to mean 'getting the right people and the right equipment in the right place at the right time'. Military language tends to be just a bit stuffy at times, I've noticed.

The major problem Narasan's men encountered lay in the fact that Gunda's wall was only about thirty feet wide at the bottom and even less at the top. Since he had to move about a hundred thousand men off to the ridge that lay to the east, it was obviously going to take more time than I was positive we really had to get them to safety.

Fortunately, the young officer named Keselo came up from the barricades Narasan's men had built to delay the creatures of the Wasteland when it was beginning to be more and more obvious that Narasan's men would *not* reach the east ridge in time. His solution was so simple that I could hardly believe that it hadn't come to Narasan or any of his senior officers. They *did* look a bit sheepish when the young man said, 'Ladders, maybe? We *do* have quite a few of those rope ladders, and every man who climbs down to the ground on the south side of the wall is one less who'll have to run along the top of it.'

'Are we keeping score, Narasan?' Padan asked his friend. 'If we are, I think you'd better mark another point in the Keselo column. The ground on the south side of Gunda's wall is flat and wide, and walking on dirt is easier on a man's boots than walking on rocks.'

'Don't beat it into the ground, Padan,' Narasan said. 'As soon as the rest of Andar's men get up here, roll up the ladders and take them across to the south side. Let's move right along, gentlemen. There's a strong smell of disaster in the wind, and we don't want to be here when it arrives.'

'The church armies are coming up from the south, Narasan,' Gunda reported a couple hours later.

'Have our men reached safety yet?' Narasan demanded.

'Most of them,' Gunda replied. 'There are a few dawdlers, of course, but I'm fairly sure they'll move right along when Lord Dahlaine rips a big hole through my wall. She was a pretty good wall, I suppose, but it's probably about time to say goodbye to her.'

Narasan glanced at me. 'Should my men and I take some kind of cover?' he asked. 'If there's going to be rocks flying all over—? I'm sure you get my point.'

I looked at the rough black wall and made a few rough computations. 'I don't think there'll be any danger, Commander,' I assured him. 'I'll bring my toy in from the south instead of right overhead. She'll knock all the stones on down the north slope.

Actually, that should work to our advantage. A sudden storm of flying rocks will force the creatures of the Wasteland to take cover, and the church soldiers will be right on top of them before they have time to reassemble.'

'What a shame,' Narasan replied with a wicked grin.

'You'd better cover your ears, gentlemen,' I warned them. 'Loud sounds can damage your hearing, and things are going to be *very* loud in just a minute.' Then I summoned my pet and unleashed her against the south side of Gunda's wall.

As she almost always does, my pet overdid things a bit, and a goodly number of the rocks that had formed Gunda's wall went spinning off to the north for miles, and when they came down out in the Wasteland below, they stirred up large clouds of the glittering yellow sand that the church soldiers found so attractive.

The noise was shattering, of course, but as it began to subside, another sound came rumbling up from deep within the earth, and the ground below shuddered once more.

Then a peculiar thought came to me. Was it in any way possible that Longbow's unknown friend was feeling a bit competitive? I'd just unleashed a very loud sound, but *hers* was even louder.

'Impressive,' Narasan murmured. 'For a moment there, I thought you might have decided to send Gunda's wall all the way to the ravine in your sister's Domain.'

'That wouldn't really be very polite, Commander,' I said. 'I always try my best not to offend my sisters. They complain for *years* if I happen to make a mistake.'

'It looks to me like the *ears* of the church soldiers shut down at about the same time that their minds did,' Gunda noted. 'They didn't even falter when those crash-booms hit them. They're still running this way as hard as they can.'

'They're such *nice* boys,' Padan added with a grin.

The tower where we stood watching was slightly higher than the remains of the wall were, so we had a clear view of what was happening below. The red-uniformed church soldiers came streaming through the gap my toy had provided. They *did* falter slightly when they saw that huge desert of glistening sand lying below them, however, and I could almost smell their overwhelming greed. Then their mindless charge continued as they ran down the slope and clambered over the first of Narasan's barriers.

'And here come the bug-people,' Padan observed, peering down the slope. 'In just a minute or two, we're going to find out if Longbow's friend knew what she was doing. If those churchies turn around and run away, things might start to get very interesting around here.'

'There's not much chance of that, Padan,' Gunda said to his friend. 'I'd say that by now, the bug-people are much more intelligent than the churchies. There's a whole lot of stupid in the air around here.'

The oversized 'bug-people' the Vlagh had spawned for this particular war were quite obviously almost totally inept. They came blundering forward to meet the charge of the better-armed Trogite soldiers, and very few of them survived. An exultant cheer rose from the Trogite ranks.

'Well, well,' Padan said then, 'I *do* believe I just saw a familiar face. If I'm not mistaken, scrawny Jalkan has just returned to the Land of Dhrall. It hasn't been at all the same without him.'

Then Veltan's friend, the farmer Omago, came forward from the other side of the tower with Keselo at his side. 'Where?' he asked Padan, his usually friendly voice gone bleak.

'Over near the west side of the breast-works,' Padan replied, pointing.

'Where's Longbow now that we need him?' Narasan murmured.

'I wouldn't be too hasty, Commander,' I suggested. 'If you look a bit more closely, I think you'll see some rather filmy threads just on the other side of that barrier. I think Jalkan and that fat man who's with him are in for a very nasty surprise in a moment.'

'As a matter of fact, I think I do see those threads,' Narasan replied as he peered down at the slope. 'That suggests one of the spider-turtles, wouldn't you say?'

'More than "suggests", Commander,' I said. 'I've got a strong hunch that Jalkan's approaching the end of his career – whatever his current career might be.'

'What a shame,' Padan added sardonically.

'Does anybody happen to know what today's date might be?' Gunda asked.

'What do you need a date for, Gunda?' Padan asked curiously.

'I was talking with Andar back in Castano a while back, and we both agreed that Jalkan's deathday should be a national holiday in the Empire.'

'Deathday?' Padan asked curiously.

'That's like a birthday, but when it involves Jalkan "deathday" *is* a lot nicer than "birthday", wouldn't you say?'

'You won't get any arguments from me there, Gunda.'

Jalkan helped his grossly fat companion over the barricade, and then he numbly followed – for almost three feet. Then he abruptly stopped and began to claw at the fine-spun web that had just snared him. His gross companion ignored his cries for help and rushed on toward the gleaming desert of imitation gold reaching out to the horizon from no more than a few feet ahead of him.

Then he too came to an abrupt stop as the silken web snared him as well.

'Is that webbing really *that* strong?' Gunda asked.

'*Very* strong,' I assured him, 'and it stretches. The more those two struggle, the more they'll become snarled up in that webbing.'

Then the hard-shelled spider came scampering out from what appeared to be a hastily constructed hiding-place just beyond the barricade and quickly spun more and more webbing to hold its two captives more securely.

'Why's the spider wasting all that time spinning webs?' Gunda asked curiously. 'Why doesn't it just kill them and have done with it?'

'I don't think you really want to know, Gunda,' I advised him.

'Yes, as a matter of fact, I do,' he said stubbornly.

'All right, then,' I said. 'Spiders spin webs to snare creatures to eat, but spiders don't have mandibles like other insects do, so spider-venom contains a very powerful digestive fluid that liquefies the internal organs – and the flesh – of its victim. Then the spider sucks that liquid out of the victim.'

'The venom kills them though, doesn't it?'

'It paralyzes them, but it's not instantly lethal like snake-venom is. The spider uses its web and the paralyzing venom as a means to store food for later.'

'That's horrible!' Gunda exclaimed.

'It's very practical, though,' I told him. 'If a spider has its web in the right place, it almost always has a supply of food available.'

Jalkan and his gross companion, now completely wrapped in the spider's webbing, were screaming for help, but their soldiers ignored them and continued their mindless charge down the slope, drawn by the vast desert of glittering yellow sand far below.

Then there came yet another of those loud rumbling sounds from deep within the earth and an even more violent earthquake.

'Move back!' I sharply warned Narasan and his men. 'It's about to break loose!'

We all scurried along the top of Gunda's remaining wall toward the eastern end and – we hoped – safety.

The thundering sound from far below us continued, but it seemed to be rising up through the shuddering rock.

And then, perhaps a hundreds yards on down the slope, there came a thunderous eruption that was *not* molten rock.

It was water, and it gushed forth in a vast wave that swept the church soldiers and the servants of the Vlagh away indiscriminately.

From far, far out in the Wasteland there came a shriek of frustration that rapidly faded off into the distance as the servants of the Vlagh rushed to carry our enemy off to safety.

Several things came together for me at that point, and I was shaken to my very core by what Longbow's unknown friend had just achieved. *This* was why the geyser that had been the source of the River Vash had suddenly gone dry. Unknown Friend had moved it from the center of the basin to the upper end of the north slope to eradicate the servants of the Vlagh *and* the five church armies with a single stroke. I glanced over my shoulder and saw a steadily rising body of water down on the floor of the Wasteland. Unknown Friend had just replaced her 'sea of gold' with a sea of water that would permanently block off my brother's Domain from any further attacks by the creatures of the Wasteland.

The now-horizontal geyser produced a great deal of mist, naturally, and the sun was high above, so the sudden rainbow that appeared over the growing sea down in the Wasteland *could*, of course, have been nothing but a natural phenomenon, but I chose not to believe that it was something that simple. Unknown Friend, it appeared, was very pleased with her pretty invention, and a rainbow *is* a sort of blessing, after all.

'Well, gentlemen,' I said to our friends with feigned casualness, 'I guess that pretty much takes care of everything up here. I suppose we might as well pack up and go on back down the hill.'

It was about two weeks later when we gathered again in Veltan's map-room. My brother's map was now seriously out of date, and there was no real reason for us to be there rather than in some other part of the house, but for some reason, we all seemed more comfortable there.

There was quite a bit of storytelling at first. Our friends had been widely scattered during the actual war – *if* what had happened up there had really *been* a war. To my way of looking at things, our contributions this time had been minimal at best. Longbow's Unknown Friend had done most of the work. Of course, Ashad's dream *had* produced the flood, but the more I thought about it, the more I became convinced that Unknown Friend had been tampering with Ashad since the very beginning. The 'second invasion' in Ashad's first dream had provided a huge force that had met the invasion of the servants of the Vlagh with enough force to hold them in place until the flood destroyed *both* enemies.

'Let me tell *you*, old friend,' Sorgan was saying to Narasan, 'we ran on up out of that basin like a fox with his tail on fire. Those earthquakes that set everything to bouncing around raised a lot of memories about the fire mountains back in the ravine, and the notion of getting cooked alive can make a man run about twice as fast as he ever thought he could.'

'It was a sensible thing to do, Sorgan,' Narasan said. 'None of us knew exactly what was going to happen, so getting out of the way made a lot of sense.'

'I seem to remember that "get out of the way" was something Longbow's dream lady told him forty or fifty times every time he closed his eyes,' Rabbit added. 'She knew what she was talking about, all right.' The little man squinted slightly. 'Whatever happened to that greedy one who started that second invasion. Did he get drowned like all the other church people did?'

'I don't think he was still around when the flood broke lose,' Padan said.

'What happened to him?'

'He got et.'

'Et?'

'Eaten,' Padan explained. 'He and that fat friend of his were trying to run on down the slope to gather up buckets-full of that pretty but worthless sand out there, but they got all tangled up in a spider web along the way – and the spider most likely had them for lunch – while they were still alive and screaming for help.'

Rabbit scratched his chin. 'That sounds about right to me,' he said. 'They deserved something like that, I suppose. I'd say that they'd earned something more than an arrow in the forehead or a sword in the belly.'

'Omago seemed to approve,' Keselo added.

'This is all over and done with,' my sister Aracia said tartly. 'I think it's time for us to move on. The first thing we should consider is just where the Vlagh will strike next, and start making preparations.'

'Don't we have to wait until one of the children has one of *those* dreams?' Zelana suggested. 'We won't really know where the Vlagh will strike next until we have a dream to work with.'

'I think you're overlooking something, little sister,' Aracia replied. '*Your* Domain, and now *Veltan's* as well, are both permanently blocked off. The Vlagh only has two options now – Dahlaine's Domain in the North, and mine in the East. That narrows things considerably, so I think we should prepare for both possibilities.'

At that point Aracia's hired warrior queen Trenicia stepped forward. 'Ekial and I have discussed this at some length,' she told us, 'and we pretty much agree that the presence of Narasan and Sorgan could be very useful when our enemies attack the North and the East. They've had much experience with those monsters, so they'll be able to warn us if we're making mistakes. Then too, if their armies come with them, we should have more than enough warriors to eliminate the creatures permanently.'

'What do you think, Narasan?' Sorgan asked.

'As long as we get paid, I don't see any problems,' Narasan said.

'I'm sure we'll be able to work something out,' sister Zelana told them with a faint smile.

Then the door opened, and the beautiful wife of Veltan's friend Omago came out onto the balcony. 'Dinner's ready,' she announced in that vibrant voice of hers.

Then something came to me that set my senses to reeling. It had been the appearance of Ara that had stirred Jalkan to the point that he'd said things that nobody in his right mind would have said, and those remarks had moved Narasan to the revocation of Jalkan's commission and his imprisonment on board one of the Trogite ships in the harbor. Then, when Jalkan had escaped, he'd gone off to the south and had returned with the five church armies that had, in effect, defeated the servants of the Vlagh. It was remotely possible that there had been no connection between those various events, but—

I stared at the beautiful lady in awe. Could it possibly be that *Ara* was our Unknown Friend? If she *was*, her powers went so far beyond mine or my brother's or sisters' that I couldn't even comprehend what she might be capable of.

Then her voice spoke to me in the silence of my mind. 'Not now, child,' she said. 'We can talk about this some other time.'

Also published by *Voyager*

Book Three of The Dreamers
By David and Leigh Eddings

THE CRYSTAL GORGE

Extract from Part One, The Reluctant Chieftain

1

It was summer in the lands of the west, and the young boy with red hair woke up even before the sun had risen above the mountains to the east of the village of Lattash and decided that it might be a good day to go fishing in the small river that flowed down from the mountains. There were quite a few things that he was supposed to do that day, but the river seemed to be calling him, and it wouldn't be polite at all to ignore her – particularly when the fish were jumping.

He quietly dressed himself in his soft deerskin clothes, took up his fishing-line, and went out of his parents' lodge to greet the new summer day. Summer was the finest time of the year for the boy, for there was food in plenty and no snow piled high on the lodges and no bitterly cold wind sweeping in from the bay.

He climbed up over the berm that lay between the village and the river and then went on upstream for quite a ways. The fishing was usually better above the village anyway, and he was sure that it wouldn't be a very good idea to be right out in plain sight when his father came looking for him to remind him that he was neglecting his chores.

The fish were biting enthusiastically that morning, and the boy had caught several dozen of them even before the sun rose up above the mountains.

It was about midmorning when his tall uncle, the eldest son of the tribal chief, came up along the graveled riverbank. Like all the members of the tribe, his uncle wore clothes made of golden deer-skin, and his soft shoes made little sound as he joined his young nephew. 'Your father wants to see you, boy,' he said in his quiet voice. 'You *did* know that he has quite a few things he wants you to do today, didn't you?'

'I woke up sort of early this morning, uncle,' the boy explained. 'I didn't think it would be polite to wake anybody, so I came on up here to see if I could catch enough fish for supper this evening.'

'Are the fish biting at all?'

'They seem to be very hungry today, uncle,' the boy replied, pointing toward the many fish he'd laid in the grass near the river-bank.

His uncle seemed quite surprised by the boy's morning catch. 'You've caught *that* many already?' he asked.

'They're biting like crazy this morning, uncle. I have to go hide behind a tree when I want to bait my bone hook to keep them from jumping up out of the water to grab the bait right out of my fingers.'

'Well, now,' his uncle said enthusiastically. 'Why don't you keep fishing, boy? I'll go tell your father that you're too busy for chores right now. A day when the fish are biting like this only comes along once or twice a year, so I think maybe our chief might want all the men of the tribe to put everything else aside and join you here on the riverbank.' He paused and squinted at his nephew. 'Just exactly what was it that made you decide to come here and try fishing this morning.'

'I'm not really sure, uncle. It just sort of seemed to me that the river was calling me.'

'Any time she calls you, go see what she wants, boy. I think that maybe she loves you, so don't ever disappoint her.'

'I wouldn't dream of it, uncle,' the boy replied, pulling in yet another fish.

And so it was that all of the men of the tribe came down to the river and joined the red-haired boy. The fishing that day was the best many of them had ever seen, and they thanked the boy again and again.

The sun was very low over the western horizon as the boy carried the many fish he'd caught that day up over the berm to the lodges of Lattash, and all of the women of the tribe came out to admire the boy's catch, and even Planter, who seldom smiled, was grinning broadly when he delivered his catch to her.

And then the boy went on down to the beach to watch the glorious sunset, and the light from the setting sun seemed almost to lay a gleaming path across the water, a path that seemed somehow to invite the boy to walk on out across the bay to the narrow channel that opened out onto the face of Mother Sea.

'Are you still sleeping, Red-Beard?' Longbow asked.

'Not any more,' Red-Beard told his friend sourly. He sat up and looked around his room in the House of Veltan. It was a nice enough room, Red-Beard conceded, but stone walls were not nearly as nice as the lodges of Lattash had been. 'I was dreaming about the old days back in the village of Lattash, and I'd just caught enough fish to feed the whole tribe. Everybody seemed to be very happy about that. Then I went on down to the beach to watch the sunset, and I was about to stroll on across the bay to say hello to Mother Sea, but then you had to come along and wake me up.'

'Did you want to go back to sleep?' Longbow asked him.

'I guess not,' Red-Beard replied. 'If I happened to doze off now, the fish would probably start biting my toes instead of the bait I'd been using. Have you ever noticed that, Longbow? If you're having a nice dream and you wake up before it's finished, your next dream will be just awful. Is there something going on that I should know about?'

'There's a little family squabble in Veltan's map-room is about all. Aracia and Dahlaine have been screaming at each other for about an hour now.'

'Maybe I *will* go back to sleep then,' Red-Beard said. 'You don't need to tell anybody I said this, but the older gods seem to be slipping more and more every day.'

'You've noticed,' Longbow said dryly.

'Do you have to do that all the time?' Red-Beard demanded, throwing off his blanket and struggling to his feet.

'Do what?'

'Try to turn everything into a joke.'

'Sorry. I didn't mean to poach in your territory. Shall we go?'

'It's fairly certain that the creatures of the Wasteland will come east now, Dahlaine,' Aracia was saying as Red-Beard and Longbow entered Veltan's map-room. 'After Yaltar's volcano destroyed the ones in Zelana's Domain, they turned south to attack the nearest part of the Land of Dhrall, and east is closer to south than north. They'll attack *me* next. That should be obvious.'

'You're overlooking something, Aracia,' Dahlaine disagreed.

'The servants of the Vlagh are cramming thousands – or even millions – of years of development into very short periods of time. If we assume that they're still thinking at the most primitive level, I think we'll start getting some very nasty surprises. I'm almost positive that their "overmind" has come to realize that the attack here in the south turned into a disaster, and that would make "closer" very unattractive. I'm quite certain that their next attack will be as far from here as possible.'

'Aren't we wandering just a bit?' Zelana suggested. 'We won't know which way the bugs will move until one of the Dreamers gives us that information. I'd say let's wait. In the light of what happened in my Domain and Veltan's, we just don't have enough information to lock *anything* in stone yet.'

'Zelana's right, you know,' Veltan agreed. 'We can't be sure of anything until one of the children has one of "those" dreams.'

'May I make a suggestion?' the silver-haired Trogite Narasan asked.

'I'll listen to anything right now,' Dahlaine replied.

'I'm unfamiliar with the lands of the north and the east, but wouldn't it make sense to alert the local population to the possibility of an incipient invasion? If the people of *both* regions know that there's a distinct possibility that the bug-men will attack, they'll be able to make some preparations.'

'That makes sense, Aracia,' Dahlaine conceded. 'If what happened here and off to the west are any indication of what's likely to happen in your Domain or mine, the local population will probably play a large part in giving us another victory.'

Aracia glared at her older brother, but she didn't respond.

Longbow tapped Red-Beard's shoulder. 'Why don't we go get a breath of fresh air,' he quietly suggested.

'It *is* just a bit stuffy in here,' Red-Beard agreed. 'Lead on, friend Longbow.'

They went on out of the map-room and then some distance along the dimly lighted hallway.

'Is it just my imagination or is Zelana's older sister behaving a bit childishly?' Longbow asked.

'I don't really know her all that well,' Red-Beard said, 'and I think I'd like to keep it that way. It seems to me that she's got an attitude problem.'

'Or maybe even something worse. Remember what happened back in the ravine? Suddenly, for no reason at all, Zelana jumped up, grabbed Eleria, and flew on back to her grotto on the Isle of Thurn.'

'Oh, yes,' Red-Beard said. 'Sorgan almost had a fit when she ran off like that without giving him all that gold she'd promised him. If I remember right, it finally took a bit of bullying by Eleria to bring her back to her senses.'

'I don't know very much about Aracia,' Longbow admitted, 'but I'm starting to catch a strong odor of irrationality in her vicinity. Her mind doesn't seem to work any more.'

'I wouldn't be too sure about that, Longbow,' Red-Beard disagreed. 'It might just be working very well. From what I've heard, anybody in her Domain who doesn't want to do honest work joins the priesthood and spends all his time adoring her.'

'That's what I've heard too.'

'Soldiering is one kind of honest work, isn't it?'

'Not as hard as farming is, maybe, but it's still harder than adoring somebody.'

'If that's the way things are in her Domain, doesn't that sort of suggest that she doesn't have anything at all like an army over there? Wouldn't that explain why she wants all the soldiers Zelana and Veltan hired to come on over to her territory to protect her if the bug-people decide to come her way?'

'Very good, Red-Beard,' Longbow said. 'Maybe she's not quite as irrational as it might seem. If her Domain is totally undefended, she'll need just about everybody with a sword or a bow to come there to protect her. It's very selfish, of course, but I don't think that would bother her. She seems to believe that she's the most important thing in the whole world, so from her way of looking at things, we're all obliged to rush to her defense.'

'There's not much that we can do about it right now, friend Longbow – except possibly to suggest to Zelana that she'd better keep a close eye on her big sister.'

'I'm sure that Zelana already knows about her sister's peculiarities, but we might want to caution Sorgan and Narasan about this.'

'You're probably right. Should we go on back and listen to the screaming? or would you rather go fishing?'

The squabbling of Dahlaine and Aracia continued for another half hour or so, and then Ara, Omago's beautiful wife, joined them on the balcony of the map-room. 'Supper's ready,' she announced.

'That's just about the best news I've heard all day,' Sorgan Hook-Beak declared. 'Let's go eat before everything gets cold.'

They all trooped on down the hallway to Veltan's impromptu dining-room. That was one of the characteristics of the elder gods that Red-Beard had never fully understood. There was a certain practicality involved in their lack of a need for sleep. If some kind of emergency came up, a sleeping god might not be able to deal with it, but Red-Beard couldn't for the life of him see why they didn't eat. They didn't need nourishment, of course, but there was more to eating food than just satisfying the grumbling in the belly.

Dinners in particular were generally something along the lines of a social event that brought people closer together and smoothed over various disagreements. Red-Beard was almost positive that the elaborate dining-room in Veltan's house hadn't even been there before the outlanders had arrived, and he was fairly sure that the dining-room Veltan had added to his house had originally been Ara's idea. Omago's wife was quite probably the best cook in the entire world, but she was wise enough to know that getting people together and establishing friendships was even more important than eating. There were several peculiarities about Ara that Red-Beard didn't fully understand – yet.

He was still working on it, though.

Oddly, Veltan and Zelana were accompanying them to the dining-room. Since they didn't need – or want – food, they obviously had something else on their minds.

The conversation at the dinner table was fairly general, but after they'd all eaten – more than they really needed, of course – Zelana and Veltan took Sorgan and Commander Narasan aside and spoke with them at some length.

Red-Beard nudged his friend Longbow after supper. 'I could be wrong about this, I suppose, but I think Zelana and Veltan might have come up with a way to make peace in their family, and it's probably going to involve Sorgan and Narasan.'

'What a peculiar sort of idea,' Longbow murmured.

'You saw it too, didn't you?'

'It *was* just a bit obvious, friend Red-Beard. I think it might disappoint Holy Aracia a little, though.'

'What a shame,' Red-Beard said with a broad grin.

'That's a nasty sort of thing to say.'

'So beat me.'

When they returned to the map-room, Sorgan Hook-Beak cleared his throat as a sort of indication that he was about to make a speech. 'Narasan and I talked this over, and I think we might have come up with a way to deal with the problem that's been nagging at us here lately,' he announced. 'Since we can't be certain sure exactly where the bug-people will strike next, we'll have to cover both possibilities. Since Lord Dahlaine's territory is farther away than his sister's is, Narasan and I pretty much agreed that *I* should cover that part of the Land of Dhrall – not because my men are better warriors, but because our ships move faster than Narasan's can. Of course, that's why we built them that way. Chasing down Trogite ships and robbing them is the main business in the Land of Maag, but we can talk about that some other time. Since my people will cover the north, Narasan's will cover the east.' He gestured down toward Veltan's "lumpy map". 'If that map's anywhere at all close to being accurate, it'll only take Narasan's fleet a few days to reach Lady Aracia's territory, and he can protect *that* region. That means that we'll have people in place to hold the bug-people back in either the east or the north, and our employers can zip from here to there in no time at all. If the attack strikes the east, I'll sail on down around the south end and join up with Narasan in just a couple of weeks. But, if the bug-people come north, my people will be able to hold them back until Narasan arrives to help *me*. When we add the horse soldiers in the north and the women warriors in the east, we'll have enough people to bring any bug invasion to a stop. Then, when the rest of our friends arrive, we'll be able to stomp all over the invaders and win the third war here in the Land of Dhrall.'

'It'll be something on the order of the way we handled things before the war in Lady Zelana's Domain,' Narasan added. 'There'll be enough of our people in either region to hold off the invasion until our friends can join us. Then we'll move directly on to stomp-stomp.'

'What a clever way to put it, Narasan,' Sorgan observed.

'I've always had this way with words,' Narasan replied modestly.

'I don't want to intrude here,' the scar-faced Ekial said, 'but how are we going to get *my* people – and their horses – up to Lord Dahlaine's territory? Horses can run fast, but probably not quite fast enough to gallop across the top of the sea.'

'I think I know how we can do that,' Narasan said. 'Gunda's got that little fishing yawl that *almost* knows how to fly. He can take you on down to Castano and hire ships. Then the two of you can sail on over to Malavi and pick up your men and horses. Then you'll go north to Lord Dahlaine's territory.'

'I think that maybe I should go with them, Commander,' Veltan added. 'When you hire Trogite ships, you need gold, and I know of a few ways to keep that much gold from sinking Gunda's yawl.'

'I think we've pretty much solved all the problems now,' Narasan said, looking around at the others. 'When do you think we should start?'

'Have you got anything on the fire for tomorrow?' Sorgan asked him.

'Not that I can think of,' Narasan replied.

'Tomorrow it is, then,' Sorgan announced.

Red-Beard had been watching Zelana's sister rather closely as Sorgan and Narasan smoothly cut the ground out from under her. It was quite clear that she wanted to protest, but the two clever outlanders hadn't left her much to complain about. She obviously still wanted *all* of the outlanders to go east to protect her Domain, but Sorgan and Narasan – at Zelana's and Veltan's suggestion, evidently

– had dismissed any protest she could raise.

'I don't know if you've been watching, friend Red-Beard,' Longbow said quietly, 'but doesn't it seem to you that the warrior queen called Trenicia is staying very close to Commander Narasan, and she appears to be *very* impressed by him.'

'Do you think it's possible that she's having *those* kind of thoughts about dear old Narasan?' Red-Beard asked.

'I couldn't say for sure,' Longbow replied, 'but that would be a *very* interesting sort of thing to crop up along about now, wouldn't you say?'

'Not as long as my head was on straight, I wouldn't.'

2

———◆———

At first light the following morning, the farmers of Veltan's Domain began carrying large amounts of food down to the beach to stock the ships of the two fleets. There was a steely quality about that early morning light that always made Red-Beard's instincts seem more intense. 'This might be a good day for hunting,' he said to Longbow as they watched the farmers come down the hill.

'I don't think Veltan would like it much if you started shooting arrows at his farmers,' Longbow replied.

'Funny, Longbow, very funny,' Red-Beard said. 'There's something about this first light before the sun comes up that always makes me feel that this might be one of those perfect days – you know, a day when nothing can go wrong.'

Longbow looked up at the still colorless sky. 'You might be right, friend Red-Beard,' he agreed, 'and if you're very lucky, things won't start to fall apart until mid-morning.' He looked out at the ships of the Trogites and Maags. 'It's likely to take them most of the morning to load all that food on their ships,' he said. 'Let's go talk with Zelana and find out if there's something she wants us to do before we leave Veltan's territory.'

Zelana and her two brothers were watching the farmers from a hill-top some distance back from the beach when Red-Beard and Longbow joined them.

'I'm not trying to tell you what to do, baby brother,' Zelana told Veltan, 'but I think you might want to consider a bit of 'tampering' to get Gunda and Ekial down to Castano as quickly as possible. We won't know for sure exactly where the creatures of the Wasteland will mount their next attack until one of the children starts dreaming. It's only a short distance from here to Aracia's Domain, so Narasan should arrive there in just a few days, and it's just a short voyage from Aracia's temple to the Isle of Akalla where Trenicia's warriors live. It's much farther from here to Dahlaine's Domain. Sorgan's ships are fast enough to reach that part of the Land of Dhrall in plenty of time, but you'll be spending quite a few days in Castano hiring Trogite ships and more days sailing on down to the land of the Malavi. Then you'll have the long voyage from there to Dahlaine's country on those wallowing Trogite ships.'

'I'm very good at tampering, dear sister,' Veltan told her with a faint smile. 'Mother Sea is lovely at this time of the year, and I'm sure that the Malavi will enjoy their voyage enormously, but sight-seeing isn't really all that important right now, so we'll hit a few high spots and hustle right along. It's going to *seem* to Ekial's Malavi that big brother's Domain isn't really all that far north when they get there, but that's not particularly important.' Then he turned to look at his older brother. 'Will the local people in your Domain be at all useful if the Creatures of the Wasteland decide to go north?'

'The natives of the Tonthakan region are fairly good archers,' Dahlaine replied. 'Their territory's very much like sister Zelana's Domain, so the Tonthakans are primarily hunters. The central region, Matakan, is open grassland and the game-animals there are bison. They're quite a bit larger than the deer in the forest, and their fur's a lot thicker. Arrows wouldn't be too effective against animals like that, so the Matans use spears rather than bows and arrows.'

'Wouldn't that limit the effective range?' Longbow asked.

'Bison aren't as timid as deer are,' Dahlaine explained. 'They don't panic the way deer do. The Matans use what they call "spear-throwers" to increase the range.'

'I don't think I've ever heard of a "spear-thrower",' Red-Beard admitted. 'How does it work?'

'Basically, it's an extension of the hunter's arm. It's a stick with a cup on the end. The hunter sets the butt-end of the spear in that cup, and then he whips the stick forward. The added length increases the leverage, and it nearly doubles the range of the spear. The stone spearhead's quite a bit heavier than your arrowheads are, so it cuts through the fur and the thick skin of the bison. It sounds just a bit crude and primitive, but it *does* keep the Matans eating regularly. You'll probably have an opportunity to see how well it works when we get there.'

'Isn't there a third region up there as well?' Veltan asked.

Dahlaine made a sour face. 'I should have done something about Atazakan quite some time ago, but I've been just a bit busy here lately. The Atazaks have an elevated opinion of themselves – which probably derives from what's referred to in that region as "the royal family". I've never had occasion to study the notion of "hereditary insanity", but the term seems to fit in the case of Atazakan. The current chief, leader, king – whatever – is totally crazy. He's absolutely convinced that he's a god, and that I'm just a usurper, and that I'm trying to steal what's rightfully his.'

'Oh?' Zelana said. 'What *is* this precious thing you've filched, Dahlaine?'

'The world, of course – or possibly the entire universe.'

'Why don't the citizens just remove him – with knife or axe?' Red-Beard asked.

'Because he has thousands of guards,' Dahlaine replied. 'I'd say that every third man in Palandor is a member of what Holy Emperor Azakan calls "the Guardians of Divinity" – which gives those "guardians" an easy life. About all they have to do is stand around scowling threateningly at sunrise and sunset.'

'What's the weather like up there?' Red-Beard asked.

'Autumn isn't too bad,' Dahlaine replied. 'There's a warm stream of water out in Mother Sea that modifies the autumn weather, but it sort of veers off at the end of autumn, and things get very cold. Blizzards go on for weeks at a time, and the spring thaw comes much later there than in the rest of the Land of Dhrall. Summers are fairly nice, but every now and then we get spells of bad weather. Huge storms build up in the sea to the east of my Domain, and they come screaming in to hit the coast of Atazakan.' He smiled faintly. 'Holy – or crazy – Azakan always tries to order those storms to go away, but they never seem to listen for some reason.'

'Storms don't ever seem to listen, big brother,' Zelana said. 'When Mother Sea gets grouchy, it's time to take cover.'

'Fortunately we should be near the end of what the people of Matakan call "the whirlwind season".'

'My people call those storms "cyclones",' Veltan noted, 'probably because of the way they spin around.'

'We don't see those very often in my part of the Land of Dhrall,' Zelana said.

'You're lucky then,' Dahlaine replied. 'Those spinning windstorms tend to rip things all to pieces. They're fairly common in Matakan, because that region doesn't have very many mountainous ridges to disrupt them. The Matans usually take shelter underground.'

'Caves?' Longbow asked.

'Not exactly. The Matans dig deep cellars with thick roofs, and when they see a whirlwind coming, they all go underground to sit it out.'

Rabbit came up from the beach at that point. 'The Cap'n told me to tell you that the *Seagull's* ready to go whenever you say it's all right,' the clever little iron-smith advised.

'Tell him that we'll be along in just a few minutes,' Dahlaine said. Then he looked at his brother and sister. 'We could probably go on ahead,' he told them, 'but it might be better if we stayed with the Maags. They'll want directions, and we can give them information they'll probably need before long while we're sailing on up to my Domain. It's going to take quite a while to get there – even on those fast Maag longships – so we might as well use that time to our advantage.'

'Could you have a word with Narasan?' Longbow asked Veltan as they walked on down to the beach. 'I think we might want to have Keselo with us in the north country. He spent a great deal of his time studying when he was younger, and he carries a lot of information in his head that we might need in Dahlaine's Domain.' Longbow smiled slightly. 'Rabbit and I came to realize that if we named something, Keselo had probably studied it.'

'He *is* quite learned,' Veltan agreed. 'I'll have a talk with Narasan before I join Gunda and Ekial in that little yawl. I'm fairly sure that Narasan will agree. I'm sure you noticed that Narasan's going off to the east just to mollify sister Aracia's sense of having been offended because everybody didn't rush over to her Domain to defend her.'

'I don't think that's entirely true, Veltan,' Longbow disagreed. 'Red-Beard and I were talking outside your map-room when Aracia and Dahlaine were arguing, and we sort of agreed that your older sister's problem wasn't so much offense as it was fear. If the descriptions we've heard of her part of the Land of Dhrall are anywhere close to being accurate, she doesn't have anything that even remotely resembles an army. She has farmers, merchants, and priests, but no soldiers. If the creatures of the Wasteland attack her Domain, there's nobody there to resist. *That's* why she wanted both the Maags and the Trogites to go east. She's more than a little self-centered, of course, but it was fear that was driving her.'

'Now *that's* something we hadn't even considered,' Veltan admitted. 'It *does* sort of fit, though. We all get a bit strange and confused at the end of one of our cycles, and the rest of the family assumed that she was being driven by pride, and that being adored by all those priests had dislocated her mind. We never even considered the possibility of fear. You might want to pass this on to Dahlaine and Zelana and see what they think. It could explain Aracia's odd behavior here lately.'

Things were a bit crowded on board the *Halies* as they sailed south from the house of Veltan in the late summer. Sorgan obviously wasn't too pleased when Zelana and Dahlaine appropriated his cabin, but it *did* make sense, since they had the children, Eleria, Ashad, and Yaltar with them. Maag sailors frequently spoke to each other in colorful terms, and it was probably best to keep the children in a place where they couldn't hear certain words.

Also, for some reason that Red-Beard couldn't really see.

Dahlaine had insisted that Omago and his beautiful wife Ara should join their party. There was something about Ara that Red-Beard couldn't quite understand. She was beautiful, of course, but very peculiar things seemed to happen quite frequently when she was around. It could just be coincidence, of course, but Red-Beard was more than a little dubious about that.

For right now, however, Red-Beard had something a bit more serious to worry about. Once the *Seagull* and the rest of the Maag fleet were past the south coast of Veltan's Domain, they'd be sailing north along the coast of Zelana's part of the Land of Dhrall, and there was a distinct possibility that they'd pull into the bay of Lattash for any one of a dozen or so reasons.

It took him a while to work up enough nerve to speak with Zelana about the matter.

'Are you busy?' he asked her one bright, sunny morning as the *Seagull* raced down along the east coast and Zelana was standing alone near the bow.

'Are we having some sort of problem?' she asked him.

'Well, I hope not,' he replied. 'Do you think you could see your way clear to persuade Sorgan Hook-Beak to avoid the bay of Lattash?'

'Is there something wrong with Lattash, Red-Beard?'

'*New* Lattash,' he corrected her. 'Old Lattash was just fine, but it's not there any more. It's New Lattash that's got me worried.'

'And why's that, dear boy?'

'Boy?' Red-Beard found the term to be a bit offensive.

'It's just a relative term,' she said, smiling. 'What's troubling you so much, Red-Beard?'

'I'd really be much happier if word that I'm here on the *Seagull* didn't leak out anywhere in the vicinity of the new village.'

'It's your home, isn't it?'

'Well, it *used* to be. After my uncle White-Braid came apart when Old Lattash was buried by that lava flow, the villagers decided that *I* should be the chief.'

'It seems that I'd heard about that. Did I ever congratulate you?'

'No, and I think I'd like to keep it that way. To be honest about it, I didn't *want* to be the chief, and I still don't. If I'm lucky, these wars in the other parts of the Land of Dhrall will go on and on for years. I've never wanted to be the chief of the tribe, and I still don't.'

Zelana laughed. 'You and my sister make a very odd pair, Red-Beard. She *wants* all that authority and adoration, but you keep running away from it.'

'How can she *stand* all that foolishness?'

'It makes her feel important, Red-Beard, and being important takes some of the sting out of the fact that our older brother outranks her in this particular cycle.' She paused, looking thoughtfully at Red-Beard. 'You *do* know about our cycles, don't you, Red-Beard?' she asked.

'Sort of. As I understand it, you and your family stay awake for a thousand years, and then you hand your task off to some younger relatives and take a long nap. Is that anywhere close to what happens?'

'Fairly close – except that your number isn't quite right. Our cycles are twenty-five times longer than *one* thousand.'

Red-Beard blinked. 'You've been awake for *that* long?' he asked her in a voice filled with wonder.

'Not quite yet, but it's getting closer to nap-time. When our current cycle began, people – your species – were at a very primitive level. They hadn't even discovered fire yet, and their most sophis-

ticated weapon was the club. In many ways, this is the most important period in the history of the world. The man-things – your
species – spend most of their time changing things. That makes this
particular cycle very significant – *and* very dangerous. There are
some things that should *not* be changed – and that brings us to the
Vlagh. Do you know anything about bees?'

Red-Beard shrugged. 'They make honey, and they sting anybody who tries to steal it. Honey tastes good – but not so good that
I'd want to get stung a thousand times just to gather it up.'

'Wise decision, Red-Beard. Bees – and a number of other varieties of insects – have developed very complex societies that are
designed to expand their territories and their food supply. That's
what these wars here in the Land of Dhrall are all about.
Unfortunately, the Vlagh is an imitator. When one of the creatures
of the Wasteland sees a characteristic that seems useful, the Vlagh
starts experimenting, and its next hatch will have a variation of that
characteristic.'

'So we end up with bug-men who know how to talk.'

'Not exactly bug-*men*, Red-Beard. Bug-*women* would come
closer to what's really happening. There aren't really very many
males among the creatures of the Wasteland. They're almost all
females, *but* the Vlagh herself is the only one that lays eggs –
thousands and thousands of eggs at a time.'

'I don't think baby bug-people would be very dangerous,' Red-
Beard scoffed.

'Maybe not, but they grow very fast.'

'How fast?'

'They're adults within a week. Of course, they only live for
about six weeks, but a new generation is already in the works. The
outlanders we've hired to help us don't fully understand this, but it's

not really necessary for them to understand. It's probably better that they don't. If they knew that the Vlagh can replace all the ones our friends kill in about two weeks, there isn't enough gold in the whole world to have persuaded them to come here and help us.'

'Why are you telling me all this, Zelana?' Red-Beard asked her.

She shrugged. 'A few people need to know what's *really* happening, Red-Beard, and you just happened to be in the right place at the right time. I'll have a word with Sorgan about your problem, and if it's really necessary for the *Seagull* to go on into the bay of Lattash, we'll find someplace to hide you so that the people of your tribe won't be able to find you.'

'That definitely takes a load off my mind.' Red-Beard hesitated. 'You *do* understand why I don't want any part of being the chief of the tribe, don't you?' he asked her.

'It has something to do with freedom, doesn't it?'

'Exactly.' He frowned slightly. 'You went right straight to the point, Zelana. How did you pick it up so fast?'

'I've already been there, Red-Beard. That's why I went off to the Isle of Thurn a long time ago. If you think that being "chief" would be unbearably tedious, take a long, hard look at being "god". Just like you, I didn't want any part of that, so I ran away. I spent thousands of years in my pink grotto composing music, writing poetry, and playing with my pink dolphins. Then my big brother brought Eleria to me, and my whole world changed.'

'You love her, though, don't you?'

Zelana sighed. 'More than anything in the whole world. That's what Dahlaine had in mind when he foisted the Dreamers on us in the first place. In a certain sense, it was very cruel, but it *was* necessary.'

'Well, I'm not really all that necessary where the tribe's concerned. They can find somebody else to sit around being important.' Then a thought came to Red-Beard, and he suddenly burst out laughing.

'What's so funny?'

'I know who'd make the best chief the tribe's ever had,' he replied. 'The tribe might not *like* it very much – at least the men wouldn't – but Planter really should be the chief.'

Zelana smiled. 'She already is, Red-Beard. She doesn't need the title. The tribe does what she wants done, and that's what really counts, wouldn't you say?'

'Not out loud, I wouldn't,' Red-Beard replied.

The wind was coming out of the east when Sorgan Hook-Beak's fleet of longships rounded the first peninsula jutting out from the south coast of Veltan's Domain, and when that wind caught the sails, they billowed out with a booming sound. It seemed to Red-Beard that the longships almost flew toward the west. He had a few suspicions about that. Zelana and her family frequently spoke of 'tampering,' and a wind coming from the east was very unusual. West winds and south winds were fairly common at this time of the year, but east and north? Not too likely.

The *Seagull* rounded the third and last peninsula on the south coast of Veltan's Domain a few days later, and then the Maag fleet turned north. The weather seemed to have a faint smell of early autumn now, and Red-Beard began to feel that seasonal urge to go hunting. Autumn had always been the time to lay in a good supply of food to get the tribe through the coming winter.

He was standing near the slender bow of the *Seagull* with Zelana's older brother about midmorning one day when Sorgan Hook-Beak came forward to join them. 'I got to thinking last night that it might be a good idea for me and my men to know a bit about the people of your Domain, Lord Dahlaine,' he said. 'My cousin Skell discovered that it's not a good idea to turn Maags loose on the natives of this part of the world when they haven't got the faintest idea of what the local customs are.'

'You could be right about that, Captain,' Dahlaine agreed. 'I suppose a little conference in your cabin might be in order along about now. There *are* few peculiarities in my Domain that you should all know about.'

Sorgan's cabin at the stern of the *Seagull* wasn't really very large, so things were just a bit crowded when they gathered there about a quarter of an hour later.

'Captain Hook-Beak spoke with me a little while ago, and he wanted to know a few things about the people of my Domain,' Zelana's big brother told them. 'It's not a bad idea, really. I'll give you a sort of general idea about my people and the general layout of the country up there, and then I'll answer any questions you might have.'

'He sounds a lot like a chief of one of our tribes, doesn't he, Longbow?' Red-Beard said quietly to his friend.

'Some things are always the same, friend Red-Beard,' Longbow replied. 'A chief is a chief, no matter where he lives.'

'When we get to the north of sister Zelana's Domain, we'll go ashore in the Tonthakan nation,' Dahlaine began.

'Nation?' Zelana asked curiously.

'It's an idea I came up with quite some time ago, dear sister,' Dahlaine replied. 'It was the best way I could think of to put an end to those silly wars between the various tribes. There are three significantly different cultures in my domain, so I set up three "nations" – Tonthakan, Matakan, and Atazakan – and the various tribes in those nations settle their differences with conferences instead of wars.'

'What an unnatural sort of thing,' Red-Beard said in mock disapproval.

'Be nice,' Zelana chided him.

'Sorry,' he replied, although he didn't really mean it.

'The nation of Tonthakan lies along the western coast of my Domain,' Dahlaine continued, 'and it's very similar in terrain – and culture – to sister Zelana's Domain. The mountains are steep and rugged, the forests are dense and mostly evergreens, and there are several varieties of deer roaming through those forests. The Tonthakans are primarily hunters, and they're quite good with their bows. I'm sure that Longbow and Red-Beard will feel pretty much at home in that region – except that the winters are longer and colder than they are farther to the south. It won't be quite as noticeable in the autumn, but the days are longer in the summer up there and shorter in the winter.' He glanced at Keselo. 'I'm sure our learned young friend from the Trogite Empire can explain that for us.'

'It has to do with the tilt of our world, Lord Dahlaine,' Keselo replied. 'Our world isn't exactly plumb and square in relation to the sun, and that's what accounts for the seasons. She spins, and that's what gives us days and nights, and she travels around the sun in what scholars call "an orbit". If she didn't spin, half the world would live in perpetual daylight, and the other half would live in the dark, but it's that slight lopsidedness that gives us the seasons.'

'I've always known that there was something wrong with this world,' Rabbit said with no hint of a smile.

'I wouldn't really call it "wrong", Rabbit,' Keselo told him. 'If it weren't for the changing of the seasons, I don't think anything alive could be here. Perpetual summer might *sound* nice, but I don't think it really *would* be.'

'Pushing on, then,' Dahlaine said. 'The central region of my Domain is a large area of meadowland that's primarily grassland with very few trees.'

'That turned out to be very useful last spring,' Longbow said.

'I don't think I quite follow you there, Longbow,' Dahlaine said with a slightly puzzled look.

'It has to do with certain customs in Zelana's Domain,' Longbow replied. 'There are certain tasks that we call "men's work" and others called "women's work". Men are supposed to hunt and fight wars, and women are supposed to plant vegetables and cook supper. It might *sound* sort of fair, but it seems to give the men of any tribe a lot of spare time to sit around talking about hunting and fighting. When the fire-mountains won the first war for us, Red-Beard's village, Lattash, was buried under melted rock, so the people had to move to a place on down the bay from the old one. There was open land that should have given the women plenty of room for planting – except that it was covered with thick sod. Cutting away the sod would normally be "women's work", but Old-Bear, the chief of my tribe, told us that he had once visited that grassland you just described, and that while he was there, he saw the lodges made of sod rather than tree-limbs. Building lodges is "men's work", so after Red-Beard's tribe had settled in their new village, the men built the traditional tree-limb lodges, but the wind blew quite a bit harder where the new village was located, and one night, all of the lodges were blown down.'

'That must have been a very strong wind,' the farmer Omago said.

'Not quite *that* strong,' Longbow replied with a grin. 'Red-

Beard and I gave it a bit of help. Then the next morning we put on long faces and told the men of the tribe that tree-limb lodges weren't strong enough to stand up in "windy-village", and we suggested sod instead. The men grumbled a bit, but they went on out into the meadow and started digging up sod for all they were worth, while the women came along behind them planting beans and other things that are good to eat. Nobody was offended, and nobody will starve to death this coming winter.'

'You two are a couple of very devious people,' Omago's wife Ara observed.

'One should always do one's best when the well-being of the tribe's involved,' Red-Beard replied sententiously.

The pretty lady actually laughed.

'Pushing on, then,' Dahlaine continued. 'There are a few herds of those various deer near the western mountains in Matakan, but the most numerous creatures in Matakan are the bison. They're quite a bit larger than deer, and they have horns instead of antlers. Since the winters are very cold in my Domain, the bison have dense fur, and their hides are quite a bit thicker. Arrows *might* penetrate that fur and hide, but spears seem to work better.' Dahlaine went on to describe the Matans 'spear thrower' again.

'Something like that would be very difficult to aim, it seems to me,' Rabbit said.

'The Matans practice a lot, and they're good enough to bring home a lot of bison meat.'

'That's what counts,' Longbow said. 'Their spearheads are stone, aren't they?'

'Of course,' Dahlaine replied. 'The only metal we have anything to do with here in the Land of Dhrall is gold – and I don't think gold would make very good spearheads.'

'I'd say it's almost time for me to go to work again,' Rabbit added with a glum sort of look.

'About all that's left now is "crazy land", right?' Red-Beard suggested, being careful not to smile.

'Does he always have to do that, Zelana?' Dahlaine asked his sister.

'Do what, dear brother?'

'Turn everything into a joke.'

'It keeps him happy, Dahlaine, and happy people are nicer than gloomy ones. Haven't you noticed that before?'

He gave her a hard look, but she just smiled.

'All right,' Dahlaine continued. 'The nation on the east of my Domain is Atazakan, and as our friend who hasn't yet learned how to shave just suggested, the ruler of that region is fairly insane – which isn't really his fault, since the last five generations of his family have also been crazy. The current ruler of Atazakan has taken crazy out to the far end, though. He's absolutely convinced that he's god. He goes out to the public square in the city of Palandor every morning and gives the sun his permission to rise. Then, late in the afternoon, he goes back to the same place and permits her to set.'

'She'll do it without his permission, won't she?' Rabbit asked skeptically.

'Of course she will,' Dahlaine replied with a faint smile, 'but that absurd business makes "Holy Azakan" feel more goddish.'

'I don't think there's such a word as "goddish", Dahlaine,' Zelana suggested.

'You understood what I meant, didn't you, dear sister?' Dahlaine asked her.

'Well, sort of, I suppose.'

'That means that it's a word, doesn't it?'

'Not one that *I'd* ever use.'

'You're a poet, Zelana, so your language is nicer than mine. Anyway, crazy old Azakan desperately *wants* divinity. Whether he truly believes that he has it might be open to some question, but his subjects – or maybe worshipers – have learned to accept his announcement that he's a god, because their very lives depend upon it.'

'Is there anything at all resembling an army in that part of your Domain?' Sorgan asked.

'Not really,' Dahlaine replied. 'Azakan has a goodly number of guards that call themselves "the Guardians of Divinity". Their primary duty involves intimidating the populace of Palandor so that they'll applaud and cheer each time the sun rises or sets at Azakan's command. They carry poorly made-spears and clubs, but they don't really know how to use them. I'd say that their primary contribution to a war with the creatures of the Wasteland will involve staying out of the way.'

3

***

The *Seagull* and the rest of the Maag fleet sailed on past the narrow channel that opened out into the bay of Lattash without bothering to stop, and Red-Beard heaved a vast sigh of relief – touched with just a faint hint of shame. He was fully aware of the fact that he was evading certain responsibilities, but he knew that the tribe would survive without Red-Beard of Lattash serving as chief.

As they moved on farther north it became more and more obvious that summer was coming to a close. There were aspen trees and birch scattered among the pine, fir, and spruce, and the leaves of those particular trees had begun to turn, spattering the evergreen forest with patches of red and gold. Autumn was the most beautiful season in the forest, but it also gave a warning. Winter was not far away, and only fools ignored that silent warning.

It was about three days after they'd passed the bay of Lattash when Longbow advised Sorgan Hook-Beak that he was going to paddle his canoe ashore so that he could speak with Old-Bear, the chief of his tribe. 'If anything unusual is happening up in the land of the Tonthakans, Old-Bear will have heard about it.'

Sorgan seemed to be just a bit surprised. 'Are your people really *that* familiar with the natives of Lord Dahlaine's territory?' he asked.

'I've gone up there a few times myself,' Longbow replied. 'It's always a good idea to get to know the neighbors. There *are* a few restrictions, of course, but we can usually step around them. As nearly as I can determine, we won't need the archers of Zelana's Domain up in her brother's country – *unless* the creatures of the Wasteland attack in millions, but it's probably a good idea for us to stay in touch with Chief Old-Bear. If an emergency comes along, he'll be able to pass the word to the other tribes. Help will be there if we happen to need it.'

'I'll lend you a skiff, if you'd like.'

'Thanks all the same, Sorgan, but I'm more comfortable in my canoe.'

'Could you use some company?' Red-Beard asked his friend. 'Boats are nice, I suppose, but I'd like to put my feet on solid ground for a little while.'

'Ships,' Sorgan absently corrected.

'You missed me there, Sorgan.'

'We call them "ships", not "boats".'

'Well *excuse* me.'

'I'll think about it,' Red-Beard replied.

Red-Beard followed his friend out onto the deck of the *Seagull*, and then the two of them carried Longbow's canoe up out of the forward hold and lowered it over the side.

It felt good to be in a canoe again, and Longbow's canoe was one of the smoothest Red-Beard had ever sat in. He rather ruefully conceded that no matter what Longbow did, he was always the best. Some people might have found that irritating, but it didn't particularly bother Red-Beard. Longbow was his friend, and he almost never tried to compete with him.

It was a balmy autumn day, the waves were gentle, and Longbow's canoe seemed almost to skim across the surface toward the pebbly beach.

Red-Beard noticed that the men of the Tribe seemed to avoid Longbow, which wasn't really all that unusual. He'd noticed in the past that *most* people tried to avoid Longbow. 'It's probably that grim expression of his,' Red-Beard said to himself. 'I'm sure he'd be more popular if he'd just learn how to smile now and then.'

Chief Old-Bear's lodge stood alone on a small hillock that looked down over the beach. Red-Beard thought that was very unusual. Most tribe-chiefs set up shop right in the center of the village, but Old-Bear seemed to want to be separate – and alone.

He greeted Longbow rather formally, it seemed to Red-Beard, but different tribes have different customs.

'How did things go in the Domain of Zelana's brother, my son?' Old-Bear asked.

Longbow shrugged. 'It was a bit more complicated there than it was here, my Chief,' he said, 'but things turned out quite well. It seems that we have a friend who can do things that Zelana's family can't, and she does them without the help of the Dreamers.'

'The old myths are true, then,' the chief observed.

'So it would seem, and she was using *me* as her spokesman. That got to be just a bit tiresome after a while, and it took me a while to catch up on my sleep.'

Old-Bear looked a bit startled. 'I must have misunderstood the myth. I'd always assumed that she'd use one of the Dreamer-children to pass her commands on to the outlanders. What did she want you to tell our friends?'

'Her speech in my dreams was just a bit formal, my Chief, but it more or less boiled down to "get out of the way". She knew what she was doing, and she didn't want us to interfere. We had two separate enemies, and they were very busy killing each other – right up until she destroyed them both.'

'Fire or water?'

'She used water this time – a *lot* of water. The creatures of the Wasteland won't be going south any more, because there's a large inland sea between them and Veltan's Domain.'

Chief Old-Bear laughed. 'I imagine that might have upset the Vlagh just a bit.'

'More than a bit, my chief,' Longbow replied. 'We could hear her screaming from miles away.'

'Is there something happening that I should know about?' Red-Beard asked curiously.

'It's a very old story that's been handed down in our tribe for years and years,' Longbow explained. 'It has to do with a crisis that lies off in the future and what we'll have to do to meet that crisis. There are some references to strangers in the myth – probably Sorgan and Narasan – and to some elemental forces – fire, water, wind – that sort of thing. The story's possibly been garbled just a bit over the years, but down at the bottom, it seems to be very close to what we've encountered so far.'

'Are there any hints about what we ought to be looking for up in the north or off to the east?'

'Nothing very specific,' Longbow replied. 'Visions of one kind or another tend to get just a bit garbled as time goes by.'

'Do you think the outlanders will need our help if the creatures of the Wasteland attack the Domain of Zelana's older brother, my son?' Old-Bear asked.

'Probably not, my chief,' Longbow replied. 'The Tonthakans are fairly good archers, and if the Maag smiths cast bronze arrowheads for them, they should be able to do what needs to be done. If things start getting out of hand, though, I'll send word to you.' He paused. 'How is One-Who-Heals getting along?' he asked.

'Not too good, my son,' Old-Bear replied. 'It would seem that age is one of the diseases that he can't heal.'

'That's too bad,' Longbow said. 'He is – or was – a very good teacher.' Then he looked at Red-Beard. 'I'll be back in just a little while and then we can paddle on back to the *Seagull* and join our friends.' Then he left Chief Old-Bear's lodge.

'Where's he going?' Red-Beard asked Longbow's chief.

'To visit Misty-Water, probably,' Old Bear replied.

'Oh,' Red-Beard said. 'I don't think he's ever mentioned her to me – or anybody else – but some of the men in your tribe spoke of her on occasion. People who don't know about her don't understand Longbow, and he frightens them. Of course, sometimes he even frightens *me*.'

'He was not always like he is now, Red-Beard,' Old-Bear said. 'The time will come, I think, when he'll draw his bow with the Vlagh for his target.'

'I hope he doesn't miss when that day comes.'

'I wouldn't worry, Red-Beard,' Old-Bear replied. 'Longbow never misses when he draws his bow.'

'I've noticed that.'

'I'm sure you have. Everybody who's ever met him notices that.'